T0065362

GUS LEE is the only American-born member of a Shanghai family. He grew up in San Francisco and attended West Point for three years until his failing performance in then-mandatory electrical engineering gave him the involuntary opportunity to become an enlisted man. After receiving his law degree from the University of California at Davis, he rejoined the army as Captain Lee and served as general counsel. He resumed civilian life to become a deputy district attorney in Sacramento, then served for some years as Director of Attorney Education for the State Bar of California. He is married and lives with his wife and two children in Colorado Springs. *China Boy* is his first novel.

GUS LEE

CHINA BOY

A NOVEL

A PLUME BOOK

PLUME
Published by the Penguin Group
Penguin Group (USA) Inc., 375 Hudson Street, New York, New York 10014, U.S.A.
Penguin Group (Canada), 90 Eglinton Avenue East, Suite 700, Toronto, Ontario,
Canada M4P 2Y3 (a division of Pearson Penguin Canada Inc.)
Penguin Books Ltd., 80 Strand, London WC2R 0RL, England
Penguin Ireland, 25 St Stephen's Green, Dublin 2, Ireland
(a division of Penguin Books Ltd.)
Penguin Group (Australia), 250 Camberwell Road, Camberwell, Victoria 3124,
Australia (a division of Pearson Australia Group Pty. Ltd.)
Penguin Books India Pvt. Ltd., 11 Community Centre, Panchsheel Park,
New Delhi – 110 017, India
Penguin Group (NZ), 67 Apollo Drive, Rosedale, North Shore 0632, New Zealand
(a division of Pearson New Zealand Ltd.)
Penguin Books (South Africa) (Pty.) Ltd., 24 Sturdee Avenue,
Rosebank, Johannesburg 2196, South Africa

Penguin Books Ltd., Registered Offices: 80 Strand, London WC2R 0RL, England

Published by Plume, an imprint of Dutton Signet, a division of Penguin Books USA Inc.
Previously published in a Dutton edition.

First Plume Printing, January, 1994

 REGISTERED TRADEMARK—MARCA REGISTRADA

LIBRARY OF CONGRESS CATALOGING-IN-PUBLICATION DATA
Lee, Gus.
      China boy : a novel / Gus Lee.
            p.   cm.
      ISBN 978-0-452-27158-6
      1. Chinese American families—California—San Francisco—Fiction.
2. Chinese Americans—California—San Francisco—Fiction.
3. Family—California—San Francisco—Fiction.   4. Boys—California—
San Francisco—Fiction.   5. San Francisco (Calif.)—Fiction.
I. Title.
[PS3562.E3524C47   1994]
813'.54—dc20   93–27236
                                                            CIP

Set in Janson
Designed by Steven N. Stathakis

PUBLISHER'S NOTE
This is a work of fiction. Names, characters, places, and incidents either are the product
of the author's imagination or are used fictitiously, and any resemblance to actual persons,
living or dead, events, or locales is entirely coincidental.

To Diane, Jena, and Eric. The book began as a summer's tale to our seven- and five-year-old children, and resulted in our collaborative work. It is a moral lesson for myself—a father's reminder of the purpose of life, the need for both parents' love, and the everpresent opportunity for redemption.

ACKNOWLEDGMENTS

To Mah-mee, for love; to Father, for guidance; to my stepmother, for English; to my sisters, for caring.

To those who encouraged my work, with particular thanks to Lee Hause, Ying Lee Kelley, Mary Ming Zhu and Maralyn Elliott, to Susan Leigh and Alfred Wilks; to my peerless agent, Jane Dystel of Acton & Dystel and to Arnold Dolin, Vice President and Associate Publisher, and Gary Luke, Executive Editor; to Mrs. Marshall and Captain Piolonik, my high school and West Point English teachers; to H. Norman Schwarzkopf, whose faith in callow youth is still valued; to Bill Wood; and to HMR and MTH, who set the standard for excellence.

To the men and women staff and volunteers of the San Francisco Central YMCA, who ministered for low pay and long hours to the needs of youth: Karl R. Miller, Tony Gallo, Bruce Loong Punsalong, Bobby Lewis, Sally Craft, Dick Lee, Ken Cooper, Pete Joni, Don Stewart, Keith Gordon, Dave Friedland, George Wong, John Lehtinen, Leroy Johnson, Harry Lever, George McGregor, John Mindeman, Art Octavio, Buster Luciano Weeks, Dan Clement, Sherwood Snow, Dan Moses, Ralph and Lela Crockett, Lola and her cafe, and my other teachers and coaches of youth whose names could not be held as closely as the lessons they imparted. And to Toos, wherever you are.

And, to the Central YMCA Boys Department on Leavenworth—a place where all youth were of the same color, and every lad could be a hero. A place now so desperately needed, and now so sadly closed.

CHINA BOY'S FAMILY

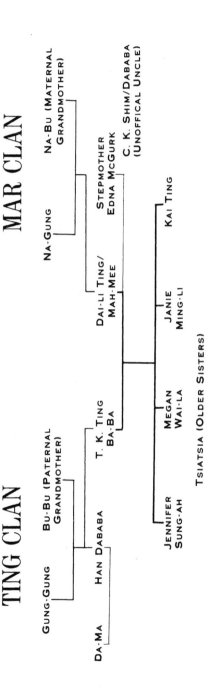

TING CLAN

MAR CLAN

HOUSEHOLD STAFFS

CHINA
BOY

1

CONCRETE CRUCIBLE

The sky collapsed like an old roof in an avalanche of rock and boulder, cracking me on the noggin and crushing me to the pavement. Through a fog of hot tears and slick blood I heard words that at once sounded distant and entirely too close. It was the Voice of Doom.

"China Boy," said Big Willie Mack in his deep and easy slum basso, "I be from Fist City. Gimme yo' lunch money, ratface."

"Agrfa," I moaned.

He was standing on my chest. I was not large to begin with; now I was flattening out.

"Hey, China Boy *shit*ferbrains. You got coins fo' me, or does I gotta teach you some *manners?*"

In my youth, I was, like all kids, mostly a lot of things waiting to develop. I thought I was destined for dog meat. Of the flat, kibbled variety.

In the days when hard times should have meant a spilled double-decker vanilla ice cream on absorbent asphalt, I contended with the fact that I was a wretched streetfighter.

"China," said my friend Toussaint. "You'se *gotta* be a streetfighta."

I thought a "streetfighta" was someone who busted up pavement for a living. I was right. I used my face to do it.

I had already developed an infantryman's foxhole devotion; I constantly sought cover from a host of opportunities to meet my Maker. I began during this stage to view every meal as my last, a juxtaposition of values that made the General Lew Wallace Eatery on McAllister my first true church. Its offerings of food, in a venue where fighting was unwelcome, made my attendance sincere.

The Eatery was a rude green stucco shack. On one side was a bar named the Double Olive that looked like a dark crushed hat and smelled like the reason Pine Sol was invented. On the other flank was an overlit barbershop with linoleum floors in the pattern of a huge checkerboard.

The Eatery's windows were blotched mica of milky greased cataract, its walls a miasma of fissured paint, crayoned graffiti, lipstick, blood, and ink. I always imagined that Rupert and Dozer, the Eatery's sweaty, corpulent cooks, were refugees from pirate ships. They had more tattoos than napkins, more greased forearms than tablecloths. They were surly, they were angry, they were bearded and they were brothers, bickering acidly over what customers had ordered, over the origin of complaints or the mishandling of precious change; enemies for life, and so angered by countless hoarded and well-remembered offenses experienced and returned that no one would consider even *arguing* inside the Eatery, lest the mere static of disagreement spark a killing frenzy by the angry cooks.

"Flies, please," I said to Rupert, who was the smaller, but louder, sibling.

"*Fries!* Crap! Boy, how long you *bin* in dis country? You bettah learn how ta talk, an' you bettah have some coin, and don be usin no oriental mo-jo on me. Don job me outa *nothin!*" His voice churned like a meat grinder that had long been abused by its owner.

The Lew Wallace Eatery's proximity to dying winos and artistic kids, its daunting distance from the Ritz, its casualness in differentiating dirt from entree—all were of no consequence to young folk who had tasted its fries and salivated to worship them again. Inside, food was ample, aromas were beguiling and my scuffed and badly tied Buster Browns were drawn like sailors to Sirens.

The Eatery was central to the nutrition of the Panhandle, but it failed to draw critics from the papers, gourmets from other nations, or gourmands from the suburbs. Passersby in search of phones, tourists seeking refreshments, the disoriented hoping for directions would study the Eatery's opaquely cracked windowpanes, the cranky bulk of its grill managers, and steadfastly move on. The Eatery had not been featured in the convention bureau's brochures. The Panhandle was the butt end of the underbelly of the city, and was lucky to have plumbing.

San Francisco is possessed with its own atmosphere, proudly conscious of its untempered and eccentric internationalism. With grand self-recognition, it calls itself "the City." It is foreign domesticity and local grandeur. It is Paris, New York, Shanghai, Rome, and Rio de Janeiro captured within a square peninsula, seven by seven miles, framed by the vastness of the Pacific Ocean and the interior half-moon of satellite villages rolling on small hills with starlight vistas of Drake's Bay.

The City's principal park is the Golden Gate, a better Disneyland for adults than anything Walt ever fashioned. It has aquaria, planetaria, stadia, museums, arboreta, windmills, sailing ships, make-out corners, Eastern tea gardens, statues, ducks, swans, and buffalo. The park runs east directly from the Pacific Ocean for nearly half the width of the City, traversing diverse neighborhoods as blithely as a midnight train crosses state lines.

The Panhandle is where Golden Gate Park narrows to the width of a single block. It looks like the handle of a frying pan, and is almost in the dead center of the city. On this surface I came to boyhood, again and again, without success. I was a Panhandler. Panhandler boys did not beg. We fought.

A street kid with his hormones pumping, his anger up, and his fists tight would scout ambitiously in the hopes of administering a whipping to a lesser skilled chump. That was me. I was Chicken Little in Thumpville, the Madison Square Garden for tykes. It was a low-paying job with a high price in plasma. I had all the streetfighting competence of a worm on a hook.

Streetfighting was like menstruation for men—merely thinking about it did not make it happen; the imagined results were frightening; and the rationale for wanting to do it was less than clear.

Fighting was a metaphor. My struggle on the street was really an effort to fix identity, to survive as a member of a group and even succeed as a human being. The jam was that I felt that hurting people damaged my *yuing chi,* my balanced karma. I had to watch my long-term score-card with the Big Ref in the permanently striped shirt. Panhandle kids described karma as, what go around, come around.

"Kai Ting," my Uncle Shim said to me, "you have excellent *yuing chi,* karma. You are the only living son in your father's line. This is very special, very grand!"

I *was* special. I was trying to become an accepted black male youth in the 1950s—a competitive, dangerous, and harshly won objective. This was all the more difficult because I was Chinese. I was ignorant of the culture, clumsy in the language, and blessed with a body that made Tinker Bell look ruthless. I was guileless and awkward in sports. I faced an uphill challenge with a downhill set of assets.

I was seven years old and simpler, shorter, and blinder than most. I enjoyed Chinese calligraphy, loved Shanghai food, and hated peanuts and my own spilled blood. It was all very simple, but the results were so complicated. God sat at a big table in *T'ien,* Heaven, and sorted people into their various incarnations. I was supposed to go to a remote mountain monastery in East Asia where I could read prayers and repeat chants until my mind and soul became instruments of the other world. I had a physique perfect for meditation, and ill-suited for an inner-city slum.

God sneezed, or St. Pete tickled Him, and my card was misdealt onto the cold concrete of the Panhandle, from whence all youth fled— often in supine postures with noses and toes pointed skyward.

Some who survived became cops, but more became crooks. We played dodgeball with alcohol, drugs, gambling, sharp knives, and crime. As children, we learned to worry about youth who held hidden razors in their hands and would cut you for the pleasure of seeing red. We avoided men who would beat boys as quickly as maggots took a dead dog in a closed and airless alleyway. The compulsion to develop physical maturity long in advance of emotional growth was irresistible. It caused all kids, the tough and the meek, the tall and the small, to march to the same drum of battle.

It was a drum tattoo that was foreign to the nature of my mother, but all too familiar to her life. This beat resonated with the strength of a jungle tom-tom in my father, but it ran counter to the very principles of his original culture and violated the essence of his ancient, classical education and the immutable humanistic standards of Chinese society.

Almost to a man, or boy, the children of the Panhandle became soldiers, until the Big Card Dealer issued a permanent recall, with the same result. Noses up.

As we struggled against the fates, Korea was claiming its last dead from the neighborhood, the 'hood, and Vietnam and every evil addiction society could conjure were on the way.

2

EARTH

My family arrived in San Francisco in 1944, in the middle of the most cataclysmic war the planet had ever suffered.

The family called the trip to America *Bob-la*, the Run, which is like thinking of the Hundred Years' War as a pillow fight. The Run was a wartime journey across the Asian landmass, from the Yellow Sea to Free China, to the Gangetic Plains of India, across the Pacific Ocean to America.

Even today, this journey would be a hardship. In 1943, it was a darkly dangerous, Kafka-like venture into the ugly opportunities of total war. A million extremely hostile enemy soldiers blocked the thousand miles of twisting river road from Shanghai to Chungking. From there, with a major assist from American aviation, my family continued to India, and from India, with the help of the U.S. Navy, to the United

States. It is the type of exercise where one hopes for more than a cold beer at road's end. Since I was born in California, I missed the trip.

My family was not built for the road. My eldest sister, Jennifer Sung-ah, was fifteen. She was already tall, with long slender bones and a chiseled high-cheekboned face for which fashion models pray. She possessed unimpeachable status, for she was the Firstborn. She was resourceful, but was also a patriot, and experienced deep conflict in leaving China.

Megan Wai-la, my second *chiehchieh*, or older sister (*tsiatsia* in Mandarin), was twelve, and possessed of a charming and mirthful spirit. Megan Wai-la was as beautiful as the elegant Jennifer Sung-ah, but was poorly dressed. She possessed the strength of iron, for her pleasant disposition had been formed without the benefit of enduring care from our mother. Mother had, of course, wanted sons. A first daughter, with some good fortune, could be endured. But two daughters! This augured bad luck, and Mah-mee passed this ill fortune to the little baby girl who could be blamed for not being a son. Worn, secondhand clothes in a wealthy family were symbolic of a powerful devaluation.

Janie Ming-li was four, and enjoyed the dual status of being unbearably pretty as well as a near casualty of the diseases of China. She was at an age when crying was normal, but in a situation where a cry at the wrong time could draw a soldier's gunfire.

In 1943 my mother and sisters were alone in a world at war. All they had to fear were Japanese Imperial troops, brigands, typhus, *dufei:* bandits, rapists, thieves, deserters, and the unclean. My father was a Nationalist Chinese Army officer and joined the family in San Francisco after V-J Day.

"Earth, wind, water, fire, iron," said my mother. "This is what makes the world. I think I am earth. I crossed it, and became it, in the Run. I look at my fingernails, so clean, and still see the earth's dirt in them. Farmers' hands have soil embedded in the pores, so they are like the paddies. I can still feel the *Bob-la* in the little grooves in my fingers."

My mother's favorite belongings had been deposited into a crate that had been hauled across the world, defying the curiosity of interlopers and the efforts of thieves. It was a treasure trove of books, photos, clothing, and memorabilia.

Notice had come in the early morning of November 5, 1943: "*Kampetai* coming for the family of Major Ting Kuo-fan!" the short Salt Tax prefect cried breathlessly. "Tomorrow—dawn!"

The Kampetai, the intelligence arm of the Japanese Imperial Army, had identified Major T. K. Ting, Kuomintang Army, as an officer assigned to General Stilwell's Rangoon Headquarters. He was now known to be running in the hills of Hupeh province with renegade American soldiers, shooting Kwangtung Army infantrymen. He was being sought by their gestapo in retribution for his warlike acts. Our dogs would be killed if they barked. Sons would be bayoneted and hung from poles, the women shot.

Mother turned to Paternal Grandmother, her mother-in-law. "Please. My respects to you, and my father. Please tell him I had no time to say good-bye. I must take my children from your home and seek another. Tell my husband!

"Tell him we will go upriver, to the Cheng clan in the Su Sung Tai. From there, Chungking. I would like, please, the old vegetable cart behind the tailor's outhouse. Please tell Yip Syensheng that the wheels should be oiled. We leave before dawn."

In that one tear-streaming night my mother and sisters tore through their belongings, putting all they could into the crate. Mementos went in, sacrifices came out, but the loss was not material. They were leaving the people of their blood and the home and hearth of their ancestors, and their efforts were like waving good-bye to the world. They were leaving everything, from love itself to the best kitchen staff and cook in the maritime provinces.

"How can this be?" my mother asked.

"Everything beneath Heaven is disturbed," whispered Da-Ma, her sister-in-law, who was higher in rank and therefore possessed the answers. Their children cried as they said good-bye to each other, fearing the eternal loss of irreplaceable friendship, dreading death and the loss of the clan's lineage.

When the cocky roosters called forth that morning, sitting atop empty dog kennels, my mother and her three daughters were already five hours upriver, stirring cool road dust with the chef's finest provisions and the house's best guard dog in the cart.

Jennifer, my eldest sister, looked forward to reaching Free China, and even America beyond, with the fierce determination common to the young in 1940s China. She did not want to leave the most exciting city in Asia, but her duty was to Mother.

Father had been born in 1906, six years after the foreign powers had seized Beijing in the Boxer Rebellion. Two years after his birth, the

Empress Dowager Tz'u-hsi died, leaving P'u-yi, the infant Last Emperor on the throne of the Empire of China. P'u-yi and my father had been born in the same month of the same year, in the last dynasty in Chinese history. When my father was five, the Empire fell, and the warlords appeared. After the popular student democracy movement of 1919, my father's mother, who ran the Shanghai Salt Tax Companies Office in the name of her husband, foresaw a Western-influenced future. She promoted a younger man to be house interpreter and chief of tutors.

He was Luke Hung-chang. He was from Fukien province, was missionary-trained, and had bright, penetrating eyes. All my sisters remembered that. He spoke English, French, and German, was a ferocious reader, and represented the hope of a new China. He gave my sisters their Western names on their last night at home.

"Sung-ah, I give you the name Jennifer. It is very classy, very tremendously musical! A name Amadeus Mozart would have composed!" said Tutor Luke, smiling while tears glazed over his fiery eyes.

"Wai-la, close your eyes and listen. Listen to this sound: Megan! Is that not dramatic, and beautiful! A name of love.

"Wai-la. It is a tremendously special name. And your honored mother appreciates the effect of name-changing. It will bring you her affection, and change your *yuing chi*. It is an excellent name change! I will think of it, and the sound of it, as you wear it in Free China!"

The tears now streamed down Tutor Luke's cheeks, the dark comma of his forelock continuing to fall into his glistening eyes. He knew their chances of reaching Chungking were not good. If they succeeded, he also knew that Major Ting wanted the family in America, a place he would never go. His duty was in China.

Chinese men are only allowed to shed tears when the cause is great. He was losing the girls of his dreams. My sisters remembered his passion that night, and how his tears and hair fell as relentlessly as his hopes. He knelt before his smallest student.

"*Syau* Ming-li. Little Ming-li. I name you Janie, the name of an empress queen of *Yinggwo*, England, the name of strong and good women of foreign literature. No one pushes around a Janie! So! Remember to keep your head tall, and straight. I expect you to remember me, and to keep this name. This would honor me, *Bobbobbei*, Little Precious.

"Say it," he whispered.

"Jen-nii," she said, sadly, reaching forward, touching his tears.

"Remember me, my beautiful students," he whispered.

In the vegetable cart that was their transport, Megan, drama in her name and cursed with being Second Daughter, looked back, fearing a future without the greater family's protection from an uncaring mother. She was twelve.

Jane, four years old and not to be pushed around by anyone, slept in our mother's arms.

Mr. Yip, the barrel-chested horsemaster with a German self-loading Mauser in his belt, spat on the road as they left the delta, heading for the danger of Japanese lines, the hope of sanctuary with our clan's allies, the Chengs of the Su Sung Tai, and the heady promise of Free China near Chungking.

My mother wept silently, not looking back to the east. She turned to the north, to her father in Tsingtao. She carried an unpaid debt of *shiao*, piety to parent, in her breast, as heavy and as foreboding as the rock of Sisyphus.

She also carried a wealth in diamonds, pearls, and rubies in the lining of her clothing. Smaller gems had been sewn into the jackets and pants of her daughters. The thumbs and fingers of my mother's and sisters' hands were numb with the accidental prickings of the desperately rushed needles. The jewels were their passports to safety in a world gone mad.

Mother feared that Father would never find them, wherever the fates compelled them to stop. The world was insane, and very big, the Yangtze longer than the Great Wall itself.

I later asked Megan about their flight from China.

"Oh, Little Kai, it was frightful, and *horrid*. The fear was—*hateful*. Mah-mee cut off all our hair, smudged us with charcoal, bound our chests, dressed us like peasant boys. We pretended to be stupid as we hiked the Yangtze gorges so men would not look at us."

"Why no want men look at you?" I asked.

"It took six months," said Jennifer from across the hall. Megan licked her lips and shook her head, her long hair shimmering in the light from the bright ceiling lamp in her room. She loved having as many lights as possible illuminated. "We really were in terrible danger," she said. "Mah-mee wore a butcher knife on her forearm, tying it against her, like this," showing how it lay on the inside of her left arm, always within reach. "She threw it at bandits once. We were always frightened.

Then we lived with the *Gungtsetang*, the Share Wealth Party, for over a month. Mother convinced them that we were peasants, and they accepted us." Megan peered into the distance.

"It was safer with them than to be on the road. But we left the Share Wealth village for the Nationalist capital in Chungking."

The *Gungtsetang* were the Reds—the communist enemies of our father and General Chiang Kai-shek. I could not understand it. "We saw so many people who were going to die." Her fingers rustled through the hair on my head. "Father met us near Wuhan. He said to Mahmee: 'I know you; you never give up,' and he gave us troops to escort us to Chungking, but they were killed. *Dufei*, bandits, and *tucbun*, warlord soldiers, attacked us. That's when Mah-mee threw the knife. Ayy," she concluded.

They had bounced and swayed in the old, unpainted cart, clutching the crate, listening to the hooves of the horse, ignoring the men on the river road, hearing the rippling tides of the Yangtze as it rushed to the sea, the dog barking anxiously at his new world.

"Quiet, dog," said Mr. Yip. He evaluated the road people. Refugees, spies, thieves, misplaced farmers, homeless, hopeless. He curled his eyebrows and his lips, promising death for their interference, placing the menace of his guardianship into their fantasies of finding wealth in the crate.

One of the best prizes of the redwood crate was a book written by Mother's tutor for her. Years later, she pulled it out to show me.

"See," she said, "the character, Tang, my tutor. Oh, son. He was so wise, so deep. He always wanted to train a prodigy to become the tallest scholar in *Chingsu*, the Forest of Brush Pens, in the imperial capital. Instead, he got a girl who could never take the examinations. And I revere his memory because he also taught me about Mozart."

My mother wept for him. As she related this family history to me, I twitched and rubbed her arm, which only made her cry louder. I asked her the key question about the escape story.

"Yip Syensheng and doggie kill bad guys?" I asked.

"Here is the character, Mar," she continued wetly, "my family, and Ahn Dai, my name then. The book explains the great philosophers K'ung-Fu-tzu, Lao-tzu, Meng-tzu from a female viewpoint." Later, I learned that K'ung-Fu-tzu was known in America as Confucius, which is as East Asian a name as DiMaggio.

"You change names, Mah-mee?" I asked. My mother's name was Dai-li.

"Oh, yes, My Only Son," she said, sniffling and giggling and pulling my ear. "We change names at our pleasure. For *foo chi*, good luck, or for better luck. Luck is everything. *Foo chi* is controlled by gods and spirits. Only clan names and family titles, like Mother and Oldest Daughter and Father and Uncle and Auntie and Firstborn's Tutor, are unchangeable, for these ranks were established by the gods themselves in the beginning of time.

"Your father has had many names. He was such a dashing, handsome rogue at Taoping Academy that he had a series of them, each from a different teacher. I changed my name only once. When the first Japanese sentry at Hangchow Gate outside Tungliu asked where we were taking my crate and pressed his long knife into Megan's face."

"You care for Megan?" I asked.

Mah-mee's face said: Wrong question.

"Father name, real name?" I tried.

"Of course it is. It is the last one he adopted at the academy. It came from his college roommate, from the powerful Cheng clan, of the Su Sung Tai up the Yangtze gorges from Shanghai. Father now works for the daughter of the Chengs."

"Where Yip Syensheng? Where doggie, Mah-mee?"

She shook her hand at me, since the horsemaster's fate remained unknown, but he was a powerful, smart, and resourceful man. He was a survivor. He was probably shoeing a horse as we thought of him.

"What doggie name, Mah-mee?" I asked.

"Name? He was a dog. His name was Dog," she said.

"Doggie live, Mah-mee?"

"The guard dog ran away in Free China. Tsa, tsa! You are so much a boy, worrying about a dog! He salivated constantly after the Run, and peed on everything in Chungking everytime the Japanese bombed us."

As I grew older and came to see fighting as a way of life, I wished that I had been born earlier, so I could have participated in that grand odyssey. My father understood that sentiment, but it made my sisters think me daft. In many ways, as a child, I prepared myself for an epic test, an adventure that would measure my worthiness to be the only son of the American extension of the Ting clan.

The Panhandle and the Haight, our mirror 'hood south of the park, were standard-issue wartime blue-collar districts where shipyard workers and longshoremen returned after back-busting, long-shift days at Hunters Point and Fort Mason. The Handle and the Haight were in the sunbelt, unique San Francisco districts without fog, thunderstorms, or people of Chinese or Caucasian descent.

When I arrived squalling—no doubt prescient about my imminent fate—the streets were half black. By the time I was in the second grade and in the center of the frying pan, I was the only Asian, the only nonblack and the only certified no-question-about-it nonfighter in the district. Black families, tired of being hammered by the weight of history and pressured by the burden of being members of the wrongly hued tribe in Georgia and Mississippi, were heading west armed with hope and cheap gas.

That same hope brought my family trekking eastward on a U.S. Navy Liberty ship called the USS *George Randall*, which my sisters, accustomed to great wealth but sobered by war, regarded as the *Queen Elizabeth*. My father's service as infantry liaison to the China–Burma–India Theatre and Army Ground Forces Commander, Joseph "Vinegar Joe" Stilwell, had earned him a place in the general's heart and berths for our family on an American airplane and a naval vessel.

These families from Macon and Kiangsu met in the Panhandle, a new and voguish rendezvous point for those interested in building life from the rubble of sundered cultures.

Our families arrived gasping, recoiling from shock, happy to be alive but unsure about all else. There was a feeling that something was owed them for this outrageous upset, for nothing that had been done during the preceding years could have justified the insult of war, the hidden costs of relocation, the tariffs of change, the loss of life.

Blacks, for more than a hundred years, had been fighting and bleeding under their nation's flag, hoping for a share of the fruits of victory. They had all the optimism of Dickens's Mr. Micawber, with none of his chances.

During that same century, the Chinese were beset by government corruption, foreign invasion, civil, religious, and ethnic wars, revolution, famine, drought, flood, and excess population. They had suffered countless blights. The Taiping Rebellion, whose fourteen years of steady siege coincided with the American Civil War, had killed 60 million people. Foreign powers ruled China's coast and imported opium to pay for exports. Legalized opium was laying waste the aristocracy, splintering the social fabric, and threatening even those too poor to purchase it.

China, of course, is not what a billion people call their own country. It is *Chung Gwo*, the Middle Kingdom, the central state, the center of the universe, the axis of the world, the home of the celestial heaven's chosen people. It is the home of the tamers of dragons, the sailors of the sea, the students of the moon. Until the eighteenth century, its armies and navies did their will, needing only whim to lash out with lance and sword to carve new boundaries and conquer new worlds.

The land of my heritage was like Big Willie Mack—its personality was that of an unfairly large bully. And karma had come calling, for all of us.

3

ELDERS

My mother was nearing forty, her rather perfect face concealing a third of those years.

Her five-feet-and-seven-inch frame was usually in dynamic motion, her delicately featured pale oval face, framed in thick black hair, was quick and precise in its expressiveness. Her eyes cast the mood for the house, and they lay above a molten and active personality that had the reflective calm of Vesuvius. Mother had endured family division, seen war and the destruction of her society. But the marks of loss were not in her delicately thoughtful face.

She was smart and probably more beautiful than wise, a woman who saw passion as life itself. She was like Sophia Loren or Anna Magnani, ignited by the surging and crackling impulses of life, inserted into a society of women sworn by Confucian edicts to apparent silence and conspiratorial whisperings.

My mother did things that most Chinese women would not imagine attempting in a state of final extremis. She refused obsequiousness, rejected submission, and exchanged restraint for spontaneity, stating the contents of her mind at the moment of the thought, however transient. She acted as if she were an enfranchised male.

This was the propensity of persons seized by *quab*, curious behavior, or of molten Italian actresses captured by drama. It was not the recommended mode of highborn Kiangsu gentrywomen. Worse, Mother used this unsanctioned license to speak her mind to criticize her own mother.

Her sister-in-law, my *da-ma*, the wife of my uncle the Firstborn Son, saw Mother as a revolutionary. That is akin to a Mother Superior suspecting a novitiate to be a Protestant. My aunt's cranium was analytical, mathematically driven, and poorly suited to coexist with Mother's passionate persona. Da-ma, it was said, believed that Mother was a repository for tortured spirits whose descendants never honored them in *ching ming*, filial worship, and were therefore never satisfied and would never know peace.

As Firstborn Son's Wife, Da-ma held higher rank, a position fortified by her bearing a son while my mother produced daughters. Da-ma punished Mother by ignoring her and encouraging her part of the household staff to do the same. These sisters-in-law lived on the same floor of the ancestral home in Shanghai, sharing space and tasks. Their enmity was poisonously patent, disturbing the geomancy of the house and causing the renowned head cook to tremble and overseason main platters. When Grandmother complained about this grievous failure in cuisine, she directed the head cook's assistant to make the sauces, and *he* overseasoned as well in order to protect his boss. Often, in China, it was difficult to fix problems.

Mother came from an aristocratic line that had more money than affection and more pride than skill. Mother's mother had scorned her work-loathing husband and denied his existence.

My mother was the firstborn, a station of unquestioned majesty and responsibility. She sided openly with her abandoned father against her mother, and did it seriously, maintaining the commitment in the face of popular disapproval. She persevered in her choice long after the death of Grandmother and the separation of an ocean from her father.

"Loyalty *is*," Mother said. "Loyalty *never* dies. Women who do not revere their husbands do not merit loyalty. Of course, I revere *my* husband, but love him more than I respect his authority."

Emphasizing her eccentricity, she dabbled with the spices of foreign languages and European music. To the horror of both her parents, she studied the Christian God and seemed genuinely affectionate about a poor prophet named Jesus Christ. Mother's portly maid, Round Pearl, accompanied her to the mission for English lessons. Round Pearl was very conservative and anti-Christian and feared the foreigners, but her presence did not impede Mother, or calm her parents. Mother's parents knew that Christ Syensheng had been hung with thieves for his opposition to traditional authority, and were only too aware that their sparkling daughter had married a soldier. They used to argue about which condition was worse, each blessed with the energy which only the self-righteous possess.

In contemporary terms, my mother came from a badly dysfunctional family.

My father was a descendant of warriors, whose line had atrophied in the three centuries of peace that China had won by war.

When militant Italian Jesuits arrived in China in the seventeenth century, they saw mounted shock troops of regimented and color-coordinated Banner warriors, bristling with razor-sharp weapons and quivers of iron-shafted arrows. The warriors rimmed the horizon with blood-red armor, pounding glinting tools of death against their chests and flashing cold ivory smiles as they anticipated the pleasures of homicide.

These men killed for the joy of blood and performed all functions, except the writing of sentimental sonnets, from their worn and battle-scarred saddles. They eventually suffered from an embarrassment of riches: they laughingly killed all their enemies and created their worst nightmare. A world at peace.

By the nineteenth century, Bannermen used saddles as drying racks for silk costumes and gourmet braising pots. They carried swords that had been blunted to avoid accidental cuts. Disputes were resolved by rash games of gambling and false threats rather than by combat.

When confronted by the modern armies of invading European imperialists bent on taking all the tea and silver in China, the descendants of the first armies to use field organization, maneuver, and gunpowder blinked dumbfounded, threw fine porcelain teacups in the air and ran hooting in a flapping of silks for their latrines, crying upon the Seat of Heaven to unleash the celestial furies.

That army, unimaginably, would worsen under the goading pressures of famine, overpopulation, and bribery. My father had all the attributes needed to be one of the great captains, but he was as out of place as a bishop in a liars' contest. It was my dad's sad fate to be a great officer in the lousiest military organization since the Children's Crusade.

My father's father, Gung-Gung, was a tremendous poet and artist who showed great fidelity to classic calligraphy, to high-throated, gilded-tongued *dongszi* singsong concubines, to his *kang*, the teak hardwood bed where he smoked opium, and to his fine, high-priced gum burners where the drug was softened for the pipe. He absorbed the poppy in a self-destructive fury. He pretended that he had no children. He was a product of wretched excess, when the very purpose of living had been lost through the oppression of wealth.

He was a matinee-handsome man who could have been an actor on the Mandarin stage. My paternal grandfather died the way he had lived: in disorder, with his sons facing the end of the world, their wives at war, the clan's wealth whisked to the winds of the poppy, his wife forgotten, his body turning on itself, the angered and exploited peasants at the gate unfurling red flags and asking for heads.

My mother believed in spirits, in bartering with capricious ghosts, in burning joss sticks to them in moments of reflection, in conversing coherently, and aloud, with her beloved father in Tsingtao while she was in a bathtub in San Francisco.

"The tub is perfect," she said. "I have come across the sea like the Ming admiral, Cheng Ho, to find this perfect tub. It is because of excellent deals I have made with the spirits of water and wind. The tub allows my feet to point to the west, toward Father, where the *feng shui*, geomantic forces, inspire calm and peace and allow the sun to sleep."

She once said at the dinner table—the center of life—that she wished I were a speedy forest and sea spirit who could deliver messages to my grandfather by air, wisping through space in the direction of her toes, toward the setting sun.

She trusted spirits in principle and distrusted people in general. She kissed the joss sticks to ensure that any carelessness in calling spirits to the fragrant paste during their manufacture would be repaired by her own attention to detail. She was superstitious, her respect for the unseen ranging from mild acknowledgment to hysterical drama.

A leading family belief—begun by rumor and concluded in reality—was that the only male child in Mother's first cousin's family in Ningshia had died horribly after eating peanuts. Whether it was anaphylactic shock from a unique allergy or asphyxiation from catching the peanuts in the throat, this is unknown.

But peanuts—eating peanuts—became the equivalent for me of spitting on an ancestor's grave.

I was eating a *chienkuo*, a peanut. *"TII-IINNGGG!!!"* Mother cried, making my entire body jerk in a massive, involuntary lurch.

The Chinese are wizards at homonyms; one word has a hundred definitions. *Ma,* for example, means "mother," "horse," "locust," "frog," "thirty-six English inches," "hemp," "agate," "question mark," and "numb." Old and venerable societies need not bother with the invention of new words; the old ones will do, and can be reissued for new concepts if absolutely necessary. The Chinese, who outnumber the rest of the world in multiples, have only one hundred family names for all of them to share. Italians, I later learned, have a relatively small population and more family names than stars in the night sky.

Our family name means, among other things, "stop." So I wasn't sure if Mother was telling me to desist or was calling my name.

Mother picked me up as if I were a rolled blanket and whisked me to the bathroom, inserting her finger into my throat, causing me to deposit the contents of my stomach into the unsuspecting sink. Then she beat me on my back. Gagging and gasping, eyes wild with this insult to my digestive process, her hand pounding me, I heard her sob:

"Please, please, Only Son! *NO, NO PEANUTS!* It weakens your *shigong,* your vital spirit! Here! Take some *Chiing chun bao,* the liquids of life!" she cried, pulling the plain brown bottle from the medicine cabinet and pouring it into my mouth. *"No* peanuts! No no no no no! I did not wait my entire life to finally have a son, here, in this remote world, to have you die of *peanuts!"*

The liquids of life were extract of baleen whale pancreas, or supreme glorious squid tentacle essence, or somesuch, and always tasted worse than the malady it sought to cure. It advanced the use of shock to cure anything by scaring it out of your body, with immediate effect. It encouraged health, since fear of the remedy could exceed the harm of the ill.

"Mah-mee," asked Janie. "Why do *we* eat peanuts, but Kai cannot?"

"Kai is My Only Son," said Mother.

Even today, the name *Chiing chun bao* sends a shiver up my spine.

But the whiff of a peanut-butter-and-jelly sandwich makes my stomach quail. Eat peanuts or suffer death-by-a-thousand-cuts? I would have to think about it.

My sister Janie Ming-li also enjoyed the benefits of deep-seated superstition. When Janie fell victim to infantile dysentery in China, Mother marshaled all the forces of the spirit world to keep her suffering child in health. She posted violent scripture all over the house, on every floor. She hung the sayings from the alternating peach trees and weeping willows on the street, and on the *wutung* oil, magnolia, and mandarin orange trees in the central courtyard. She burned money as sacrifices to needy gods and refused no petitioner her unique counsel. She advertised positive thoughts in a specific campaign to show the weak gods that she was not given to fear.

"My little baby girl is in *wonderful* health!" she declared with loud overconfidence to all who greeted her.

She offered to make peace with every woman with whom she had warred in the house.

"Honored Mother," she said to her mother-in-law. "I have wrongly criticized you for bathing in the front hall. This has been unforgivably dishonorable and disloyal. I appreciate your showing your daughters how beautiful your skin is, and compliment you on being the most beautiful lady in all of the Central Kingdom."

"Honored Elder Sister," she said to my da-ma. "How could I have questioned your wise judgment? Of course, I suffer from *quab*, for I hoard within me the despair of free-floating ancestors, abandoned by their unworthy clans! Please forgive me."

"Sung-ah," she said to my eldest sister, Jennifer. "I have confessed to my elders as they have wished. My yuing chi must now be indomitable and will save our little baby!"

"I have a sick baby," she told the best herbalist in the International Settlement. She described the symptoms.

"This is all for a girl, Lady?" replied the herbalist.

"You will treat this 'girl' as if she held your own life, Learned Doctor," she said.

"I will take your failure in her treatment personally," she added, using all her powerful nonverbals, silently focusing her fiery intent. The herbalist adjusted his wide, white medical headband. I know how he must have felt—as though the dragons of antiquity had come calling, the flames only hinting at the level of disaster promised. Mother had a way of making men touch their hats or make discreet lower-body movements to ensure they still possessed their manhood.

The herbalist provided thick paper packets of spotted-deer antler horn, Tian Shi Pian royal-red Korean ginseng root, griffin essence fluids, crushed foxglove, and Beijing royal gelatins for mixing into Janie's foods. Mother applied Zheng Gi Shui liniment and Dragon balm analgesic to her daughter's skin.

Unlike some, Mother did not cut her own flesh and add it to the pharmaceuticals. She understood the difference between form and substance, and knew that flesh-adding was all show with little curative value. The herbs had a pharmacological base; she was becoming a new-world scientist. Mother burned joss as she fed Janie the gentle, medicinalized rice gruels, bean pastes, and soy bean curds. She enclosed Janie's bed in heavy mosquito cloth to seal her from the spirits of sickness lurking within the family and required her other daughters and their servants to fast once a week to appease any jealous gods from striking the baby.

Friends were barred from the children's quarters in the house until Janie was three.

Episcopalian missionaries, to whom Mother was a mercurial darling, offered the magical elixir of Western culture to save the little girl. Mother used this as well. It was Cream of Wheat, from Passaic, New Jersey, and Mother always treated this particular cereal as if it were something found inside the Holy Grail by crafty archaeologists. Even Round Pearl liked this high medicine and she thought the *lao mao tze*, the Old Hairy Ones, the European foreigners, were evil incarnate.

"I'm not feeling well, Lady," Round Pearl would moan. "Please— one prescription of *lao mao tze* porridge medicine?"

"Here, toast," Mother would say to us at breakfast in America. "And," with brio, "Cream of Wheat!"

When Janie was old enough for hard-fiber foods, like inland broccoli, beef, chicken and long-bean, Mother softened the food by chewing it first. Janie was surprised when she discovered later that all food did not arrive in paste form.

Had Janie been born healthy, she ironically would have become the new Worthless Daughter, freeing Megan from that rank. Janie would have been the child with a living nonmother, cursed with being yet another in a line of honorless females and unborn sons. Yuing chi's, or karma's, downside is the utter ignorance of what one had done in the previous life to deserve the pain of the current rotation.

When it was unmistakably clear that Janie Ming-li would not only recover, but that she was probably the most robust child in two provinces, Mother revisited the herbalist.

"Doctor, I am in your debt. I gave you cash money for herbs; you gave me my daughter's young life. I owe you," she said, bowing. "Our clan would be honored by sharing any task or burden that falls into your road."

My mother's father, Na-Gung—the Outside, In-Law Grandfather—was a big, shambling broad-shouldered scholar with a large estate. He was generous with books, kindly to his daughters, quick to laughter, and slow to work. He appreciated the outrageous—a wonderful trait while traditional, Imperial China went to hell in a handbasket. In America, his lawn mower would have been hidden in the corner of the backyard in weeds and rust while he played checkers with children. His wife was not amused.

My mother, as was the custom, left the home of her father to join the household of my father. But her father had likewise left the home of their ancestors, taking his great library and Wang the fish cook to the northern port of Tsingtao, where the Germans were training dockworkers to become brewmasters. Here the crushing condemnation of an angry wife could be nullified mug by mug, fish by fish, book by book, chuckle by chuckle.

Tsingtao, from whence China's best beer would emerge with a Bavarian accent, is six hundred miles north of Shanghai, hard on the upper curve of massive Shantung peninsula on the Yellow Sea coast.

"Spirits," my mother said, "are perfect because they never die and never leave you. Women, My Only Son, have the great spirits. It is our gift."

Daughters, sisters, wives. In parts of society, a man and wife were merely a permutation of a boy and his dog. Women were expendable birthing organisms for the glory of the family. Mother resisted this status.

"Why must you always argue with me!" roared my father, shattering wine goblets on the other side of the city.

"Sweet honey," she said. "I am the one who left my dear father and brought our children to the Pretty Country. I did not argue about leaving that night. We left, and here we are. Your yuing chi is to hear my argument now, and to agree with me later."

She scrutinized naked male Rodin statues while thinking reproductive thoughts in an effort to make her fetus a son. Fearlessly, and in opposition to the embarrassed grumblings of her husband, she pinned pages from art books on the walls of their bedroom. The selected art was representative of the European masters, but the variations shared one trait: they all displayed the male organ. My sisters would enter our parents' bedroom and cover their eyes, bumping into the furniture with their shins.

Mother would hum her favorite Christian hymns while looking at the pictures, praying in her wonderfully eclectic way to God Almighty, Michelangelo, and the Yin, the Goddess of Fertility. She lit joss sticks, with some difficulty, and closed her eyes, visualizing male babies. She shelled peanuts, crushed them, and threw them away with the announcement, "For you, Watching Gods!" Most Chinese, like the gods, enjoy peanuts, and Mother was banking on the gods not knowing that she personally hated them. She attended Episcopalian churches and overdonated, murmuring, "For my Son, whom You will give me, thank You."

Hardly likely, of course, but here I am.

She did not hesitate to express herself fully to any person, be it the president of the Chinese bank where my father worked so arduously or a toddler, with equal force and elocution.

Men who made passes at her were not rude ruffians but agents of evil river spirits. She would shop at Old Petrini Market on Divisadero Street and wonder why men stared at her. In China, men of my parents' social grouping developed peripheral vision and would not gaze openly at women.

"River–Spirit–Men!" she cried after returning from Petrini's, throwing her tiny purse at her second undaughter with the flair of Sandy Koufax. "Why do they stare at me so? Why do they lick their lips like Gobi nomads at a well?" She put her hands on her hips, frowning at their misbehavior.

Even at the age of five I knew why. She was beautiful and wore tight, side-slit, high-collared, short-sleeved Mandarin dresses. She carried a parasol to keep the sun from her face.

She was an expert in nonverbal communication. Her lips, eyes, nose—these were the instruments of discourse. Spoken words were not crucial because people should be able to divine the next move. For me, initially, it was like learning how to play patty-cake without a partner.

Unlike most of the known world, Mother did not like American cigarettes. But she enjoyed the eccentric radio commercial that featured a high voice yodeling, *"Call for Phi-ilip Mor-riss!"* and having Megan light them for her.

"Call for Phi-ilip Mor-riss!" she sang in a high voice, and Megan delivered a cigarette with a flaming match. Mother delicately puffed the expelled smoke, lips pursed as if she were kissing a newborn, and she would pose as if she were a European lady, gesturing with the cigarette. Mother could have delivered the Gettysburg Address in pantomime, using the motions she made with a lighted cigarette in her hand. When the smoke burned her eyes, she doused the cigarette with a thoroughness that was unnerving.

Mother knew that I had trouble seeing, so she would move her silently expressive face—the medium of discussion—close to me if she wanted her features to say something, so to speak.

Father, to introduce us to American culture, got the family hooked on the cinema. My sisters enjoyed the movies that featured Bette Davis or Barbara Stanwyck. Mother loved the escapism that films provided her, for she allowed her spirit to reach out to the women on the screen, urging them to success, to leave the undeserving men, to kill the bad ones, to protect the children. She felt she could influence the outcome of the screenplay by her concentrated thoughts as the story unfolded. Father went to absorb the values and the symbols of American culture, but never succeeded in making the diet a pure one of Westerns and war films.

"See here," he would say. "This man [John Wayne, Robert Mitchum, Victor Mature], strong like my army friend, Na-men Schwtz'd." Father was fortunate in his friends, but not in the friendliness of their names.

It was an American ritual in the fifties, when the studios still produced a new movie every week, to go to the movies as regularly as to church. Before Mother realized my nearsightedness, she buried my head in her bosom at moments of great drama, to protect me from the frights of the screen. I had no idea what stimulated her actions. I thought people went to movies to listen to them.

When something confused her, which happened as regularly as the ticking of the magic clock, she giggled brightly, delighting in the mysteries of the world. She used to say that there was a small god inside the doorbell, and she called him the Chime God. We could hear her laughing from anywhere in the apartment. She, like Archimedes, had just experienced a close encounter with a truth from the endless excitement of the world of physics.

"Mr. Westinghouse and General Electric," she said, "are *great* men! They have absolutely superior *shigong*!"

Mother loved ice from our kitchen freezer. Shanghai summers were hot and humid, and the two middle weeks in August were insufferable. Although San Francisco summers are cool and foggy, she always kept ice in bowls throughout the apartment in August, like votive candles in a chapel, small perpetual ice floes to ward away the sticky-handed gods of humidity that, across the ocean, had robbed everyone of the pleasures of sleep and dryness.

"It is *so* hot in Shanghai now!" she intoned. "It is . . . is—hateful! Megan Wai-la! More ice! It melts!"

Father bought her a new Kelvinator refrigerator-freezer on New Year's Day on the lunar calendar, February 4, 1950. I was five that year in Chinese counting, which counts one year for the mother's hard work in pregnancy. I was four years old by the American standard.

Mother stood in front of the freezer, standing on her tiptoes, her hands clasped together, jumping, giggling, touching it.

"It's perfect! I'm so happy!" she cried. "I want a party!" While she happily cavorted, I crept up to the huge white smooth box and gingerly touched it. It did not bite, nor did it give me food. Mother's smile was huge, and I smiled at her, moved by her joy.

"Oh, no, My Only Son!" she hissed. "Don't smile so broadly for gifts! The Teeth God will want all your bright teeth, which you show so bravely! Remember—moderation in all things." I immediately clapped a hand over my mouth.

"Oh, Mah-mee," moaned Jennifer. "There is no such thing as the Teeth God! He would have taken your teeth and mine and Ba-Ba's and Megan's and Janie's teeth by now! And *you* are not moderate or Confucian in all your thoughts!"

"Tsa, tsa, daughter," she scolded. "How you argue! The Teeth God does not want women's teeth! And he is afraid of your father, who is a warrior! My Son, however—he is a musician and scares no one! And of course I am Confucian; I respect my father."

That night we recelebrated my Red Egg Ginger Party. "Red Egg Parties are held one month after birth," my father said. "To celebrate the male baby and his mother surviving birth. It allows recovery before the barbarity, the social invasion, of the family. And of friends. It allows time against disease, to know that the infant will live."

Red paper, reflecting good fortune, with bright, bold, gold calligraphy, was hung in the kitchen. The largest banner bore the name of her father, Na-Gung, and she prepared a special seat for him at the other end of the table from my father's chair.

Mother invited Uncle Shim, who brought groceries and helped make pigs' feet in vinegar, baked dumplings, and steamed cakes—special dishes that reflected the honor of the moment. Uncle Shim was a wonderfully elegant, silver-haired man with bright metal spectacles and a mind that seemed to contain all the wisdom of China. He had been a famed scholar by profession in the old days, in the old land, and had been nominated by my father to be my tutor in America. Uncle Shim used to call me *Hausheng,* his personalized and shortened way of saying Able Student. He had done great honor to my father by calling me Hausheng on the day of my birth, before I had evidenced the slightest potential for scholarship.

Jennifer and Megan made the special Mother's Chicken Soup. It brewed inside the brown earthenware soup vessel with the nipplelike lid handle emblazoned with the characters for double happiness. Dozens of eggs were boiled in bright red dye. The soup was medicinal for the mother's recovery; the shape of the bowl was suggestive of reality, and the eggs spoke for themselves. Father was a great cook and seemed to use every pot in San Francisco. He made long-length longevity noodles—not for their superstitious value, but for their taste.

He especially enjoyed this party because it was flouting tradition—it was four years after its customary time. He was a proud iconoclast, meeting the rigidity of the past with equal fervor.

"Why Na-Gung not here?" I asked, pointing at the empty chair.

"Oh, but he is here, Kai," said Mother.

I stared suspiciously at the empty table setting. Na-Gung was alive, so he could not be here as a spirit. Everyone said that I had trouble seeing. No one else seemed bothered by Grandfather's absence, or tardiness, or invisibility. His serving of food grew cold, and no ghostly, unseen chopsticks attacked it.

So we ate for hours, laughing and full of the joy of family. At first, I was afraid to smile, but Mother said that the Teeth God was dangerous when you smiled from greed, and that people laughing at food would never offend the touchiest of spirits.

Uncle Shim laid lavish praise on my parents for the quality of the food, the effort in preparation. Then, after tidily wiping his mouth—which in no way impaired the perfect cleanliness of the napkin—he told jokes. Everyone laughed at his humor, although Janie and I were merely imitating the noises of others. Mother cackled, covering her mouth with one hand, in the Chinese way, and slapping her thigh with the other hand, in the American way. But Father's laughter boomed through the house, filling the air in the dining room. I blinked and grinned when I heard it. It was a huge, wonderful, spontaneous sound, suggestive of whales calling vigorously to each other across oceans. It was the sound of a dying race, the call of a species bound for extinction, laughing at the moon while karma closed against the throat. After these days, I was not to hear his laughter again.

After the jokes, Uncle Shim recited poetry in a lyrical, singsong voice full of great, shaking drama and octave-spanning cries, his face floridly contorted with the effort of creating a total spectrum of earth-shaking emotion from the force of his recitation alone. He did not use his body. The Chinese language requires great intonation, and Uncle Shim was the cat's pajamas of tones. I thought his poetry was funnier than his jokes, but I often got things wrong in those days.

That year, when I was four, I asked permission to escape the suffocating confines of our darkened apartment. To the street. Into the air, to the magically beguiling sounds of other children.

Mother looked out the cracked window of our secretive second-story walk-up apartment. She lifted a blade of the graying venetian blinds as if it were made of fragile gossamer thread, as if she herself were under observation from an ominous, watching god.

Our apartment was a block from the Municipal Railway Car Barn, six blocks from the park, and ten thousand miles from Shanghai. She saw the teeming clutter of squalling children, the routine combat at the corner of Masonic and Golden Gate Avenue. Our neighborhood looked like a refugee camp, bursting its seams. It was. She shook her head.

Kai, said her face, you are not going outside. Bad river spirits there; I can feel them, in command of the street.

"All those children that fight out there hurt their karmas," she said. She ran her hands through her long and pretty hair and then looked thoughtfully at my chest. Karma. God kept score.

Westerners look up to God. My mother looked at the chest, the site of the true scoreboard, where all the ganglia and veins congregate, preparing to make final judgment on their host.

"There are fine musicians in America; you are to be one of them. I feel it," she said, nodding with a grand smile. It was infectious, and I grinned back at her. She hummed Mozart's *Jupiter* Symphony. Her face said: If you go outside, you will lose the music and become a ruffian and the sun will bake your skin and make you the same as the urchins on the street.

"*Wupo*, witches, outside," she whispered. "Devils." Accented by a shaking head, her hands, fingers pointing, gesturing, directing.

Wupo! Here! In the streets of America! I had thought they lived only in China. I trembled in fearful excitement.

Chinese believe in shaping children like clay. I still wanted to go outside, to see the witches, their evil little horns, wicked white hair, and red, gleaming rat eyes.

Don't make that face! she said with her eyes.

I stopped my face.

Her face was lovely, oval with large, deep-fired brilliant eyes, cheekbones chiseled softly from pale soapstone to hold haunting shadow and a mouth that seemed perfect in its fine linearity, its connectedness to the dimples that had been the common pride of her divided parents. A wonderful, joyous mouth that could laugh and grin and smile in a hundred expressions of precious, life-giving mirth.

She said the things that protect children from their fear of night, their anxieties about change, the terror of abandonment. I was so happy to be her son, her strength and beauty a shield against the glare of complicated and misunderstood days. She used to rub my ears with her fingertips, my cheek with the backs of her slender fingers.

"I love you so much, My Only Son," she whispered, clutching me to her as if she feared I would run away.

"I love you, Mah-mee," I managed, breathlessly.

She had the light, shade-cultivated complexion valued by Chinese aristocratic gentry. The portrait of her that was commissioned in Shanghai by the famous Japanese painter Nishio in 1932 shows a Madonnalike visage that stops the casual observer and begs reflection. I think it made happily married men review their vows.

She was proud of her rigorous classical literary education, but paradoxically cursed by a mind that could not grasp the simplest physical fundamentals of the Newtonian world: she would look in mirrors, bewildered by the image. She could never understand why the gardenia in her hair appeared on the left in the mirror and on the right in photographs. "Magic," she whispered.

I shared her confusion. Bread went into the toaster and disappeared. Burnt toast came out; so where was the bread?

She had come from a preindustrial society, where running water represented the New Age, and servants struggled red-faced with the crazed implements from Western forges, such as cars, irons, victrolas, and radios.

My father came from wealth but chose to fly airplanes, to jump out of them with parachutes made from silk, to march with armed and illiterate peasants in the yellowed *loess* muds of Chinese rivers, to accept Western military science, and to shoot guns at people for political reasons. He claimed Na-men as his best friend—a huge hairy foreigner whose clan name sounded like a summer mountain thunderstorm rolling down the Yangtze gorges.

Father loved the Americans. They were unspeakably competent with machines, were far friendlier than the Germans in the China Military Mission, and generously shared the best cigarettes in the world. They spoke easily in front of large groups—always a sign of deep inner strength. They chewed gum like tall, two-legged cows and laughed as easily as the wondrous, multivoiced, rubber-faced street storytellers in the International Settlement who spun gymnastic tales of lost lovers, lucky peasants, seasick sailors, and hardworking students, and rewarded the most appreciative members of the audience with the treasured white rind filament membranes of ripe oranges. Even better, the Pretty Countrymen, Americans, came from a country so young—less than two hundred years old—that they possessed no rock-bound traditions. In fact, they had no truly independent traditions at all.

Father had understood the present moment of China's history. He knew that the *Sheng-Yu*, the Sacred Edict of Master Confucius, could not provide the answer. He took to aviation lessons and the mechanical introduction to industrialized war as if born to the role. He was what the U.S. Army had prayed for—a tall, tough Chinese soldier who was fascinated with machines and could smile at death.

The American cadre clapped him on the back, shook his hand like village idiots and took his picture every five minutes.

My father's closest friend from those days was Major Henry Norman Schwarzhedd, an amiably capable Infantry officer of the American

Regular Army. H. Norman's father had been a China missionary, and
the entire family spoke several Chinese dialects. He could laugh at being
a *lao mao tze*—an Old Hairy One—at the age of ten. He liked Chinese
culture, Chinese agronomy, Chinese food. He could squat like the short-
limbed, long-backed farmers of China's paddies and understood the basic
elements of earth, water, air, iron, and fire. He knew the cycle of rice
of southern China, the milling of wheat in the north, the occult kalei-
doscope of the *Tao I Ching*, and the dominion of the weather gods over
all life. He did not leave China until he was fifteen, his mind broad and
grasping, his spirit kind and Christian, his tolerance unlimited, his tongue
dexterous and international. Na-men could sit on a farmer's dirt floor and
listen to stories of the Monkey Spirit for hours, laughing, nodding,
commenting like an elder when he was only a child of eleven.

Na-men, as H. Norman was called, was fascinated by Father's strong
grasp of Chinese history and had always asked for deeper discourse on
history. Father and Na-men talked about K'ung-Fu-tzu, the moralist, and
his *Analects*, and Sun-tzu, the Chinese theoretical master of battle and
author of *The Art of War*, with a degree of animated sophistication that
Father never had achieved during his earlier studies.

Father liked this big, beefy American who spoke Chinese in a strong
and loud voice, and accepted the eccentricity of his family name. Na-
men worked at his craft of military leadership as hard, as durably, as
uncomplainingly, as Imperial Scholars preparing for their examinations.
Na-men was a New-Age Man of China; he had no fear of steel machines
or of the host of deities that populated the world. He knew that men
struggle and that gods rule.

Most important, however, was the deep sense of honor, of integrity,
that lived inside Na-men as it was supposed to in all men of moral
Confucian rectitude. Na-men made sure all his men were paid and did
not steal. He always ate last, after his men. He was the first to deny
himself comfort and sleep. He did not use his position of rank for his
own advantage. He treated all noncommissioned officers and enlisted
ranks as men of ultimate worth, whether they were Chinese, Senegalese,
Indian, or *lao mao tze*.

The men in my father's family had not worked since the discovery
of fire, and it had been even longer since his forebears had labored in
the public interest. "Serving the public" invoked in their minds an image
of busy waiters wincing under the blows of demanding diners. Honor
and high purpose drew my father with irresistible attraction.

"Where did you go to school to learn this behavior?" Father asked.
Na-men said, "China. And West Point."

My father nodded. He had heard about West Point at Taoping Military Academy. West Point had been depicted in American movies.

"Hmmm," he said.

Father was trapped by human nature. After abysmal treatment at the hands of his father, Major Ting had been left vulnerable to the weaknesses of the human spirit. He could not help but respond to respect, kindness, and comradeship. Father fought alongside Americans. Na-men saved his life; my father saved his.

Father honored the United States, and its most learned and splendid school of schools, the U.S. Military Academy, located at a place called West Point on the Hudson River in the state of New York. Beyond that, the Americans made movies, which, prior to the Japanese occupation, had appeared within weeks of Hollywood premieres in the Bund theaters of Shanghai. Movies were picture windows into a brighter, newer world, where courage was honored and happy endings were routine.

So Father's heart belonged to Lillian Gish, the Barrymores, Thomas Jefferson, Joseph Stilwell, H. Norman Schwarzhedd, the Springfield '03, the T-2 parachute, the Vought O2U pursuit biplane, C-rations, and the hot dog. His choices could not have frustrated his own father more. Grandfather was deeply indifferent to the future and disdainful of the successes of his forgotten sons. Their failures or disappointments, however, merited his critical attention, which he would generously share with family, with his sons' friends, and with utter strangers. My father and his brother Han, it was rumored, had been beaten by their father when they were small children. This, of course, could not possibly have been true, but the very existence of the innuendo was evidence of a great moral ruin. I think I know why my father became a soldier, a professional fighter, and an iconoclast.

My mother was not impressed with Father's career choice.

"Ay-ya! *Soldiers* are killing our friends! And you *still* want to be a soldier?"

My father knew that the coming revolution would settle his class's long-term debt to the peasantry. The house of his father contained all the acquisitiveness and greed that promised the paroxysm of class war. The aristocrats would be the kindling for a roaring fire fueled by the fats of social exploitation.

Father wanted to live in America, where second sons could begin anew, washing the curses of five millennia from their blood and taking an oath to this new land that accepted everyone.

Mother accepted the decision to live in Indian country as gracefully as babies accept inoculations on their bottoms. She could not believe that the typhoon winds of change could alter our family. She cared little for wealth but believed that the powerful political connections of the Ting clan and her own wisdom about people would ultimately save them from destruction.

Mother had been a counselor to others in China. She had been called "Mother" by those unrelated to her. She was a social problem solver, a source of guidance to women and, through them, to men. She would have bargained with the victors, reasoning here, pressuring there, compromising in the middle, respecting balance, harmony, geomancy, truth.

"I am not a Nationalist, or a Red," she had said to my sisters. "I am, first and foremost, an honoring daughter. Second, I am learned in letters, as good as any man. And, of course, I am Chinese."

Mother and my elder sisters had lost everything—extended family, ancestral home, conventional roles, tradition, friends, teachers, wet nurses, cooks, wealth, servants, advisers, tailors, nation, customs, continuity, harmony, status. I do not think I have left anything out.

So being in America made no sense to her. Her inability to conform to the requirements of Chinese custom and family protocol, her helpless relegation to living without the extended family, and the continuous affront to her filial duty to tend her distant father, made her face flash with bolts of white-hot anger. Sparking with the unresolvable frustrations of the twentieth century, she threw dishes and tossed pots like the Yankees' starting pitching rotation.

A series of terrible explosions made me jump. I ran into the kitchen and the youngest of my three older sisters, Janie Ming-li, pushed me out.

"I want see!" I shouted.

"Don't go in! Mommy's angry and turned the room upside down!"

"Wow! Upside-down room! I want look!" I cried in Shanghai.

Mother had no fear of revolutionaries, of high office, or of broken dishware; she wanted to go home. Soon.

She loved electricity—ghost spirits in positive action. It was an affection shared by my sisters; electrical lights were icons of peacetime, of luxury, and of the ecstasy of nighttime reading. While interior decorators were becoming critical of the aestheticism of ceiling lights, Jennifer and Megan left them blazing in the glory of unsubtle illumination.

Reading one night under a lamp, Mother shrieked in abject horror when the light bulb exploded, showering her with small glass shards.

"Angry ghost!" she cried, throwing her book high in the air, snapping the binding and exploding pages across the living room like schools of frightened white bats.

Jennifer rushed in to make sure Mother was all right. She unhooked the lamp. Using a small towel, she unscrewed the hot bulb and inserted a new one, replugged the lamp and turned it on. She then swept up the glass and reassembled the book, clearing the room of the tepid bowls of water that had once held ice.

Mother rushed to Jennifer and fiercely seized her arms the way a feral bird locks talons on food. She looked at her as if she had turned ox dung into diamonds or had explained the ancient mysteries of the kitchen toaster.

"Jennifer Sung-ah! *Promise me* that you will be an engineer!" she cried, peering intently into her Firstborn Daughter's eyes as she marveled at her ability to harness the forces of Heaven. "Ah Tiah always loved you so, and now it is clear that he was so correct!" Ah Tiah was Gung-Gung's formal name, and in his later years, my paternal grandfather had remained aloof from everyone in the clan except my sister Jennifer.

Mother drove a car the way an orangutan would operate a tank. Alarm clocks startled her with their surprising janglings, ice was overproduced, and our toast was always burned.

"Dark toast is considered quite elegant," she suggested.

"I have seen workers along the Yangtze Gong turn black in the sun. Not you. You are My Only Son, and not toast. Do some reading."

The neighborhood was changing before our eyes. Whites were moving out as blacks moved in. To my mother, being in Africa was no worse than being in America, for the greater family was in neither and the mother tongue was absent in both. But she knew that she did not understand the culture of the street, although she studied it through the blinds as later generations would watch soap operas. I did not know what culture meant.

"These people. They have been in the sun too long. War has been hard on them, too. Their clothes are old, like ours."

Mother walked me to school on the first day of first grade, my heart slugging with pounding anxiety. I wanted to go out, but I had been held out of kindergarten. I did not want to go to school. That lasted for *hours*. I wanted to see other children, not be with them.

"This is My Only Son," she said to the principal, an innocent named Mrs. Priscilla Wyatt. My mother recognized the type. Mrs. Wyatt was like a missionary, a brave and dedicated soul who ventured into the Third World with precious medicines and heavy, dog-eared, mildewed books.

Women could answer a moral calling by going to places like Hunan and the Panhandle. They could brave any responsibility for little or no pay, with only death or disappointment as the risks. Na-men Schwarzhedd's mother had been one of those brave souls. Mrs. Wyatt could not have become a school principal in Presidio Heights or Cow Hollow or the Sunset. Want rank and opportunity, Mrs. Wyatt? Go to the slums. Too rich for your blood? Go home and have children of your own.

"He has some trouble with English," said my mother. "I appreciate all you can do for him, in giving him very special help. We are not going to be here much longer," she added cryptically, her face saying, And do not ask why.

"He has a delicate and rare skin condition that worsens in sunlight. Please. Keep him inside the school building while the other children are outdoors. Not knowing English, or having too much sun, could be very dangerous for him."

I did not know whether to look at my mother or at my skin in surprise. I hoped it was not serious. My skin condition was this: poor little Chinese hothouse plant.

"My husband joins me in this wish, if that means anything to you. I would respect his wishes. You see, during the war, he killed people."

I do not know when Mrs. Wyatt uncrossed her eyes after that parent–teacher conference.

I was kept indoors until the age of seven, and as a result I knew nothing about children my age. Mere speaking and the use of my body in physical games and sports, as forms of social interaction, were unknown arts, as distant from my experience as the rings of Saturn.

I understood calligraphy, and I valued food. Of course, I valued food—the Chinese had mastered the creation of sauces when France was still Gaul. Small, children's chopsticks became my best friend when I was four.

· I could, by placing my nose against the floor, and by being very patient, find the smallest button or lost item that evaded my family's search. I painted calligraphic characters with my eyes only inches from the soft graph paper, and learned from Uncle Shim the basics of Chinese chess, *shiang-chi*, with its bold, charging elephant, its austere general and his five *ping* soldiers. I could play American checkers by myself. I would laugh, for I never lost.

Uncle Shim had told me that I was to be *tsong lian*, an Inspector General of Imperial Viceroys, a scholar of historic proportions.

"The boy is perfect," said Uncle Shim. "He has a scholar's eyes already, built for reading and not for archery, and is only a toddler! He will be a great friend of books, unenticed by horses and the games of peasant boys! He will be safe from the physical world!"

I looked at the boys the way a Neanderthal would look at a dressing-room mirror in Macy's—not understanding the reflection, the resemblance, the connection, or the purpose.

Instead of possessing the native instincts of the hoped-for musical prodigy, I would prove to be nearly tone-deaf. This could have been occasioned by my later entry into the street, where my ears, and other things, were routinely boxed. For whatever reason, fists in the environment or genetic links missing in the DNA, Mozart's place in history was secure for another century.

Mother was a great believer in education. "My father," she said, "gave me Tang Syensheng, who was a Hanlin scholar, willing to retire from high office after the chest disease captured him. Tutors are for boys only, but Tutor Tang taught me for *eight* years before I had to share him with Younger Brother!" Her face was bright. "*Syensheng* means literally 'before born' and is an honorific. Age is *very* important, for it means the gods have smiled on your face every day of your life.

"I am happy that you like books. Comic books are good for you. What a cute little mouse! He will help you read music."

4

MOTHER

The Chinese are unabashedly social, for China's hard terrain and its labor-intensive rice, grain, and potato economy requires full cooperation for survival.

The Chinese lend new meaning to the concept of social interaction. Anyone can relate to other people, but traditional Chinese honor the dead. *Ching ming*, which means "shiny bright," is a ritual of paying homage to ancestors. Only the Chinese—who use the color white for funerals, speak to the dead, and leave elegantly spiced gourmet meals by cold gravestones—would use glittery adjectives to describe death.

Grave sites are swept, flowers placed, food offered, meals arranged at the headstones. The living explain new developments, emphasizing accomplishments, to the dead. Apologies are offered for imperfections in a Confucian world that expects flawless behavior. An unforgiving managerial continuum reaching from the father to the oldest remembered paternal relative sits in stony judgment.

Ching ming is probably the reason that so many Asians have succeeded in school, since honoring professors is simple compared to pleasing people who have been dead for centuries and who have nothing to
do but judge your behavior according to the pickiest standards known.
It was why Mother's favorite and most dramatic adjective was "perfect."

Mother could not practice ching ming properly because her ancestors were on the other side of the Pacific. No grave sites to sweep, no
azaleas and oranges to decorate a shrine, no direct communication with
the dead.

In 1951 we learned that Gung-Gung, my father's father, had died,
his death confirmed by reliable sources in Hong Kong.

Gung-Gung had been moved to a Reeducation Camp near the
outskirts of Chungking. It was a mild irony that a patriarch of the old
order had been sent to a concentration camp near the former Nationalist
capital, the place my sisters had called Free China. Grandfather's with-
drawal from opium had given him two extremely painful years of slow
death. He had always valued a simple, orderly, and fastidious life; it was
why he had maintained only one concubine at a time rather than a large
gaggle. This man of the old order, who had more wealth than he could
use, died in a dirt-floored barracks without a pillow or a last smoke.

Mother erected a shrine. A dark teak table, white pillows and
tablecloth, oranges, lilies of the valley, Gung-Gung's favorite mushroom pork dishes, glowing joss sticks, all surrounding his framed photograph. The photo depicted him in the days before he had discovered
the poppy, and he looked glorious, like someone who would never
kneel to age, communists, hard work, or death. The acrid pungency
of the incense made the air in the room heavy and sulphurous.

As the Only Son, I followed Mother to the shrine. I knelt once
for my grandfather, once for his father, and again for his father before
him. I lost count and added another, and no one complained.

"Kow tao for Grandmother?" No, said Mother's face. Respect is
for fathers, grandfathers, sons, bearers of the name.

The incense mixed with the smell of ling cod in soy sauce and
sugar, of mushroom pork, and the scent of lilies and orange peel. I felt
no loss, no sadness. Mother wept quietly for a few moments, as did
Megan.

Mother then disassembled the shrine, setting aside Grandfather's
special portions. She called Father, at the bank, and he returned home.

"Baba not like Gung-Gung?" I asked.

"Eat, eat, My Son!" said Mother, setting out all the dishes except those saved for Grandfather. She carefully extracted and then placed the valued fish's cheek on my plate. I smiled, for this meant that she loved me.

But this isolated ancestor's ritual was a unique event. Mother could not fully celebrate the Lunar New Year without the extended family. Why clean a house, pay debts, hang newly painted verses honoring the domestic deities, settle long-term disputes, and prepare feasts when the clan was not on the same continent? When one could not report to the watching dead?

We went through the motions, enough to depress my mother and sisters through the reminder of their separation from family, and enough to anger my father for the ritual's superstitious roots.

It was enough for me to become utterly confused about the relationship between the Kitchen God, who lived in Heaven and returned to the call of firecrackers, and General Electric, who operated the ice machine and only worked if money were sent to him in a white envelope with a magic stamp on it every month. As joss had to be lighted, the stamp had to be licked, and it tasted like an herbalist's mistake.

Santa Claus Syensheng lived in the North Pole, which was near Tsingtao, and returned if you brushed your teeth. But he never brought food, which was not only very strange, but rude. Instead, you were supposed to leave food for him, which should make his job very popular. If you were cursed with dirty teeth, Santa Claus would ignore the invitations to visit and leave you without toys, which had no bearing at all to teeth. I never understood why, if he were so popular, he was not allowed to use the door but had to enter the house through a cooking stack.

"What happen to Teeth God?" I asked, never receiving a satisfying answer.

Verses in bold, red characters painted on yellow banners were hung over our doors for good luck, while Janie wrote secret messages to Mr. Santa Claus and then burned them on the stove, like cash offerings to needy gods. How could Claus Syensheng read the message if it were burned? Only *wupo* could read smoke!

Great dishes were prepared for ching ming and for Christmas. But the best dishes were left to sit on a shrine for the dead in the first, and eaten until one was sick for the second. I went along with the motions, thankful that Uncle Shim, who loved to ask questions, left me alone on these issues.

The disparity between our home in America and the one known in China only bothered my mother while she was awake.

The utter isolation of our family from China was echoed by our partial estrangement from the Chinese community in San Francisco's Chinatown. We were of different tribes, and the difference was worst for my mother. Mother thought we were a microbial, disassociated satellite of the greater diaspora of Chinatown.

Chinatown was established against great odds by Kwangtung men, the resourceful and fearless railway builders and fishermen farmers from southern China. Their cultural center was Kwangchou, or Canton, and their three subdialects of *sam yep, say yep,* and *toisan* were incomprehensible to people from Shanghai.

Father spoke Cantonese because Taoping Academy, although in the north, had been strongly influenced by Kwangtung men. Mother had not gone there and did not speak Cantonese well. She could not bargain for food or order a meal in Chinatown gracefully without using English, a tongue for which she now bore little affection.

Once, I wandered away from my sister Janie Ming-li in Chinatown. Being Chinese, I entered the first restaurant I saw. I wanted a barbecued pork dumpling, a universally recognized dish. I was five. It was the Kuo Wah on Grant Avenue.

"Muhr-deh, ching," I said politely, my feet together, my head slightly inclined. Pork dumpling, please. I said it in Songhai, the language of the known world.

The hostess looked at me and said something that sounded like *"Neh ghong WAH!"* The first word rose with unlimited aspiration, the second fell precipitously without hope, the third seemed strangely complaining. She spoke in an angry volume that shrank my male unit and climbed tonal scales like a steam-driven xylophone. That was Cantonese.

I repeated myself. She repeated herself, louder.

She put her hands on her hips, like Mother, and I smiled. "Ayyaa!" she said, shaking her head, beckoning to me. I followed her through a maze of tables, through a corridor and a door. The smells were heavenly when she stopped and spread her arms. I squinted and searched, my head six inches ahead of my body. I smelled and saw the basketful of *muhr-deh.* I pointed. Ahh, she said, smiling.

"*Char siu bao,*" she said clearly, nodding.

I frowned and shook my head. That was not char-see-you-bow, or whatever. Those were pork dumplings. "*Muhr-deh,*" I said as clearly as I could, making the hostess laugh. She shouted at the cooks in the wild, exciting, undulating music of her dialect.

"Ay-yaa!" hissed Janie, breathless with her search of Grant Avenue, Stockton, and Kearney from Clay to Pacific streets. "I'll *muhr-deh* you!"

Murder was not an unknown theme in the family, because Mother had a driver's license. She refused to pay parking attendants because she felt the demands of driving horrifying automobiles were sufficient offense. After all, if she did not really drive, why should she have to pay once she stopped?

Automobiles. *Chi tz,* gas vehicles. In her hands, carts from Hell.

When the depressing un-Shanghai-ness of San Francisco and the isolation from her social niche overwhelmed Mother, she would weep while collecting us from school.

Throwing Janie Ming-li and me in the old Ford, she drove like a suicide candidate to the Pacific Ocean, releasing the straining parking brake at the halfway point when the hot scent of smoking metal reminded her to do something.

Every ten minutes or so she would hear the tortured scream of the transmission and randomly change gears. We would bob back and forth like horizontally thrown yo-yos. Her gear shifts sounded like twenty cooks pushing trays of silverware into an industrial-strength garbage disposal.

She drove with the relentlessness of a Mongol horsewoman, spectacularly indifferent to the vagaries of traffic or the subtleties of traffic signs. Even the great Jim Brown used to change directions occasionally. I think she regarded driving as something to be endured with a minimum exposure of time and space, dashing like a live duck through an arcade shooting gallery.

We looked out the windows goggle-eyed in anticipation of fiery death. Cars honked, brakes screeched, and drivers cursed, shaking fists and pointing digits. We knew how they felt.

She jerked to a wild halt on the Great Highway, bouncing us off the dashboard and flinging open her door, removing her shoes and dashing across the busy street. Janie turned off the engine and closed the doors. Mother flew past the undertow warning signs, down the graffiti-splashed concrete steps, across the thick sand to the wet beach and the surf of the Pacific Ocean, startling fishermen, jellyfish, and beachcombers.

My mother was the only woman I had ever seen who ran without Evil, the local bulldog, or a man with criminal intent in murderous pursuit. I ran with her, consumed as small children are in the passions of their mothers. She sighed as her feet found the wet sand, allowing her to accelerate while I still fought the deep, slowing mush of the dry dunes.

When I turned five the muscles in my legs learned to cooperate with the rest of me, and I could speed past her, hitting the flat wet plains of the forward beach first. Of course, she was running more slowly then, and I did not know it.

She was uncanny in her parking. There were perpendicular and diagonal spaces.

"Parking!" she cried. If we were parked straight, I knew we were in the diagonal spaces, and vice versa.

"Ma'am," said a motor police officer during one of our spontaneous appearances at the ocean. "You can't park like that."

Mother had returned from the sea, a Chinese Venus on a shell—a Ford—tears providing a liquid sheen to her cheeks. This was a woman who lied to school principals, pinned bronzed male genitalia to her bedroom wall, had a son who was going to surpass Mozart, and had produced a daughter who could harness St. Elmo's fires. She had crossed a world contorted by war, had traversed the gorges of the Yangtze, pitched hatchets, and bartered for her daughters using diamonds and rust. She did not need admonitions about *parking*.

"I am sorry, sir," she said in a voice that Marilyn Monroe was using that year, batting eyelashes that would have shamed Elizabeth Taylor. Gazing at him, drenching him in nonverbals, appealing to his basest instincts.

"Oh, please. Did I do something . . . *wrong?*"

The officer looked at her, and looked at Janie, smiling. He looked at me. He looked at her again, liking her too much.

"Ahemm," he said, tugging down his helmet visor, retreating, his motorcycle going *BrinDinDinDao!* in amplified exuberance as he roared off down the Great Highway, fleeing to safety.

Mother would sit behind the wheel of the idling Ford, shivering with her wetness, gazing at the Pacific like a fisherman with a hull-punctured boat. Her father was across the horizon.

She had put her bare, graceful feet in the frigid sea and expended two books of matches before wild fortune caused a match to accidentally ignite the joss stick. Sputtering in the cold sea wind, its sweetly acrid paste afire, it sparked to the spirits of the sea while she talked to Na-Gung, her father. The wet wind blew out the flame, allowing it to smolder and smoke, releasing incense.

Between my wildly unrestrained, unchained, free-from-the-apartment, seagull-chasing sprints up and down the beach, I caught parts of her conversations—her hopes that Wang the fish cook would bring a two-man pot of sea water with swimming yellow fish to Grandfather's home in exile in distant Tsingtao.

Grandfather would apparently cool his heels in the water on the hot and humid days of a Yellow Sea summer, letting the fish tickle his feet.

"I hope it is hot on the Tsingtao Bund today!" she cried into the crashing surf, the joss stick hissing.

"Then the water that touches my feet is the same that touches yours, and you can know how I miss you, and revere you, and respect your learning!" Mother had to speak aloud to her father across the sea, because he could not read her facial expressions from afar.

"Do you think of me? Do you forgive me for leaving you?

"I am so sorry, Father!" she cried into the cloaking roar of the waves, the mist of the sea kissing the tears welling from her eyes.

"Mother abandoned you! I promised I would never do the same! And I am now in another world! Oh, my Christian Lord.

"Do you know?" she asked the wind as it carried her words to China. "The Americans made the black people their slaves. They took them from their homes in Africa. I think the war has done the same to me."

I assumed that our family home in Shanghai was like the Mark Hopkins Hotel on Nob Hill. It housed, at high season, forty-five people. It *fed* forty-five souls three times a day, every day, including Sundays, holidays, and Leap Years.

"Mommy. Can I run in Songhai home? Like at beach?"

"Of course! There is a high, upper gallery that encircles the inner courtyard of the main house. You can run around the gallery and pick the mandarin oranges all you like, just as your father did when he was a boy.

"I will also take you by train to Tsingtao, to pay homage to Na-

Gung, who will be so happy to see you. He will give you the additions to the ancestral tablet of sons for the *ssu tang,* the family shrine.

"He will ask you to recite the Sixteen Edicts, and play magic string-knot games. Oh, yes! Let's do that soon!" she cried, crushing my arms.

"I have discussed our future with our Only Son," she announced to my father.

Father had received a letter from Amethyst Jade Cheng, who had fled from Ho-t'ien, escaping from the Japanese and the communists. She had arrived in Hong Kong in 1946, the lining of her coats filled with American corporate bearer bonds. In 1951 she had founded the China Lights Bank in Hong Kong, and asked Father's assistance in opening a branch in America. Amethyst Jade's parents had died on the Yangtze River road that my family had traversed. They had been unable either to assist my mother and my sisters or to survive themselves.

The Tings had saved the Chengs from revolutionary slaughter during the Taiping Rebellion in 1854; in 1946, the surviving Cheng redeemed the American Tings from financial ruin. Amethyst Jade Cheng was a brilliant businessperson who spent half of each year in London with English bankers. Until her death she never understood that Father, without her, was destitute. She presumed that a man with Father's abilities—flying airplanes, fixing guns and cars, being admired by American generals—meant that he could not have possibly left China without a fortune in diamonds and gems.

"Ah, gallant Colonel!" she would say, curling an arm around his. "How is the Ting family fortune?"

Father would smile painfully. "We have no fortune, Lady."

"Ohhhh! Colonel! You are so tricky! You must come to London with me! We will take all the money in the British Empire together!"

Father was seated at the kitchen table, studying his set of twelve banking-procedure manuals. He had chosen between his true profession, soldiering, and his nation of choice, America. To maintain his uniform, he would have had to live in Taiwan. So he became a banker for an institution that required as much travel as he had experienced while soldiering.

Mother said, "We are prepared to return home, while *my* father is still alive, to perform our true filial duties, *whenever* you are ready."

My father began balding about this time.

Sometimes my youngest sister cried for her cousins, friends, and wet nurse, Sweet Plum, a personal house servant dedicated to each child until either died. But my sister had more diversions than our mother. She was very good in school and had no prejudices about language.

For my sisters, America was a great adventure in learning, in adapting, and in forgetting. For my mother, it was limbo, and I was her company.

I loved bedtime, when my mother sat by my pillow, holding me in her lap to read books that she drew from the redwood crate.

She read about mounted warriors who fought pirates on the east coast of Africa during the twenty-five-thousand-man expeditions of Admiral Cheng Ho in the early fifteenth century, about Bannermen archers who walked a thousand miles, crossing the Great Wall from Manchuria. They could break rock and bring down eagles with their arrows. I liked the swordfighting lancers of Hunan, who laughed as they ate with huge chopsticks from the largest menu in the world. She read about Genghis Khan and his Golden Horde, who had swept across Russia and left almond-eyed people throughout Europe. I learned of the lush southern colonies of China, called Vietnam, where the native tribesmen had fought the armies of the Chinese emperors for over a thousand years, prevailing in the end against what was then the largest and best-equipped army in the history of the world. There were few references to women in these tales.

I would follow my mother's graceful finger as it glided up and down the characters, from right to left.

"Writing is *so* important," she said. "Many of us are in this country, *Mei-gwo*, but speak a different *hwa*. But all of us share the same writing, and it unifies the literates.

"When you write, you can communicate with any of our countrymen, from Macao to Tsingtao, from Foochow to Chungking. If you have a daughter, after having *many* sons, please allow her to have learning, as well. Maybe she will write about her paternal grandmother!"

I asked her to script the characters for: chicken *tsow mien*, oyster-sauce beef, *muhr-deh* and *kuo tieh*, potstickers (a soy-sauce and vinegar-dipped pork ravioli). I kept the paper in my back pocket, and pulled it out as though I were Billy the Kid drawing a six-gun in the Kuo Wah restaurant.

"Here," she said, "is your family name. Ting means 'human,' 'individual.' Look at how beautiful the character is—a straight, strong, two-stroke chop.

"Kai takes eight pen strokes. It means 'reform,' 'educate,' 'improve.' I will ask your Uncle Shim to teach you how to write your names, for his calligraphy is absolutely number one. Your father will be leaving for Singapore next week, and Uncle will stay with us, and you will learn the noble strokes of your noble name.

"Your name should have come from Gung-Gung, but he never met you, and I never received the high family honor of your birth—a living son—because you were born here, in Mei-gwo.

"So. Here you are, so humble and meek, because we could never report your arrival to the ancestors. Your name comes from me. It is a very smart name. Mrs. Constance Carlson, who taught me and my maid Episcopalian English, told me that Kai is a Chinese name that also sounds Western. It became the perfect name for you, here in this Episcopalian nation. Our chief of tutors, Luke Syensheng, gave Western names to my daughters even before we reached this foreign land.

"Someday, My Only Son, we will return to the Yangtze. You will be so learned, so well prepared, that your future as a musician will be beyond doubt. Your music can unify traditional and new China, and my father will weep for the joy of you."

Her eyes twinkled, saying, And my pride in you will know no bounds. She hugged me, and my heart flew into hers.

Her favorite book was *The Tales of Lu Hsun*, which had been printed manually by the communists. She acquired a copy during the Run, during their stay with the Reds, and how my father ever tolerated its presence in our house has evaded all family understanding.

Lu Hsun described common village life, which was well beneath the purpose of calligraphy's highborn intricacies. Written language was for philosophy and poetry and was itself a demanding art—matters having no connections with daily life.

"Storm in a Teacup," "The True Story of Ah Q," "The Flight to the Moon"—these were the concerns of Lu Hsun. He wrote of food, farming, animal husbandry, and village storytellers, of shaman priests and *wupo*, witches.

Mother liked the tale of Tzu Han-ren, a five-year-old peasant boy supported by his village to reach the Pen Forest and become an elevated *chuan yuan* scholar, selected through direct examination by the Emperor himself. When he turned nine, and received his customary, first true birthday celebration since the Red Egg Ginger Party, the village gave him enough cash to buy three books—*The Analects*, *The Water Margin*, and *The Dream of the Red Chamber*.

Janie and I had birthday celebrations every year, in which we could order our own dinner menus.

"Why Tzu Han-ren only have one birthday?" I asked.

"In Songhai, My Son, we celebrate every tenth birthday," she said.

"So why did he have his tenth birthday when he was only nine?" asked Janie.

"Oh, it is to outwit the clever Birth God, who expects the celebration in the tenth year, and would strike you down if you enjoyed your birthday too much. Moderation in all things," she said.

"I don't think the Birth God is so clever," whispered Janie. "Don't you think he would learn?"

My mother loved education and revered scholars and musicians. I liked soldiers and loved to run.

"Kai. Recite for me the story of the good student Tzu Han-ren while Jennifer brushes my hair."

"Mah-mee, how do you want your hair brushed—back or up?" asked Jennifer.

"Dear. Please. Brush my hair so it will look windswept, as if I were standing on the beach barefoot on a warm day, singing to my father, facing China, with typhoons coming to me from the Yellow Sea!"

I was six when our mother died of cancer. I think she regretted in her last days the separation from her father in Tsingtao and the greater extended family in Shanghai more than the deprivation of a long life in America or the permanent separation from us. Her death had begun when she left China in a cheerless lonesome dawn, without a kiss from her parents or forgiveness from her father. She was never to see them, or China, again.

If only she had shown overtly her psychic bruises, sacrificing a beautiful and ephemeral face, admitting to the ache in her heart and the loss in her soul.

I did not mourn her. As with so many things, I was ignorant of the conditions that occasioned change. Things just happened. First, I was told she was visiting friends. When she returned she looked weak and unhealthily pale. She neither drove nor spoke to her father from the tub.

She was exercising denial. If she pretended all was well, the evil spirits could not find a purchase point to take her away before she could return to China and her filial duty.

"You sick, Mah-mee?" I asked.

"No!" she whispered, her face saying: Don't ask more.

She spoke, smiling and nodding. I paid her words no heed, focusing on her bright, shining eyes, looking for the message that said: I will never leave you again.

As she had never managed to say farewell to her father, I never said good-bye to her.

I was then sent to stay with another family for a month.

When I returned, I ran into the kitchen, dashing from one set of female legs to another. Jennifer's legs, Megan's legs. Back to Megan's.

"Where Mah-mee?" I asked.

"So, did you enjoy your visit to the country?" asked Megan Wai-la.

"I no go country. I Chinatown. *Who* those people, Older Sister?"

Our mother's absence had caught me between languages. My Songhai was pitiful, my Mandarin worse. My English was fractured. My Cantonese was nonexistent.

I wonder to this day about that family, and if my visit ended a friendship. I can remember nothing of them, but I have a vague feeling of having been well cared for. I never saw them again and yet I owe them a debt, a gratitude.

Jennifer Sung-ah, elegant, confident, and firstborn said, "Well, Chinatown is *almost* like being in the country."

"Kai, did you finish the book we sent with you? Here, have some noodles," said Megan Wai-la, crying.

"Where Youngest Sister? Why Wai-la cry?" I asked. No one in our family answered direct questions very well. Janie Ming-li, seven years my senior, had also been sent away without being told of Mother's death.

This was traditional, to protect the young children from the shock of a parent's death while the adults burned incense, offered oranges, served spectacular dinners, overpaid for stupendous caskets, and prayed for the continuity of the family. Death was an important event, and respect to ancestors was a requisite, regardless of the distances that women in bound feet would have to traverse, regardless of the separation of men from their fields.

The surviving spouse and adult children of the deceased prepared to enter the prescribed periods of mourning, which ranged from a year to twenty-seven months for offspring. But without our mother, and the other keepers of the culture in distant China, these rituals were abandoned and I had only the vaguest knowledge of them. At the age of six, I was clearly within the age of nondisclosure of my mother's passing. Janie was in fact old enough to know, but Jennifer and Megan could not agree on whether to tell her, and there were no elder women to advise them.

Years later, I ran into a friend walking down Kearney Street, leaning on a cane.

"Gideon Chen! You okay?"

"My mother died. This is my mourning cane," he said.

"Oh, no. I'm really sorry," I said, sad for him. "Say, what about the cane?"

"Oh, yeah. I keep forgetting that you grew up without culture. The cane, it's to help us in the pain of losing her."

But Janie deduced Mother's death quickly. With fierce willpower, she maintained the custom and did not tell me.

"Where Mah-mee staying—I do wrong?" I asked, my speech compressed, anxious.

"What shall I read you?" Janie asked in a tight voice, while Megan rustled the hair on my head. Megan had always treated me well, despite Mother treating her as a visiting IRS agent. Megan's birth had created a family with two daughters and no sons.

Megan would become the most renowned member of the family, the one dedicated absolutely to public service, to world peace, and to the health of nations. Like all my sisters, she was beautiful. Her special attribute was her ability to draw friends and allies for a lifetime, based on fleeting contact.

She saw war in its simplest context: a man holding a steel bayonet to a girl's slender throat, and she dedicated her life forces to creating alternatives to the blade. Megan matched our father's courage in battle with fierce, gutsy pacifism.

Jennifer Sung-ah was eighteen years older than I and was emotionally, physically, and culturally the most mature. The turmoil of China, the war, the Run, and the sojourn in India had made her wise before she had seen sixteen years. By the time she arrived in San Francisco, she was facing a difficult decision: should she stay in America, tour Europe, or run for Mayor?

She was the unquestioned leader. While she flourished in America, her friends would wonder what world-shaking changes she might have wrought had she not been wrested from the homeland. I still think that she might now be the foreign minister or minister of culture, perhaps Chairperson of the Party, to the greater benefit of the world. It was a great reflection of her inner self that most people thought of her as smart first, and voguishingly stunning second. She kept her distance from me because she feared others would think me to be her offspring.

My sisters cranked thoughts like Univacs. After a lifetime of being tutored and learning the world's most perplexing language—Chinese, in three tongues—they picked up English, a smattering of French, and negotiated American public schools and college with ease.

My sisters had perfected the English taught them by Tutor Luke by spending most of 1944 in India, where they awaited passage to the States. They had loved their English instructors, who were Indian and English. Jennifer and Megan still speak English with the lilting music of the British Isles, making many suspect that they came from London, rather than the English Concession of Shanghai and the Crown Colony of India. It was also clear from their internecine teasing that they had broken men's hearts every time they left one continent for another.

They both looked like Nancy Kwan. When *Flower Drum Song* became a movie in the sixties, I said that Nancy Kwan resembled them.

"That's not a compliment, Kai," said Jennifer. "Nancy Kwan played a mindless tart, utterly dependent upon men."

In the next year, Janie Ming-li became my functional mother. She was the household manager, arranging meals and tasks with a military precision unusual in an adolescent. It was like a shipwreck, where the resourceful child passenger becomes the first mate. Father traveled, as he had in the past, but Uncle Shim did not appear in his absence.

I loved my sister's care. But a sadness dwelled in her, and I worried about it constantly. I angered her with my continuous questioning about its origin, unaware that the same sentiment lay festering in my persona, as insidiously hidden as our mother's cancer.

Typical of children who have lost a parent, we suffered eating and sleep disorders. For a while, Janie overate, then fasted. I ate less, performing an unconscious, immature child's ching ming by offering my food to my lost and missing parent. We tossed fitfully at night, unable to capture the winds of the sleep gods, and occasionally fell dead asleep in the middle of the day. Janie made our meals, laundered our clothes, darned socks, struggled to teach me religion, and made straight A's in her spare time.

Our father enjoyed Janie's home maintenance but missed his wife profoundly. It had been an arranged marriage of money to brains, and they had always argued about who represented which. But both people possessed exceptional passion for life and for each other. Father always loved Mother for braving the world to bring herself and their children to America; Mother loved Father for merely cursing when she declared her utter emancipation from the tyranny of the ancient traditions of crushing male rule. Their union was powerful, and unique, and never to be replaced.

My father began to rage over small things. Stilwell, whose mind was exceptional, had been surprisingly profane. The GIs had taught Father how to swear in English, and he got better at it. In China, his commander would have excused him from the regiment for the mourning period—at least a year. Father would have invited the friends of his childhood, his family, and his regiment, to drink *tsin boi* and reminisce with hot tears about the wonder and the beauty of his wife, the mother of his children, while he wore hemp cloth, sandals, and strode with a cane, the community allowing him to be nuts for a while.

In America he had no childhood friends, and he showed no weaknesses to his colleagues in the China Lights Bank. He had little affection for his absent family in China, and his organization, the 186th Regimental Combat Team, of 11 Corps KMT, was gone forever, obliterated in the bitterest civil war and revolution history had known. The wonderful, active alliance with the U.S. Army in China was history. He was now an American. Gary Cooper or Na-men Schwarzhedd wouldn't cry, so neither would he.

I could. I was good at it. I thought someone was hiding my mother from me.

My sisters crafted letters to me, full of details of the busy harbor esplanade, the Bund of Tsingtao, the fat yellow fish from the Gulf of Po Hai, the austere greetings of my maternal grandfather, and the exotic foods of the White Russian restaurants of Shanghai and Harbin. They read them to me, tearfully.

They were signed, "I love you My Only Son, Mother."

I wondered why Father received no mail from her, and why Mother had not taken me to accompany her to meet Grandfather and his tickling fish, to let me run in the compound's upper gallery and pluck mandarin oranges from the long branches of its treasured shade trees. I wondered if she had found Yip Syensheng, and Dog.

"When we go China, see Mother, Father?" I asked.

This no doubt made my father feel that he needed to find a mother for me, one who was older than thirteen, to cleanse the house of the complications of family consideration.

He had come from a lineage in which men had neither participated in childrearing nor generated income for a span of five generations. Such were the grand advantages of wealth.

Father had refused his roots, recognizing in American soldiery the beauty of action, the seduction of decisiveness, the satisfaction of utter and honorable commitment of dedicating his life to the safety of others.

"It is no longer good enough to measure a man by what he knows," he said. "That is the old world, the old China, standard.

"Now what counts is this: what can a man *do?*

"All the knowledge of the teachings of the philosophers means *nothing* against an airplane with guns and a pilot who knows how to kill."

So Father moved the family to safety, from a corner of the world saturated in blood. He moved his wife and children to *Mei-gwo*, the Beautiful Nation, the Pretty Country, so ripe with promise, unsullied by rapacious foreign invasion, uncomplicated by a cultural heritage that was heavier than its people.

America was blessed with a West Point, filled with movie theaters, far removed from debilitating superstition and the enduring memory of his critical father. My father had found his home.

5

EDNA

Nine years after the Run and seven years after my birth in America, Revolution arrived. It came in the corporeal form of Edna Madalyn McGurk.

She smelled like roses. She was a college graduate in English literature from Smith, was primly handsome, and had missed her calling when the SS closed its ranks to all comers after the demise of Hitler.

Our father married her for my sake, although I thought he had generously exceeded my needs. I understood the part about having a mother, because by the time Stepmother Edna was sworn into office, a year had passed since I had seen mine. My mother's letters from China had shifted from the lackluster and the infrequent to the nonexistent. I began to fear that she would neither return nor call for me and Janie to join her, and was even more fearful of the cause of her break in correspondence.

My yuing chi, my karma, was bad. Not bad. Terrible. I had not scored well in God's book. I struggled to determine what I had done to make my mother stay away for a year, wanting to never do it again. It was so baffling, for I felt as if I had behaved correctly, trying to help Ming-li raise me.

"Good morning," Edna said, with a blinding smile, the echo of her clacking heels loud on the hardwood floor of our hallway. She looked like a movie star—tall, angular, and confident. She had a very attractive, bright-eyed face and light, sunny blond hair that fascinated me. It was like looking at a well-dressed light bulb. She looked remotely like a Western version of Mother.

"My, you're just adorable. So cute!" She was wearing a dark navy pillbox hat with a veil and matching wasp-waisted dress. She demonstrated her dexterity by managing to pinch my cheek while wearing elbow-length white gloves. It hurt a little.

"You may call me Stepmother Edna." I could pronounce none of it. She was luminously gorgeous, and I loved her.

Unlike us, Edna was a direct person, providing absolutely precise answers to cosmic inquiries. We learned to dislike her answers. I listened carefully to her because she was tall, had perfect diction, looked wonderful, and scared me down to my socks.

She was *nahgwangning*. Foreign country person. Tremendously exotic. I couldn't wait to see how she drove a car. Her face was slender, illuminated in the center by pale gray eyes and shimmering in its blond outline. Her face was rather immobile. She spoke with her tongue and lips, and not her face.

Edna McGurk came from an insular inner circle of elite Philadelphia society. She came to our house the way the Germans marched into Paris, certain of conquest and totally prepared to suppress resistance.

Six years before, she had shocked her family and class by marrying a destitute Berkeley law student. He was a solid fellow, a World War II vet who was on his way to a good life with her when he was drafted for the Korean War.

Chinese communist troops killed him on the banks of the Imjin River in the winter offensive of 1950. He had died under the guns of Chu Teh's infantrymen of the People's Liberation Eighth Route Army, the same guys who had dropkicked my father's former regiments across the Formosa Strait the year before. The same guys, by their thoughtless acts, had managed to place Edna, angry and sad, into our immigrant home.

I do not know how Edna coped with her loss. As with so many military casualties, the ordeal began with reports that he was missing in action, followed by possible POW status, and concluding with final regrets. His remains were returned with military honors. I think part of Father's attractiveness to her was premised on his survival through the test of an extended war record.

Their meeting was an arabesque, orchestrated by a USO function at the Geary Theatre for veterans and widows. The prime attraction was Danny Kaye. The audience roared and punished its hands in endless applause. Amid this eruption of celebrational goodwill, manners became expendable, petting was rampant, and booze was in the air. "Thank you, thank you," Danny Kaye was saying, as Colonel Ting and Mrs. McGurk were jostled together at the lobby bar.

"Make mine Coke," they uttered simultaneously, laughing and admiring each other for their common demonstration of restraint. The recognition each saw in the other was instantaneous. The exotica of their contrasts, the attraction of shared height, the patent, irresistible marks of loss in their eyes, drew them elbow to elbow, gazing at each other. Edna was captivated by what she termed a cosmic sweetness. Heightened by the remembrance of war, softened by the light brush of comedy, strengthened by the common bond of need.

"My name is T.K. Ting," he said, passing her the soda.

"I am Edna McGurk," she replied, offering her hand, searching for confirmation of the heady spark that had illuminated the smoke-filled lobby.

He learned that she was from the East Coast, loved Shakespeare and Gauguin, believed in a God that favored no particular faith, and had read all the books of Pearl Buck. And that she was the only member of her family to leave Pennsylvania and had long fantasized about flying in the open cockpit of an airplane, wearing goggles and a scarf. She confessed to becoming giddy with a few drinks, slipping curiously into an Irish brogue.

"I'm a widow, but not a merry one," she said.

"Fate can be cruel, but in America, it can change," replied Father.

She learned that he had been classically educated in China, had fought alongside the American army, had been a pilot, and was the only member of his family to leave China. That he thought she resembled the actress Lana Turner, and that his wife had died very recently.

Edna had loved her first husband, and was swept away by her

second. She arrived in our home silently grieving for one while openly adoring Father. We mourned the absence of our mother. Both Father and Edna had lost their lives' true loves, and were doing the best they could manage. The children were to prove liabilities to their plans.

"I am going to be your mother," she announced, removing the hat while aligning the veil. "It's going to be wonderful."

Neither Father nor Edna were friends of indecision. The wedding was over and Edna had moved into the master bedroom. I never knew the impetus for their speed, but I think they were fleeing reason, preferring to throw the dice and go for broke rather than take another chance on a lonely tomorrow.

Father gained notice for marrying a beautiful foreigner, and had taken a major-league step toward cementing the American assimilation he so desperately sought. Edna proved that her first marriage to a commoner was no quirk; she picked her husbands premised on her own, very individual tastes.

Nor was Edna one to take open counsel of her fears. She joined our ragged little household with an abruptness that was unknown to it.

"I can't *stand* how *everyone* in this house speaks!" I thought she was referring to my sisters' English accents until I realized that "everyone" was me.

I also showed an early lack of communication proficiency.

"When *tsow mien?*" I asked, lacking only the empty bowl in my hands to complete the effect. Stepmother Edna looked so smart; she had to understand that I was requesting noodles, the food of the gods. Even the Italians had adopted it after Marco Polo brought the strands back through the Silk Route.

She studied me, like bird droppings on a Rolls-Royce.

"*What* is 'sow men'?"

"*Tsow-mien,*" I said, louder.

Her toe began tapping. I looked at it.

"I cannot understand that barbaric speech," she said. "Do not talk to me unless you are prepared to speak *English*. And don't look at me like that!" The toe stopped. Her fist balled.

I knew what that meant. But I was wrong; it meant much more than, yes, we have no noodles.

"Young man, you are now an American. You are very cute, but you cannot get by in this world by looking endearingly at people. You must give up your past habits and learn new ones.

"You also look quite sickly, and you make so many—faces," she said. "I will teach you English, and you *will* learn. This will save you from becoming a ditchdigger or a drayman. It should also improve your facial expressions."

Edna was placing the kitchen in order. Because Janie was not very tall, everything in the lower cabinet shelves had been organized in the year of our mother's absence. Everything above Janie's height was cluttered.

Edna seemed angry as she spoke, moving cups and dishes. She was standing on a chair, and her hair wafted across her face until she wrapped it up atop her head. Her nose was aquiline and sharp, like Uncle Shim's, although she was considerably prettier. She liked neither the kitchen's condition nor the effort involved in its reorganization. I knew she viewed me in the same light.

I marveled at her physical beauty, wanting her to like me, to read to me, to even hold me. I remembered, looking at her, that my mother used to kiss my nose in the morning, her cup of steaming white tea misting her face.

"Stepma kiss nose?" I asked, using my hands and face more than my speech.

"Pardon me?" she asked crisply.

"You need to go outside and fill your hollow chest with fresh air. Truly *normal* seven-year-olds play outside. Now, shoo! If I want you, I'll whistle, like this," and she made the sound of a London constable car siren.

I did not know that then. I thought it sounded like Mr. Carter's whistle. Mother and I had seen him use the whistle to call Evil, his bulldog, after it had started to chew on short human legs. The whistle was shrill and had to be louder than a child's mortal cries.

I stood there, ear wax melting, ear drums erupting, and eyes popping.

I tried to tell her that I had this special skin condition, which worsened in sunlight. But only Chinese Mulligan Stew, wild with crisscrossed *r*'s and *l*'s, with deep-forested diphthongs and evergreened interdentals, came out of my struggling mouth.

The street waited for me the way a mako shark awaits limbs hanging from inner tubes.

The street was filled with my peers. War babies, the Baby Boomers. There were more of us in the two-through-seven age group than in all

the others combined. We were a huge club. My membership card had
not arrived in the mail.

Some of the street kids had seen me before. I would zoom down
Central past the huge, redbrick Municipal Railway Car Barn to McAllister and pull a screaming left. I would hoof it with high-pumping knee
action to Fremont Elementary on Broderick like Pacific storm winds
howling off Twin Peaks. I left for school before most kids were up,
honing those high-achievement skills early.

During recess, I hovered near teachers, the natural allies of pint-
sized Asian students. Away from the protective radius of the faculty, kids
were being beaten dumb by other kids. These children are cashing in
their futures, I thought. During class, I pretended I was not there, a
small ghost my mother would have understood, a spirit with whom she
might commune.

The slum schoolteachers of the fifties were as resourceful as atomic-
bomb survivors, a status for which they had been trained. These were
the days of ducking and cowering under our desks to survive a direct
hit from an atomic bomb.

Mr. Isington was from England. He had a refined accent like Jennifer's and Megan's. An expatriate, he had been in the Canadian Army,
landing on Normandy and staying in the war until the end. He was
short, squat, had a feral sense of survival, and smelled of baby powder.
Kids backed off when he began tugging at the end of his nose, as if he
were extending the muzzle of a gun.

He was a no-nonsense chap. Mr. Isington operated like the Clau-
dian emperors, with his own Praetorian Guard. He formed a band of
monolithic sixth-graders, and enforced classroom discipline with flying-
wing tactics.

He called them the Bomb Squad—the first youth gang created
under color of governmental fiat since the alley mobs of Scilla. They
were guided by the axiom "Might makes right" and manned by thugs
who accepted higher authority. They were probably Young Republicans.

Mr. Isington later told me that Big Willie Mack, my enemy on
the streets, had asked if he could join the Bombers and had been refused.
That, in retrospect, was a big mistake. Cop or crook, the turn of a
screw. What if Big Willie had become a rescuing Bomber, and not a
thunderous bully? What if someone in Vienna had taken young Adolf
Hitler's efforts at architecture seriously?

Fighting in class was normal. When it became a riot, teachers cried

"Help!" through the door transoms into the hallway. The hall monitors passed the word like the Pony Express.

"By Jove, lads," said Mr. Isington on the scratchy, static-filled squawk box, "we have an incident in Room 20, Mrs. Halloran's. Be so good as to bustle down there, if you would. Hall monitors, keep to your stations. That's good, young gentlemen." And the Bomb Squaders would leave their sixth-grade seats and trash the offenders.

Mrs. Halloran showed her teeth in a sickened smile while organized battery was committed in the name of order, suspending for the moment our lesson about the wild beasts of the Fleischacker Zoo.

I came home from school as I had arrived: fast, my feet barely touching the pavement. At the age of seven, without outdoor play but with the history of the dunes, I had learned to pump my legs and arms high like a hurdler sprinting for the tape. I had learned to run as baby starlings learn to eat predigested pabulum, or as Janie had eaten pre-chewed broccoli from our mother. Because it was necessary.

Other kids were too happy at the 3:10 bell to worry about the little Chinese squirt beating feet for his life. I would enter the sanctuary of our apartment breathing hard and filled with the relief of escape.

American culture was a mystery, the evolving black subculture of the Panhandle was an enigma, and both overlapped across my struggling mind like a galloping herd of octopuses; I had trouble distinguishing the origin of the tentacles. But foreign or not, I knew I did not want to get beaten up.

Some of the preschool kids on the block did not think I was human. They had not seen my dawn runs to the school. So when Edna evicted me, they touched my hands and face, wondering where all the color had gone. And what had happened to my hair?

"Man," said one of them. "He so ugly. Doctah pull him out, doctah slap his momma 'steada him!"

"Don't say *nothin* 'bout no mommas!" said someone else.

I wanted to hear *more* about mommas. Anyone's momma.

Some of the kids were old enough to know that I belonged to a group of people who had attacked Pearl Harbor and cooked terribly stinky food in funny restaurants. I would later learn to my great relief that my mother and father did not attack Pearl Harbor.

"Jap," said one.

"Chink!" said another. "He a Chink, not a Jap!"

My heart had gone from beating two hundred times a minute to

All Engines Stop. My psychic apparatus told me that Jap or Chink, I was in deep trouble.

I thought Pearl Habba was an unlucky victim of the Fremont schoolyard. That Pearl was probably a kid who couldn't run like the wind. A kid who got thrown out of sanctuary to become dog meat. Food for Evil, the dog.

If you've got the blood, we've got the fists. It's Alpo time.

The two kids who could not agree on the ethnicity of my origin pushed each other for a few seconds. A circle formed. Then they beat each other up. This was the pattern of the schoolyard. I ran for my door. It was locked. I knew how Hansel and Gretel felt in the scary woods. I rang the doorbell as sincerely as I could, and Edna appeared, like Pinocchio's fairy godmother. We all looked at her. Even I stared as if I had not seen her before. She was blond. She did not seem to like Chinese food, made unusual noises, and was proudly violent. She was *wupo*! Ay-ya! They *were* in America! And they opened doors!

"T'ank you!" I gushed.

"Now, I didn't whistle for you. You just went out." She was staring directly at my terrified face, ignoring the mob. "Go make friends." Slam, click.

Scared but ignorant, I descended the six stone steps to the street. The fight had stopped when Edna had appeared, and the kids were a bit dazed with the appearance of a blond Anglo-patrician on their block.

"Wow!" said a huge kid, who had to be thirty years old. "Who dat lady?"

"Stepmama Edna," I said, in my eccentric accent, and those who heard me laughed. Those who had not heard also laughed. I thought laughter was good. Wrong again.

I was not comfortable talking to kids, particularly boys, and I avoided the older ones like the plague. Now they were on me like raw egg on hair.

The group of children smelled my fear and anxiety. They looked like a homogeneous mass of clothes, heads, and arms. They closed in tighter.

I tried communication. Take me to your leader.

"*Yau pungyob*," I squeaked. I want to be friends.

"*Yow?* Yow *what!?*" The laughter was deafening. These kids and I were more culturally attuned than we knew. Chinese *bwa*, language, and the black patois of the Panhandle depended on inflection and musical tone and were indifferent to conjugation. We came from societies that honored families, war, percussion, and elders. These similarities, however, were not presently evident.

"Who she be, you ratfacedshitferbrains," said the mammoth kid, towering above the mob. His name was Willis "Willie" Mack. Big Willie, "big" as a dirigible hangar. Mack, as in truck. Willis, as in nemesis.

I stared blankly, his meaning lost. He said it again, louder.

I yelled as something incredibly hurtful hit my chest and I went backward on the step, hitting the back of my head. Shocked and feeling pain, I began to cry. Something else hit me and now, convinced that death was calling, I wailed with all my might. I was calling to Janie, Megan, and Jennifer. I was so panicked that I forgot that none of them was home. I was the only kid on the block who did not call for his mother when pain came calling.

I had been hit by two people. The first blow landed on my heart and was terrible; the second had absently glanced off my arm. I had not seen the blows coming because I was dramatically nearsighted. I used to think that punches were natural phenomena that just appeared, and came with your face, like bad breath in the morning.

When the second fist only made me cry louder, gurgling like a Listerine junkie, the group lost interest and passed on.

I knocked on my door. I rang the bell. I screamed loudly with enough heart to shatter panes in a glazier's shop. A disembodied voice filtered down to me from an upstairs window.

"I didn't whistle for you," it said.

I irritated someone else about an hour later, and discovered that screaming, crying, and making other disgusting, self-effacing noises were no bar to beating. In fact, they added spice.

"It hurt!" I cried, convinced that the punches would end if their sponsors understood that pain was the result.

The boys on the block were accustomed to blows and did not see them as cause for drama. My screams goaded them to greater effort. It opened no doors. I looked at my front door, the former gateway to sanctuary, the portal to safety, as if it had betrayed me.

The spirit of the door had changed, as had the spirit of my mother.

At first I thought I was being punished in a universal way for language incompetence. Stepmother Edna hated my dialect, which was at the me-Tarzan level, and it was unmistakably clear how the neighborhood children viewed my communication patterns.

They dubbed me "Yow!" Later, because even "Yow" did not fully express my Martian nature, they settled on China Boy. China, in our neighborhood, was more bizarre, more remote, than a distant planet.

I knew that China Boy was not intended as an affectionate moniker. I didn't get it. My family was Chinese, a fact of which they seemed proud.

"China Boy" sounded the dinner bell for a knuckle sandwich buffet. Being the China Boy outside the house was like being chum bait at a shark feed, an honor I could easily live without. In fact, I had to shed the honor before it consumed me.

I told Janie about the jungle outside our door. She had not been bothered by anyone in her long walk to the redbrick Roosevelt Junior High on Arguello. Her friends were in another neighborhood, one without a title, a nickname, a streetfighting ethic, or a death squad.

Why wasn't she China Girl? Why didn't they punch her nose and stand on *her* face?

"Ming-li. 'China Boy'—it bad name?" I asked.

"It's not good," she replied.

I thought about it.

"But I boy. From China. Sort of. I think."

She watched me leave our stoop for the street one day, seeing the kids gather around like a lynch mob after a child molester.

"Edna. Um, Stepmother. Please, Kai is really getting beaten up outside by all the street kids. He could really get hurt. He needs to be inside."

"Oh. *Well,*" she said, the dual exclamations a promise of trouble. "He *needs* to be inside. How wonderful. He pesters me. He asks me questions I do not understand. He asks for food that Irish would not give to pigs. He looks like a refugee, and looks *stupidly* at *everything.* Now, he *needs* to be inside. What are *you,* Jane, his *mother?*

"Listen to me very carefully. You will interfere with my responsibilities regarding this very lost little boy only at supreme hazard to yourself. Do I make myself clear?"

She turned to me, hands on hips. "You are to remain in the street from the end of school until supper, and from after supper to bedtime. Out, now."

As I was being propelled again into my daily catastrophe on the sidewalk, Janie invited me to join her friends, north of the Panhandle.

Stepmother Edna said, "No. You belong on your own block, where I can whistle for you. You can't hear me on Encanto Way."

"No rike me, why make me be here?" I asked.

"Of course I don't dislike you. If you don't step outside *this* moment, you are going to be whipped silly."

Later, she told me that my father's job was so demanding, so hard, that he needed the comfort of his wife when he returned home.

"Seeing you and your sourpussed face only makes him sad," she said. "We are having a wonderful life, without you. You and your *sister*—" she said this as if it were a classic profanity—"are ruining it for us. You children are just *burdens.*"

"Hello, darling," she breathed, as Father returned, taking his hat and acting as if the two of them were alone in the house.

I watched her sit before my mother's vanity. Edna was brushing her own hair. Mother seldom did this—it was my sisters' work. The light platinum of Edna's hair, undulating beneath the strokes of a golden brush, enchanted me and I entered their room on silent feet to sit behind her. I marveled at the nearness of her size and shape to that of Mother. Now, at this moment, she did not seem like a *wupo*. I closed my eyes and listened to the sound of her brush wisping through her hair, taking comfort from hearing distantly familiar sounds from my stepmother without suffering injury or fright. I think she knew I was there, but I was never sure. After some minutes, I rose and left the room.

Stepmother Edna was like a living statue, obviously capable of all human activity, but limited for unclear reasons to a restricted range of interaction. I had really needed Mother, and then found myself wanting a mother, any mother. I could tell that Edna thought I was a bad, small person, probably of the wrong color, undoubtedly of the wrong personality, operating badly with the tongue of a monkey.

It was not her fault. She had not wanted us—her connection was to Father. Nor had she wanted stepmother status any more than any rational person might. She simply wanted a happy marriage.

I wanted to be a fighter pilot. With my eyesight, I would have operated Thunderjets the way Mother had driven Fords, but I would have crashed and burned in the joy of flight. With Edna's sadness and anger, after losing her husband to Chinese infantry in Korea, she was not destined to be Mother of the Year in our once-Asian household.

While I understood none of this, Edna was tied to the yoke of undesired motherhood.

It was her karma. My karma was to help her expunge her personal devils by being smaller than she was when she was angry.

Without running for office, I had been made the Poster Boy for Corporal Punishment, enjoying all rights and privileges thereto pertaining, and with all fists, feet, bells, whistles, and sirens appropriate to the station.

My youth seemed interminable because my personal identity was unclear, and in the resulting fog the gauge of time became unmeasurable. Time seemed to lag because the neighborhood was committed to the idea of child warfare, and I was an early pacifist. My stepmother was an agent of emotional estrangement, of war by proxy, combat by youth, and chronic discipline.

I had embarked on my first rite of passage into boyhood, into violence and the realm of the fist.

6

REVOLUTION

While the manly stage of development on the street would last a decade, only the first year was dehumanizing. At home, however, the process of reconstruction began badly and soon worsened.

To an unformed child, Edna Madalyn McGurk Ting was like nuclear fusion. Awesome power, few controls, and no reasonable comprehension for the technically uninformed.

I think she liked me until she heard me speak, watched me walk, saw my clothing, observed my skinniness, and realized that I ate Chinese food willingly.

She had come from wealth and had mistaken Father's moneyed past as a precursor for the future. She had never before met a poor banker. We were waiting for a number of good things to happen, such as winning the Irish Sweepstakes or discovering uranium under the staircase. None of these events occurred. Edna pretended that they already had. She used denial the way Big Willie Mack used fists.

"Tell me again," she sighed languorously to my father, "about the servants who bathed your mother." Or about the live-in cook's family, the splendid fish cook, the live-in tailor who could fix Western watches. About the Sikh house constabulary, the personal maids, the servants who swept the outside verandas and journeyed to the burial grounds to sweep graves, the servants who stood silently against the walls of the dining room during meals, waiting to offer the gold tongue scrapers and gargling bowls before dessert, the *amahs* who tended the many raucous children of the Ting clan.

The geocultural distance between Shanghai and Philadelphia describes all the differences in the world, but she completely understood one major element in our domestic practice: the hallowed protection of family secrets.

When Stepmother Edna's younger sister Eileen visited us, I was instructed, "You will smile and obey me absolutely while Aunt Eileen is here. If you do not, if you show that dull, ugly, scowly little Asiatic expression in her presence I will make you sleep outside in the street and will tan your bottom black and blue."

She could not have learned to think like that at Smith.

When Aunt Eileen arrived with her family, Janie and I smiled like beauty-queen contestants until our faces ached. We were ready to do toothpaste ads for Ipana or Pepsodent.

"Don't you wish you looked like our cousin Kate?" I asked Janie. I had wanted to look black, but Eileen and Kate had more food, nicer clothes, and apparently had never been beaten.

"Shhh!" hissed Janie. "Speak in English! No! Why would I want to look like a *lo fan* ghost? Her hair is so light, it looks like it's not there." She paused.

"It's weird; Eileen doesn't seem anything like Edna. Something really bad must've happened to her."

True, I thought. Me.

"I am *so* lucky!" cried Edna to her sister. "These children are *wonderful*. They are the blessings of my life."

"See that you maintain this comportment at all times," she instructed after Eileen left.

To keep a secret, Edna sacrificed truth and took no prisoners.

"As far as anyone else is concerned, we are *not* poor. We are merely saving for future purchases."

I feel sympathy for her now, when my regrets can provide her no comfort, and the memory of my growing antipathy sits like corrosive guilt on the linings of my heart.

She expected to be the happy wife of a good lawyer, without any intent to have children. She instead became a lonely bereaved widow. Then she anticipated joining a sophisticated Chinese society family and living comfortably, and ended up in a mother role without the money, the temperament, or the training.

In making our family a victim of her cultural chauvinism, she administered a self-inflicted wound and denied herself the love and affection that could have been the sustenance of her life.

Father, known as the Colonel, was a celebrity of sorts in Chinatown. He was a decorated war hero, a former biplane fighter pilot, a paratrooper trained by the American army, an infantryman trained by the Germans. He worked for Madame Amethyst Jade Cheng, who had as much wealth as Croesus and whose parents had possessed impeccable political connections to Chiang Kai-shek. She had a deep, rich laugh that showed all her teeth. She was a free person, invigorated every day by the undeniable fact of her freedom, elevated by the inestimable breadth of her material wealth. She loved success, adored money, and learned charity. It was only the latter fact that drew my father to her in any personal way: charity was American.

I remember Madame Cheng as two people. First, as an alabaster goddess who was almost spritelike, a young woman prancing in the world of mature financiers, giggling as I and other young sons of her employees knelt and pressed our foreheads to the cold, red-tiled floor. Within the space of a few years, she had abandoned her ivory complexion for the burnished bronze of a frequent traveler to the south of France and would laughingly pull us to our feet whenever the kow tao seemed appropriate.

"Young gentlemen!" she said in her Shanghai-accented Mandarin. "You are Americans! Don't bow! Chew gum!" and she would laugh as she lifted her chin, her ebony-black, short-cropped, Dutch Boy coif falling back from her prominent forehead.

Father was poor, handsome, direct, and dashing. He was utterly unconventional. Father saw what had become of traditional Chinese values in the modern world. He had suffered the chaos, the irresponsibility, the waste, and the obsolescence of a culture that could not fashion an airborne corps, run a modern railway, operate a film industry, or defeat superstition.

His father, a friend of the poppy and an escort for concubines, a man who had not worked a day in his life, had been Chinese. My father was going to be American.

"We are in America!" he roared at his colleagues in the China Lights Bank, causing inkwells to jump and paper stacks to crash to the tiled floor.

"No more ancestor worship! No more stinking joss sticks! Firecrackers to chase spirits! No!! We should be celebrating Thanksgiving and Fourth of July! And memorizing goddamn Constitution! To form more perfect union, establish justice!"

So Father was in a unique position—a society notable whose rabid pro-Americanism placed him on the daring edge of the social register. Neo-hero, counterculture rebel. A middle-aged Jimmy Dean.

The president of the bank was a hard-faced aesthete with cheekbones so deeply indented that he appeared skull-like under harsh ceiling lights. He had been a Cheng kinsman in the Su Sung Tai and had honorably carried a fourth of the wealth of the clan out of war-torn China to the Bank of England, in his patron's name. Amethyst Jade knew that Mr. Lew could have forgotten his duty and disappeared in storied opulence in Zurich. But he was the ultimate in loyalty, drawn to his boss by her entrepreneurial courage, her charismatic capitalism. He was also amused by Father's unconventionality, and clearly marveled at him for his lack of focus on wealth. I think he regarded the marriage to Edna McGurk as a supreme coup, since Edna looked like the women who made movies in Hollywood and advertised kitchen soaps in the magazines. But there were some in the community who did not share his cosmopolitanism.

When the later woes of the China Lights Bank became common knowledge, Edna discovered that we were genuinely poor.

Victoria Lum Ting, one of the powers in the local family association, visited our house. She made a point of speaking to all of us in Songhai, and dealing with Edna as if she were the village idiot. Victoria, who had all the compassion of a toad after flies, knew that Father's fortune was waning while her wealth increased. The word was out on

Grant Avenue: Amethyst Jade is restructuring and will base her operations henceforth in Singapore and Hong Kong. All staff who wish can follow. Those who stay possess their own joss.

"Edna, would you want to live in Singapore?" asked Father.

"Oh, darling, you can't be serious!" she exclaimed. "The communists would *love* to take Singapore. It fell to the Japanese in—hours! You can't possibly want me to be so close to the Reds!"

Victoria wore her most sumptuous mink coat, her fingers winking with every diamond ring she could borrow from the Ying Yum Jewelry Mart. Victoria's rude demeanor did not promise improved East–West relations.

"Ah ha, Ting Taitai," said Victoria. "You like mink, or you like sable? Thank golly my husband, when he alive, no put his money in China Lights Bank! So, you think go, Singapore? Ha-ha. Nice ring, ehah?"

So my pushing and hustling for Chinese food in what was regarded as a hostile tongue must have set the worst possible tone for positive coexistence. The sound of the Chinese language had become Edna's talisman for poverty, exclusion, isolation.

This set up the Sunday punch. This was the Western world, where to spare the rod was to spoil the child. On the other hand, the Chinese think that if you continually beat a youngster or slap him in the face his brains will seep through his ears. And you will be rewarded in later years with someone who fires burning arrows into everyone's barns.

"Why must you make those terrible faces at me when I tell you to do something?" she asked.

I struggled for the words.

"You're frowning again!" Stop that! said her hand against my cheek. The nonverbal tradition of the family was being upheld.

She discovered that fate had rendered her a missionary, tasked with the salvation of a heathen band of lost souls, without offerings at the altar or solace in the prayers. Missionaries should have willing flocks. It is tough to reform something that is shapeless and indifferent to improvement, like Jell-O in the hands of a carpenter.

We had lost our cultural glue in the Run. The keepers of the flame of custom were dead, absent, or in college.

Edna McGurk valued the suburban look. This was the ascent of the Golden Fifties, when *Good Housekeeping* was more than a magazine

and the concept was grander than a golden seal. Suburban thinking was
in vogue, but totalitarianism was better. It was also more affordable.

"Sit up taller. Put your knife on the back of the plate. Keep the
napkin square on your lap or it will fall off, and you may not drop
anything on the floor. Cut small pieces and chew methodically with
your mouth *totally* closed. No speaking at the dinner table. Elbows off,
wipe your mouth." There was much to learn.

Whipped by bad fortune, surrendering to the inexorable gravity of
downward-sliding consequences, Edna enforced home order without
compromise. Discipline was the staff of life. It became our true religion,
more impressive than the magical fries in the Lew Wallace Eatery, more
eloquent than the heavenly chorus in the neighborhood Holy Christian
Church of Almighty God.

But the application of discipline was uneven. Edna was intimidated
by Jennifer and Megan's maturity, and they were in college at Cal.
Jennifer Sung-ah was studying music; Megan was in education. Jennifer
liked Edna because she was smart and honest. Megan liked Edna because
she did not torture her, as our mother had.

Jennifer could have outwitted Einstein and was the safest from
Edna's interference. That left the short sprouts of Janie and me. Edna
was not reluctant to beat us for an endless series of capital transgressions,
usually involving facial expressions, illegally spoken Chinese, poor table
manners, and miserable carping about being slapped, hit, and kicked, in
that order.

I had never been hit before. I think my sisters used to squeeze my
arms or other appendages when my crying became insufferable, but face-
slapping was not appropriate. Nor was kicking. Or punching.

The first time Stepmother Edna hit me I was convinced it was a
mistake and waited dumbly for an apology. She was waiting for mine.
When I realized that she *meant* to hit me, I trembled and let loose the
tears of the Last Flood. Edna discovered, to her surprise, that more,
emphatic hitting did not terminate my crying. I felt pain, outrage, more
pain, hot anger. Then, a flat disassociation. I am not here, I said, limiting
my involvement in the world to the range of my myopic eyes. Edna
wondered if I was retarded, but the thought was not enough to save
me.

Megan hinted that slapping children in the face was not Chinese.

"We are *not* in China, Megan," Edna would say through her teeth.
"That is precisely the point I am striving to make."

Then Janie announced that if Edna ever touched her again, she would kill her. Janie had turned fourteen without a party, a noisemaker, or a hot cup of tea. She looked twelve, and had been as innocent as Mary's little lamb. Like all children, she was not inherently violent; she was adapting to the culture of her home. We thought we were becoming European.

"How would you kill her?" I whispered in Songhai while Janie read the Hunan chopsticks story to me.

"I will drive the *chi tz*, the car, and run over her," she said. I nodded. That idea made sense. We respected driving as others regarded natural catastrophes.

Edna figured she could not afford to call Janie's bluff. After all, what if she meant it? So I became the sole target of corporal punishment. I was beginning to see a global purpose to Edna's plan. Beat him on the inside, whip him on the outside, and pretty soon he'll cooperate and tell us everything. You know, spill the beans.

I just couldn't figure out what the information was.

Edna stormed me with words—an incessant, articulate torrent of elevated vocabulary uttered with careful diction and unmistakable menace. My ears began to ring in response to her anger. I did not understand her, and she could barely tolerate me.

But her true weapons were emotional. Oh, Kai, did you not pick up your room? Fine. See this model airplane? Crunch! It was a balsa Curtis P-40 Tomahawk, carefully completed just a few days before. Is this your creamed corn unfinished on the plate? Very well, no dinner tomorrow, and I will take your firetruck away. Take that look off your face! Slap! Crunch! to the firetruck, and Smash! again as it resists her stomps. Whap, I told you to keep your elbow from the table. I gave you three minutes to be in the bathroom and you have taken four. Kick. You did not move your bowels at 7:30 as I instructed. How else can you become regular? Kick. Oh, you did not go to sleep as directed, at eight? Slap. Very well. You may not speak to Jane for one day. Your clothes look terrible, almost as bad as you, be that possible. I don't care how it happened. Don't make that face! Slap!

I watched her destroy my toys, numb in the face of loss and helpless in the tide of history.

Janie stood up to Edna, and was rewarded with progressively worsening life conditions.

"Edna, would I be able to invite Donna Riley over?" she asked. Janie did not look at our stepmother, controlling her face.

"Please address me, Jane, as 'Stepmother Edna.' "

"Stepmother Edna. Can Donna Riley visit?"

"When?" asked Edna.

"Whenever. This weekend?"

"No," said Stepmother Edna.

"Some other time, then?"

Edna did not answer.

Edna provided me two gifts. The first was respite from peanuts. Mother's conditioning had worked; when I ate them, I became violently ill. Edna hated acceding to my weaknesses, but she hated the consequences of forcing her way with peanuts. The other gift was allowing me to keep my blankie, the one positive fugitive from the law of averages and an enduring survivor from the forces of assimilation. I looked at my blankie with hope; if it could survive, then so might I.

7

WATER

Our home was linguistically disarrayed. We sounded like elevator talk in the Tower of Babel, with a smorgasbord of Chinese dialects on the ground floor, a solid base in Songhai, a strong layer of Mandarin, and a smattering of *sam yep* Cantonese veneered on the top. Ascending, we found Father's unique hybrid blend of Chinese, English, and German accents employed in his pronunciation of English. Then came Jennifer and Megan's high English aristocratic accents—the products of Tutor Luke's original instruction and the year of speaking Empire English in India. Of course, had we been at the fount of the tongue, in Great Britain, their speech would have represented the apex. But this was America, and Janie's rapid grasp of American dialogue placed her just beneath the perfect enunciation of Edna, who rested at the pinnacle. My gibberish of eclectic sounds was actually not part of the structure and lay in the subbasement, in the antediluvian terrain of cave-dweller grunting.

When Kaiser Wilhelm II lost the Great War, the Allies at Versailles demobilized the German Army. That was so the Germans would never make war again in Europe, which reveals the practical value of political science. Chiang Kai-shek then hired three thousand unemployed German officers and NCOs as cadre for his Kuomintang Army. This was the China Military Mission, headed by the brilliantly capable General Hans von Seekt, a man my father admired despite his lack of American citizenship. Von Seekt was a professional, what the U.S. Army called a Regular.

Thus, before Pearl Harbor brought America into the war, Father had been trained for battle by the kaiser's veterans in North China. They taught in the universal language of war: military English, with a German dash, a monocled eye, and artillery, which is globally understood.

We had the customs of a family uprooted from its ethnoculture and dropped on its head in the wrong neighborhood in the wrong country. We should have gone to Germany. I still wanted to go to Tsingtao, and I didn't even like beer.

Edna knew that we, like the soldiers of Bonaparte, lived on our stomachs. The heart of the matter, in a Chinese household, is food.

How are you? ask the French and other Latins. Americans ask: How's it going? Tibetans say, I pray for you. The Chinese ask: Have you eaten? So Edna found our Achilles heel—in the abdomen.

Janie had become a great cook and provided us pleasure in her meals. But that was now *finis*. Behind Edna's Irish roots lay three things: potatoes, a German maid, and an unconscious dislike of cooking. I called potatoes *Dai-fan*, or Big Rice Kernel. Janie called sauerkraut "rotted pig poop."

> *Bye-bye, food. Bye-bye* mu shu *pork.*
> *Hello, cauliflower, I think I'm gonna die.*
> *Bye-bye, sweet food, good-bye.*

Jennifer and Megan's visits home on weekends became infrequent.

I began staring at mirrors, wondering what it was in my face that made Stepmother Edna so violent, so angry. Edna's cultural offensives were launched when our defenses were weakest—at dinner. Communication to Janie and me arrived with the boiled squash in the presence of our father. Her pronouncements were delivered with the formality of a Vatican edict. Edna attacked the incomprehensible gibberish of the house.

"We are only to speak English henceforth," she announced. "Absolutely *no* Chinese, in any form. The removal of this *foreign* food will help, since I understand that no proper words exist to describe it.

"Kai, that means no singing songs in Chinese. Jane, that means that you will say nothing behind my back that I cannot understand. There will be no breaching of this policy."

"What," asked Jane, who had the courage of Daniel, "will Father do when Uncle Shim or Mr. Soo Hoo call from the bank, and he has to talk to them in Songhai?"

"Your father's conversations are private. Besides, that is not Chinese. That is banking.

"Furthermore. 'Uncle Shim' is *not* your uncle. And he calls this house too frequently. He has such a curious voice. That reminds me. Why, sweetheart," she asked Father, "does this Mr. Shim want to call so often?"

"Darling, he's a friend, as good as Na-men, uh, Norman Schwatz'd," he replied, still daunted by the linguistic pretzel of Na-men's name. "His family know my family in China. Shim is a top scholar, very, very smart. He, uh, teach Kai how to write Chinese."

"Well, obviously, *that* must stop! Your son must be *American*, and not be confused by conflicts in culture!"

Clothes were next. She dressed Jane in rags to make her look bad to establish clearly the undesirability of another female in the house. Our family was the only one I knew that had designated two separate daughters as Cinderellas, under different mothers. Edna dressed me in Little Lord Fauntleroy outfits to make me look good. In our neighborhood, it was pinning a bright red bull's-eye on a sitting duck. Kids who want to live to morning recess do not wear blue velvet outfits with white neck-buttoned shirts. I could not have done worse if I had worn a placard saying, SCREW ALL YO' MOMMAS, TWICE.

Eventually, economics saved me. Little Lord clothing was costly, and it was being trashed by my community beatings as soon as the tailoring was complete. Edna stopped buying such clothes for a while. This did not stop my daily cultural goofs and the resulting creamings, but it saved me from poundings by kids from other neighborhoods who saw me for the first time from across the schoolyard.

Once, as I was fleeing some street bullies, I sprinted past my own door and saw that it had been left ajar. Edna went out no more frequently than my mother, but she must have cracked the door for a look and forgotten to lock it. Feeling the luck of the Irish, I braked hard, jammed inside and latched the door, panting. Edna appeared immediately and forced me outside with paddling hands and helping feet.

"I hate you!" I cried, as the pack closed in.

She hit me so hard with an open palm to my face that the herd stopped, incredulous that the pretty blonde had done its work. For free. The blinding violence of her hand was so public, the shattering impact of her blow so immediate, that I felt my spirit blanch in panicked retreat. My sense of internal self evaporated and my brain rocked as tiny lancets of ice-white light sprinkled across my optic field.

That night she whacked me with a belt.

"You *never* tell your *mother* that you *hate* her!" she cried, her belt singing. "Only little beasts, *animals*, say things like that! And that is what you *are!*"

"You not my mah-mee!" I wailed with desperate logic.

The beating worsened, frightening me more with her fury than the actual blows, which alone were crowding my screaming panic with the fear that she would not stop.

"*Arguing won't help,*" she hissed, panting with her effort. "I *am* your mother. By God, it is the best thing that ever happened to you! If you knew how corrupt your illiterate mother was! You will know this someday, and regret this horrid, devillike resistance to me! Can you do nothing about that morbid, defiant face!"

Therein lay a fundamental problem: animals versus her unique interpretation of Philadelphia Society. Edna wanted meals to resemble the paintings of Rembrandt—silent, stately, admirable, full of shadow and tint, and quietly aesthetic.

The Chinese eat with the joy of abandonment, the relish of a pride of lions. The object of a Chinese meal is eating. It is not a spectator sport, and the theme of the exercise is free pleasure after a long day's work. Chinese food is complex artistry in preparation, and simple, unrestrained celebration in eating. People talk, shout, laugh, and enjoy what must modestly be viewed as the most complex and diverse cuisine in the world.

The Chinese are smart; they reserve aristocratic airs for the business of court and permit the child within us all to romp freely with happy little chopsticks at dinnertime.

Edna must have viewed her first meal in our home in nauseous dismay, a rapid descent into Dante's kitchen. The snuffling, the talking with food in the mouth, the elbows on the table, the unknown taxonomy of the strange things on people's plates probably had the same effect on her as a Milk of Magnesia–and-mustard-based emetic.

The purpose of a meal with Edna was protocol. We learned an elaborate preparatory procedure that made scrubbing for brain surgery seem dilatory. No talking, no grinning. Death to laughers. Food to a fascist is somber business. After all, it eventually produces waste matter. Unless no one eats.

Chairs just so. No wrinkles in the tablecloth. Without funds, we purchased silver and glassware. Knife first at your right, water glass centered on its tip, one inch away. Water in each glass two inches from the lip. Dinner fork, left, napkin artfully displayed. Knife, spoon. On left and right, outside, like tackles in a standard pro-set, were salad fork and soup spoon.

"Salad forks on the *outside!*"

A bloodcurdling scream would issue forth, then a sharp slap on the cheek would bring all the blood in the body into the face.

We never saw a salad and had little soup. But the utensils were patiently in attendance, in case the missing victuals were airdropped by the 82d Airborne or Mr. Campbell Soup visited without calling first.

The marks of childhood endure. Today, when I see silverware improperly aligned, I feel a jab of fright, a small, tender sliver of pain, a threat of disorder and possible doom.

We prayed.

Mother had joined the Episcopalian Church in prewar Shanghai when she realized that daily missionary English lessons were part of the deal. She loved learning, and English seemed so much the vogue. My father often spoke of Rice Christians—that is, Chinese who accepted the teachings of missionaries in return for the meals. I understood that. Mother had been a Keats Christian, a Dickensian parishioner, a Shakespearean Follower of Jesus, enduring the Old Testament for lessons in the new tongue of English, the language of new-age Chinese college students, the currency of the brave new world.

The missionaries could have laughed last, had that derisive senti-

ment been in them. When Mother arrived in America and realized the
distance from China, her family, and her father, and that the passing
fancy of British words was now the dominant tongue of her physical
world, she began attending church regularly, asking God's forgiveness
for past insincerities. But she resented the tongue. It was a reminder of
her losses.

Now Jane Ming-li had assumed the role of conscience in our mother's absence, and tried to find an explanation for Edna in every book in
the Bible. We both were fascinated with Exodus. Megan Wai-la, abandoned by our mother and seemingly by the gods, was understandably
drawn to agnosticism. Jennifer Sung-ah, like our mother, adored Mozart.
Father was a Confucian, which is a nonsecular ethical faith and involves
ancestor rituals inappropriate for the dinner table.

Edna was an eclectic adventurer in religion. Except for Episcopa-
lianism, she never met a faith she did not like. Her present passion was
Christian Science, and she was unsure of its blessings before meals, so
she directed us all to pray individually. Edna's religious adventures were
vicarious, for her explorations meant that someone else would be the
dutiful pilgrim attending services. She never went.

I did. Edna had sent me to the Holy Christian Church of Almighty
God—a place I found by location and not by name recognition—and
anxiety pressed on me as everyone under the roof sang their hearts out
in mind-sweeping melodic majesty. When I first heard the rich, emotive
singing, I did not realize that the people in the congregation were producing it. Nor did I know the words, except for "Jesus" and "love,"
but the huge crescendo of feelings—of safety, and caring—that rushed
through my small body made me weep. Somehow I knew that I could
cry in these pews without fear and without shame. Others, taller and
older than I, also wept.

Reverend Stamina Jones was a tall, stately, white-haired man
with clear eyes in an extremely dark round face. His voice was so
low that it tickled my tailbone. He had a softness to him that
made men open their hands and surrender their fists. He ministered
with a capability as deep and wide as his voice, singing the song of
love.

I reminded myself that Mother had attended an Episcopalian
Church in China, as well as in the City, and I imagined her strong
musical voice in the choir, singing, secretly, for Na-Gung.

But of all the churches I attended—Methodist, Community, Apostolic, Baptist, Foursquare Gospel, and Catholic—the most unique was the Church of Christian Science. It was the Ninth Church of Christ Science on Junipero Serra Boulevard—named after the famous Catholic friar—in the all-Anglo mansion district of St. Francis Woods. This was just two miles from Ocean Beach, with its diagonal and perpendicular parking slots that had always confounded Mother. Four blocks away was Sigmund Stern Grove, where the parks department presented free summer Sunday concerts and Pine Lake was stocked with fish for the children to catch.

In the Handle, we had Fist City concerts and nocturnal meetings of the Righteously Pissed Males' Knife and Gun Club, and the streets were stocked with broken people.

In the Ninth Church, I was the only nonwhite. I was openly accepted, though no one had a clue from whence I had come. Edna said that she had picked the Christian Scientists for me because the founder was a woman, and because it seemed that the faith was premised on strength of belief. I suspect that the true reason was that St. Francis Woods was far away and provided another automatic day when I would be gone. She had given me the directions and I had left, taking buses like a maestro of the Municipal Railway. I sat quivering in the back of the Church.

I worried when everyone turned whisperingly to stare, the sound of bottoms twisting on wooden pews accentuating the words of the minister. I looked behind me to see a pure white wall. But I was not scared and my legs did not tense with the need for flight. I did not smell that biting, salivating mob drive that communities often generate when people of the wrong club enter without invitation. No fascists, stepmothers, or rabid dogs here.

It was safe and ordered. The organ music was beguiling, and probably matched the gothic horror of our home. The singing was much quieter, more subdued, less motivating than the congregation's work in the Holy Christian Church. My body did not keep rhythm with the hymns by crying, and Jesus did not move me. The music was exterior to me. People seemed to be holding on, not letting go. They were protecting something, and I did not know what it was.

After the subdued service, which was no more understandable than Reverend Jones's, a man in a light tan suit approached.

"Bob Lamport," he said, offering his hand. I shook it.

"What's your name, young man?"

"China Boy Kai Ting," I said, as honestly as I could. A hesitation.
"What shall I call you?"

I shrugged. I was trying to think that names were not so important.
"May I call you Kai?"

I nodded.

"Let me take you to Sunday School. I'm one of the teachers."

He led me from the pew to a side room, separated by a clean,
deep blue curtain. Blond, blue-eyed children were seated in the room,
and Mr. Lamport introduced me to them.

These kids were like Kate Potts, Aunt Eileen's daughter. They were
dressed like royalty and were as orderly as a drill team in final competition. They were chubby and unbruised.

The Sunday School lesson dealt with Joseph's coat of many colors.
The story involved brothers killing each other.

A girl with hair the color of sunlight, wearing clothes from *T'ien*,
Heaven, played the organ, and I had the same magnetic pull to her as
I did to Anita Mae Williams, a stunning older girl in the Handle whose
face was so pretty it made me feel weak. I loved the blond girl in some
strange and inexplicable way, watching her fingers make the music my
mother would have adored.

The kids in the Ninth Church had mastered life itself.

The organ player said good morning to me, and I pretended that
I was deaf, staring straight ahead, filled with hope and fear. I am not
sure what Mary Baker Eddy thought of the outcome; I knew with every
fiber of my being that Christian Science could not alter the sum and
substance of Edna's kicks or Big Willie's fists. But I got to travel on
Sundays.

I was facing daily death in the streets and was the only true believer
at the dinner table. I needed to have faith in a merciful God, knowing
that he was keeping score, and that I had not been doing well. I needed
help. I wanted my mother to return. I prayed to Him with a zeal that
wrinkled my brows, drew most of my forehead into my eye sockets,
and worried casual observers.

We endured all of this for fresh breadsticks, boiled cabbage, flinty
lima beans, hardy brussels sprouts, and undercooked hamburger stew.
Edna loved to have a carefully set table. She hated to cook, for it had
been an unlearned skill in a house with a live-in German maid. I missed
Mother's burnt toast.

Edna did not do these things to make us miserable. Well, she did them to make Janie miserable, but she merely wanted to improve the home.

"Janie," said Edna. "When you learn to enjoy brussels sprouts, I will allow you to buy that dress at Sears."

"It's gone," said Janie. "The sale ended months ago, and it's not on the rack."

"Well. It was very ugly. Because you have black hair, there's little you can wear. As I said, when you *like* brussels sprouts, if you do not criticize me again, I will look for another. Meanwhile, I am taking away your green coat, as a reminder of your responsibilities to be respectful to your family."

"I don't care!" cried Janie, running headlong into the maw of the consuming enemy.

"Very well," replied Edna. "Then I will take your poodle skirt."

"That's not mine! It's Margaret Apodaca's!" she wailed.

Worse for Edna, however, than the brooding resentment over the slapping, kicking, and hitting, the food revolution, the loss of possessions, the religious reformation, the casting out of tongues, the ancient art of German clothing torture, and the onset of team depression was the lingering memory of the first Mrs. Ting.

Mother's presence was palpable. We could hear her voice, her call to spirits, her effervescent laughter; we could smell the memory of joss sticks and her hundreds of matches to ignite the paste. We stared at the empty bathtub, the toaster, the clocks, and touched the steering wheel of the 1950 Ford as if the fervor of our eyes could animate her return. I would rub the bedspread where she sat when she read to me, holding the books, carving into my memory the texture of her caressing voice. I felt the warm slenderness of her patrician fingers as they traced the characters in her tutor's book, their special spirit shimmering in my immature memory.

Janie Ming-li and I looked out the attic window to the ocean, where I thought she might be visiting. I always peered for her at the beach, my heart racing if I saw a running figure.

"Don't you think," Edna asked brightly at one of our customary funerallike medieval dinners, "that Dai-li was a *terrible* mother?"

"She wasn't so bad," offered Megan, who was visiting and the only one at the table who could have honestly agreed with the question.

I smelled smoke, and for one thrilling moment I thought it was Mother making toast in the kitchen. But once seated, we could not move.

"Janie. Mommy at toaster?" I asked.

Janie looked at me as if I had asked her if she were Bob Hope. But when she looked into the kitchen and didn't shout for joy, I knew that something other than toast was burning.

"Your mother," said Edna, "was *also* a terrible cook."

The normal hush at the table was replaced by a silence that every mother of newborn triplets prays for, and never receives.

"Her very moral fiber was rotten to the core. She had *servants* cook her meals in China. *This* is America," she said slowly, "where individual dignity is a hallowed principle."

Please, Janie, I thought, don't mention Stepmomma Edna's German cook. Arguing won't help.

"For which good men have died."

She was referring to her first husband. I thought she was speaking about me.

I was cutting up the sauerkraut to hide it under the liver. I tasted the liver and shuddered, storing it in a corner of my cheek. Then I tried to hide the liver under the sauerkraut, wondering how I could empty my mouth. Early Rubik's Cube.

"Edna," said Megan, "you should ask Jane that question."

I looked up. Megan had not lived with Edna. No, no. *Don't* ask Janie what she thinks! Edna will hear her answer!

Jane's face illuminated, and she said, in a big rush, "She was a *wonderful* Mom. She *loved* us. She *fed* us and didn't beat us and she let us sing. She would never slap . . ."

"*Silence!*" cried Edna as she sprang from her seat and slapped Jane, and I involuntarily jumped, catapulting a hideous piece of liver across the table, splatting it onto the silver butter dish, which was always empty. But clean.

I expected death. I had few toys left. I wondered if Janie, her face livid with the mark of Edna's hand, was going to drive the Ford into the dining room and flatten Edna into the pancake she was striving to form from me.

"Henceforth, there will be *no mention* of Dai-li," Edna screamed like a priest in a whorehouse.

"I have taken the photo albums that she dragged here from China and *burned* them! I burned the whole crate they were in! All that trash is now *smoke*! This is America! And *she does not exist*!" She was standing, stamping her feet on the floor.

"This hurts my feet!" she cried.

Everyone screamed but me. My father swore. The crate contained some of his identity papers, photos and letters from war buddies, his old uniforms, and Sam Browne belts.

"*Goddamn!*" he roared. "There was live .38 Super ammo in box! It could have cooked off and killed *everyone*! Why not *ask* first!"

"Because you would have said no!" she yelled back.

For years, my sisters' friends did not believe this story. "Incredible," they would say. "Impossible!" they would exclaim. "She *couldn't*!" they would cry.

Our mother's wedding gown had been in the crate and my sisters expected to use it someday. My sisters' proof of Edna's spectacular act of cultural violence was the absence of the famous gown on each of their marriage days. I know that my sisters cried at their weddings, and I at first thought it was because of our stepmother's arson.

The albums were Jennifer's favorite possessions in the world, but this night she had chosen the dust of the Cal library over liver and sauerkraut. She was spared the trauma of dinner, the object lesson in human dignity, and the smoke of Revolution.

I must have looked too calm, for Edna looked at me with wild eyes, pointing a finger that seemed to have the friendliness of a Flash Gordon death ray.

"Dai-li Ting is *dead*!! What a stupid secret to keep!" she cried. "And don't think I didn't know about those filthy foreign books! And those awful Chinese pens and dirty inks! They were in the crate, too!" That made me join in the community cry. So much for Uncle Shim's treasured calligraphy, the notions of Santa Claus, the domestic gods of our kitchen, and *The Tales of Lu Hsun*.

"Stop it!" she shrilled at our orchestra of wails.

My father rose and left the table. I wished he had asked me to join him. His departure was dignified, orderly, and sensible.

Whenever Mother had severely criticized Megan Wai-la, Father was at work. My worst beatings by Edna occurred when he was overseas, at the bank, or at meetings. This was Woman's Work.

I felt the imbalance in duties, the unfairness of responsibility, but it was the best argument I knew for possessing the status of a grown man.

The crying stopped, the sniffling and nose-blowing began.

"Mah-mee alive, not dead," I said to myself, my hands between my legs, rocking back and forth, again and again that night. I sat up in my bed until dawn, my mind and legs aching, unable to sleep, wanting to turn on all the lights in the house, knowing I lacked the authority. Mother had loved electricity.

I comforted myself with Reason. Ma-ma had brought my sisters out of wartime China. She used to throw knives at bad guys and could live with communists and survive the attacks of warlord *ping*. She was still practicing knife-throwing, in Tsingtao. She never gave up. She would never give up, would not give me up. Nor Father. Nor Jennifer, nor Janie. Maybe Megan. But not me.

I followed my father into the bathroom the next morning.

"Ma-ma dead, Baba?" I asked in a whisper, fearing suspicious spirits, listening gods, and Edna. I knew then that it would be okay if he didn't answer.

He lowered his head into his hands, fingers rasping whiskers. He raised his head up slightly, and brought it down decisively, his lips tight, bloodless. Yes. And now we have said it.

"Cancer. Cancer killed her," he said in the voice of a small mouse.

"Who Cancer, Baba?" I asked.

"Cancer is a disease," he said.

"Like god? Cancer god?" I asked.

He nodded. "Yes. The Cancer God." It was the only time that Father acknowledged the existence of spirits.

The rest of that week and that month became a blur of weeping, of my body becoming one of the base elements. Mother had been earth; I was becoming water.

I surrendered to emotional rages that lacked genesis and closure, blurred memories of beatings sparked by failed tasks and violations of Edna's protocols. I uttered spontaneous Chinese phrases, sent heated prayers to all authorities, and tried to understand the logic of Mother's death. I recited the Sixteen Edicts of Confucian Thought, tripping and stumbling awkwardly in Songhai, softly moaning with the realization that my native speech was becoming unfriendly, sliding out of the reach of my tongue. What would Uncle Shim say? Uncle Shim missing. Not even phone calls anymore. Father, going to Hong Kong next week, to be gone for two weeks. Then to Singapore.

Death, like in China. Finality. The Good-bye Forever. No Mother. You have a mother. A new mother. The first one is gone, for all time, and your vital essence, your *shigong*, has followed her.

Sometime in that first week, or the second, following our Banquet of the Burning Crate, I tried to run away.

I was caught in the stairway by Edna. I had one worn blanket, an extra set of underwear, a broken flashlight, and twenty cents. I had no plan, no vision, no concept of where to go. I just wanted to be somewhere else.

I lost the last of my toys.

I could not sleep. The thought of my mother not returning made my body thrash on the bed in an agony of failed denial.

She is in Tsingtao with Na-Gung, Maternal Grandfather, and the two of them are playing with yellow fish while Wang the fish cook laughs until tears sparkle in his eyes.

They are preparing a place for me and Janie and I will learn music and be a *chien shur* scholar and will relearn Songhai and I will never do anything that could make her leave me again.

8

DOG MEAT

Catch, China Boy!" shouted Tyrone Sykes as an antipersonnel grenade disguised as a rubber kickball caromed off my head.

"You sucka!"

The abuse inside the house was being reenacted by different players back on the street. The following months were filled with dramatizations of my almost universal incompetence. Three main areas of cultural failure appeared, refusing to be corrected by my merely being on the street.

First was language. My speech was bonkers. I lacked the words, the pronunciation, and the body language. My voice resembled marble-mouthed Esperanto chants. I lacked the thoughts that precede speech. I was too far behind to close the cultural gap by osmosis. I was like a water-skier without the skis, dragged through the wake of an uncompromising culture by my neck. I missed the nuances and the signals that accompany social existence in any milieu.

I didn't know what the kids in my neighborhood talked about for nearly a year. When I found out, I was disappointed; they discussed fighting and sports.

"Reginald, he beat tar outa dat cat from da Haight," said one.

"Nuh-uh!" said another. "Reginald, he tore inna dat boy, but he loss all his blood. Dat boy from da Haight? He a muthafucka, I promise you dat, and no Reginald no how got no chance wif him! Ya'll see da *guns* on dat boy? Reginald, he skinny lika rail! He dog meat!"

"Reginald, he dun *thump* dat boy. You lissena me!"

"Reginald, shee-it! No way! Dog meat, boy!"

"Naah. Is not!"

"Yeah! Is!"

"Is not, and da Yankees, dey gonna win jus like Reginald, an' make yo' ma'fuckenDahjers dog meat, too!"

I wanted to talk about food and hear about their mothers.

"Who ma'fucken?" I asked.

"China Boy," said one, tiredly. "Don be buttin in, fool. Don hurt yo mouf when ya'll don know *shit.*"

"Name Kai, no China Boy," I said accurately. "I from China," which was untrue. I was from the Panhandle.

Second was sports. The kids in the Handle played ball and fought. They ran, they jumped, they argued. They laughed. I understood the running part, but it brought me neither honor nor status.

After my peers had been born and weaned, round spherical bouncing objects had been placed in their hands until the relationship between them and the balls became a unity. I met my first ball at the age of seven. I discovered that it was a slippery reptile that came at high speed to smack me in my face without notice. It cleverly went left if I went right, went up when I went down. My swearing in Chinese at the cursed sphere did not seem to help. The ball became my enemy and made me the Martian the kids already suspected me to be.

The third area was the bottom line. Fighting was the final test of life on the street. It measured a boy's courage and tested the texture of his guts, the promise of his nascent manhood, his worthiness to live and bear friends on poor streets. It was the ultimate *chien shur* examination, for instead of merely facing the Emperor, one faced himself.

Kids who could play ball but were chicken fighters did not belong on the block. They were supposed to stay in their homes. Kids who could do neither did not belong in the *world,* and were supposed to be banned, killed, or worse.

It took little time to discover that I was in a new category. I was the kid who knew nothing, played ball like a goat, had no fighting spirit and less ability, and would not stay in his house, leave the block, or die. Edna had locked the door and kept me within a whistle's reach.

The kids, too numerous to remember or name, tested me, hoping for a real fight, searching for evidence that I was human or that I possessed human potential. I occasionally swore in Chinese, which showed defiance to Edna. It inspired derisive laughter and never improved my station.

I responded to the challenge of combat with the tactics of avoidance and flight. The flights of the China Boy worked with the marketing aplomb of the Edsel.

I would try to elude notice, but I stood out like a white rat at a tomcat convention. A cultural gaffe would invite a pounding. I wouldn't say hello; I did say hello. I was sneaking around; I was strutting too proud. I didn't return a ball, or I touched a bruiser's holy kickball when I didn't have a right to. I took cuts like a girl; I made a face when called a name. Then Jerome, Jerue, Keith, James, J.T., Tyrone, Maurice, Big Willie, or Wally Junior would be in my face. A push on my chest, which, because of its limited area, required great accuracy.

Hey, I would squeak, unconvincingly, my head bouncing in whiplash.

There were about a dozen who got into the ritual of having the China Boy for lunch. Or, if I were really slow that day, for breakfast. I was sunshine Wheaties for an entire generation of future boxers.

Jerue had to push four times and recite a litany of four epic profanities involving my mother before he kicked for the groin. He liked to keep the banquet to one course. Keith Scott was the opposite, never quite sure how he would start, focusing on dessert, when he would finish with certain foot stomps. Reginald Tufts, whose fighting ability was frequently the topic of heated debate, hit me until I cried. I learned to cry quickly with him, and we were both satisfied.

Some kids gave two pushes, some five, building up. But protocol called for the opening push, like soup before the main course. Then a fist, then two. First the arm, then the gut, then the face. Sometimes a kick. Each tormentor had his habit.

Jerome was like the Twelve Celestial Heavens full-course Chinese banquet. He would scream obscenities, loud enough to scare me half to death just by the sound of them. Then a push on the chest, followed by punches and *then* kicking.

J.T. had a push that knocked me into next week. He'd laugh, which was worse than the physical hurt, for it imprinted itself on the brain longer than muscle could hold a bruise, and that, with the long-lasting memories of his heckling giggle, was the fight. And so on.

As my concrete internship gained momentum, Father drove me to Big Recreational Field in the park, known as Big Rec. He parked and when I got out he was holding two baseball mitts and a hardball. I put the small glove on. Instead of descending into the bowl of the field itself, which was filled with Little Leaguers, we stayed on the bike path, next to the curb. He backed away, and I winced as the ball hit my chest.

"Bring glove up, catch ball," he said.

I smiled, found the ball, and rolled it back to him.

Once again the ball arrived from nowhere in particular, to hit me on the arm. It stung a little. Again, I smiled, wishing Father had brought calligraphy instead of ball torture. Four or five times later, the ball hit me on the shoulder and rolled down a storm drain. Quietly, Father retrieved my mitt, put both of them in the trunk, and drove us home. I knew something had just happened, and that it was neither positive for our relationship nor good for my karma. I knew he was trying to reach me and that I was slipping away from him. I loved him so much for trying, hoping that the ball had not cost too much money and that the gloves could be returned.

"You need to be in good physical shape in America," he said. "Try to practice catch."

"Tyrone," said Maurice. "We be bashin China Boy from da get-go an he ain't laid a lick on us. Le's fuck dis shit an leave da slanteye sucka be."

"Dat who we *be*! We be da *Bashers*!"

When a group organized around torment gives itself a name, bad things can only worsen. I knew who the first Grand Poo-Bah of the China Boy Bashers was going to be. It was the Honorable Willis "Fist-In-Your-Face" Mack.

Big Willie was the worst of an evil band. He kicked and usually punched, but his size and strength produced blows that jarred the body and caused lapses in consciousness. He fought from meanness, and few things could please him more than tripping a smaller kid into kissing the pavement with splayed lips. It was so cheap in exertion, so productive in humiliation. But he was really his own gang. The meanest kids appreciated his hegemony and stuck to him like magnets on a refrigerator. In a way, I was their reason for being. I gave Willie something around which to organize.

Big Willie persisted in the belief that because I was a China Boy, I had to be special. And special people, like whites, had to have money, somewhere. For years I struggled with the sense that Big Willie and Edna were related to each other.

A dime taken from any other kid was a good deal. A dime from me would cause Willie to expect more.

"No have no mo'!" I cried, enraged that my words had no effect.

"Boool*shit*!" said his fists, with grand eloquence.

My yelps and tears did nothing to stop the whippings; the blows ended with the passing of the honor of the moment. As the months unrolled, the protocols changed, becoming briefer and more efficient. I had to relearn the system while making new book on the short little punchers who were coming up in the ranks, pounding their way up the order.

I knew that this was my fault. Bad karma. Some epic insult to Heaven. I wrestled with its etiology; what exactly had I done to make all this necessary?

I went to the attic, looking out the window on the right.

"I sorry!" I shouted in my mind. Okay, I bad boy say all things wrong with bad face and Mah-mee not come back! I understand! No more lessons!

Christian churches seemed to be of little benefit. I took control by becoming an informal Buddhist, drawing from the well of our unconscious past and Mother's pre-Christian ideals. I stopped stepping on ants, and, unlike other kids, did not throw rocks at birds in the park or skip stones at ducks at Stow Lake. I was infinitely kind to babies. I even said hello to Evil, the voracious bulldog.

"Don eat me, doggie *pungyob*," I said.

I went back to the attic to look into the sky. I saw little detail of anything in those days, so seeing God was as easy as perceiving anything else. I knew I had yelled at him earlier, and regretted it. But even when I had God's undivided attention, and was not motivated by frustration, and had mouthed songs in a score of his churches bearing different names and honoring different tribes, I doubted the benefit of devotion. I sat beneath the attic window, waiting for God to lay a soft-edged parallel-ogram of light on the bare wood floor, shifting to place my body within it. I used Songhai, God's language.

"I trying hard, God, like Han Tzu-ren the good student," I said, referring to the smart, fabled boy with the single birthday from *The Tales of Lu Hsun*. I spoke into the light from the pane. "I no hurt living things. I set table *hao dao*, right way, fork on left. I listen in your temple house, in all temple house you have. I like sing songs to you. I like Jones Syensheng, Lamport Syensheng, Hogan Syensheng, Lowry Syensheng, Cutler Syen-sheng, all temple teachers. McCready Syensheng, from St. Ignatius, too. You stop beatings. No more beating, please, please God. I do what you say. Promise, hope die."

I looked at the sunlight. I could see the tiny dust particles in front of my eyes. I perceived no sign, but could hear Edna stirring below. I blinked several times and held myself very still, so he would know that I was attentive and studious. Nothing happened. I took a deep breath and prepared for the street. God was busy with other people, probably firstborns.

I became adept at avoiding the first punches, but could never dodge all of them. When the first blow landed, I took to my feet. I ran with all the motivation my little psyche could gather. But flight was uncool, and it galvanized the other kids to a packlike response, my speed a spur to their own efforts. I was as fast as any kid on the block, but I ran stupidly, unable to plan moves because everything in front of my eyes was a generalized blur while everything in my brain had evacuated to my lower intestines.

They chased, blocked, and channeled me into a fence or a wall, there to perform the honor of single combat with the one I had fled, serving sentence for violating every rule on the street. The crying con-fused them, for it was the culmination of too many street taboos in a single child.

"China Boy, you'se a chinkface clown, a *joker*," said Tyrone. "You'se a gimp. You'se stupid as jasper. Can talk none. An you'se deaf, too. Can fight. An man, den you *cry?*"

Younger kids coming up in the ranks could learn how to hit another kid in the face—a rite of passage from arm and stomach punches—by practicing on me. I served a purpose in the community, the way hydrants do for dogs.

"Ming-li," I said. "Boys fight in China?"

"Boys!" she said. The sisters had been born with good looks and had always drawn boys' attention. She was now at an age when she began to suspect the reason, and she didn't like it. "I don't remember too much about China. But I think they fight everywhere!"

"I don't like fight. Don't think Mother want me to fight. She say bad for karma. What you think?" I asked.

"I think it's worse for your face," she said softly.

9

TOUSSAINT

A rail-thin nine-year-old named Toussaint LaRue looked on during these beatings and only hit me once. I therefore assumed that he occupied some lower social niche than mine. Like a snail's.

He took no pleasure in the China Boy rituals. He instead talked to me. I suspected that he had devised a new method of pain infliction.

"Toussaint," he said, offering his hand. "Ya'lls supposed ta shake it." He grinned when I put my hand out with the same enthusiasm with which I would pet Mr. Carter's bulldog. Toussaint, like Evil, had a big gap between his front teeth.

Toussaint would become my guide to American boyhood.

My primary bond to him was for the things he did not do. He did not pound or trap me. He never cut me down. Or laughed with knives in his eyes. Then he opened his heart by explaining things to me, giving me his learning, and taking me into his home.

"China. Don be cryin no mo'. Don work on dis here block, no sir, Cap'n! Give 'er up. When ya'll cry, hol' it insida yo'self. Shif' yo' feet an air-out, go park-side. Preten ya'll gone fishin. Don run, now. Ain't cool."

"Fish in park?" I asked.

"Cheez! Ya'll don colly nothin! Ferget da fish, China. Dry yo' tears."

He told me about the theory of fights. That kids did it because it was how you became a man later on.

"Momma tole me," he said, "in ole days, no Negro man kin hit or fight. We belongs to da whites, like hosses.

"Man fight 'notha man, be damagin white man goods. So he get whipped. An I mean *whipped.*" He shook his head and rubbed the top of it, easing the pain of the thought.

"Now, ain't no mo' dat," he said, smiling. "We kin fights, like men." He was speaking very seriously. Fighting was a measure of citizenship. Of civilization. I didn't think so.

"China, stan up."

"Why?" I whined.

"Putchur fists up. Make a fist! Right. Bof han's.

"Dis one—," he said, holding my left. "It fo' guardin yo' face. Dis here one—dat's fo' poundin da fool who call ya out. Here come a punch, and ya'll block it. China—you listenin ta me?"

"No fight, no reason!" I said hotly.

"No reason!?" he yelled. "You can fight wif no *reason*? Boy! Whatchu *talkin* about?"

Uh-oh, I thought. Toussaint's hands were on his hips.

"Evera kid on dis here block like ta knock you upside da head and make you *bleed* and ya'll got no *reason*? China. Ain't no dude in da Handle got mo' cause fo' fightin *evera* day den *you*!"

"Too many boy fight," I said, drawing back from his heat.

"Uh-*uh*! No sir, Cap'n! Big-time nossir! Lissen. Some kids, dey fight *hard*. But ain't *never* gonna be no gangin up on one kid. *Dat* ain't cool." He shook his head. "Kid stan on his feet. No one else feet. Ain't *nobody* gonna stan inaway a dat. An youse best colly dat."

"Hittin' long," I tried.

"Say what?" he said.

"Long. Not light!"

"Wrong? Ya'll sayin fightin's *wrong*?"

"Light," I said.

"Howzat?"

"Bad yuing chi," I explained.

"Say *what?*"

"Bad, uh, karma!" I said, finding the East Indian word often used by my sisters.

"Well, China, ya'll thinks awful funny. Don have nothin ta do wif no *caramels*. No matta Big Willie take yo' candies. Ain't *candies*. It not bein *chicken*. Not bein yella. Ya'll don havta like it. Sakes, China, no one like ta Fist City. Well, maybe Big Willie, he like it. But like it or don like it, no matter none. Ya'll jus *do* it."

He invited me to play in his house. Many of the games involved capturing cockroaches. "Ya'll ready?" he would ask, and I would nod, nervously. Toos would kick the wall next to the sink, and roaches would slither out of the dust and the cracked plaster. Toos would use his plastic cup, smacking it quickly onto the floor, smiling as he watched the captured roach's antennae struggle to escape, its hard body clicking angrily against the plastic.

He made his closest buddies tolerate me. His mother took me to the church of Reverend Jones on Sundays until Edna changed my religion. The simple presence of his company, and that of his pals, saved me from innumerable trashings and gave me time to breathe.

I had never had a friend before, and I cared for him as few lads have for another. My heart fills now when I think of him. That will never change.

Toussaint was, next to me, the skinniest kid on the block. He ran no faster than I since he lacked the sincerity of my efforts, but he was as tough as a slum rat and had the guts of Carmen Basilio. Basilio, the big-headed middleweight who fought while his blood ran down his bruised face like cascading crimson rain in a summer monsoon. Basilio, whose busted face was on the front page of every pinned-up sports section in every barbershop in the city. Kids respected bravery above all else. It was what allowed you to put your pants on in the morning.

My courage was so low that putting on my big-boy underpants was a task. Toussaint was deemed crazy to buddy with me. But he was my friend because I needed one. He got nothing for himself, in the hard world of our peers' respect, for his generosity.

Outside of a table service, we had few possessions and less cash, but Toos's home made ours look like a gilded palace of Babylon. The

LaRue family lived in a windowless converted storage room in a shambling tenement on Masonic, next door to Brook's Mortuary. The stone steps to the main door were chipped, crumbling, and dangerous for old people and toddlers. The entryway was a garbage dump for rotted food, and the stairways reeked of old and pungent uric acid.

A sad, small alcoholic named Sippy Suds lived next door to Toussaint. Suds's apartment produced the worst smell in the Panhandle, a rancid sour waft of vomit and urine so strong in the closed space of the hallway that it made you crazy with the badness of it. He used to mess on himself. Suds was one of several people in the 'hood whose speech evaded understanding. I thought it was related to my eyes. Whenever I concentrated and tried to fight through his thick, inebriated Mississippi babble, my eyes watered from the pungent toxins in the air. Suds had everything no one wanted, down to flies that liked his clothes and odors that would cause others to change jobs.

Many of the kids on the block despised Suds, taking his pitiful coins by incessant begging.

"C'mon, Suds, gimme nickel. Yeah! Gimme dollah!"

Toussaint respected him.

"Leave da man be," he said to a whole battalion of yammering kids. "Ain't cool, takin poor man's coins. C'mon! Back off!" he shouted, pushing them back. " 'Sides. Man yoosta be a fighta," he said.

Heck, I thought. *Everyone* around here is a fighter.

I had seen dead rats before in our house, looking pitiful and scary in the traps, their little feet tucked up in death, thick round tails looking like remnants of ancient lizards. But I had never seen families of them alive. They were on Toussaint's stairs, sluggish, bunched up, and squeaky, and the first time I saw them I stopped and cried. Toussaint looked at me, nodding his head. The rats were pushy and one ran over my foot, small, heavy, sharp-clawed, and warm.

"Won hurtcha none," he said, taking my arm as I began to faint.

An elderly and toothless woman lived in a shamble of newspapers and produce cartons on top of the stairs in the hall. Toussaint called her Missus Hall. She wore old shawls, discarded and unmatched men's shoes, and staggered on broken hips with wriggling loose shoelaces, aided by a short stick wrested from a fruit crate. She would sit on the neighborhood stoops, her crackled fingers pulling splinters from each other, her aged and wrinkled face scrunched with the effort of finding the torment in her hands. During these efforts, her fleshy nose could touch her lips.

She was missing clumps of hair, eyelashes, eyebrows. Missus Hall did not look like someone who had been very pretty in her youth. But her durability, her will to survive, were attractive, and I liked her very much.

My mother had been beautiful. And she had died.

Missus Hall would relieve herself on old newspapers in the alleyways on Central Avenue. She never spoke to anyone but would nod at Toussaint, who brought her shares of their meager food. The LaRue and the Ting families did not look even a little bit alike, but we had the same caloric intake, while enjoying strong differences on the meaning of Christian charity.

Mrs. LaRue offered to feed me as well, and I was inclined to eat anything that wasn't going to run away from me. This easily included plain, unbuttered grits, which resembled *tze*, rice gruel. But Toussaint's friends never took food from his mother. Her son was too thin.

One Halloween night, after I had been friends with the LaRues for more than five years, Missus Hall smiled at me. I remember that when she showed her teeth I thought she was angry. It took a moment to realize that she was greeting me with a smile, and I beamed back at her, offering her witches' teeth candy, the world full of light.

I asked Mrs. LaRue why Missus Hall never spoke.

"I honestly don't know, Kai," she said. "I figure somethin almighty drastic happened in her life, and it probly happened twice. Once early, and once late. She's not gonna do nothin fancy with her life. She's jes getting ready for the next blow."

The LaRue home had no furniture, only milk cartons and fruit crates that his momma got from the Reliance Market.

Toussaint had no toys and never asked to play with those belonging to others. He had no father. His mother was wonderful and caring and had convinced Toos that toys and living fathers were not necessary in this mysterious physical world. She carried the whole load, all the way. Toussaint had the gift of love, and they shared everything they had. I was testament to that fact. His smile, shining from a high-cheekboned, high-foreheaded, almost skull-like face, was beatific and had the force of the Prophet. I thought he was the handsomest boy in the world.

As a streetfighter, Toussaint was unusual. He cared nothing for style, which was becoming an extremely big deal to the others.

"Toos," said Jerome Washington. "Ya'll fights like a ole' lady. Ya'll fights like Missus Hall." He giggled. "Ain't dat right, Toos?" Jerome was not looking for a fight. He just enjoyed stirring feces with his tongue.

"Dat probly be true, Jerome," said Toussaint, slowly. He was smiling, frustrating Jerome in some mysterious way. Jerome cursed and moved on.

"See, China? Jerome don mess wif me. He wanna hurt mah feelins, an I jes talk blahdee-blah trash back at 'em. 'China Bashers.' Dat's a lota *crap*. Misser Pueblo, in Cutty's Garage. He tole me: fight fo' da fight. Don pay no mind ta no lookers. Style, dat fo' *girls*.

"Fists. Be fo' da boy dookin Fist City wif ya."

Toos threw unending series of berserk punches, ignoring incoming rounds as if they were raindrops on a pleasant spring day. He would punch until the fight was over—until Toussaint collapsed or the other kid stopped. I didn't know how he could do that.

When he fought, the smile beat feet, and he became all business. He did not have to do this often. It usually occurred when a Haight kid crossed the border of Fell Street and strutted north up Masonic, looking to break some bones.

Toos's home was on the cross-'hoods thoroughfare. It was Indian Country; trouble came calling with the rising sun.

Toos was skinny and occasionally got picked. He would stand up straight, like an older boy, and roll his shoulders back, like a grown man. He would measure the challenge, giving the Handle crosser a chance to move on. Sometimes his quiet, unfearing gaze was as articulate as my mother's face. When parley failed, he met aggression with his own fury. He was never called out twice by the same youth.

The Haight, six blocks south, was bogeymanland. Boys carried knives, men had zip guns, and women looked more dangerous than twenty San Juan streetfighters with switchblades. Some of the Haight boys wore old-skinned Big Ben coveralls and carried barber shaving razors in the cup of the hand, hiding the flash of steel inside their arm-swaying struts. They could punch a guy and move on. It took a moment to realize that the face had been opened, blood everywhere, the searing pain following long moments after the incision.

"Ya'll stay outa dere," said Toussaint, pointing with a long and skinny thumb at our rival 'hood. "Be boogeymen, big-time."

Until I learned English, I understood it as The Hate.

The Panhandle lay between our 'hoods like no-man's-land, a DMZ that operated without U.N. intervention. Panhandle boys entered the park with great care and only in daylight. It was a jungle of thick eucalyptus, corpses, tangled azalea, and memories of aimless nocturnal screams. Men gathered there at night to smoke and drink and discuss this new land of California. When they disagreed, people died.

The Haight was largely populated by trekkers from Alabama and Louisiana. Mrs. LaRue said their heartaches came from not having a minister. Reverend M. Stamina Jones had followed the LaRues, the Joneses, the Scotts, and the Williamses—the Panhandle families—from Georgia. Others in the neighborhood hailed from Mississippi, Maryland, and Tennessee. I thought they were names of streets.

"No ministers in the Haight, just knife fighters," she said. "They'se lost. Toussaint LaRue and Kai Ting, you listen to Momma! Don't be goin into the Haight, no how and no way. Now. *That* be gospel."

Toussaint taught me about music. He tried to translate the words of the chorus in the church of Reverend Jones, but I always suspected that he lacked certainty in his explanations. But he knew that the chorus moved me, and would rub the hair on my head whenever I found myself weeping in time with its singing. I did not have to be an Imperial Scholar to know that crying in this temple house was accepted; the congregation's choral majesty was salted with tears and accented by open weeping. Sobs often served as confirmation of the truth of Reverend Jones's ministry. A dry-eyed assembly meant that his delivery was off the mark.

Toos also introduced me to Mr. Carter, who owned Evil the bulldog. Mr. Carter was a shipyard worker at Hunters Point who lived across the street from us, with the LaRue home around the corner. He had a platoon of exwives, no prospects of any more, two radios and a record player, and everyone on the block liked him while hating his dog.

Evil was moody. Somedays he raised his black-and-white head to you on a loose leash, anxious for a pat, his eyes half-closed, his teeth looking sadly overused and brownishly old.

Other days he growled, the fangs angry and huge and brightly wet. He would run around like a broken top with his jaws open, all the kids screaming as they scattered. Evil never caught me; I was the flight expert. He would clamp his maws around a kid's leg and throw his neck back and forth and Mr. Carter would blow that whistle in Evil's ear until he let go. He would then use a fat clothes-hanger dowel to beat the starch out of the dog, and I was the only one who felt sorry for him.

"Oughta jes give dat dog *away*," said Toos.

I shook my head. "Give doggie mo' food," I said. "He too much hungry."

"China, you'se a very funny boy," he said. "Now. Don let no dog

smell yo' fear. He smell dat, he get feared hisself and eat yo' pants in a
big hurry."

The men who had been in the army would sit on the wide stairs
of Mr. Carter's place and sing "What the Best-Dressed Man in Harlem
Is Wearing Tonight," "The Blues in the Night," and I could close my
eyes and sway to their unearthly beautiful voices. They also sang songs
they called Jodies. I knew them; my father used to chant them while
he chopped vegetables in the kitchen when our mother was still alive.

> *"Yo' momma was dere when ya lef"*
> *"YO' RIGHT!"*
> *"Jody was dere when ya lef"*
> *"YO' RIGHT!"*
> *"Sound off—"*
> *"ONE-TWO!"*
> *"Sound off—"*
> *"THREE-FO'!"*
> *"Bring it on down—"*
> *"ONE-TWO-THREE-FO'!"*
> *"ONE-TWO-THREE-FO'!"*
>
> *"Jody got somethin dat you ain't got"*
> *"I'S BIN SO LONG AH ALMOS' FO'GOT"*
> *"Yo' baby's as lonely as lonely can be"*
> *"WIF ONLY JODY FO' COM-PANY"*
> *"Ain't it great ta have a pal"*
> *"TA HELP KEEP UP HER MO-RALE"*
> *"Sound off. . . ."*
> *"Yo' not gonna get out till da enda da war"*
> *"IN NINET'IN HUNDRA' AN' SEVENTY-FOUR. . . ."*

Adults and kids gathered on Mr. Carter's stoop to sing and clap hands,
or to gently swing to "Harlem Nocturne" and the high throaty jazz of
Billie Holiday's "Strange Fruit," "The Way You Look Tonight," and
"God Bless the Child." Toos told me that the words to that song meant
that if God did not love you, you were soon dead, because little came
to short people without God's grace.

"Good news is, China," said Toos, "dat God love all chilun."

"Me, too?" I asked.

"Dat *gotta* be true," he said. "God get dibs on all da little chilun he kin find. And," he said, elbowing me, "you'se little."

We would keep time and tap with one foot while keeping the other ready to exit stage left if Evil felt the urge. The muse didn't come cheap in the Panhandle.

"Mista Carter," said Toussaint's mom. "That's not right, namin a dog Evil. You can come up with a better name'n that, I know you can. Callin somethin a name sometime make it so."

"Charlotte, you think it be a big favor to all de chilun on dis block be comin up ta dis here dog an callin 'em *Spot?* or *Fido?*"

"See. His firs' name, it was Winston. The name offered no warnin. Folks like ta pet 'em. Den he start ta eat kids? He gots too much crust. I call 'em what he is: Evil." He whacked his pants leg with the dowel.

Kids learned to make their own music, without radios. I thought this was because of Evil, since the price of listening to radios could be a pint of dog-drawn blood. But I was wrong. Kids, even poor and unhappy ones, love to sing, warbling the purity of expression, the unsullied and miraculous poetry of a child's honesty. Happy kids sing better. Toos sat on his crumbling steps with Titus McGovern and Alvin Sharpes—boys who had pledged their lives to him—to sing the "Papa Ditty," and other rapadiddle tunes from the not-so-distant South.

> *"Well, I don know but I been tole,*
> *Papa gonna buy me a pile a coal.*
> *If dat coal don burn fo' me,*
> *Papa gonna take me to da sea.*
> *If dat sea don make me wet,*
> *Papa gonna sink us deeper in debt.*
> *If dat debt don eat our food,*
> *Papa gonna thank da good Saint Jude."*

And so on.

Each kid would sing a two-line stanza, making it up as he went. I always shook my head, lowering it as I blushed when it was my turn.

"Dang!" cried Alvin Sharpes. "Lookit China's face. It all red! How you do dat, China?" It was easy. I couldn't rhyme.

"Missa LaRue," I asked, struggling to align the *L*'s and the *R*'s. "Kin rearn me 'Papa Ditty'?"

"The 'Papa Ditty'? I don't think I know that, Kai. Can you sing a little of it for me?"

I tried. She laughed and hugged me.

"Oh, sweetnin, that's 'The Mockinbird's Song.' Listen to me," she said, bending over, her smoothly angular and pretty face bright with life, looking at me with a great smile, singing in a deep mystic voice that scratched the itches in my heart.

"Well, I'll tell you what I've learned:
Papa's gonna buy me a mockinbird.
If that mockinbird don't sing,
Papa's gonna buy me a diamond ring.
If that diamond ring don't shine,
Papa's gonna buy me a bottle of wine.
If that bottle of wine don't pour,
Papa's gonna take us to the shore. . . ."

"My momma rike shore, rike ocean," I said.

"Well, Kai, that big blue sea, it's somethin, all right."

Toussaint told me that Big Willie Mack, the glandular error in the guise of a twelve-year-old, had been the first to punch me on my inaugural day on the street. Big Willie was the toughest dude on the block, a bad combination of vicious clothes-taking bully and mean, gutsy fighter.

Toussaint had hit me on the arm that day with that second, harmless blow, to make sure that Willie didn't wind up and do it again.

"China, ya'lls gotta fight. Pretty soon, he be takin yo' clothes."

"No. Crows too small. Him long size," I said.

"China. He don't take 'em ta wear. He take 'em to *take 'em*. You'se gotta punch it out wif him, China."

"Ohnry make worse, mo' hit."

"Den *you* hit back mo'. Dat how it is. It hard be livin, be a stan-up-boy on dis here block, ya'll don fight. Don havta *win*, jes *fight*. Make it so's da other boy think fightin you's too much work! Make it easy on *bof* of us."

"Kin *you* whup Big Wirry?" I asked.

"Nah, don think so. But he know I fights 'em, won give in. He wan *my* shoes, he gonna havta give me some *blood*."

We both looked at Toos's shoes. I didn't think Toos had to worry about anyone taking them unless Evil went crazy or a starving rat was driven to extreme means.

I tried to explain yuing chi, the responsibility of the future, God's ever-watchful scorecard, to Toussaint, but the concept exceeded my vocabulary. I had understood the idea so easily when it was conveyed by the dark, shimmering, expressive eyes of my mother. I was so anxious to explain that fighting was wrong, and would cause later pain, but winning this inarticulate debate was as difficult as prevailing in its subject matter.

I thought desperately about fighting but could not figure it out. I would be noticed, cut down, called horrific names, shoulder-bumped or shoved into the soft tar of the old streets of the Handle. A kid would challenge me and fear would rise inside my stomach like fog on the Bay and swamp me. My lights would get punched out and I would bawl like a newborn.

Flight always overcame Fight.

The very best I could do was control my tears, to a point. It was my only victory over the weakness of my body, the paucity of my combat power, the horror of fighting.

"China, I need yo' help someday too," said Toos.

I looked at him, confused.

"Say dude from da Haight strut here wif a razor, break mah bones and bleed me. Hustle to yo' door, ya'll lemme in. Right?"

I thought of Edna. Edna wouldn't let *me* in.

"Hmm," I said.

Toussaint was a preacher of the handshake. He already knew at this tender age that people got by because they gave each other the biggest gift in the book: time. His momma provided it for him whenever he wanted it. They had a handshake on it, and it gave him the strength of angels.

"You'all lookin at me kinda strange, Kai. Whatcha thinkin?" said his momma, as Toos went out the door.

"Toos ask fo' wata. You *give* wata."

She studied me for a bit, passing me a sad little cup of water, as well. I drank. "Say that again?" she said. So I did.

"Kai. I love my son. Now look here. *Everybody* love their kids. Yo' daddy and his wife, they surely love you, too. Jus' everabody don't know *how*.

"If the Good Lord took my boy from me I would curl up and die;
I truly would," she said very solemnly. "He sent me Toussaint LaRue
so's I could *love* him, give him my life, my heart." She smiled. "I have
the Lord Jesus and I have Toussaint, and they'se my joys.

"Kai. You 'member this, chile. Someday you'all gonna have yo' own
little Kai, a little Janie Ting. When yo' child want yo' time, you *give* it.
That's our—our *callin.* I *love* my boy, but sometime he want ta play the
cockroach game and I'm jes sick of it? Oh, Lord, *really sick of it.*" She
looked down at the old floor, clicking her tongue. "Or, he tell me the mos'
borin, stop-your-mind stuff *ever?* My little man, Toussaint, he tell the longest
and mos' unfunniest jokes in the world! But I *listen,* and I laugh fo' his joy,
and I play him roaches, cuz I'm his momma, and he's my son. It's my God-
given duty."

She dried her hands on a rag, and exhaled, looking away from me.
"Toussaint's daddy got killed in truck acciden' in Benning," she said
softly. "He was an officer. He went inta the army a private, and came
back a cap'n, two bright silver railroad tracks on his collar. Lord, what
a man he was! Well. The war, it was over, and he made it back from
overseas, a pure hero, and he gave me Toussaint, and then we lost
him. . . ." Her voice faded.

"He was a good man, Little Kai, and I miss him *evera day.*" Her
voice was choked. She stopped to blow her nose, shaking her head, hot
tears coursing down her cheeks. "God wanted him bad, and took him."
She looked toward the door. "Oh, Lord. What a price You exact. . . .

"John LaRue made a promise to me. I think his son done made
one to you. Promises be powerful things. I take care of my son's wants.
Then he give water to other men when they need it. And we'll have
another John LaRue in the world. You want some more water?"

That was yuing chi, karma! And she let Missus Hall and the rats
live on the stairs, and roaches in the wall. Mrs. LaRue was Chinese! She
just didn't *look* it.

Could you give water to children who asked for it *and* beat the
stuffing out of them if a fight was offered? I frowned with the difficulty
of the riddle. She was offering me more water.

I took the plastic cup from Mrs. LaRue again, looking at the liquid
within it as I drew it to my mouth. The plastic was old and scarred,
with a history probably longer than mine. Innumerable scratches and
half-cracks made it look tired, as if the serving of its masters and the
catching of roaches had somehow cost too much. The water inside the

cup sloshed, like the surf in the ocean, and for a transcendent moment all the scale and sense of proportion in the world dissolved, and I could see my mother placing her feet in the roaring waters of the cup. She was communicating with Na-Gung, an ocean away, and with me, from another world. My eardrums tickled, making me shudder, with her reaching for me. The cup was against my lip, and I stared inside it, cross-eyed. I could not drink this water.

"Tank you. Momma," I said. "I keep wata?"

"You want ta take it on home?" she asked.

"No. Want keep here, on sink. Same wata," I said. "Special. Uh, big-time, special."

"You can take it, chile."

"No," I said, shaking my head. "Mo' betta here." I heard Toos come in. Mrs. LaRue took the cup and placed it on the sink.

"China. Ya'll wanna be mah fren'?" asked Toos. Mrs. LaRue smiled and moved away from my field of vision. Maybe three feet.

"Chure, yep," I said. I sensed something weighing in the balance, an unasked question, a favor awaiting fulfillment.

"Den shake on it," he said, extending his hand. Again? I wondered. He took my hand and molded it into his. His was so hard, so rough.

"Squeeze, squeeze hard, China," he said, "like milk'd come out if ya squoze hard. You'se gotta know how." I gripped, and he smiled.

"Now. We'se frens, fo' sure," he said.

"An you can ask him yo' question, honey," said Momma.

"China," said Toos.

"Toos?" I said.

"China. Tell me 'bout yo' daddy."

I frowned. "Tell what?" I asked.

"Anythin, China. Jes *talk* 'bout him."

I began breathing heavily, not knowing what to say.

"I think yo' daddy was in the war, right?" said Mrs. LaRue. I nodded. "He in China army, for war," I said. "He fry airprane wif guns, bomb. He—" I made motions with my hands—"fall in pallashoot. Shoot gun. Save my ma-ma." I was licking my lips. "He very smart. Read books. Pray catch wif me. . . ."

There was a long silence.

"Thanks, chile," said Momma. "Listen. You share yo' daddy with Toussaint, here? Dat's what frens do."

Toussaint was all smiles, and I halfway grinned at him, trying to hide my teeth so the Teeth God would not want them.

It was now another day, and my friend, my friend of the handshake, my friend of the water, was staring at me. I jumped a little when I realized he had been staring at me.

"China, ya'll knows how ta laff?" asked Toos. We had been playing marbles. I was pretty good at marbles, for the short shots. I was also becoming something of a demon in penny-pitching, and card-tossing. Parlor games, not at the level of the Bigs of street-thumping and ball-playing, but something, after all. It was all in the wrist.

"Chure, yep," I said, worried by his question.

He opened his eyes wide and showed his teeth. He giggled. It was high, and silly, and warm.

"So les hear yo' laff!" he giggled.

I started to explain to him about the Teeth God, realizing that I could neither describe it nor prove its existence. I didn't even know if it was a boy or a girl. This was, like karma, a matter of faith. I suddenly wondered what all this god-fearing was worth. Mother had respected every god known, and they had taken her.

I opened my mouth and tried to make a laughing sound. It must've been ridiculous, because Toos bent over and guffawed, slapping his knees and putting his head between his knees while making a wonderful sound of a strange animal. My ears perked as I heard what I could later favorably compare to a spasm-ridden rum-crazed jackass. Now I was hearing something that reminded me of the distant laughter of my father. I giggled with him, still holding back.

Even through the laughter came the whistle of my stepmother. She never called when I needed her.

I could not discuss my street whippings at home. Stepmother Edna pretended that no problem existed, washing out the blood from my clothes with astounding tolerance. I began to believe that she took pleasure in my fear. I felt that my shame was mine, and somehow my father's and even my mother's, and did not see it as transferable.

Janie was involved in a struggle for survival with Edna. It was a war between two de facto mother figures. One by blood and death, one by marriage and expectation, neither by choice.

As the lastborn kid of four, I did not understand Janie's tenacious resistance, to Edna's supreme power. Kids in the lower birth order, like me, seldom resisted parental authority as did the firstborn, the vanguards. Jennifer Sung-ah and Megan Wai-la were in Berkeley; Janie was now the functional older sibling.

Edna was a grown-up and could slap you silly and dance fandangos on your face. But she hadn't touched Jane for months. If Edna had left me alone like that I would have written poetry for her.

"Kai. I'm doing this for both of us. She is *not* our mom."

"I know dat," I said. I just didn't know what it meant. Janie's eyes were bright in anger.

"Edna told me not to read this to you," she said, pulling a stained and torn book from her aging schoolbag. "It's called *Hansel and Gretel*. It's about a stepmother who gets the father to get rid of the kids. Edna threw it out, and I dug it out of the garbage." Janie looked very intense, very determined.

We sat on the front stairs of our house. I pretended to look at the book, but was watching for Big Willie and the Bashers.

"You China Boy sister?" asked Reginald Tufts.

"His name is Kai," said Janie.. "Can you say that? Kai."

"Kai," said Reginald. My mouth was, again, as open as the Red Sea was for Moses. Hearing a boy say my first name was astonishing, and I squinted with the pressure of it, waiting to see what else in the world might change next.

"I'm going to read a book. Want to listen?" she asked.

"A book? Yeah!" he cried, and I glared at him, not wanting to share Janie with a Basher, or a friend of a Basher. Even if he had said my name.

Janie opened the book, which was missing its cover.

"Once upon a time," she began, "there was a poor woodcutter who lived at the edge of a large forest with his wife and two children. The boy was named Hansel, and the girl was named Gretel. Many years before, his wife had died, and he had remarried. They had always been poor. . . ."

Toos and Alvin Sharpes arrived and sat on the stairs to listen to the story and stare at the storyteller. Janie smiled at them and received their smiles in return. I grinned.

The stepmother in this story gave the two children a last meal and left them in the woods to be taken by wolves. She had done this to allow the father and stepmother to live without the burden of the kids, whose voracious appetites were consuming too much of the limited food. It was a credible tale.

I later asked Toos what he would do if his momma left and another mother moved in.

"My momma, she no go nowhere wif out me. Dere ain't no other momma," he said.

"But she go bye-bye anyway," I said.

"Den I goes wif her."

"If she jus, *gone?*"

"I fin her," he said.

"Can fin her, den . . . ?"

"Keep lookin," he said.

"Where rook?" I asked.

"Dunno, China. Lord. *All* over." He looked at me. "Ya'll miss yo' momma, doncha. Yeah." Then he looked up, squinting. "I 'member her. She yoosta tote da um-brella when dere was no rain. Ya'll was a big saprise, comin outa dat 'partment. Didn know you'se in dere."

I looked down at the stairs.

"Ya'll don like yo' stepmomma?"

I shook my head, fearing that somehow, even around the corner of buildings and the rise of streets, she knew I was admitting it, and that this knowledge would hurt me.

"She be a white lady," he said, and I nodded. "Wif yella hair," he added. "Don think she like *us,*" he concluded.

"What I do, Toos?" I asked.

"She yo momma, now. Dang, China. I get it; dat's hard." He studied it for a bit. "I'd as' da Lord."

"I did dat," I said.

To my father, the combat between the females was Women's War, the incomprehensible tensions between disenfranchised females. In Shanghai, there was an unquestionable hierarchy, an immutable order of rank. It did not call for the involvement of men, and he had no experience to make himself Ward Cleaver, who in any event was a fantasy designed to sell Mapo. He could not find an intellectual guide to the current problem and knew that he did not wish to reestablish the old order. I found guidance in comic books.

I loved Superman and Mighty Mouse. I had lost my funnies in the revolutionary storm. Alvin Sharpes had a deep and endless collection and I began to draw from his castaways. I read them, two inches from my face, again and again. I began to imagine myself as a fighter. Who did good for others and beat the crap out of bad guys. Good karma. I projected myself into the cartoon sequences. I was unconquerable. Here I come, to save the day. . . . It means that Mighty Mouse is on his way. . . .

After my stunning victories over evil incarnate, I received the appreciative accolades of my family, laurels from a grateful nation, a citation from the President of the United States, free milk at our doorstep, and a new copy of *The Tales of Lu Hsun*.

After a pounding on the street, I would take out my comics and pore over them with shaking hands and a teary face, trying desperately to incorporate their messages into my body. But the correspondence-school method of streetfighting proved unsuccessful.

Then I tried reason. Be pal? I would offer. Pow! I don wan twubble wit you. Wham! Here, candy? Snatch!

Forget reason. I returned to comics and running.

Then Edna rediscovered the comic books, and they were gone.

I wondered if I was going crazy. I would awaken at night, crying from a dream in which I was fleeing my stepmother. Edna would enter my room and slap me in an effort to stop the weeping, which had awakened her. By the time I figured out that the dream had merged with reality, she was gone and I would squint at the closed door, trying to separate images of light and dark.

Despite the fact that I now had Toussaint and his mother in the periphery of my life, I tried to run away again.

Knowing that silence was imperative to successful flight, I took my time. It was not difficult to sneak down the staircase, my footfalls absorbed by the carpet that had through long wear become part of the risers. The front door made a sound like a cherry bomb when opened by the remote handle. I had seen Father lubricate it. I put oil in the hinges and gave the task five minutes, and the door opened with all the sound that a mouse makes when it sniffs cheese.

Golden Gate Avenue was utterly dark and surprisingly cold, the lone streetlamp at the corner of Central Avenue offering few clues and no warmth. But the street was mine, surrendered only for blinding moments as cars with overbright headlights passed.

The first time a car approached I ran from it, thinking it was an agent of Edna in hot pursuit. I could run very fast on a cold night on an empty sidewalk, my lungs bellowing as I humped arms high and hard to let my legs pump, my head vibrating synchronously with the effort as I fled my fears.

I roamed McAllister, leaning against the cold steel doors of Cutty's Garage, peering into the barred windows of the Reliance Market, missing the winos who kept guard at the Double Olive Bar, trying to recapture the now departed aromas of sizzling french fries in the General Lew Wallace Eatery. I wondered if Rupert and Dozer, the fratricidal siblings, argued after they closed the Eatery and went home to the large apartment building on Grove. Without the aromas of food, McAllister smelled sour and old. I played imaginary checkers on the linoleum grid of the barbershop floor. I projected the more complex figures of Chinese chess, *shiang chi*, onto the black-and-white squares, but could not remember all the moves for both players.

I strolled to Broderick Street, over the pavement where I had once raced when I had a home in which to hide. I looked through the iron-grate fence of Fremont Elementary, retracing beatings by Big Willie and the Bashers. I surveyed the kickball-field benches, the lunch tables, where food had been taken and little bodies stomped. I looked at that spot of the yard, knowing a truth lay in it. I looked away.

Cats chased shadowy rats on the street where Big Willie had stood on my chest. Dogs rousted garbage cans. One growled at me and I froze, waiting ten or fifteen minutes like a man who has stepped on a pressure-release-trigger landmine, until the dog had taken his pleasure with the waste. With light feet, his mangy tail down, he padded away from me and I breathed again.

This was my street, McAllister. Now, in the solace of the night, with its bullies and angry words and fists absent, I liked it. I wanted to sleep by day and to walk McAllister to the east at night. It felt safe, the biting cold welcome and fitting. For an instant, I did not want to go any farther, my feet immobilized by the vast, dark unknowns that surrounded the 'hood. I wondered if *wupo*, witches, awaited me in side alleys, or if *dufei*, bandits, were hoping to snatch the only son of the Ting clan tonight.

Ah, I thought. The *wupo* is *inside* the house, not here.

Feeling mildly suicidal, I crossed McAllister to Fulton, which was bold for any kid north of the park. I headed south, keeping to the shadows, crossing Grove, Hayes, and Fell, the final boundary between sanity and simple stupidity. I watched the night traffic on Fell, a big, wide thoroughfare. Where were these people going? Could I go too?

Now I was in the tall eucalyptus trees of the Panhandle itself, the glare of the streetlights swallowed in the darkness of gnarled, interwoven trees. I was in the demilitarized zone, the place of mysterious human sounds, secret passions, and dark bleeding. This was not a child's place.

I crept through the brush as only a boy with bad night vision can. Slowly, patiently, silently, over a detritus of cans, wrappers, boxes, papers. If I made a noise, I stopped. I crawled past a man and a woman, whispering to each other with an intensity beyond comprehension. I shimmied up to a group of talkers sitting around a burning trash can. The fire crackled and cloaked my advance.

I listened to the men in the park. "Boogeymen" from the Haight, with deep, gravelly, bitter voices, raspy with old rumbling hungers. The humor was strained. Some of the speakers were drunk and flared at each other like the trash fire finding fuel to combust in gunfirelike consumption.

What would they do if they found me? I wondered. Nothing, I decided. They didn't care about little boys. There was little talk about sports and fighting. Someone mentioned Joe Louis, and I heard Di-Maggio's name.

They were mostly concerned with women, and their meanness and beauty. The mystery of women. These men blamed women for all their woes. Always taking things, wanting more, refusing love, yelling, complaining, comparing. I nodded my head, watching the shadowed figures gesturing, belching in hunger, nodding heads, tippling bottles.

One man held their attention as he spoke of the great Southern Pacific trains that ran from the China Basin docks to Mexico with empty freight cars, no railroad police, and a free meal at the train stops for veterans. I was the son of a veteran. Did that count? I didn't have a mother. Did that matter?

China Basin. It was somewhere in San Francisco, and it sounded like China Boy, like me. It was *my* train. I could go to Mexico. No Edna. No Willie and no Bashers. I would be leaving Janie. Could I do that?

In my mind I heard the wail of the engine calling, its thunderous power promising fast, determined movement, high-pumping wheels chugging tirelessly, taking me away even while I slept in its cars.

I watched the firefly sparks of the trash fire flicker into the night sky, looking like the stack flames of a southbound freight, disappearing into the swallowing blackness. For years I would deride myself, assailing my manhood, for not taking the China Basin train. The decision had been in my hands, but I lacked the ability to seize an early opportunity to die a boy's lonesome death on a distant track.

When I reached Masonic and Golden Gate, I was drawn to Toussaint's apartment building. I climbed the outside stairs with great stealth, thinking of Mrs. LaRue, wanting a glass of water, happy with the mere thought that she was on the other side of the door, resting. Truly there, actually alive, to be seen and heard again. I touched a leg. A big leg. I knew that I was dead from fright and would be beaten afterward for clumsiness.

It was Sippy Suds, his horrendous odors mysteriously absent in the cool of the night. He stirred slightly and began to snore softly. He looked huge lying down, folded inside his faded, moth-eaten, navy pea jacket. In his bent, inebriated, staggering postures on the street, I had thought him as short as Missus Hall. He was actually a tall man. His hands were pinned between his drawn-up knees. They were huge, the fingers bent and black with the dirt of past labor. His wrists were bony but very thick. Hands that gave precious coins to greedy children.

His face looked as if it had been hit often by hard objects or by an angry stepmother. It was square and hard, different colors shading it. Bruising colors. His nose was very flat at the bridge, the bottom of the nose turned to the side, as if an anvil had been dropped on it from an angle. The closed, trusting eyes were surrounded by scars and small mounds of built-up skin. The rough pebbles of scar tissue interrupted the deep lines that laughter had once carved into his temples.

He was a fighta, Toussaint had said.

I sat next to him, looking at him, edging closer, absorbing his kindly silent companionship, feeling safety, defeating loneliness with every moment in his company. I held my breath.

Then we breathed together, and I matched his cycle, my small puff of air emerging with his thicker cloud, both of us slowly exhaling our fatigues with bright, streetlit, vaporous breath into the foggy night. My lungs filled with soulful strength.

I wanted him to awaken and to tell me about his fights. I wanted to hear that he had won, somehow, somewhere, in his past. Together, I thought, the two of us could do anything. I sat until my bottom ached from the hardness of the stairs, and I began shivering, my thin body capsized in cold.

Bye-bye Suds, I whispered, smiling as he stirred again. I returned with small steps to the house of my stepmother, ready for neither the beginning of sleep nor the start of day.

10

HECTOR PUEBLO

,

Salvation arrived near the middle of my first term on the street. It happened during my worst beating.

Little Aaron Williams was five and twice my size. Blessed with a roundness of body and limb, a breadth of chest and shoulders, he presented like a thoroughbred fighter, but fought like a dray horse. He had been scuffed a couple times in his first fights and had cried too loudly. His stock on the street was down, and he was itching for an opportunity to redeem it. That was my job.

As he looked at me, Aaron must have thought: Here come Chicken Little!

I cannot remember what stimulated the event, but I was in the middle of a routine panicked run and somehow, as I faced the motor traffic on the bad corner of Fulton and Masonic, Toussaint's urgings broke through, and I got tired of flight.

I felt my buddy's handshake, and I stopped. I stuck a fist in Little

Aaron's face. I think the surprise of it exceeded the hurt, but he cried
like a stuck pig while I shook my wounded hand, marveling at the fact
that I had somehow won. I had avoided a pounding. I should have said,
Not so fast, hotdog. . . .

Anita Mae Williams was a tall and swift-limbed ten-year-old. She
was beautiful, with a smile that tugged at the hearts of boys and a
careful, watchful grace amplified by an elegant swan's neck that suggested
unattainable royalty and wonderful, confusing, mesmerizing girlhood.
She also had a sincere right cross. She was responsible for raising her
baby brother Aaron. There were a lot of kids with that responsibility
on the block. Janie was one of them, and these young girls shared in
common the fact that they were serious about it.

When Anita Mae Williams found out that the China Boy had
punched out her Little Aaron, she tracked me down. Later, when I
discovered Western literature, I recognized in Inspector Javert the stead-
fast resolution of Anita Mae when she put me in her cross hairs.

I was on my return leg from Fremont, hustling down the clutter
of McAllister, just past the drunks at the Double Olive Bar. I was stupidly smelling the fries at the door to the Eatery and wondering how
angry Rupert the cook might be when she got me.

"Flies," I said, hesitantly. "Fl-ries. Uh, fl—"

Anita knocked me down and wasted me from the Reliance Market,
on Lyon, all the way to Cutty's Garage on Central. She was stripping
the skin from her knuckles, but all she could see was her baby brother's
cut lip. I tried not to cry and then she hit me square in the nose. I hurt
enough to scream, startling the winos and causing one of them to drop
his paper-sacked Tokay on the street with a wet explosion of cheap glass
and bad grapes. "Aww, shee-itt!" he complained.

This was a serious licking and it worsened when she tired of chasing
me and picked me up, stuffing me into a square metal garbage can, the
likes of which once adorned the streets of San Francisco. She began
punching me methodically in the face, her grunts of effort so ugly, so
unlike her delicate, angelic face.

I was hurt past crying, and I could sense in Anita's blows the
momentary hesitation that all people feel when they are about to kill
someone. She kept hitting my forehead, and penumbra replaced myopia,
and my arms fell away, no longer offering interference.

A Mexican mechanic named Hector stopped it.

"Hey, girl," he said. "Park yo' fists! Boy don have no *sangre*, no blood lef fo' you. You made yo' point. You keep swingin, he gonna fo'get why you hate him. You bein a *pendeja*, chica.''

Anita nodded, not knowing the foreign word but recognizing the truth. I knew it had stopped but the pain seemed to worsen. I tried to thank him but my lip was split, and a dislodged late baby tooth impeded articulate expression. I couldn't crawl out of the can. His rescue allowed me to sob and cry weakly, all I had left.

Hector extracted me from the steel box, which was like pulling a barbed fishhook, and took me into Cutty's rest room and cleaned me up, using fresh oil rags. The rags turned heavy with blood. My cheek was swollen like I had misplaced a tennis ball. My ears rang off and on like a broken telephone deep in my cranium and my lips began to swell toward Sutro Heights. Every now and again I sat down involuntarily. In the middle of all this I got the hiccups, and as he gave me a glass of water I tried to look for waves inside it, half cross-eyed. I began to laugh hysterically.

"Sorry I cly,'' I said to the world.

I felt safe in the garage. It smelled of dead grease. My blood was on his hands, on his T-shirt, and on his floor. He was not angry. Nor was Joe Cutty when he pulled out the engine from an old truck and walked over to inspect my body damage. I kept trying to wipe up the drops of blood on his concrete floor.

"Man, oh man,'' he said. "Don't sweat that. This here's a garage, not an officers' club. That cheek could use a stitch. You gonna live, son?''

"Ah could sew that rip up,'' said a third man. It was Tom Molineaux, a small, wiry, jumpy sort of person who had just graduated from Polytechnic High. He called wrenches "spanners'' and liked to spin them like batons. He was always eager to do what Joe called the "shit details.'' He always was in a rush, working fast. He had received his draft notice for Korea.

"No, no,'' said Joe Cutty. "That'd hurt more'n the tear.''

I was ready to move in.

"Hector. Who pounded this boy?'' asked Cutty.

"Anita Mae,'' he said. *"Hombre*, she was plenty P-O'd!'' There was a silence. A girl had just trashed a boy on McAllister. Wonders would never cease.

"Why she screw wif you so bad, chico?'' asked Hector.

"Hit bruddah,'' I squeaked.

"She hit her brother?" asked Tom Molineaux.

I shook my head, and it hurt. I pointed at me. The men nodded. They knew that Anita Mae really watched out for Aaron.

"When yo' daddy come home, *niño*?" asked Hector.

"Six," I said.

"Yo momma expec' you home now?"

I shrugged my shoulders and he nodded. Hector went into the office and came out with a stack of *Argosy* magazines and some Donald Duck comics. I smiled and he smiled.

I was reading about Huey, Louie, and Dewey's Woodchuck Guide and the Magic Flying Radish while Hector pulled chains, banged tools, hummed Navy tunes; Joe cranked ratchets; and Tom moved around the garage like a zephyr.

Then Anita Mae said, "Hey, I'm sorry, China Boy. Doncha be hittin mah Little Aaron no mo'."

I nearly jumped out of my socks. I was afraid of talking to her. I nodded, my throat jammed, all the hurts in my head, mouth, and stomach coming back, with the hiccups. Her knuckles were skinned from tagging my face. I started to cry and she shook her head, her drop earrings bobbing, catching the fading light from the open garage doors. She walked off on her long legs.

Later, when I was twelve, and driven by blind ambition, and she was fifteen, and knew better, I asked her to marry me. She laughed in a deep rich woman's tone that made rejection both interesting and bearable.

Hector Pueblo was from Guadalajara, making him an outsider as well to the main culture of the Handle. He spoke blackgang Navy and black street with a Hispanic panache. He had been an unemployed carpenter until Joe Cutty hired him.

Cutty was huge, formed from a template that would have served two normal adults. He had a round face made jovial by bright, almost boyish eyes and eyebrows ridiculously small for a man his size. His biceps were as big as his head.

Joe Henry Cutty was like most of the men in the Panhandle. He had returned from the war, relieved to be alive and unsure about the future. With his savings, bolstered by intelligent poker play across the breadth of the Pacific, he managed to buy the garage from a redneck who viewed the black migration into California as the end of the free world. The seller had said to him, "Glad you're not like them other niggers. I can trust *you*."

Cutty smiled his slow smile that expressed no joy. He then lowered his offer to the owner by half, and the man took it, cursing himself and the black nation.

"Bastards trying ta get a good deal. Can you believe that shit?" the seller muttered to his god.

Cutty hired Hector after seeing his tattoos. Both of them had been Navy machinists. In Lingayen Gulf in 1944, their carrier groups had fought next to each other, and that had cemented it. Hector was heavily muscled with long arms and big, high-knuckled hands that caught sharp and hot metal surfaces and absorbed grease. He and Joe Cutty were top mechanics, artisans with wrenches, and they smelled like engines on a hot summer day.

"*Joven*," said Hector. "C'mon. We gonna hump dis hill, go to your home." He pulled me out of the deep couch, and kept his hand on my back as we trudged up Central to my house.

"Lissen. Say *tío*. It mean 'uncle.' You unnerstan'?"

"*Tío*," I said.

"*Joven*. You call me Tío Hector, hokay?"

I nodded. "Uncle" was *dababa*. Now I had two uncles. He and Uncle Shim did not resemble each other very much, and looking carefully at Hector while we climbed the hill did not change the perception.

Edna did not want to let Hector or me in the house. My father opened the door. He knew Hector and invited him in. Father and Edna looked at my face and my clothing. Hector, wearing a nice Navy khaki shirt, jumped right in.

"Missa Ting. Yo' boy, he need lesson in *boxeo*, in *pugilato*, fists. I see him tussle, and ees *ugly*." Hector glanced at Edna, licking his lip nervously.

"He's *muy rápido*, you know, bery quick. Black boy get in his face and firs' t'ree punches, firs' kick, yo' boy go lik' dis an lik' dat, no touch." Hector twisted his upper body, his arms up.

"But his eyes, dey get *muy grande* and he take to feet an try to run home. Den dey take him down and dey beat him."

He looked down at me and rubbed my hair with his hand. He looked at me. I smiled, but only halfway; Edna did not like Hector, his shirt, his speech, or the hair-rubbing. Beatings were okay in our family, but touching was taboo.

"Now wors ting, dis boy tink," pointing at me, "ees cryin. Ain't bad, cryin." Hector could see that Stepmother Edna was not buying it.

"*Los jóvenes*, de children, dey cry. Ees natural. You know, dey say, 'Cry Lika Baby'?" Hector smiled engagingly at Edna, a great, shining, teeth-gleaming, Cesar Romero, Gilbert Roland heart-warmer.

My father grinned. I smiled.

Edna's face said: No sale, you common laborer.

"Hokay. Not fightin, dot's bad news," Hector said forcefully and directly to my father, making my guts jump. I had a feeling our house confused him. He was not alone.

"Chinee boy gotta fisticuff, maybe mo' dan odder kids. He stand out, bery big-time. Yo'll better tell him dot, cuz cryin ain't de problem. *Boxeo, dot* de problem."

My father's face was impassive, but I felt grand relief. The reality of my life had come before him.

"Thank you," my father said, and I tried to keep my face passive, too.

Hector was trying to figure out Edna, whose stern disapproval was patent in the hallway. Hector's advice regarding the saving of my life did not belong in this house, either. His tattoos and muscled arms also felt out of place, and he put them behind him. I think he liked my father, because he said, "Missa Ting. I teach yo' boy *un poco*. But firs', you sen him to de Y.M.C.A. Dey teach him de basics, *las reglas*. De boy, he can come to Cutty's to learn. But, no way he come to hide." His arms were out, and I watched them, fascinated. He made a fist and cocked his right arm up, a gesture of strength and defiance.

"Den, I teach him *street*," and he pumped it. His biceps bulged; the long muscles in his forearm popping. Edna glided out of the entryway and Hector ignored her. I breathed again.

The Y.M.C.A. cost twelve dollars every two months. At first, Stepmother Edna balked. But she realized that further beatings could result in medical bills. She had just discovered that we were not only poor, but very poor. She had restated her position that she did not want me in the house between school and dinner, or during sunlight on weekends. Six dollars a month. An investment in childcare.

Hector said good-bye. My father pointed to the old round leather hassock. I sat down and he turned on a table lamp. The hassock had once been green and red and was now a uniform brown. He cleared his throat. We had the best talk of my life to date.

"I was in Chinese Army," he said in a gruff voice, looking out the window, toward China, his posture militarily erect, shoulders square.

"We lost to *Gungtsetang*, the communists. To the Red political chief, Mao Tse-tung. Very smart man. He reached the peasants, and they went to him, like fish to sea. We lost to the Red generals, Chu Teh and Lin Piao, who fought like Sun-tzu, master of war.

"That's why we're here. We did not fight so well." The pain on my father's face was profound. His features did not move, but his eyes looked so vacantly sad, so ineffably alone. It was a war he needed to win and could not afford to lose.

"Your mother missed home." He coughed a little, squaring his shoulders to the window, filling his small, dark pipe with Edgeworth, a prize in wartime China. Sometimes I thought that the Nationalist Army had fought the war for Virginia tobacco. He lit the pipe, his own shadow playing on the walls, and he slipped into Songhai.

"In a way, the war goes on. The Reds might still be kicked out, and we could return to Kiangsu, where everyone but you was born. The Nationalists, my old army, are not a lot better than the Reds, but they won't kill *us*. I don't want to go back. I am American. But it might be better for you."

Better for me. Father, talking to me in our true tongue, talking about Mother. Oh, Mah-mee. I wanted him to keep talking, to never stop. Drunk on his words, intoxicated with the communication. He was talking about somehow returning to China. But I was having a hard time figuring out how to be black, how to be American. Now I had to learn to be Chinese? To go to China now, with our mother dead.

Here I had Toussaint, and Titus McGovern and Alvin Sharpes. I had Toussaint's momma, who hugged me, spoke to me with laughter in her voice, and had sung to me. A number of other women on the block were likewise kind, wiping my blood with white hankies. Hector had just saved my life, and he and Joe Cutty had great coin on the street. Reverend Jones always smiled at me, welcoming me to his church. I was not sure that I would be so lucky on the streets of Shanghai, trying to get by as a cultural Chinese. I could hardly speak Songhai anymore. The idea of backtracking on the Chinese tongues made me ill.

I, of course, in my eclectic upbringing, would have an opportunity to try that, as well.

"When you are older," he said, "I can teach you to use a gun and to knife-fight. To patrol and ambush, call in artillery fire. Military combat." He chuckled, an unusual sound. "But these are things the Army will teach you."

He shook his head. "But I am not expert at fighting with my fists." He unlocked a drawer in his desk. He pulled out a huge gun, snugged inside a light tan shoulder holster. He untied the restraining straps, the dust rising softly in the lamplight.

He looked so strong, so handsome, his jaw square, shoulders broad, the scar on his temple pronounced, his eyes far away, thinking, seeing memories, touching China and his former world.

The gun came out of the holster, complaining against the leather. It was a Government Colt Super .38 on a .45 frame. It looked heavily used, with the dark bluing worn away down to cold steel around the trigger housing and the hammer. It fit in his muscular hand like a big Thorson wrench in Hector's grip. I smelled the light oil on it. Given to him by Na-men Schwartzhedd after the Japanese invasion, it had become a talisman, an invitation to fight the enemy and survive, to find new life in the New World, to become one with the gun and with the country that had forged it from the hardest elements in the earth.

Jennifer Sung-ah had told me stories about Father during the Run. So I knew this gun had been inside his peasant jacket on the Yangtze River road, when he had found Mother and my sisters at the edge of Free China, when he had lowered his recently injured forehead to rest it against my mother's face, nine years ago.

"I know you," he had said to Mother that day in 1944. "You don't give up. You would never give up."

He snapped the action, locking it open and removing the well-worn magazine, verifying that it was empty by inserting his little finger into the breech. I was nervous, looking at it. This gun had killed people.

"When you go in the Army, this will be yours. This is not to be touched until then. I am showing this to you, because weapons are for war, for death. Never confuse this with *wu-shu.*"

I didn't know that I was going in the Army. I thought they gave you a gun, which was the only reason I could think of for joining.

He frowned at me, releasing the lock, which made the slide snap shut with a startling metallic punch. He locked the magazine into the butt of the handle, slid the weapon into the holster, and put it away.

"You have been beaten badly. Children expect parents to fix things. But you need boxing, to stand on your own.

"My older brother Han was a good boxer. The Chinese invented boxing, *wu-shu*, and are the best at it, a secret foreigners do not know. Chinese boxers are almost like magic, they are so good.

"Uncle Han's nose was broken and our mother stopped his lessons, and mine before they began. Han is a very handsome man, like a movie actor, and Mother feared for his looks. I am sorry you have never met my brother. Uncle Han and I. We, we were not friends. But I am his Younger Brother, and always will be, regardless of what I do. You have not met your grandfather, grandmother. Your aunts. The tutors. The cooks, servants."

"Where Han Dababa now?" I asked.

"Aahh," he sighed quietly, like dying seltzer bubbles. There had been no word about Uncle Han at all. He, and Da-ma, my aunt, and Round Pearl, Mother's servant, Wang the fish cook, Chief Tutor Luke, the Hanlin master, Tutor Tang, and the horsemaster Yip, and Janie's wetnurse, Sweet Plum, all were lost in the distant haze of invasion and the Chinese revolution. Gung-Gung, of course, had been terminally reeducated. But Father missed the staff of his family more than the management. His father had treated him like yesterday's newspaper.

He went to the kitchen, where he blindly rattled in the cupboards. The kitchen smelled of sauerkraut and scrapple, a flat, cerealed, pork Pennsylvania Dutch sausage that Edna was trying to sell to our palates.

I was intoxicated with the information he had provided me, and my bruises were forgotten. I felt shaky, shuddering in emotion, electrified by his communication.

My father, his other life, a big gun in our house, a boxing uncle named Han, a nation of fighting Chinese, the Army. Was I to join his Kuomintang Army, or the U.S. Army, which was taking so many men from the neighborhood for Korea?

Wu-shu. Fighting talent, or fight arts, something like that. Something deep in my shallow years, so mysterious in my utter simplicity, so ancient in my youth, connected to a distant land and long-dead ancestors. Deep racial memory. *Wu-shu* was magical fighting. Combat by ghost warriors, faster than dreams, stronger than concrete, war using wind, iron, and fire.

From the kitchen, where the intense bare bulb cast light that was both too bright and insufficient, he said, "I am going to send you to the Y, the Young Men's Christian Association. I think my wife will agree."

I coughed, and said, softly, "Ba-Ba. Stepma Edna my ma-ma? And Janie's ma-ma? *Real* ma-ma?"

Silence came from the kitchen. He approached me, looking down. I looked up. "She thinks of you as stepchildren," he said. "But you must give her the respect that you would give your mother."

"Stepma Edna want me go Y.M.C.A?" I asked.

"I think so," he said. "The Y will teach you to fight, how to protect yourself. I want you to try very hard and learn. It will probably hurt.

"It was the same for me. At St. John's College, and Taoping Academy, I was eighteen when I started learning about the ways of the West." He switched to English, clearing his throat.

"See here. America. It has the answers." His shoulders hunched and he made a huge fist, banging into the open palm of the other hand. "It has *the answers!*" His voice rang passionately through the apartment, and I knew that Edna and Janie were listening, from different levels in the house.

He looked up at me. More quietly, he said, "If you are very good—terrific, terrific, good—you can make application to West Point, someday, to make us proud. I will find Major Na-men, and ask his advice. He is West Pointer. Maybe he help get you in. It is something, the only thing, I pray for."

Father *praying?* Praying for me to be an American *ping*—a soldier. A small, white ivory figure on a dark teak Chinese chessboard. My heart pounded.

"Where Major Na-men, Father?" I asked.

"He is in Korea. Ahh. How I worry about him." Father's face said everything, with all the articulation Mother had used. And I knew, with sweeping, insightful clarity, that Father would have been long in Korea, with his true comrade, fighting the Reds, laughing at death, if he had not had children. Or a dying wife. Or a new one. That his family was a barrier to a greater destiny. He was passing time with us, while greater events marched past his window.

More solemn shadows flared as he lit his pipe, the sound of the drawing air strained and high.

Our magical talk was over. I found myself crying helplessly. This was so hard, crying in front of him, but his words, his sharing, his interest, the weight of his own loss caused by me, were more than I could bear. My shoulders shaking, my arms trembling uselessly by my side, I snorted and snuffled as I tried to stop myself.

My crying discomforted him. I sensed that he wanted me to shake his hand and say thank you in a manful way, and not turn into a quivering, protoplasmic blubber of tears.

I thought of my mother. He had said "us." I stood and left the room, going to the place in the hallway where her portrait had hung until Edna had removed it. I closed my wet eyes and mentally drew in every detail of her face and smiled when I reached her mouth.

11

BANQUET

My father was feeling no guilt, when there were those who felt he should. He had enjoyed a certain beau-geste reputation in Chinatown, a condition only enhanced by his tragic widowerhood. But he married a *nahgwangning* widow with flaming blond hair and a chest designed to make the majority of Chinese women on Grant Avenue look at their mirrors twice.

The new bride wrinkled her nose at the best Chinese banquet dishes outside the Far East, made no effort to learn the Chinese language or customs, and kept expanding her chest at people when she felt threatened.

The Ting Hui, our Family Association, was notable for its broad spectrum of personalities, its unique domination by Northern Chinese, and its consistent ability to mistakenly order unbalanced banquet dishes. For reasons unknown, there had been no Ting Hui in north China, while there was one in the south. Our Association had no deep tradition of ordering routinely for seventy people.

Banquets should involve correct ratios of fish, fowl, beef, and pork, vegetables and soup, tea and rice wine. But our Hui, or *tong*, often spoke Cantonese with the clarity of Sippy Suds reciting *Hamlet*. A misplaced tone, an awkward emphasis, and chicken wings appeared in lieu of Peking duck. When the unparalleled elegance of birds'-nest and sharks'-fin soups was appropriate, we got egg drop broth. If the final fish dish were supposed to be ling cod, we had rock. Squab was ordered but extra portions of abalone wrapped in Tientsin cabbage appeared.

As an American variant to Chinese food service, each table sported a bottle of Johnnie Walker Red, a bottle of Johnnie Walker Black, and a bottle of crème de menthe. Our Association almost never broke the seals and rotated turns for taking the liquor home. Later, these bottles would be circulated as constantly unopened, repassed, reused, and recycled gifts for weddings, the New Year, graduations, births, or ching ming. The trick was acquiring matching gift boxes from liquor stores and making a five-year-old circulating bottle of alcohol appear as a new purchase. Of course, no one was fooled, but the effort was considered essential.

"Ohh, Auntie! This looks *new!*" cried one innocent.

"Elaine! Of course it's new! It's never been opened!"

When Father brought Edna to the Family Association Banquet celebrating the Double Ten, the new bride was received like royalty. October 10, or Ten-Ten, is the anniversary of the formation of the Chinese Republic in 1912 under Sun Yat-sen, a man admired by both Nationalists and communists, by Chinese citizens, and by the overseas communities. Jennifer Sung-ah and Megan Wai-la also appeared, to honor Father, to respect his new marriage, and to have a great meal.

Edna wore a deep celestial-blue, Chinese cheongsam, a side-cut mandarin-collared dress of the same style affected by my mother when she shopped for Cream of Wheat at Old Petrini's. This was the uniform of the Chinatown banquet circuit after the war, before many of the women decided to liberate themselves from dresses that made breathing a struggle. The blue set off Edna's shining blondness, and she seemed to have arrived with all the fanfare of a UCLA cheerleader, complete with tinseled searchlights, a roll of drums, and a blare of trumpets. The gallant iconoclastic killing machine, Colonel Ting, had married Marilyn Monroe and had brought her to dinner.

My sisters looked grand, and I marveled at their beauty in their similar dresses. Jennifer wore teal, Megan was in red, and Jane, because her older sisters knew she would arrive in rags, had brought her a classy, elegant black cheongsam. Our family must have looked like something out of Hollywood. Or Shanghai. The young men in the *tong* flocked around my *chiehchieh*, calling them *hsiaochieh*, or honorably desirable high-ranking unmarried misses, and I was delighted for Janie. She was having a Cinderella-like evening. Hearing her hesitant giggle, and then her fulsome laughter, made me smile with wet eyes.

I had been to banquets before and had been allowed to run around the tables with other children. I knew a few of the boys my age by name, and had missed seeing them. Edna's rule was to remain seated, and I did not know if I could move. That's not true, I corrected myself: if in doubt, don't. I strained my ears to listen to my sisters, and with a sinking sensation realized that their Songhai was too fast for me. I was losing my language. But I enjoyed looking at them whenever they passed near, and both Jennifer and Megan took time to sit next to me and tell me how handsome I looked. Janie had already explained to them why my face looked like Route 66 after a bad rain.

Leo Soo, one of the brightest kids in Chinatown, dropped by the table and sat next to me. I poured him a short cup of tea, and as he filled the balance of the cup with sugar, he asked me how our family was surviving the loss of our mother.

I smiled, putting on a brave face.

"I'm sorry, Kai," he said. "Very sorry. Mah-mee invited you and Ming-li over to spend weekends with us. But your new mother said you were too sad to leave the house."

Chinatown banquets, like West Point meals, seat ten souls in family-style tables. So I sat, poured huge mountains of sugar into my tea cup, and drank away. The food arrived, the families took their seats, our table drew all the stares, and Father explained the dishes.

"This," he said, pointing, "is called 'sea cucumbers.' But they are not vej-ah-taybles. They are ocean slugs. Yes, yes. It's terrible. See there. Chicken heads. Not cut off, since that's bad luck. So stupid! These superstitions! Cutting off heads mean, not giving *everything* to the guests. Like, holding back something valuable. So we have the head, looking back at us. Make no sense! Not cutting off fish head okay, since cheek is special. There. There is Peking duck. This is plum sauce, for the crispy skin . . . and the small bun . . . see, it breaks like this. First sauce on, then skin. . . . No, no. No waiters for this table! We serve ourselves! We're American!'' He waved them away.

Jennifer helped Father serve the dishes, first for Edna, then for Megan, Janie, me, and then themselves.

"We serve the tea in the opposite order of the west," said Megan, pouring. "The first-poured tea goes to the youngest; the last-poured tea, which is the richest, the fullest, the best-steeped, goes to the eldest, or highest-ranking family member. Tonight, Edna, that is you. So I serve Kai first, then Janie."

At the earliest opportunity—after seven courses had been served—several women of the Association broke ranks and approached the elegant couple, offering greetings while frankly assessing the bride's goods.

Edna did not care about the food; she worried about the approaching women. She was extremely suspicious, but gracious, delighted to find so many bright and conversant women interested in meeting her. She made five friends in one night, talking about current events, history, and literature. Most of the women were college graduates, thought highly of Smith, and were pleased that this stranger was so smart.

Edna and my sisters spoke to these brightly dressed women with the familiarity of Bob Hope chatting with Bing Crosby. Father smiled from ear to ear, and he and I both ate like fiends.

Western smorgasbords and conventional salad bars present the least-valued foods at the front, inviting the diner to fill the plate with mountains of iceberg lettuce and leaving only a smidgen of room for the roast beef at the end of the line. A Chinese banquet begins with the costliest delicacies and marches down the order to the lower-caste condiments. Dessert was usually *babofeb*, the Eight Precious Preserved Glutinous Rices Cake.

This sequence was good for adult palates, since the most sophisticated tastes were sated first. But it was less appreciated by children. We wanted noodles and rice, and these were the last to arrive, hours after the appearance of complicatedly exotic soups such as birds' nest or sharks' fin. Jennifer, of course, was the genius. When the good dishes arrived after the soup, a magic bowl of rice arrived, just for me. I smiled at her with all my heart.

On this October evening, squab had been ordered and had arrived. I later learned that Jennifer had called the Association Secretary to learn the desired menu. She then phoned Mr. Kan and reviewed the menu in detail. As the dishes arrived, the staff's best waiters lined the walls, ready to assist in the serving of the dishes. There was one person who had a different idea in mind.

Victoria Lum, one of the dragons at the gate of the Association, had already plagued Edna's peace of mind with incessant Songhai pronouncements and a flashing of crass wealth in our poor, evolving, German–Irish home.

Victoria Lum Ting watched Edna's diplomatic entry into her political arena the way a Doberman tracks a burglar. This *lo fan* devil woman with the mountains packed into her front was going to divert the intelligence of the clan from its organizational mission. First, all this squawking about chicken wings. Now, when we finally get squab on order, we get wide-eyed tributes to Western breasts.

In the past, when the misordered food appeared at the banquet tables, Victoria would moan, knowing that the tables would be consumed with food chatter and customary griping. My mother, facing the same sight, used to sigh and look at the wonderful, ghost-driven chandelier lights. Tonight, Edna tried not to look at any of the dishes, correctly ordered or not.

Victoria was a fiery mystic, a Stanford graduate who intimately understood the ward politics of San Francisco. She wore vermilion lipstick like a neon sign in downtown Reno and displayed a beauty spot on her right cheek like the posting of a pirate flag. She was of medium height and weight with rectangularly cornered shoulders and a waist the diameter of a garden hose. She wore her hair in three buns with a dramatically large and fragrant gardenia pinned on the right side. Her husband, Cornelius Ting, had died some years ago. It was well known that Victoria was interested in our father. I was not inclined to like her.

The agenda for the Ting Family Association, as seen by Victoria Lum, did not include perfecting its ability to order the correct banquet dishes. Nor was it the invasion of China, toy drives, or crazy talk about bringing a major-league baseball team to San Francisco. Nor should it be the New Year, the grand *foo chi* of the birth of a new son, *ching ming*, a decennial birthday, a wedding, or the start of a new business— the common causes for a lavishly extravagant family banquet that could wipe out a family's savings.

For Victoria, the agenda for the Ting Hui was city politics and political contributions, period.

Through a remarkable compact between her hips and her torso, and between the laws of inertia and harmonic vibration, she approached our table, her bright rosebud lips pursed.

"Colonel," she said carefully to our father, lifting her right arm to demurely adjust her flower, making her chest send a hex back at Edna's. "We live here now, in San Francisco," she salvoed in Songhai. "Who cares if it is October Ten? Or if we have crab and no lobster? We should worry about the mayor, and our property taxes! Yes?"

My father looked at her. So did Edna.

"Hmmm," he said.

"Ting Taitai," said Jennifer. "What a wonderful elbow you have!" Victoria smiled sweetly at Jennifer, lowering her arm and parting her lips to retort.

"Please," Jennifer added, "Madam, do not thank me for the compliment." Victoria retired from the table, somewhat less pneumatically dynamic than during her arrival.

Victoria discreetly left a small plate of *duvu*, soy bean curd, at Edna's place setting.

Chit duvu, in Songhai, means "eat soybean," or "to make a fool of someone without his or her discovering it." Duvu, or tofu, is fine stuff. Low in cholesterol, high in protein, environmentally sound in production, and amenable to the rich spectrum of Chinese sauces. But it lacks the historic class of duck, the traditional expense of lobster. Cleverly seasoned and disguised, it tastes as good as the pricier platters. But it is not expensive, and cooks who pad an expensive dish with duvu know that a deceptive expansion of volume, a camouflage, has occurred. Eat duvu, eat dirt without knowing that it is dirt, foreigner—this was the message.

"They are so cowardly! Oh, darling, am I deserving of this?" Edna cried after having the platter explained. I think she felt betrayed, unsure if the dish had been delivered by one of those who had befriended her.

Father clearly hated this. Women's War in America, the old bad habits. Could he never run far enough away from bad family practices? He rose and approached Victoria's table. He was not certain that she had been the offender, but he took his chance.

"No more chit duvu, Ting Taitai," he said.

"Colonel?!" she cried, her hand to her graceful throat, coloring. "How can you possibly accuse me of this?" Father nodded, knowing that he had confronted the culprit.

Victoria called a sidebar of her closest allies, urging them to replace nuptial sentiment with hard political decisiveness. In other words, with hate. Victoria Lum Ting and the two members of her cell for political action now prepared to greet Edna as Europe had welcomed the bubonic plague.

When Edna went to the ladies room, Dolly Fang was waiting. She told Edna that it was customary for brides to toast the senior women of the Association, and preferably with alcohol that was poised, unopened, at the table.

"Speak loudly, so all can hear you," she said. "You are so lucky. You speak English *so well!*"

Edna nervously licked her lips. She was unable to distinguish between the women she had met and those she had not. She must have surveyed the second floor of Johnny Kan's Restaurant, filled with glittering Chinese society, with trepidation. She stood and with great clarity offered a toast to the senior women.

"To the gracious women of the Association, I toast you," she said, holding her Go-liang rice wine glass high.

I knew something was wrong. Jennifer and Megan were looking down at their plates. Father was glaring at someone, his eyebrow giving the caterpillar, his jaw flexing. I could not see Janie's expression.

Edna was met with a hushed silence fitting for only the most violent faux pas. She had been screwed, and knew it. The Ten-Ten celebration for the Tings involved only discreet table-to-table toasts offered by the Association President or by a designated host. Tonight, already, the president and his wife had circulated through the seven tables.

"Thank you for honoring us with your presence and for fortifying the unity of our clan," they said quietly, inclining their heads respectfully, holding aloft the wine and not drinking, making the sacrifice of hosts as the honored guests sipped and smiled, saying, *"Hao, bao."* Good, good.

Anything else was considered vain, disrespectful, and violative of the expectation of modest behavior. Particularly by women. Emphatically for foreign women who marry local bachelors.

Edna scanned the banquet room. One hundred and forty eyeballs stared back. They were all brown in color, and largely unsympathetic. Entrapped, she upended the glass, turned to Father, and said, "I am leaving, darling. Please escort me out?"

Father stood and took her arm. Jennifer and Megan stood, majestically, like storied princesses, and Janie followed. I chewed faster, stuffing my mouth, until Megan hustled me to my feet and escorted me away. We filed out of the banquet hall. I could hear the diminution of talk, the quieting of the clatter of passing platters, the scratchy hiss of whispering. I could hear Victoria chuckle once, clearly. And then we were going down the stairs to the lobby.

I had an extremely mature view about these proceedings. I thought that Victoria Lum was a super *wupo*. And I lamented the inability to finish dinner.

"No more dinners, please," said Edna, who had now lost her chance at having women friends. We were driving down Broadway, toward the Bay Bridge, to return the older sisters to Berkeley.

"They are oddballs, those friends of Victoria Lum," Father said. "In fact," he added reflectively, "they're the *oddest of balls!*"

Father was trying to say that parts of Shanghai society had become decadently sophisticated in their ability to spear the psyches of others, to impale them on embarrassment, to enjoy life through the crushing of the spirits of others. He was depressed that this absolutely dispensable element of the culture of his origin had followed them to the United States.

And it all came to me. Edna was afraid of the streets, and the people, and the women in the Handle, as I had been on the first day of my ejection into the greater society of Golden Gate Avenue. She was an alien in her own land. And Janie and I were her prisoners.

12

Y.M.C.A.

On the following Saturday my father gave me twelve old, softened dollars in a crisp white envelope with English writing on its face. He gave me directions and two dimes for the roundtrip busfare, and a third to call home. I repeated the phone number, WEst 1-5281, until I was dizzy. I carried the fortune of coins in a small packet of red paper in my jeans. Red for good luck, and I hoped not for blood. I was not optimistic.

Before the Borden milkman made his rounds in his tall boxlike white truck, I shivered and walked to the bus stop at Masonic. I boarded the Five McAllister, pretending that Janie was taking me to Chinatown. This was the first time I had ridden a bus downtown by myself. I watched my dime fall through the winding coin tunnel in the clear-glass-and-metal fare receptacle. The dime reminded me of myself, turning hard corners and accelerating into a final bell-ringing disappearance through a bright metal trapdoor.

As the bus carried me downtown across the hills and through the early-morning fog of the city I tried to imagine what this Y.M.C.A. place would be like. I presumed it would be like a church, where some kindly man like Bob Lamport would teach me how to kill other children and to destroy my karma for all time.

I kept touching the dimes in my pocket. I could not imagine calling WE 1-5281 unless it was to announce that I was dying. Edna always picked up the phone, to discourage Uncle Shim from talking Chinese to Father.

I had told Toussaint that I was going to the Y.M.C.A. to learn how to fight, and he knew no more than I what it meant.

"I go Y, Toos," I said.

"Why?"

"Yep."

With my ever-vigilant ears I listened for my stop, getting off on Market. I was in the cold morning sun of the Tenderloin, the remnants of the Barbary Coast of San Francisco. A place where prostitutes, pool sharks, bad gamblers, heavy drinkers, and sailors by the fleet cruised in search of a good hour in a bad life. The Tenderloin, I learned, had no kids. That was fine by me.

At seven-thirty on a Saturday morning, I was almost alone, sensing without clarity the bundled pedestrians on distant streets.

I found Leavenworth and walked uphill, north to Golden Gate Avenue, and located the old beige-gray, columned monolith of the downtown Central Y.M.C.A. This was so strange, that I lived on Golden Gate Avenue and that this ominous churchlike structure was on the same street, in a different district. I looked up the avenue, west toward the ocean, and could not see the Panhandle. I breathed deeply. It smelled different. More car exhaust. No food, more light, less fog, same distant scent of old, decayed booze. I circled the block, grinning. This was like touring the Handle at night, safe from fists. I entered the Boys' Department, on the Leavenworth side.

Two large wooden doors with windows. I could barely push one open. It was early autumn, and downtown the sun was bright in the unlit lobby. Here it smelled like school, the linoleum imprinted with the rubber from Converse All-Star sneakers, generations of bubble gum, Sen-Sen, candybars, and the kind salts of boysweat.

A glass-enclosed office to the right, white marbled stairs in the center, rectangular green tables edged in white with little nets stretched across their middles to the left, hallway with more doors in the distance in front.

Trophy cases everywhere. I imagined trophies to be special drinking glasses for very large people. I kept staring at the glass and I realized that it was clean—the whole place was old but clean. Fremont Elementary was old and soiled, waiting for terminal erosion like the bits of tire debris that trucks leave on freeways.

I stood at the counter with the envelope. I looked around for any enemy, such as kids, and was relieved; the place was abandoned.

A shortish black man in a bright white T-shirt and bright white pants appeared, walking with soft footfalls and an unusual sound—starch crackling in newly pressed trousers. When he spoke I saw that he had no teeth.

Ay-ya! I thought. The Teeth God got him!

"Not open yet, not eight o'clock," the man in white pants said. "Gotta be seven years old, be allowed come in here, anyhows." I stared at him blankly, not knowing what to do.

"You seven, young man?" he asked.

I nodded and offered the envelope.

He raised his eyebrows. They were in several pieces, broken, where skin had grown over the places hair had been, like a sentence with the center clause removed. His broad nose looked strong, and it wiggled at me as he spoke. He had soft eyes and scar tissue, distantly reminiscent of Sippy Suds, and I liked him.

" 'Scuse me," he said. "Be right back."

He returned with a tall, silver-haired, foreign white man in a suit and tie. I listened to his decisive footfalls approach me. Like Edna's, with sharp, well-defined heels.

"Mista Miller, dis here da boy. Dis," he said, "Mista Miller, 'Zecative D'rector, Central Y.' "

Mr. Miller extended his hand and my arm disappeared inside it. His hair was the color of Uncle Shim's, but he did not have the mustache or the spectacles. Mr. Miller was very well dressed, and looked like President Eisenhower. He told me that he had chatted with my father. I nodded. There was a silence. Mr. Miller looked at the man in white.

"I'm Mista McCoo," the man said, studying me. He offered his hand. I didn't like all the touching.

When I shook Mr. McCoo's hand I noticed that his knuckles were the size of small eggs, and that his fingers were stained in a wild variety of colors.

"Ah surely hope dis boy ain't here fo' da Hook," he said in a very deep voice, looking at Mr. Miller as if it were somehow his fault. Mr. Miller smiled and touched Mr. McCoo's hand.

"Come with me, son," said Mr. Miller.

"Da Hook, he be 'gainst *art!*" hissed Mr. McCoo. At least my name was not Art. Maybe the Hook would not be against *me*.

In a mildly disconnected state I followed Mr. Miller through winding corridors to an elevator, through smells of cleaners, laundry, the faint scent of food, of hot humid steam, chlorine, and soap. He said hello to people who were opening up the building. We entered a lobby and his office, which was filled with more huge cups. A short white cup of steaming coffee sat on his brown wooden desk, and I sniffed it from the door.

"Do you speak English?" he asked.

I nodded, hesitantly. "I go school," I said.

"Good, son." He took a deep breath. "Do you know that this training, this schooling that you're going to get here, is going to be hard?"

I nodded. "It hurt," I said in a small voice.

"Well," he said, smiling. "A little. Learning is sometimes that way."

"Uncle Shim say, school, hurt, mind. Father say, 'Merica school hurt."

"Uh-huh. All right," he said, kindly. "I want you to look at this photo album while we wait for the gyms to open. It's our summer camp, Jones Gulch Tolowa, near Santa Cruz. In one more year, you'll be old enough to go. Doesn't that look like fun?"

The photographs showed boys doing a lot of things with their bodies. Baseball, basketball, kickball, boys in water. I shuddered. I went through the photo album ten, eleven times, seeing nothing. I felt a slow, deep dread. I could feel the Y.M.C.A. coming to life. People chattering, doors opening and closing, loud male greetings, the level of noise rising. An ancient hungry dragon stirring for its breakfast of children. It sounded a bit like McAllister Street. I had never heard so many men talking *inside* a building before. I heard no women.

Mr. Miller returned. We went up to the sixth floor. I knew that because the white inner doors had huge painted black numbers bigger than me beneath the arms of the lock mechanism.

The elevator's jerky movements alarmed me. That was not unusual. I was worried when the sun came up. Furtively, I glanced at this powerful man, so important that he wore a tie on Saturdays. His face had all the outside features of a cruel person—strong will, hard thought, relentless intent, flinty ambition. But somehow, he liked children.

He spoke to me but I could remember nothing of what he said. My mind was trying to shut down as we rose higher through the shaft, my thoughts misfiring absently, without meaning, as my heartbeat began to accelerate.

The doors opened to a huge gym that yawned before me with ominous depth and unknown odors. I had great smell, excellent salivary glands, powerful tear ducts, and the vision of an old mole. I would have been great as a chef, a Mandarin actor, or a fence post.

An oval track ran around a mezzanine floor above us, like a circular shelf. Kids were running around it, making a loud, pounding sound that echoed with different timbres depending on the bunching of the runners and where you were in the gym. They were running in a circle, essentially, going nowhere. That seemed somehow familiar. I wondered if this resembled our ancestral home's second-story compound gallery in Shanghai. There were no mandarin orange trees here.

Some of the kids were yelling in a friendly fashion, and I was hopeful that this was not another schoolyard.

The track was smaller in diameter than the floor of the gym, producing a low-hanging ceiling around the perimeter of the main floor. From the low ceiling hung large, black metal frames with little pear-shaped leather bags and black metal pipes at right angles. And a huge, body-sized canvas bag with furnace tape around its sagging middle.

Basketball court and two side gyms. Dark wooden bars in grills with boards stuck in them and large, differently sized mirrors on the walls. Some posters advertising boxing bouts.

The huge old canvas sack on a chain looked like a real-life victim of a game of hangman. The black pipes interlocked in complex patterns from the low ceiling above mountains of mats. One wall had a coatrack, like the one in Mrs. Halloran's classroom, where we hung our yellow rain slickers.

On this long rack dangled pairs of swollen black, gray, and brown gloves. I did not know how I knew it, but I recognized the thing in the middle as a boxing ring. The floor of the ring was heavily soiled and stained. I felt dread. Next to the ring was a large box as tall as I, also filled with dead, empty gloves. I could not see far enough to discern what the far gym contained.

A tall muscular black man with the elegance of kings entered my vision from somewhere. He looked like Hector Pueblo, and sort of felt like Hector, although he had not contorted his spine to reach difficult corners of piston engines. This man stood much straighter. His hair was cut almost to the scalp. That's how Rupert, in the Eatery, wore his hair. Oh no, I thought, fearing a third hostile brother.

"Hey, Top of the Morning, Kurt," this man said in a deep, rich voice that resonated across the hardwood floor and made me look at him. It was a fantastic voice. I wanted to hear it again.

"Barney," said Mr. Miller. "This is Kai Ting, a new member. He's seven years old." He stopped to let that sink in.

"His father called me. They're in the Panhandle, and, well, it's full of hoods. Kai's the only one born here in the States. He's been an indoor lad, and he's found it hard on the street, with the hoodlums and all. He needs to know how to fight. I told his dad that we could help him. What I did is commit us to a project. A project that might be off your mark. If you don't want it, I'll do it. You know your schedule, so you tell me."

The man wore a white T-shirt with a huge red Y with CENTRAL written on it. The letters curved and dipped with the contours of his chest. He had bright white pants, black gym shoes. He looked to be all hard muscle. He was evaluating me; I knew the look. My stomach felt sour and in my mind I retraced the steps to the elevator. I wished I had left a pebble trail.

He offered his hand and I breathed again.

"Hello, son. I am Mr. Lewis," he said gravely in his deep magic voice, and we shook.

Toussaint had taught me squeezing. Mr. Lewis's hands were like hard dried leather with iron underneath. He had a great, open smile and wore the same aftershave, Old Spice, that my father bought at Reliance Market, across the street from Cutty's.

He leaned forward, looking at me and locking his arms on his knees as he spoke.

"The Y.M.C.A teaches young men how to box, to develop their character. Their spirits. We do not teach young men how to *fight*. Boxing is a means toward good citizenship, of fair play, of self-reliance. Do you know what 'reliance' means?'' he asked.

I nodded enthusiastically. It was the name of the market on Mc-Allister. I could learn how to shop in a store.

I listened carefully to Mr. Lewis. He had said that he did not teach how to fight. I was hoping for hints that I was going to be excused from this high dudgeon of physical terror.

I looked over at the boxing ring. People hit each other in it. You couldn't run out—the ropes kept you in. That sounded like fighting to me. I wanted to leave. I wanted to say, I have this rare skin condition that worsens when the crap is beaten out of me.

A huge, roaring voice bellowed, *"FALL IN,* LADS!'' and I involuntarily hopped, kinetically motivated to action, my legs jumping in spastic surprise. The kids pounded down the stairs from the track, grabbed gloves and headguards and formed ranks. They stood still in a variety of poses, donning their gear.

"Kagiwada!'' said a huge, bearlike man. "Yur Platoon Leader to-day!''

"Here,'' said a kid who looked a little like me.

"Accampo, Andrea, Bain, Bascue, Betzner, Braun, Brown, Callaghy, Carpenter, Childers, Cohen, Crouch, Culp, Deal, Donofrio, Downes, Dureaux, Flax, Ford, Forsyth, Garcia, Goin, Goldthorpe, Grossbacher, Haas, Harris, Hause, Heflin, Hernandez, Imwinkelried, James, Kelley, Kimball, Kodama, Lagios, Leigh, Melis, Murray, Peeff, Perkes, Perkins, Prentice, Rapisarda, Reed, Richards, Rico, Rosenthal, Simmons, Starr, Shakely, Stenberg, Theo, Thompson, Tice, Wahle, Wailes, Wilson, Yenovkian, Yu, Zellmann, Zimmerman. Goldthorpe! Where are ya!'' he called. "Yur late! Gimme some laps!'' So many kids, all looking like fighters, dressed for war.

"Here. Here. Yo. Present. Here. Here! Yep. Right! Here. Here. Uh-huh! Present. Yeah! He's comin!'' they cried.

I recognized the Y.M.C.A. for what it was: a place of torture, a palace of pain, a formal school where street horrors were enacted under adult supervision and children lined up for lessons like prisoners in front of firing squads.

I began to hope that the Nationalist Army would win *soon.* I was ready to try Shanghai. At least I could get some real food.

Boxing lessons were one hour, Monday, Wednesday, and Friday afternoons at four, and two hours at eight sharp on Saturday mornings.

There were thirty kids in the beginners group, weights forty-five to seventy, which matched out to ages seven and eight, for slum kids at the Central Y. No one was the same color. I had never seen so many Anglos or Hispanics. They were standing in ranks next to each other, as if being so close, ready to bash each other into Cream of Wheat, was the most normal thing in the world.

Classes had begun a month ago. Mr. Lewis would figure out how to work me and another new kid, named Leroy Jones, too big to be my regular partner, into the program. Leroy looked at me and snorted, as if the sight of me hurt his nose.

Boxing was more than learning how to hit someone else. It included endless lap running, bag work, situps on inclined boards hooked to the wooden bars on the walls, pullups, rope skipping, and individual movement practice—shadow-boxing. And then more running.

"No one. I mean, *no one*," said Mr. Lewis, "can box if he cannot run." I could run. I just didn't want to box.

On Saturdays, after boxing, the kids got instruction in wrestling, swimming, gymnastics, crafts, basketball, and dodgeball. To me, the schedule sounded like pounding, strangling, drowning, contortion, fun, enemy ball, and painful enemy ball. If you got everything done you could stack towels and play Ping-Pong.

"Bet you're pretty good at Ping-Pong, right?" asked Mr. Miller. He was grinning at me, hopefully.

I did not know what Ping-Pong was.

It took me fifteen minutes to get dressed. Mr. Lewis introduced me to Rufus Monk, who vaguely helped with the headgear and gloves. Rufus had impossibly long arms with the same type of musculature as Hector and Mr. Lewis.

My head and hands disappeared inside the gear and I did not like how it felt. The headgear was so tight around the forehead that my brain began to ache, but the ear flaps dangled. Although the gear had no contact with any of my breathing apparatus, I felt suffocated.

The gloves looked as though pillows had been laced onto my forearms up to the elbows. The headband leather reeked of the sweat of children. I felt I was being dressed for ritual sacrifice and looked for bloodstains on the gloves. I found them.

I was uncomfortable around boys, and undressing with them seemed not only bizarre but treacherous. I put my clothes with the two dimes into a little brown dented metal basket, Number 228, and slid it through a gap in a giant fenced cage where another black teenager in a blue T-shirt named Norman worked.

"Dat bin," Norman said, "hold all yo' shit. It be safe. Dis bin be yours today."

It would be mine for the next ten years.

Rufus, or Roof, was in a hurry. "C'mon, tiger, c'mon c'mon! Git it movin'!" he urged.

Rufus Monk was from the Fillmore, and was already famous. He was sixteen and would turn pro in one year with the aid of a fake ID. Time wore on him like a quick fuse.

I used to think his impatience derived from his urgency to get into the ring, to show his lightning, his bolts of leather, to flash his Sunday punch. I was wrong.

Like most good boxers, he had a deep well of anger, a reservoir of fury, accumulated and saved over the precious years of youth, a huge and cancerous ball of angry twine, the rage of life interlocking naturally with the explosiveness of the ring. The hotness in his guts pushed on him like high water against a dike, waiting to burst over the spillway onto his opponent.

Each of the three men who were about to become my putative godfathers was a former pugilist. What a unique and special generation they represented! They grew up in the Depression, when the certainty of a meal was a question mark. They were the equivalents of my father. My father, who saw an entire society, hewn from hard soil and violent history for thousands of years, crumble to dust in the space it takes to say good-bye.

Eleven million Americans entered the service and fought for the handshake around the world, for the duration—until they beat the Axis or they died trying. A fight to the finish. The combat survivors bore a unique durability.

Besides being durable, my three instructors carried the burden of not being Anglo-Protestants at a time when being different implied inferiority, and the presumption of inferiority was difficult to challenge.

On an average autumn Saturday morning, when I was seven, I met eight men of this storied generation. Three of them would share their life gifts with me until I became an adult, for six dollars a month.

Tony Barraza was huge. He looked like a big bear at Fleischacker Zoo, with fur on his arms, face, and chest. He had jet-black hair, like mine, and wore a white tank top with the red Y, cut like the plain gray

one that sat on me like a circus tent on a pole. His arms were not like
Hector's, which resembled sharp chiseled rock. Mr. Barraza's arms were
like huge round steel pipe, the stuff that was used to build the Golden
Gate Bridge. He was seated at a desk in front of an office with caged
windows.

Mr. Lewis was talking to him when we came up the stairs, and he
slapped the bear on the back. Brave man, I thought. Another big man
was walking around in the background.

I watched as some kids donned headgear in mere moments. Others
were breaking out the mats from stacks and aligning them on the floor.
They were already sweating. All of them then paired off and began
moving on the dun mats. Their movements looked like fighting. I felt
sick to my stomach. The oval track was empty. The big youth who had
snorted was in front of me; he had been in the locker room while Rufus
helped me with my gear. Of course, all kids over two looked big to me.
I wanted none of this.

Tony "the Tiger" Barraza, Doctor Hook, liked to start by changing
bad habits.

"Do ya smoke," he asked in a flat, loud voice.

"Yeah, you bet!" came the high-voiced reply. The kid was maybe
eight and a half, proud of his early maturation.

"Quit or I send ya to rasslin twice a day. Smokin is absolutely bush
league and ain't the Y.M.C.A way. Ain't Christian."

"Huh? Uh, yeah. Okay."

"Doncha mean, 'Huh, Yeah okay, sir?" Now Mr. Barraza looked
up.

He had big glittering black eyes in a solid craggy face jutting from
a boulderlike head. His flat nose, his marred and unevenly square jaw,
ragtag hairline, and thick scarmounted eyebrows were eloquently expressive. His head, almost square except for the places where it had been
reshaped through blows, looked like a rock. One eye, his left, seemed
smaller than the other. I thought he had been in a car accident that had
killed everyone else. Women thought him attractive.

"Yeah, okay, suh!" piped the student.

He had been laboring with a thick, flat carpenter's pencil on the
kid's workout chart. Mr. Barraza liked those pencils because they did
not roll. Writing was hard enough without having to chase the frigging
instrument. So far, he had entered the last name. Tough questions, like
date of birth, height, and weight, were for later.

"All right, Master Jones. I'm *Mister* Barraza. Okay. Ya got yur shoes. Ya got yur trunks. Ya got yur shirt. Ya got yur gloves and yur headgear. Yur buttoned up. Don't get a temp mouthpiece till we move ta contact. Then ya chew the wax. Don't get a dental mouthpiece till ya turn nine." He said all of that very clearly. It was rehearsed.

In England, we would have been Masters Leroy, Kai, and Eugene, instead of Masters Jones, Ting, and Phillips. This was America, where bears taught boxing, English was something you did to a cue ball, Philadelphia matrons ran Chinese families, and black men felt free because they could die early.

"Ya talk ta me, ya use my name, Mister Barraza. Ya nine yet?"

"No, suh. Can I smoke den?"

"Yur a smart bastid, Master Jones. Getchur ass inna ring."

Mr. Barraza suddenly got a pained look on his face.

"Hum. Sorry. Getchur *self* inna ring," he said.

Mr. Barraza stood and lifted the rope, helping Master Jones enter, the way the condemned took the electric chair at San Quentin. Then he followed him in and knelt on the ring floor.

Oh, God, I thought. He's going to pray for him, then kill him.

"Rest of youse," he said in a booming voice that filled the gym, to kids who had already been through the drill, "look up."

The gym fell silent.

"Okay, Master Jones. Yur gonna beat me up. I'm down here on my knees, same height like youse. So. Whaddya do?"

Take flight like crazy running dog to the elevator, I thought.

Master Leroy Jones stood stock-still. He was no more going to attack Tony Barraza than swallow a metal lunchbox.

"C'mon! Come at me! I ain't gonna hurtcha. Just tryin ta make a point. I won't lay a glove on ya and if ya touch me, or tag me, give ya a quarter."

The kid came in, driven by the high purse, throwing wild punches. Tony smiled and without moving his left knee dodged the blows, his torso jinking, neck muscles popping. Occasionally, he would move one of his arms, the small gesture unnerving Leroy from unleashing a good punch. Then the weight of the gloves pulled the kid's hands down to his sides, his breathing loud, whooshing. I knew the sound. Those were my lungs just before I got pounded on Geary Street after a long chase pinned me in the Sears Roebuck parking lot.

I looked for the door.

"Why'd I do that?" he roared at the class.

"BOXER WIN, BRAWLER LOSE!" they shouted back, vibrating the dirty glass windows at the top of the gym and making roosting pigeons flap wings. It was the first time I had seen children truly organized around anything. It made Mr. Isington's Bomb Squaders look like rabble. Their strength and unpredictability astonished me. Their unity made them seem like grown-ups. Like people who could make decisions.

Then he called Rufus and told him to take the class through left jab, from the top. The kids groaned and Mr. Barraza grinned. He had perfect teeth, and when he smiled it became apparent that everyone liked this man, from first grin to last.

13

ANTHONY CEMORE BARRAZA

Mr. Barraza looked at me, my street shoes and black socks, regulation trunks, Y.M.C.A. jersey, gloves and headgear, all the strings awry, my workout card looking like a sandwich board against my bony frame.

"Oh, kid," he said, "ya make me wanna cry.

"Ya look like ya lost twen'y fights. Like ya bin dressed by a gorilla inna dark. Rufus. Golly Jesus, a good lad, but other people's laces confuse 'em."

His accent was fascinating. Later I would know that it was light Bronx and heavy Brooklyn. Loud and brash. Fast, harsh, and confident. Sharp corners on the ends. Thick spittle in the background, the New York rush slowed, leavened by the Pacific rim blends of San Francisco.

It was a sound common in California when everyone on the coast was new and the boroughs of New York generated the character and the

sound of prewar America. Brooklyn and the Bronx fixed the timbre of
the male voice, and New York boys like Burt Lancaster and Tony Curtis
could play an Apache and the Caliph's son without making *all* the critics
scream. It is a manner of speech now increasingly rare in the world,
faded and ever weakening like a lost radio signal.

Mr. Barraza's voice reeked of character, dangling clues of his background like a careless killer. He had a boxer's voice, latent hurt in the
trachea and pain promised in the big hardened fists. Kindness, below
the gruffness, the years of punishment, the decades of roadwork and
concentrated blows. Underneath the kindness was sadness, anger's loving
sister. That reminded me of Mother, and I listened closely.

I was looking at him cockeyed, the headgear occluding my vision.
Mr. Barraza moved the headgear to clear my covered left eye. Now my
right was covered. Mr. Barraza smelled like food, and he talked funny.
So did I. I did not think I could grow to like a hairy bear, but I looked
at this man with great hope.

I probably looked as though I had been in an all-day airplane crash.
I was a mosaic of contusions. The headgear was too big. The jersey,
which was extra small, had shoulder straps that were hanging on by
surface tension and willpower. If I sneezed the tank top would blow off
my absent shoulders and become an outside jock strap, with tails long
enough to trip me. I had no muscle on me. The trunks made me look
like a toothpick inside a tutu.

Anthony Cemore Barraza looked like two Joe Cuttys. He had the
sturdy aspect of a skyscraper. He had been a gritty short-armed heavyweight, a headliner at the Cow Palace and Civic Auditorium for three
years in postwar San Francisco. He lived on his power, aggression, and
shocking body hooks. He smashed his opponents, busted their ribs, and
crushed their spirits. His legs were fast concrete—mobile and indestruc-
tible. He did roadwork like a train rolling down track.

The *paisanos* from the Wharf and North Beach loved this darkly
handsome prince of the ring. He unified them—the southerners, north-
erners, Sicilians, Neapolitans—and he had two freezers at home to keep
the fresh catches he got from the able fisher fleets of Little Rome on the
Wharf.

As a young man, he lacked the ability to say no and had no place
to store the girls. I do not think Tony was a lustful man. But he was a
romantic. When pretty girls kissed him, he became affectionate. When
his wife left him and their uptown, classy Marina home, she took their

three-year-old son, Tony Junior. Mr. Barraza gave up the carousing forever. But it was too late. She and the boy were gone.

His left arm also departed. It was a mystery explored by the ring
columnists in the *Call-Bulletin* and *The Examiner.* They surmised he
had shoulder palsy or a complication from a long-hidden ailment con-
tracted in the war. Tony's priest in the Cathedral of St. Mary's knew it
was penance for his infidelities.

Tony's defense was never his forte. Without his casual left guard
he was bucket swill, the ugly effluvia that boxers deposit from their
lacerated mouths between rounds. He had been battered out of conten-
tion, out of the good arenas, and finally out of the ring with a series of
worsening injuries. His brow began to deteriorate, threatening the eye
and its wobbly cornea, and the left jaw had required two years of surgery. Even with a full set of gleaming, squared false teeth and a smile
as big as the Bay, he only chewed food on the right.

The joy of the glove disappeared for him before the fights moved
south of San Jose. The fish kept coming from the faithful. He found
Clara and Tony Junior, but the missus tired of his tortured and illegible
love notes and the little stuffed animals and saltwater taffy at her apartment door. With all the resolve of her strict faith, she sailed with their
son to Palermo, telling Tony it was Naples. Tony's mail kept coming
back from the Napoli American consulate, unclaimed.

He missed his son and always looked for him on crowded streets.
His scars were campaign ribbons, symbolic atonements for unforgivable
sins. He accepted the hot leather fire rather than parry, seeking respite
in pain. He gave his dwindling cash to the church. Tony the Hook was
becoming beatable, but the worthy few who took split decisions winced
as the ref raised their arms, their busted ribs grating in victory. For weeks
they could pass blood in kind remembrance of having beaten the Doctor.

Before he descended to the pugilist sausage factories of Los Angeles
and Mexico City, before he became a routinely punchable round-heeled
palooka, a predictable victim of younger gloves, he gave up his locker
at Hazard's and called Kurt Miller at the Central Y. It was only five
blocks from the Civic Auditorium, which had reverberated with the
shouts of his admirers and the deep gut thuds of his gloves crushing
opponents' torsos.

The Silver Fox wanted to know why Tony the Hook Barraza
wanted to teach youngsters the Science. Why not join his old gym,
Hazard's, where he could work the upcoming pros?

"I miss my boy, Mr. Miller," he said, and, knowing him as I do now, he was probably weeping when he said it.

Later, when I was a lot older, and I learned about his life, I asked why he had dropped his defense, and his guard, during his contender days.

"My heart," he said simply, "she's on the left."

"Follow me," said Mr. Barraza in his loud rasp as we trooped down the stairs and cut left on the ground floor and went into the men's locker room in the basement.

I was amazed that someone so huge could be so quick on stairs. Joe Cutty was big, but he moved with the method of a dignified VFW parade. My tank top kept falling off my shoulders as we flew down the stairs.

He needed the good weight scale for measuring small objects. He took off my headgear.

In addition to the scale, the basement contained the weight room and lockers and it dwarfed the gym above us. This massive crypt echoed with the clang of heavy weights against metal, or iron on concrete, the hard hymn of men's fists on an adult body bag, the grunts of a hundred males exerting maximum effort. Forget the poetic image of a perspiring Olympian brow reaching storied heights. This was the remarkably disgusting interwafting of two hundred genuinely smelly armpits, the curious humid density of deep lung air blown into a basement gym by continuous cycles of competition and inner striving.

"C'MON CARL YASONAVABITCH DO IT *PUUUSH YOU ASSHOLE!!*"

"*UNNNNNGHHHH!!*"

My eyes opened wide. Oh, God. They torture adults too.

Mr. Barraza directed me onto the wet base plate of the scale, his crippled eyebrow wiggling like an agitated worm as he fidgeted back and forth with the little weight on top. The noise from the other side of the locker wall—of ironmongering, or of Christian reconstruction—unnerved me.

When he stood on the device, Tony could slap the bottom weight onto the two-hundred-pound slot on the main beam scale and shift the little dingus on top to the twenty-five in one second, the indicator at steady dead center.

"How old are ya, kid?" he asked, struggling with the tale of the scale.

"Seven," I said. I could tell he did not like my accent.

"Well. Ya weigh in like a five-year-old. Yur not forty pounds. Yur wearin street shoes, fourteen-ounce gloves—two of 'em. And, there's water onna plate."

He rubbed what was left of his ears, which he would do a lot when he was working with me.

"My *foot* weighs more 'n you. Shit. My dog's *tail* weighs more. 'Scuse my swearing," he added.

"You eat every day?" asked Tony.

"Yep."

"Yes, sir, right?" he said.

"Yessir, light," I said.

"Whaddya eat?"

I was perplexed. "Food?" I offered.

"Shit. Jeezus. 'Scuse my French."

He was looking carefully at me, with some pain. "Sebbie," he said to a big, equally hairy man dressing near us, without taking his eyes from me. As if I might evaporate.

"Gimme yur towel, go getta 'nother from the desk, tell 'em I took it." The Y, I learned, took towel inventory the way Fort Knox counts bullion.

"Don be coppin no towels," said Norman the Locker Boy.

Why cop a towel? They were inedible.

Mr. Barraza wrapped the towel around my shoulders, like a medic covering an open wound.

I did not know that "shit" was French. Did I need a towel to soak up blood? Would a beating now begin?

We went back upstairs, turning into the main lobby of the Central Y. I gaped at the expansive marbled entryway, the elegant chandeliers, and white-tiled floors. Noise bounced from a ceiling that was in the sky. It reminded me of a huge church. Later, when I first saw Grace Cathedral on Nob Hill, I thought, this looks like the Y.

Passersby were dressed in suits, and took pride in saying hello to Mr. Barraza, whom they called Tony. Men wearing hats smiled at him carefully and touched their brims, looking up. Other men in gym clothes called him Hook, or Doctor Hook.

Mr. Barraza was thinking, walking with great purpose, his brows down. I had to take many big steps to stay with him, and still fell behind. He walked like Bluto, Popeye's gigantic comic foe, his huge arms swinging freely, his head lowered in thought, a paradoxical mechanical motion that was both relentless machine and liquid jungle feline.

His attention both flattered and worried me. I could tell that I was with someone whom others respected. At first, I thought it was because of his immense size. But some of the men in the Y were actually larger than he, and they showed even more admiration. I felt guilty that he could not say hello to his greeters.

The secretaries loved Tony and sighed as we ascended the wide marble staircase to the mezzanine.

"Good morning, Tony," two of them called, with the same musically alluring voices that some of the women on Masonic used.

Mr. Barraza stopped at the top of the stairs and put a huge hand on my bony shoulder. He looked up. I looked up. A large, five-foot emblem of the Young Men's Christian Association, with the words MIND BODY SPIRIT emblazoned in dark blue into the sides of an inverted red triangle hung on the west marbled wall. "Spirit" was at the top of the triangle. In the center of the triangle was an open Bible. On its pages was written "John 17:21." The triangle was centered in a bronze frieze depicting men guiding boys on golden playing fields.

Mr. Barraza pointed. At that time, I could not see or read the words. I saw what looked like a book, shimmering in gold.

"I like ta see seven-year-olds. Good fer bein molded."

"Mind, Body, Spirit. Yur mind," he says, "not sure about. Yur body, it needs work or we're gonna lose it. Mind, body, God pretty much gives ya those."

I looked up. I knew something was up there. This was like being in school, with the teacher performing mysteries on the chalkboard.

"But spirit, we'll see." He knelt and looked into my eyes.

"Ya look like a kid afraid of a lot. I'm askin ya ta put out fer me, ta work fer me. Ta give me your *try*.

"Do this fer me, Master Ting. Do it cuz ya got choices in this. It's in yur power."

I did not know what to do or say.

He looked at me, waiting for a response.

"*Capish?* Know what I'm sayin?"

I bit my lip and nodded. He was talking about my getting hurt. To work hard, as Uncle Shim and my father had urged me. To do the *reglas* that Hector Pueblo had said the Y.M.C.A. would teach. There was not a chance in the world that I would like it.

"Ya look confused. Ya look scared. And," he said, blowing out air, "ya look hungry. C'mere."

The Y paid Tony a salary. Mr. Miller knew that Tony had lost his wife and child. The city press had treated Tony and Clara's separation as it had treated that of Joe DiMaggio and Marilyn Monroe, as if they were public enemies.

Tony had all the culinary skills of a dead water buffalo. So Mr. Miller gave Tony an all-day meal pass to the Y.M.C.A. cafeteria, America's early answer to fast food. The cafe excelled in bologna, tuna fish, french fries, and Coke, but no one complained because it was clean and the manager, one Angelina Costello, reminded everyone of the mother the unlucky ones should have had.

Tony ate five or six sandwiches at a sitting, his hulking form dominating the counter. He looked at Angelina and overate, the right side of his face ballooned like a heavyweight squirrel. He pulled a small notebook from his pants and slowly recorded his intake. He adjusted his long morning runs through the park accordingly.

"Angelina. This here kid, this kid, he needs a meal. He needs *ten* meals. So I'm ordering as many as he can eat. I ain't abused the card. This ain't abuse. This is *charity*. God's work, fer God's sake.

"Maximum effort. Mayo on his samich. No Cokes. Givem milkshakes, lotsa ice cream, and the Additive. Ya doin okay?" He reached over and rubbed the top of her hand.

"Okay, Tony," she said, smiling. "I was afraid he needed a haircut. Why the towel?"

He grinned. "Ya ever got that skinny ya'd need a towel justa keep warm. Angie. What I wanna do is load this kid up with all the starch he can take. Never taught weights ta no seven-year-old. Gonna teach 'em. Lissen. Maximum effort. I need yur help," he said, looking at her, his head cocked to the side, unbalanced.

He looked funny. He wasn't used to asking favors.

"So scram," she said warmly, looking at me as he strode muscularly from the cafe. She wore a blue-and-white-striped apron with evidence of food on it. Her body showed evidence of food. She was Hector

Pueblo's opposite; nothing was chiseled. Her form had all the corners rounded out. She smiled like she meant it, as if she liked everything around her. She controlled food. I was in love.

The General Lew Wallace was a great place, but this was Maxim's, without Rupert or Dozer threatening verbal death or aiming a sharp butcher knife at disrespectful customers. This was where good boys came after they got killed by Rupert.

She looked at me. She saw an empty stomach, her cause for existence. She reached over and removed the towel.

"Oh, honey, do your parents beat you?" She looked at me like a teacher, expecting the right answer.

"No. Rooz fight," I said, sniffing the food intently, sniffing the air like an alert rodent. No scrapple. No liver. No sauerkraut. Maybe, no hitting.

She placed silverware on a napkin before me. Automatically, I separated the fork, placed it on the left, the knife and spoon on the right.

"Whew. Who do you fight, Mighty Joe Young? You poor little guy. You *are* skinny, I'll give you that. Well," she said, "the Good Lord put me, and Charles Atlas, and Dr. Reed's Bodybuilding Additive here 'cause of the likes of you. Tony'll put you in the weight room, and I'll put the beef on you. Milkshake, additive, and tuna specials and all the starch I can scratch up, comin' up. Next thing, honey, you'll be a Junior Leader or a boxing coach and get to wear those fancy dry-cleaned white pants." She had to help me untie the gloves.

"Angie," called one of the customers who was watching us. "I'm havin trouble with the button on my fly. I'm wondering could you . . ."

"*Outta my cafe, you louse!*" she screamed, and without using my feet I jumped two feet off the stool. I thought Stepmother Edna had showed up.

I would have stayed with Miss Costello for the rest of my life, but after glutting myself, Rufus collected me and grimaced when he saw my gloves on the counter, looking like huge bloated hands belonging to Disney cartoon characters.

I loved Mrs. Costello and expected, accordingly, never to see her again. To my everlasting benefit, she would feed me for three years on Tony's card. She would watch me eat the way adult men used to watch Brigitte Bardot, excited by the vision of rounding flesh.

14

THE DUKE

Mr. Barraza led me to the far gym, a smaller room filled with big Lifesaver-like rings hanging from ceiling straps, rounded leather sausages the size of sofas mounted on iron legs, and more mats. Torture apparatus. Methods unclear, but results predictable. It too had an upper-gallery running oval, half the size of the one in the full gym. Here, it took ninety-six laps to make a mile.

He put his hands behind his back, his feet spaced, at parade rest. He took the gloves from me as I was struggling to lace them, holding their faded smelliness behind him.

"Gonna start with basics.

"Yur gonna learn boxing. Pugilistics. Sweet Science a Mr. John Douglas, the Marquee a Queensberry. He wrote The Book a hunnert years ago. Yur gonna learn those rules, same as Y.M.C.A. rules, Christian rules. Yur gonna live by 'em.

"Ya live with the Duke.

"Duke gave science ta boxing. 'Fore him, the Brits boxed bare-knuckle, an taught it ta us. Men'd stand toe ta toe, go eighty, hundred rounds, beatin crap outa each other. Then they died, brains all mush. Brits are like that. Tough-ass fighters. Uh. Tough guys.

"Slaveowners did same thing with the Negroes. Molineaux, probly the best fighter, he was a slave."

"Tom Moreenoh, work in Misser Cutty Shop," I said.

"Uh, that's a different Molineaux, kid. My Molineaux, he died couple hundred years back." He cleared his throat.

"The Duke. He brought us gloves. An rules. Ya don't foul. Ya learn ta stand on yur own. Ya fight like Gentleman Jim Corbett, an Gene Tunney. Ring scientists. Means they were smarter'n they were tough."

In the great classless society of the United States, the Marquis of Queensberry had become the Duke. It would not have sounded right to say, Put up your marquisses.

"Boxing is going inta a ring," he said clearly, his large dark eyes almost glazed, focusing on the words in his memory, pulling them out like cooperatively loose teeth.

"Alone, and nakid, like a island ina middle a the ocean. Ya got yur hands, yur skills, and yur heart. It takes a lot. It gives a lot." His jaw flexed with all the effort of so much speech.

I am going to fight naked? In the ocean where Mother ran?

"Tell ya four things. Expect ya ta remember this." He was talking very slowly, and I appreciated it.

"One. *This won't kill ya.* It just hurts sometimes. Sometimes, it hurts like leeches on yur dick."

He looked at me, curling that big hairy eyebrow—what my father called "giving the caterpillar"—when I didn't react. I didn't know that this Dick fellow he was talking about was connected to me.

"Two. Ya wanna defend yurself, *ya stay the course.* Course is three years, get from Intro through Intermediate if yur under nine. Advanced, 'at's later, an 'at's different.

"Yur under nine." I nodded. I understood that part.

"Three. *Better ta give than ta receive.* That means ya beat up the other guy and don't pay squat for what he do ta ya. If I yell at ya and say, 'Rule Three!' I'm tellin ya ta find yur lanes and deliver the goods on yur opponent."

I must have looked confused.

"That means, uh, Rule Three, it means, punch the other guy. Punch. Ya know, *hit* the other guy? *Capish?*" I nodded. I knew that part, too, nodding my head vigorously. That was the bad karma part.

"See, ya hit the other guy more'n he hits you? You win. It's absolutely *uncanny.*" And he laughed with all his teeth.

"Okay. Four. *If ya fight fair an work hard, the Duke'll love ya.*

"Duke knows if ya cheat, and it pisses him off *somethin terrible*, a kid doin somethin like that."

My head swam with the religious connotations of this new truth. God knows, Jesus is his Son. The Duke had to be a special uncle, or something. Christian gods were beginning to resemble the endless pantheon of household deities my mother had respected.

"Ya cheat, yur a bum. Yur bush league with an ugly mind, fit for spittin at and ya can go rassle yaself inta knots."

Wrestling was the competitive contact sport to boxing at the Y. It was no match. Mr. Allen Fox Layteen, the Wrestling Instructor, was disadvantaged because of a lack of tradition and an absence of interest.

The Seals played Pacific Coast baseball, the Giants were in New York, and the Dodgers were in Brooklyn. The Lakers were in Minnesota. The 49ers were big at Kezar, but seating was limited; there was no television, and it was clear that the Ice Age could return and Dewey would become President and the Niners would still fail to win a championship. College football, with Cal and Stanford, and USF basketball with a giant Negro named Bill Russell, were popular for only parts of the City. For the masses, for burgs without major-league teams, it was the Sweet Science. Names like Dempsey and Louis, Basilio and Sugar Ray Robinson, caused men's spirits to swell.

I heard Tony yell at Mr. Layteen: "Rasslers. Swear to God, Allen, I don unnerstan why ya wanna do a sport where yur nose could end up in some guy's *armpit*. It ain't *clean*. Fer God's sake."

Long before he became Director of the Central Y, Mr. Miller had boxed at Stanford. That was before the NCAA decided that collegiate deaths were unseemly and had withdrawn its recognition. The Science did not seem so sweet when ring doctors held the mortally injured head of a twenty-year-old literature major, looking into dead and unseeing eyes whose last image had been a blurred and closing leather glove.

Now, in his position of authority, Mr. Miller ran the Central Y and lent as much dignity to this hard discipline as the Science would allow. He strove to make it sporting. The Marquis would have had a big smile on his face had he walked into the Y from the Leavenworth entrance, where boys went one-on-one at a time of life when sticking chewing gum under a desk was a high crime.

No pros worked in Kurt Miller's gym. Only kids and ex-pros.

Mr. Barraza looked at me again, shaking his head, as if for a moment he had thought I might have been a bad dream. A small ghost.

"Ya 'ready know ya can take a punch and live. It's, ya know, obvious. Look like produce been rolled over by a truck. Key is knowin yur not gonna die. Yur not gonna die. I said that.

"Okay. *Everythin* begins from the Athletic Position, start point fer every sport 'cept track. Stand like this, feet shoulder-width apart, left leg leadin, just slick it up like that. See how yur balanced, so's if I push ya, like this—oh, shit, sorry. Here, get up. Ya okay?"

My first day at the Y was a day at the races. I saw a swimming pool, so-called. It looked like an early version of the Bermuda Triangle, replete with emerald green water that harbored unseen denizens of the deep and chlorine so thick it could have been sold as combat mustard gas. I saw a great crafts shop, full of clay and paints. I was taught how to do a somersault on top of leather mats as lumpy as my face after a bad fight. Kids threw dodgeballs at me and I could not sit out; I had to be a target.

I stopped at Angie's Cafe for fries in a dry, clean sack, thanking her so much that she had to ask me to shut up. It was over before it began. I took the bus home with a rumbling stomach full of food. I wondered about those people I had met. I closed my eyes and recalled the sights and smells of each person. Angie Costello came first to mind, a bright lipsticked smile above a striped blue apron. Then Mr. Barraza. I closed my eyes tightly, and saw the toothless man in the lobby with the loud starched pants, the silver-haired white man, Mr. Miller, in his suit. I saw Mr. Barney Lewis and all his muscles. The teenagers, Rufus and Norman, in the locker room. And some mysterious man in the gym. I saw food, and smelled it, shuddering in pleasure as I devoured the fries.

When the Muni stopped at Masonic I got off, regretfully. It was six o'clock. Time to go in the house. I ran up Central, past a cluster of children, and Janie answered my anxious doorbell ringing.

"I had so much fun today!" she exclaimed.

"Where you go?" I whispered to Janie Ming-li as we went up the stairs.

"I visited friends on Encanto. Kai! They just got a television! I watched *Laurel and Hardy* and *Spanky and Our Gang.* It's great! I laughed so hard!"

"Is 'bout spanks?" I asked.

"No! You nut! It's about kids. The family on Encanto—the Garcias—they're very nice." She smiled, her dimples deepening. "Their mommy's like ours. She doesn't scream and hit her kids. She kept feeding me." She bit her lip to keep her eyes dry, now a common habit. "She kissed me. On the cheek." We were silent for a moment. We thought of Mother, who kissed our noses.

"I got food too!" I cried, and Edna heard us and we got kicked apart.

"Too much talking, children," she said.

Father looked at me after I washed up and sat at the table. I felt as if I had a secret, but did not know quite what it was. I felt like smiling and knew that I shouldn't.

"How was it, Kai?" he asked.

"Good, Papa. Good." My head was nodding. I felt fear. Fear that if I said I liked it, I would lose it.

"I saw *dai ren,* very big men."

"No Chinese!" said Edna. "Honestly! You *always* manage to say the wrong thing! Now pass the brussels sprouts, please," she added.

"Did you learn boxing?" he asked.

"Yes. I rearn, how stand, but I fall down," I said.

"Well," he said. "That is a start."

Mr. Barraza spent three months teaching me how to stand and move and how to hold my arms with gloves on. He learned I was a student who hit like a new animal, called a rabbit-chicken.

"Nah, nah, yur rabbit-punchin, flappin arms lika chicken!" he snorted. Somehow, whenever I aimed for his head while he knelt before me in the ring, I tapped his throat.

"Nah, nah, not the throat!" he said.

I could tell I was driving him crazy because he used a lot of French words, which were not unknown on my block, and he rubbed his funny ears until they turned red.

As a boy who had been inserted into his wishful thinking, I inhaled food at Angie's Cafe the way a whale does plankton. The bright red stool that sat closest to the register and the threateningly sharp check spike was the least used. This seat became mine, and I could rotate on it, spinning in a happy circle. I loved the routine of the cafe, which existed to produce food. The sound of silverware being washed, the griddles sizzling, the smell of fries, the pickle relish and mustard, the cheeriness of Mrs. Costello, the availability of her food. She laughed at small things. Looking at her I had the religious experience that churches seek to inspire in their parishioners. The fries at Angie's were spiced with ketchup, not blood, and she did not mutter histories of past wrongs to others in the cafe, which was the background music at the Eatery. Nor did people speak a Chinese language that I was expected to understand. I was suffering another religious conversion: good-bye Kuo Wah.

I began throwing punches whenever I thought no one was looking. In the bathroom, I punched air mindlessly until Edna knocked on the door and told me that my time was up. There was a synchronicity to the world, for both her sense of allocated bathroom time and the period of shadow-boxing, and of rounds in the ring, was three minutes.

I began to imagine throwing punches at the Bashers. Ha, I thought. That very, very crazy idea.

Father saw me throwing imaginary punches on the stairs, and asked me to show him. I demonstrated the basic stance, but he could not hide being underwhelmed by my attempts at punches.

"Keep trying, Kai," he said. "Never give up."

15

IRON

Gonna teach ya some bodybuildin," said Mr. Barraza.

Mr. B taught me how to lift weights. He taught me the movements. It was like boxing. Form was everything. It was very disciplined, and when it was done correctly, it hurt.

"When yur a kid, there's only *one* way. *My* way.

"When yur a world champeen, ya pick yur own path. Then you teach kids *yur* way, and yur right till they become growed men. Form," he said. "Stretchin. Breathin. Interval. No cheatin."

The Duke was everywhere.

Mr. B used dumbbells with three digit numbers and worked so hard that other lifters stopped to watch him. He flipped the black iron forty-five pound York plates like Eatery eggs over easy and could bench four hundred pounds on an even-keel press without a spot. He blew compressed air out of his mouth like the smooth steel hydraulic lifts in Cutty's Garage.

Men watched him press, and curl, and extend, in those suspended moments when the mind leaves the body, and there is no self-consciousness, no awareness, that one is staring. Tony focused when he was at his work, and infected those near him with his fearsome ability to concentrate.

I was too skinny to wear the smallest weight belt. They did not make them for kids, even big kids. I tried one on when no one was looking and it fell from my head to the floor without touching anything, the huge metal buckle clanging on the locker-room floor like the commercial waste cans on McAllister on garbage pickup day.

I was too skinny to sweat; my body couldn't support the effort. Tony produced sweat quickly and voluminously. He watched me as I studied his sweat glands.

"Ya want water on yur body when the glove lands. Shows yur loose. If it's not a true blow, it skids off. Takes a pro shot ta get through yur water." He studied me for a moment.

"Chinese kids sweat?" he asked.

I shook my head and raised my shoulders, so to speak.

"Yeah. 'At's right. Ya dunno."

I lifted his personal five-and-eight-pound wrought-iron bells that he used for bag practice. He held them in his big hairy fists while doing three-minute shadow rounds, the air in the empty ring popping with snapping punches and his trademark body hooks. When he was done he pitched them into a small, red-handled, green leather grip, flicking them with his wrists as others would toss car keys.

I struggled to hold them in my trembling hands.

He taught me about breathing, stretching, and thinking about practice. "Ya got a brain, I know it, so this'll add up. Ya ask yurself: 'Why am I here?' "

Big Willie Mack, the Bashers, and Hector, I thought. Edna, too. Chinese Communist Army and that man, Mao Tse-tung.

"Yur here, Master Ting, ta make a man a yurself. 'At's why. Ya come ta the gym, 'at's in yur mind. Ya curl the iron, 'at's in yur mind. Ya don think 'bout crap, or nothin. Jus 'at."

I was not very communicative. He would cock his head and peer into my eyes the way Marine Drill Instructors check rifle actions for

lint. The way Mr. Lewis would look into the eyes of a kid who was
KO'd, to see if anyone was still home.

"*Capish?*" he asked.

He taught me the basic exercises. Bench, military, and incline
presses, curls, flies. Some of the men looked at me funny when I used
an incline to press ten pounds, gasping with effort.

"Never mind those other lifts. Jes' do bench," he decided.

"Ya need a chest. Golly Jeezus, Master Ting, do ya ever need a
chest. Every chance ya gotta breathe, ya take a deep one fer Mr. Barraza.
Do that. Reg'lar deep breathin expands the cavity, simplest exercise inna
world. Someday women'll figger it out, an all the Vic Tanney Gyms
inna world gonna be filled with broads."

He stopped for a long moment. He was rubbing his eyes, and then
he turned his back to me.

"Sometimes, Italians sweat in the eyes. Don't think Chinese do
that," he said, sniffing.

I wanted to say: my sister Janie and I sweat in eyes all the time,
and I don't think we're Italian. We're stepchildren.

"Chest. Build ya a base for the other stuff ta hang on."

He emphasized triceps and shoulder development second.

"Tricepts," he said succinctly, "yur work muscle. Alla punches ya
learn, got tricepts makin 'em happen. Ya step inna ring and touch gloves
with yur opponent, use yur tricepts. Ya jab, ya cross, ya hook, and ya
cut, use yur tricepts. Pull yurself outa a hole, ya open a door. Tricepts.

"Gonna give ya more tricepts exercises than Carter got little red
liver pills. Tricepts work shoulders, too, which God ain't see fit ta give
ya. Good thing yur arms so skinny, cuz with no shoulders ya got nowhere ta pin 'em. Tricepts. It's two-thirds a yur arm.

"All other lifts, bag 'em, but don't ya ever bag yur chest or yur
tricepts. Work muscles. Naa, naa—don't stop! Don't rest so long 'tween
sets! Challenge 'em muscles!"

One of the walls in the gym had dual pulley cables. I learned a
triceps pulldown on them. Occasionally my arms would pop and I would
lose a pulley or smash the bell into my face. Mr. Barraza would smile
and chuckle, and would show me again how to avoid having the ma-
chinery kill me. He gave the dignity to youthful labor that only good
teachers can provide.

My arms and chest exploded with tiny laces of pain when I moved the weights the way he instructed me. If I cheated on the form, the burning pain was less.

"Do it like I showed ya," he said evenly.

My body ached and Mr. Barraza taught me to stretch out the spasming, tightened muscles afterward. He gave me Irish Green Liniment, a pungent salve, to rub onto myself. It smelled toxic, looked like pus from the creature from the black lagoon and burned like hot coals on the skin. I actually turned green, like an amphibian.

"This here stuff, it's best fer cuts. Draws out the poisons. Stops infection. Also's good fer bruisin and fer torn muscle. See, Master Ting, yur tearin down yur thin muscle. At night, when ya sleep, proteins from Angie build it up bigger, stronger, tougher. Rub this on," he said.

Edna thought I had fallen into a chemical toilet.

"Whatever that is, whatever is making that smell, do not bring it into this house again." She had a point.

"Janie, I like Y," I said as I prepared to leave for my bus after school.

"Why?" she asked.

"Are we 'Italian'?" I asked.

"Italian? Golly, Kai, I'm not understanding *anything*! We are *not* Italian!"

"Okay," I said. Just asking.

"Now what was it that you liked?"

"The Y," I said.

"Oh. *Why* do you like the Y?" she asked.

I hesitated. *"Hun hau ren,"* I said. Very nice people.

"Don't tell Edna," I said.

"Don't tell Edna *what*?" she asked. I jumped, a small, involuntary hop in place, my heart pounding. My mind raced. What will she break? What will get hit? What's the answer? What was the question?

She repeated the question, loudly: "I said, 'Don't tell Edna *what*?' "

I gulped. "I rike people at Y," I murmured.

"Oh. Well. That's all? My God, is *that* bad?"

I shook my head and then nodded, unsure of the answer.

"Children. Your father thinks we ought to do something together. He suggests a picnic. We will go this next Saturday."

"Y.M.C.A.," I said.

"Not next weekend. We're going to have fun," she said.

We looked at her solemnly.

"Phone Y.M.C.A., say no come?" I asked.

"Phone them? Don't be silly. You're just a . . . *child*. And it's quite obvious that you're *terrible* at whatever they're striving to teach you. Children do not use telephones. They'll never miss you," she said.

"Come, children, time for the park!" Edna announced, brightly, her voice brimming with false joy. She was using willpower on us. She employed a relentless, deliberate, upward emotionalism that would have left Norman Vincent Peale feeling mild depression. Usually, this was after someone had been hit. Mind over matter, willpower over reality. There was a distant familiarity, a faraway ringing, something about Mother, and illness, which made me doubt Edna's cheerleading.

We motored down Park Drive. Father spoke about the bank; Edna talked about the origin of picnics. They were designed for health, she told us, to allow deep breathing of forest air, while a family enjoyed the conviviality of togetherness.

Golden Gate Park was bright and sunny this Saturday morning, and we arrived early enough to be able to park at our pleasure. Father drove around Stow Lake, past the Buffalo Paddock, Spreckles Lake, and the Portals of the Past—a pair of columns saved from a mansion that collapsed during the 1906 quake. We stopped at the Association of Pioneer Women of California log cabin, and their garish statue.

Edna directed us in laying out a calico tablecloth, and she prepared the food: bologna sandwiches and potato salad. They were delicious, and in ample portions, which was confusing. There was no conversation for some time. The birds chirped, ants scurried, and we ate studiously until the food was gone.

The Association statue was immense. A massive granite block topped by a woman pushing two children before her. A boy and a girl, larger than life, and absolutely naked. The woman was fully dressed, and even had a wide-brimmed sun bonnet. A light green metallic patina covered her head and shoulders, while the children looked more darkly bronzed. At the four corners of the block were bronzed steer skulls, and the front of the block showed a sailing ship. I didn't know what the statue was for, but the meaning seemed foreboding. Where was this woman pushing the children? Why weren't they dressed? What would Edna say about the boy's wee-wee showing?

Father and Edna spoke quietly about the park, the tourists, and mentioned some veterans' gatherings and the World Series. They spent a great deal of time talking about Eisenhower, and Republicans and Democrats. I wondered why was this not as much fun as eating at Angie's Cafe, because we were eating a tremendous amount of food.

"The Korean War is going to end, T.K.," said Edna quietly.

"Yes, it is, dear," he answered.

"It's good that it's going to be over, finally. Was it worth it? Did we do any good?"

"*Ha!*" shouted Father, startling us. "North Koreans cross thirty-eight parallel, push us to the sea! We fight back. Well, U.S. Army, and Na-men, Second Infantry, fight back. Now South Korea safe again. You ask the South Koreans! Of course it worth it!" he roared.

As the echoes of his booming voice faded into the air, I looked at the broad expanse of green behind Edna, the soft blur that usually meant trees. It was like a forest, and I suddenly remembered the story Janie had read us. I looked at Edna, and at Father. The boy and girl had been fed before being left in the woods. The stepmother had wanted the father all for herself, for there was not enough food, or love. I turned to Janie, a glimmer of understanding about picnics dawning upon me.

"We stay here, rike Hanserr and Greter?" I asked.

"Where did you hear that story?!" cried Edna.

"My fault," said Janie, before I could answer. I closed my eyes as Edna tossed a cup of apple juice into Janie's face.

Unlike Hansel and Gretel, we were not left in the woods, but brought home.

"I want Janie read me story," I said while Edna unpacked the food. "Is my fault," I added, faintly.

"Silence!" said Edna. "There is *plenty* of fault to go around! I will *not* be defied in my own house! We have a perfectly *lovely* picnic and you children, you *step*children, manage to utterly spoil it! I do not know how your father is going to deal with you for this, but I assure you, you will not like it!" She was packing away some clothes. They were Janie's.

We waited for Father's punishment, but it did not materialize. We lived in an obverse world, where we did not have to wait for Father to return home for imposition of sentence.

The following Saturday I returned to the Y. Edna did not mind fruit juice in Janie Ming-li's hair, but disliked my swim lessons with Coach Richard Lee because my trunks stank of chlorine. Blood, no problem.

It did not smell. Richard Lee was from the Big Island, Hawaii. If I lived on an island, I would want to know how to swim, too. The city—we called it the City—had water on three sides, but *only three sides.*

I did not like the lessons because I was trying, however fitfully, to be a human being, and had no desire to be a fish. I was in daily agony, afraid of drowning, fearing a quick and final future.

Survival in Beginner's only set you up for worse. Then it was Minnows, followed by Fish, Flying Fish, Shark, Junior Lifesaving, and Junior Leaders, each bringing a new terror of skill requirements. Then, you were dead, had gills, or miraculously had reached eighteen and could then take Senior Lifesaving and Water Safety Instructor. I trembled with anticipation.

My skinny body shivered in the cold of the basement pool.

The pool was twenty-eight yards to the lap and had caged ceiling lights and swim lanes for the One Hundred Mile Club, and half of the shallow three-and-a-half-foot end for the kids. The industrial-strength chlorine burned in my myopic eyes and made all the lights radiate wildly colored rainbows.

The water demonstrated my lack of coordination and I wondered why, if we had to drink it, they had made it taste so bad. That's why it felt so awful when it went up your nose and tried to drown your brain.

Coach Lee was Chinese–Hawaiian. He taught swimming. That was a misnomer. He was in charge of drowning. Swimming lacked the long traditions and the gloried violence of boxing, probably because most of its advocates were on the bottom of the sea. People did not call each other "Master this" or "Mister that."

Coach had two rules: "Get in and outa water when I say. And don't pee in the pool. Absolutely no whizzin in my pool. I can tell," he added, craftily. So we peed in the showers, giggling, our hearts racing with the forbidden act.

We called him Coach, a title that replaced the high honor of syen-sheng, before born. Coach never used our names.

"Hey, *you*," he would say, and we all figured he was talking to us. The basement, its tiled floor and walls and high ceiling, reflected sound and bounced it back, in defiance of the laws of nature, with increased energy.

The noises produced in the pool during beginner's lessons sounded like complaints from a world gone mad. Echoes inside of echoes, screams and gurgles inside a vortex of growing aquatic noise as Coach tried to reverse evolution and push us back into the sea.

"Hey, *you*, don't drink my pool," he said. We all looked guilty, hanging on to the edge like fading shark bait, delaying our drowning to cough it out in great liquid, rolling hacks. Few Olympic swimmers came from ghettos; most drowned first.

But swimming was an equalizer. Other kids were not very good either, and we all inadvertently inhaled the pool again and again. I was a gimp, but so were they. How I loved being normal, even at the risk of becoming a Red Cross water-safety statistic.

Coach Lee was accustomed to seeing kids who feared water.

Coach Butch Oliva, Basketball, was not prepared to see kids who feared Wilson roundballs. While Mr. McCoo taught the Good Book and Mr. Barraza gave money to the church, Coach Oliva revered Bob Cousy, the ball magician of the Boston Celtics. He figured Cousy was Jesus Returned and thought that anyone who did not love the Celtics prayed to Stalin and had a Russian radio transmitter in his closet.

"*What*," he roared, "are you afraid of?"

"Ball," I said.

Gymnastics was taught by a small, compact man named Langston Enright. I was very good with tumbling, and not so effective with the apparatus. Langston was the only member of the faculty who wanted kids to call him by his first name.

"Ever read any a my books?" he would ask us. We all shook our heads.

"Langston!" shouted Mr. Lewis. "You are *not* going to confuse these young gentlemen about literature!"

Langston Enright sighed and rubbed the back of his muscular neck.

"Ya'll keep pushin da tumblin, Master Ting. Pretty good, fer a squirt."

But my primary responsibility was boxing.

"Yur doin good," said Mr. Barraza. "Yur movin through pain an sufferin. I like it.

"Talked to Mr. McCoo." He was the short man whom the Teeth God had punished. He was the first member of the staff I had met on my first day. He was also an expugilist who was, beneath his ring scars, an artist. The color and emotion in his paintings were things that spoke to my tiny and immature soul. I entered his paintings, abandoning the Handle, Edna, and Big Willie Mack. It was 1950s methadone.

Hardly breathing, I sat on a high and well-worn wooden stool and watched his gnarled swollen-knuckled hands create transporting mood from blank construction paper.

Mr. McCoo knew I loved drawing, painting, papier-mâché projects, and rope lanyards. I had inherited a fragile thread of my father's and grandfather's artistic abilities, and hints of my forebears' talents appeared occasionally in the crafts shop. Mr. McCoo let me use his personal paints and brushes. When finished, I cleaned them as if the future of world hygiene depended upon my attention. This was my retreat from the hard classes involving my body.

"McCoo, Mr. McCoo thinks yur too young and too little ta be playin with weights," said Mr. Barraza. "He says little guys should not be liftin. No liftin, he thinks, till ya got yur growth an yur bones are set. When whiskers come in, like when yur 'leven, or twelve." Ten years later, Tony would still be galling me about my clean cheeks.

" 'At's alota crap. We gotta do radical treatment on yur bones, make 'em bigger so's they can host muscle. McCoo thinks ya oughta be learnin *oil paintin an Ping-Pong.*" He said it as if he had been referring to cigarette smoking and pederasty.

"He's afraid fer ya, specially down inna basement, where ya could get hurt. Says if a member dropped a forty-five plate on ya we'd never find ya again. So I says ta him, McCoo, Master Ting oughta move inta the basement and *sleep* there, he needs bodybuildin so bad. Never seen a kid like ya. It's like someone took someone and cut him in half an saved the head, and hands, and feet. Lissen to me. These weights, gonna save yur life. Ain't gonna kill ya."

He looked down at me. "But *never* go down there without me. *Never* go in there with no shoes. Keep yur distance from anyone doin military presses or squats. Always do yur stretches and don't never overextend yur elbow. *Don't rest an always* go fer the burn.

" 'At's the test fer yur *try. Capish?* Gonna take ya outa crafts," he said. "Steada crafts, do bodybuildin. Don't thank me too hard," he said, smiling with his bright teeth.

"With yur extra time, ya can do pullups," he added.

I could do none. Black, iron, elbowed pipe hung from the low ceiling of the main gym's north corner, under the oval track. All the kids had to hang from the bars and do as many as they could. I dangled, like bad laundry, mortified with the lack of movement. I used to hang from anything, trying to build up points for pullups. Edna would scream at me.

"Oh my God! What are you now? A bat?! Get down from there this instant. Oh, Lord, you strange thing! Get out of here!"

But the Main Event was boxing.

"Master Ting," he announced. "Yur the only kid I ever seen 'at's so bad ya don't even got two lef feet. I think God got mixed up an put yur hands on yur legs and yur feet on yur arms." Then he chuckled, happy with the image. I already loved Mr. Barraza's laugh, which was a bit like Chinese music and some Cantonese sauces—sweet and sour. I smiled in the hope that he would laugh again, later. I loved laughter, the music of safety, of soft feelings. Few people I knew had a normal laugh, and for some reason that gave me relief.

"Only thing gimme comfort is, yur puttin on weight. Ya gained seven point five pounds, easy. Ya took ta weightliftin good, and yur movin the scale but don't look no different atall. Like all the weight went inta yur liver or yur pancreas, where I can't see.

"But ya got good wind. Yur a strange kid. Stick n' move. Keep yur left up and glide your trailin foot light, don't drag it like it died las week. Yur leavin rubber on my mat."

Teaching me the punches was difficult. My right leg finally made an appearance in the correct locale, opposite my left and below the hip joint. I could shuffle forward and shuffle back. I could circle to the left with good speed and steady feet.

Rufus taught me the rope. Roof could whip the rope like a circus trainer. His wrists would whir and the rope would slap the floor in a staccato storm of rhythmic whaps.

At first I jumped like a kid without hamstrings who had ingested rat poison for breakfast. But jump rope is an activity for the slow and steady learner. Solo practice generates neither injuries nor humiliation. I could do it in the small and abandoned ninth-floor gym. Rufus showed me how to get in by jimmying the laundry-room lock down the narrow hallway, which provided a lateral entry into the gym through the laundry chute.

"Be ghosts in here, Kai," he said, smiling, and I smiled back, entering with delicious joy a place where Mother and her spirit-world allies might be.

The gym was dark, the electricity shorted from rain leaks and now permanently switched off. Wire mesh covered the stained and permanently soiled windows. Roosts of pigeons packed the outside sills, and their constant movement threw eccentric faded shadows on the dark gray walls and brought accents to the sagging, defeated cobwebs in the corners. Their constant billing and cooing brought me a sense of peace, a remembrance of past lives, a distant suggestion of not being alone. The floor was bare and unfinished concrete, and I could jump rope without self-consciousness, without interference. I liked the peace and privacy of the small, forgotten gym.

I could also jump rope in the LaRue home, where Toos, Titus, and Alvin Sharpes would watch. They didn't laugh. Watching me skip rope was like watching a circus act—a cat cooking breakfast or a dog reciting the ABCs. Seeing China Boy do something other than weep and bleed was the stuff of the *Movietone News*.

Rufus didn't care if I tripped on the rope or stepped on it. Mr. Barraza did; he was concerned about protecting property, saving the equipment for the next generation. He said that was important.

The left jab was a quick learn. Its mechanics are the simplest, and fit my personality. I hated to expose myself, to emerge, to stick out. The jab snaps out straight from the shoulder and bounces back immediately into high guard. There is no windup, the jab normally hits a glove or an arm, and the risk of self-injury or public notice is minimal.

The right cross is the payoff punch of the entire science. It requires physical commitment to drive the glove across your own chest to the opponent's face. Mine lacked juice. Mr. Barraza tried a number of things. He wrapped my hands so they wouldn't swim inside the gloves. He put cotton in the glove's thumb to keep it from catching other digits. He held my left guard high against my cheek for the security that was the foundation for pitching that high, hard, reckless right cross. But the risk was too great, the injury it might cause to an opponent, in pure, unmitigated theory, unbearable.

My hooks, which were Mr. Barraza's house specialty and designated to be the best punch for my so-called physique, were AWOL.

"Master Ting, how many fingers I got up? Hey, over here, my hand. No, *this* hand. Good Lord, kid, yur blind. Golly Jeezus ya got a bicycle tire fer a body and then God takes yur eyes.

"Ya *gotta* learn ta hook.

"Hook comes in with yur back behind it," he said clearly. "Closest punch ta the opponent's body in The Book. No extension. Bein blind, ya need the close hook.

"Ya shorten the arm ta the side by droppin it like a bird"—he actually said, "boid"—"and this," grabbing the arm, "is yur wing. See, here, do it, see how it sits there, pretty?

"Now cock it, like this, and *hammer* 'at puppy in like clap a Judgment an push halfway in 'fore ya stop.

"See, ya got no reach. No vision. Master Ting. You'se as choice a piece a boxin material I ever seen. Probly need a seein-eye dog. Youse *might* need a goddamn seein-eye *horse*, 'scuse my French.

"Yur gonna be like me. Shortarm puncher, body digger, close quarters, just outsida clinch."

I was going to be like him? Built like Bluto, like a skyscraper, a hairy bear with sweating eyes? I think my pupils opened like the Red Sea. It never improved vision but it released the tension of surprise.

"Yur too blind ta play long ball with a puncher, tradin blows over the horizon." He put his hands on my headgear and shook me, like a rag doll. "Lissena me. Yur gonna havta go in close and hook, hook, hook! Use both hands ta find yur man. Punch left till ya make contact, then pin it with yur right. It's gonna be scary fer a little shit like youse, being so close, but it'll give ya points."

He demonstrated. I practiced.

I wanted to get it right. Very badly. The hook was risky, but it resembled me. I had trouble facing things straight on.

" 'Member ta keep movin, stick n' move, swim insida yur man. Jes like Cowboys n' Indians. Shoot n' move. Jes like in them Hollywood war movies. Don't letchur opponent 'member where ya wuz when ya busted him."

At first, my sides, the latissimus dorsi, were racked in pain, along with my chest and arm and shoulder muscles. My torso and my wrists felt as though Edna had beaten them with sticks. The liniment could not defeat it. When I lay down to sleep, it mattered little where I put my worn blankie; it still hurt. It was that way when I got up. Later, the pain was replaced by a dull ache, and I got hard little bumps on my arms.

" 'At's muscle; ain't gonna hurtcha atall," said Mr. B when he caught me studying it. I had been looking at myself the way one would inspect a sucking chest wound.

My uppercut, or "cut," was sad. Cuts require the greatest exposure and compromise of defense. The glove has to be dropped low and then brought up high into the opponent's chin, clacking the jaw and the brain. It is a single bout-ender, the only one children can possibly convert into a knockout. It takes torso and arm coordination. My cut was a joke that inspired no laughter. My combinations, the mark of pugilistic practice, were ugly little flag-waving exercises that threatened to wear Mr. Barraza's ears from his head.

Mr. Barraza was giving me gold. He gave me time, much of his experience, and all his patience, hinting that I was worthy of effort, a keeper in the bout of life itself. I was beginning to be embarrassed with my riches in human contact.

I would shuffle forward, on the approach, my head down, my guard up, my feet light, mechanically shifting my shoulders.

"Jab jab jab," he would say, and I would snap them out, straight from the shoulder, no telegraphing and no preparatory windup, fast as he liked, moving hesitantly forward.

"Jab jab, move, right cross, move, jab jab, right cross, jab jab, left hook, move. Parry left jab," he would say, offering a slow-motion left jab and I would duck hard to my right.

"No no no. Don't jink. Don't feint. *Parry* so's ya can counterpunch."

He did it again, and I would duck. Five, six more times.

"God, Master Ting! See this freeway? This freakin highway I'm givin ya ona plate for yur counterpunch! Any lousy thing! Jeezus!"

Then he said his French and rubbed his ear, his whole rocklike head shuddering, trying to rid himself of the image of the little Chinese kid unable to take an opening with ribbons and neon lights blinking from the grandness of it.

Tony had a danger inside him; other men saw it and gave him steerage. But he never had physical anger for his students, even me. He just punished the French tongue, burning Balzac's ears from across an ocean and an era.

He did not give up, showing the tenacity that had made him the people's choice. All of us who learned from him got some of that commitment to endurance, like spiritual plasma to formless youth.

"Gotta be a counterpuncher. Ain't *all* bad. 'Bout as interestin as watchin grass grow, like watchin wagon wheels go round, but ya *really* can't see shit, 'scuse my French. So's let the other guy open up, take his chance. Then belt 'em."

Mr. Barraza bent from the waist, showing what he meant with his words.

"Opponent gives ya a lane when he bashes ya. Use the lane and follow that puppy, that glove, up the road ta where it come from. *Yur* glove follows it quick and presto! Champ, ya laid a glove on 'em an got yurself a point, doin the Duke credit.

"Think a this, Master Ting. Ya know Sebbie D'Angelo, the big guy inna weight room? He's fat, okay?" Tony stretched his arms, approximating the size of Sebbie's waist. "He's gonna work fer the rest a his life an be strong as an ox, and he'll still be fat, cuz he eats like a pig. Yur skinny. Yur a *stringbean*. But everythin ya add s'gonna be U.S. Steel. Ya don't havta strip no fat off first. 'At's a good deal. Ya know all that iron down there? In the weight room? 'At's what *yur* gonna be. You keep thinkin 'at."

16

PROGRESS

After about twenty hours of instruction, I showed signs of progress in the Handle.

Tyrone Sykes's ballistic missile bounced off my head.

"Hey, China Boy. Got hit upside de head wif my ball! Go get it, sucka!"

I looked toward him as I rubbed my head.

"China Boy, whatdafuck you lookin at?"

I was stuck for an answer. But Mr. Barraza and the Duke would not want me to retrieve the ball. At least, not without having my brains bashed in for the sake of the Rules.

I was, by not doing what Tyrone wanted, adding cod-liver oil to sauerkraut—worsening a situation that at its best was not attractive. But I was neither retrieving nor running. Tyrone and I marveled at that.

He pushed me, and I rocked back. I tightened my mouth, saying nothing. Usually I whined. He swung at me and I brought my guard up, too late, taking a hard sharp punch in my gut, but waving my fists back at him.

Tyrone stopped. This was weird. Like watching a pigeon attack Evil.

He threw some more punches and I glanced one of them away from me with a parry, and as he cursed me I ran, then stopped, and ducked, and parried. When he delivered his last blow, he avoided my face, and looked worried. I had persevered, and I shed tears more in relief than in pain.

The word was out. China Boy was showing hints of being human. The effect was dramatic; little kids stayed away. The beatings ceased to be daily events. Even my second-grade teacher, Mrs. Gwendolyn Halloran, commented on my weight. "You're filling out, Kai," she said, and I smiled uncontrollably, having to turn my back and bury my face in my hands.

Pride precedes the fall. My attitude showed, and Edna told me to rid myself of that "disgusting demeanor of arrogant superiority"—which, no doubt, was merely the timid appearance of nascent self-belief.

I wanted that feeling too badly, and would not take it from my face. She slapped me and I willed myself to endure it, blinking as if a thousand strobes were exploding between my ears, behind my eyes. I used to duck and cover my face, receiving ten blows instead of one. My mouth turned into an inverted U, but I did not cry. I felt anger, rage, then nothing as my face turned red. There was no triumph in this.

She looked at me carefully and then inspected me. It was not the added weight; I think it was the change in effect. I was beginning to have a place in the world, and it probably worried her.

Oh, God, she must have thought: another Jane. Next, this little skinny pidgin-tongued etiquetteless Asian ragamuffin would be saying to her, Don't Tread on Me, with all the conviction of her colonial Pennsylvanian antecedents.

"Do not do that again," she admonished. I was not sure what she was prohibiting.

I had thought for an instant of boxing her. No. She was as dangerous as Big Willie. Fighting either of them would have been a cultural impossibility, physically unthinkable.

I told Tío Hector Pueblo what I was doing and tried fitfully, with wild pantomime, to describe the boxing faculty and my lessons. Hector had said that he was going to teach me "street," and I expected to learn a secret kick or power punch. I remembered his muscular arm pumping in our house.

"I ready, Tío," I said. I flexed my right arm, showing him my new, developing bicep.

"Say, *soy listo*. Dat mean, 'I ready,' " he said. "Dat's a mighty fine muscle, my fren'," he added, nodding his head and pursing his lips in stern approval.

"*Soy listo, Tío,*" I said. "Teach me secret kick?"

Instead, he taught me how to walk.

"*Joven,*" he said, "you *walkando como un armadillo* dat go from four leg to two leg."

Through a quirk of nature, I, a reptile, had suddenly been rendered a biped. I looked funny, awkward, bent as if bearing a heavy shell on my back and out of place. I guess that fit.

"*Joven*, you gotta show some *prestigio*. You gotta roll yo' shoulder *back*. Now, put up yo' head, *tu cabeza*. Lif up high. Keep yo' back mo' straight. Don forget yo' shoulder. . . . Jesus Cristo, wha's wrong wif yo' body, chico? Now, you try, take step same time—"

Hector gave that up and went to my facial expression, which was bland in the extreme. It was that way to hide the fear.

"Cho' *anger*, niño! *Enojado!* You pissed! All dese kids poun you, you *angry!* Even if yo' li'l body all shrivel' up an bent, no matta! Mean mug, dat's good. Now, you practice yo' *anger* face."

I tried, but I really didn't hate the kids on my block. My effort made Hector roar. Hector's laugh was infectious—one of those free, melodically hysterical things that sweeps up innocent bystanders in the wake of the sound, the victim uncaring about the origin of the humor.

"I wan rearn secret kick," I said, still giggling.

"Niño, firs' you need a face. *Tu cara bonita*, it look so empty. Dat piss kids off, dey tink dey got no effec' on you.

"Yo' *cara*, she start more fight den no secret kick can finish, you get my meaning," he said.

I thought he was talking about cars in his shop.

"*Cara bonita*. Han'some face. Yo' han'some face, *niño. Hombre!* You so much work! I gotta teach walkando, yo' face, gotta teach yo' *secret kick*, gotta teach you *Español, también!*

"*Escucheme, joven.* You get big, someday, you 'member Hector Pueblo, hokay?" He smiled and rubbed my hair.

When I started taking formal Spanish language classes in junior high, I persisted in the belief that *walkando* was the correct idiomatic gerund for the infinitive *andar,* to walk.

"Señor Losada," I said. *"Yo aprendí Español cuando era un joven, y la palabra correcta es 'walkando.' "*

My lessons in Y.M.C.A. sports, Panhandle *walkando,* street face, and Spanish were wiping out my afternoons and Saturdays at home. I was not missed. Janie had found a cluster of friends near Anza and Encanto, where people had lawns, cars, and televisions. Edna encouraged her to spend as much time away from home as possible. Overnights were encouraged.

Mrs. Halloran was at my desk. "You're wanted in the principal's office," she said.

My father was there, carrying a suitcase. He smiled at me. I grinned back; I had not seen him for two weeks. We got into the Ford and drove through the hills of the City to the bank on Jackson Street in Chinatown.

In the dark and high-ceilinged back offices, Father handed the suitcase to Curzon Fong, the executive vice-president. While Fong Syensheng spun the series of multiple combination locks on the case, I stood against the wall and gazed upward at the golden framed portrait of Madame Amethyst Jade Cheng. Click-click, click-click, sounded the tumblers. Inside the locked case were stacks of English currency, bound in yellow wrappers imprinted with uncut red Chinese chops, signature stamps. The money smelled stale, and humid.

I could feel my father reaching out to me, trying desperately to make a connection, to impart knowledge and wisdom. This was not playing catch; this was important. I looked up at him as suddenly as if he had spoken to me, and he glanced down and nodded. He was telling me something about money, about himself and Mr. Fong, that was somehow connected to me.

When we were outside of the bank, he said, "Never steal." While driving me back to school, he added, "Always work hard. Then you can name your ticket. You understand?"

I shook my head, worried. I did not know why I would want to name a ticket something else. A Muni bus ticket? To change its name?

"What new name for 'ticket,' Baba?" I asked.

"Agh!" he said, "Uh," his hand gesturing, making small rotating circles, "work hard."

He did not know how to decode children, for he had never seen the process in his own home. I wanted to help him, but I felt constricted, struggling against the limitations of understanding and language. I was looking for a way of saying, "Just talk. Say anything. Don't ask if I understand. Tell why Mah-mee died, what I did to invite the Cancer God into our home. How I can live with Edna. If we'll have Chinese food at home again," but the way was not clear.

"Okay, Father. I work hard," I said, not believing that this provided the answer. He nodded, and I breathed again.

The continuing struggles of the China Lights Bank required my father to travel. He went to Hong Kong, Singapore, Jakarta, and Taipei. He usually returned with money for the bank, but none of it filtered to our home. Later, when the embezzlement scandal of the bank became common knowledge, I realized how impeccably honest Father had been.

To see Toussaint during school hours, I had to play with him during recess and lunch. That meant leaving the protective circle of the yard teacher. My lack of athletic abilities made that difficult.

Periodically, one of Big Willie's cohorts would punch me a few times for grins or my lunch money, driven by greed or the imprints of indelible practice. I tried parries, but they were tight, tense, and ineffective. The Bashers tightened lips, hunched shoulders, and let fly.

The beatings were not as frequent as in the beginning of my street education, but I still had headaches and a bad stomach after any encounter with Willis Mack.

"China Boy, you'se jus a stupid fool ofa chink. You'se standin here in my schoo' yard, like ratfacedogshit. I'se gonna teach ya'll some Fist City, China Boy." He laughed. "Gimme yo' face. . . . " Willie Mack was a talker. He had a promising future as a charismatic political orator, and I always wished that he had moved on to politics, at the cost of junior terrorism, sooner.

But my Y.M.C.A. dodgeball practice, with dive-and-rolls, and tumbling, which taught shoulder rolls, were paying off. In dodgeball.

Robert Chill was the Y.M.C.A. fix-it man, and one of the reasons why I was improving in sports. He sounded like a junkyard dog jangling through refuse when he walked, his tools, wires, hammers, clamps, and plumb lines jangling like uncoordinated pogo sticks. He wore long dirty hair. In the fifties, that was as cool as saying you sought sexual congress with ostriches.

We loved his tool bag as much as we did watching our boxing faculty give demonstrations of its storied, professional past.

Mr. Chill liked to offer himself as a dodgeball target, yelping and giggling as we tossed the ball his way. He was special to me, because he was worse in dodgeball than I. Even *I* could hit him.

"Kai," said he. "Athletics is just *trying*. All you gotta do is put out, and you can play *sports* anywhere." I didn't believe him. But of course, he was right.

"China," said Toussaint, "ya'll lookin less like a gimp in dodge. Got less spaz in ya."

"Rearn dodgeball an roun' ball at Y. Rearn swimmin."

Toussaint's eyes opened wide. No one in the 'hood knew how to swim.

"Dat's cool," he said, not meaning it.

"Rearn box, too, Toussaint," I said. I had kept it a secret from kids. It was the kind of disclosure that could only lead to more trouble. Someone would say, Oh yeah? So show yo' stuff, ratface! I must have thought that I was learning something, to have told him.

"Ya'll fought back 'gainst Tyrone Sykes cuz a da Y.M.C.A.? Not cuz *I* teaches ya'll how ta fist?!"

"Toos. Ya teach me good. Y help, too. Big man. Name, Misser Baza. Misser Baza rike Sippy, Toos. He be fighta," I said.

"China—ya mean a *pro*, wif *gloves*, an a *ring*?"

I nodded. I imagined Toussaint having Mr. Barraza and Mr. Lewis as his teachers. Toussaint could be another Rufus Monk. He had such courage—what Mr. Barraza called Heart. What the Y called Spirit. What I called Wishful Thinking.

Toos's wild punches, if coached, could flatten houses.

"Toussaint—ask Momma sen you Y, wif me!"

His eyes lit up with the thought. Then he said, "Nah, not fo' me. Don't dig fightin, jes' fo' fightin. Ain't cool." He didn't say: China, whatever the Y costs, whatever the bus costs, we don't have it.

J.T. Cooper came up to Toos.

"China Boy be bad luck, Toos," he said.

"Howzat," said Toos.

"No way our charms gonna work wif him," he said. "China Boy ain't black. Ain't fey, ain't white. He a voodoo ghost!"

"J.T., you'se a crazy dude wif dat charm an voodoo."

J.T.'s mother was an unlicensed necromancer. She had left Stamina Jones's Holy Christian Church of Almighty God, our only congregation, to rattle stones, shuffle chicken feathers, and speak to roaches on the kitchen floor. Reverend Jones had asked Mrs. Cooper to return to the flock, to no avail.

She had done the necromancy with a modicum of debonair detachment until the Army called out her husband for the second time. He had served already in World War II.

His departure for Oakland Army Base was preceded by wild parties and loud music, which I remembered watching, and hearing, from our window before Edna came into our home.

"Lucian, he went to Ko-rea. But his spirit? It here, in my kitchen."

She began to cast horoscopes for her friends. Initially, her predictions were so wildly entertaining that many of the women who scoffed at her rejection of Jesus for the love of poultry bones cast aside their disbelief and hiked up her stairs.

"My momma know *everythin*," said J.T. "Ain't *nut'in* da womanfolk on dis block don tell her."

Mrs. Cooper missed her husband and told others that he was sending her messages through the radio and through the copper plumbing in the upstairs apartment bathroom. My mother would have liked her a lot. A delegation led by Mrs. Timms and backed up by Mrs. LaRue went to the Cooper house, straggling up the steep wooden, slivered stairs, to petition her to return to the church.

Mrs. Cooper, besides having the corner on the neighborhood gossip, supported an outlandish sense of humor and possessed the superior alto in the choir. In her absence, the less qualified voices in the congregation were obtaining entirely too much purchase, and her laughter was missed on bingo night.

The delegation left looking somber, with a great shaking of heads. Mrs. Cooper would not kill any of the cockroaches that infested her house. I understood that completely; Mrs. Cooper's karma was *excellent*.

"Oughta fix these here stairs," said Mrs. Timms.

One day the whole neighborhood came out when J.T.'s mother flew screaming from their door in her nightclothes. She stood at the top of the stoop and bent from the waist, her hands between her knees, gathering her nightie.

"My husban's bin kilt in Ko-rea!" she wailed in a voice broken with wild grief. "Da roaches tole me dat!"

But the Army people didn't come to pay a visit, and she got no star on her window. Her status as a prophet went the way of the 1929 stock market.

Her coin was down, and J.T. stopped calling me a ghost.

"Cool, Toos, cool. China Boy ain't no ghost. But, he still be the China Boy, and it be the same fucken thing! He ain't got no color in 'em, wif all dat voodoo in dere."

"J.T., sometimes yo mouf gimme a headache in mah neck!" said Toussaint.

"China. Someday ya'll gotta start talkin like me. Save some skin on da hans. And yo' face. Now, China, lissen. Say dis, 'I ain't fo' yo' pushin on, no mo'!' Go 'head—say it!"

"Uh. I no, uh, I ain't fo' no push me, uh—pushin, uh, on you? Me?" I tried.

"Lordy. Momma save us bof," said Toos.

17

MR. PUNSALONG

Mr. Barraza continued to provide individual lessons, carrying out Mr. Miller's commitment to my father. After Labor Day, however, he brought in Mr. Punsalong to help.

Bruce Punsalong was the Mystery Man. A goulash of Filipino, Japanese, Chinese, and French, or "Pilipino, Nihon, Jungworen, and Français," as he would say. "Haay, Ting. You say, Pilipino: No 'F' in the Pilippines," he said. He said little and moved furtively. His body carried the aura of the Bogeyman, for his massive torso seemed to transport itself on dainty feet. He gave us the willies. He was built like a black widow spider, his chest and shoulders so large that it diminished his limbs.

We would wonder where he was and discover him behind us.

His face was smooth as a bowling ball, the skin tight and bright, masking hard inner muscle. He had a very small mouth and fine little nose, with large, liquid, darting eyes and thin eyebrows. He looked like a man with a glass tumbler to his ear, intently listening to conversations on the other side of the wall. He seemed more alert than a cat after a sparrow. He was, Rufus Monk often said, a man with no back, only fronts. There was no sneaking up on this man. I would walk into the lobby of the Boys' Department, grinning at the other kids, and feel my heart stop when I saw Mr. Punsalong sitting like a mannequin at Mr. McCoo's desk, watching.

He was far from sinister, for he was as caring a man as I have known. But his wariness, his incessant powers of observation and vigilance, set him apart from others.

Pinoy Punsalong was far better in judo and karate than Western boxing. He would highkick and spinkick the body bag, and when we thought it would snap from its chains he jumpkicked it and we said, "Oooohhh!" as the bag shook and strained at its steel lanyards. The boards in the low ceiling would groan like lost souls shackled to the oars of ancient galleys.

"You want win?" he asked. "Learn *defense*. No one else here know that. *I* know that. Boxing. It *entertainment*! Not fighting."

As a Manila *barrio* streetfighter, he had drawn more blood than Dracula in a year of Halloween nights. But his first two skills paid squat, while the Y revered the ring like the Holy Mother.

Kids getting out of Intro thought they were hot, anxious to get the first Kilroy, or punching knockdown. They hungered for the first knockout. They wanted to free themselves of Tony's heavy hand and waste another kid. They were ready to give up listening.

More patient than the sea, Mr. Punsalong polished the basics, using unending effort. He taught speed and quickness, using hand and feet drills.

"Put hand on top mine," he said, his palms uplifted. After we rested our hands facedown on his, he flipped his hand over and slapped the tops of ours.

"Owwww!" we cried.

"Move hand, faster," he suggested.

In Intro, pupils punched *away* from blood injuries. In Intermediate, students were allowed to exploit cuts, and got hurt for the first time. Mr. P had a doctorate in the administration of pain, and could tend the injuries as well. His swift hands would probe here, touch there, wiping away blood and laying the Vaseline, the curative greases, on cuts the way carney magicians produce dimes from your ear.

He provided more than technical learning. He worked on our resolution. He used his expressive eyes to teach us.

"Resolution," he said. "That all you need."

"Say it," he said.

"Lezalushen. Uh. All you need," I said.

His barrel chest glided into shoulders and neck without hard breaks. He had smooth arms, which I originally mistook for being without muscle.

He detested weightlifting.

"Weights slow you down, take snap outa arm," he said. "Build big muscle, here," pointing to his bicep, "make arm short, fat. Slow. Then you, musclebound. Then, you lose," he added.

He treasured ring speed, arm speed, foot speed. He thought that Mr. Miller's romantic notions of boxing, and Mr. Barraza's love affair with the Duke and his fixation on weightlifting were claptrap.

"What's boxing, Ting?" he asked brusquely.

"Rive wif Duke rules—"

"Naaa, naaa. Not it, kid. Boxing is *hurt other guy.* Got it?"

He was the most dangerous man of the three.

As one of life's former victims, Mr. Punsalong saw me as a kid on the edge of bad promise.

When I listened to him speak, and saw his relative similarity to me, I thought I was hearing the voice I would have as an adult. He sounded like an Asian Peter Lorre, all foreign notes in a whispering, slightly nasal, and clearly menacing voice.

His wet eyes darted, shuttered, flexed, moving in ways that even my mother's fluent pupils had not learned. They drew our attention, the tension within him causing me anxiety.

Mr. P doubted I would live to adulthood.

"Ting got sickness. Bad heart. Somethin not right in him, inside him, deep down," he told Tony.

"Master Ting looks bad, Pinoy, cuz he gets fed like a friggin canary," said Mr. Barraza.

"Naa-uh. He got somethin bad in him. Somethin sour, not right. He should be in TB ward. In Shriner Children Hospital. Something. Something inside, or he be better. He a *very* crummy student, very crummy boxer. Like he dead already."

"Fer God's sake, Bruce. Knock that shit off. Ya gimme the creeps."

Bruce's life was filled with unknowns, his secrecy and his stealth representing a way of life more than just a manner of movement.

In St. Bonifas Church, the Tenderloin chapel, Bruce met people who resembled the men who managed the hookers in the Savoy Victory Hotel—the men who toiled on pavement after all the cheap neon signs switched off. These men in dark suits gave Mr. Punsalong money— probably the only cash the church saw. I thought he was a bootlegger or a gunrunner to Mexico, and that he honed his martial arts as part of his second, secret career. A career that called for the ability to kill.

Something made him live with fear, with paranoia, and he hated to see it in others. It was a reminder of his own mortality, of the hazards of living beyond the fast lane, of subsisting on adrenaline. He saw in me the inadequacies of survival skills, the promise of early death by inept- ness in the world of struggle he had come to know too well.

"Ting. Why so clumsy? I tell: you *afraid*. Waitin for hurt, for fist. Mr. Barraza don unnerstan. He so much heart, don see it gone in you. *I* see it, loud n' clear.

"He think bruises show you can take punch. Oh, no. They show dog kicks, from you lyin in gutter, like possum taking bites, waiting for hungry animal go away. You kid, never saw a wet paper bag you liked. You get that?"

I didn't get it.

"You inside wet paper bag, right?" he said, his wisping, sandpaper voice louder. "An try to fight your way out an lose. Now you get it?"

I shook my head, worried.

"Okay, kid," he sighed. "Not funny. Man, you groun chuck, all the way. See, kids come Y, got inner fire, to win. You don. You got no fire. No matches in your pocket, even, heh?" His eyebrows went up.

"You jus don wanna get hurt. That invite bad times, and you get hurt wors'n *anyone*. And that, *that's* stoopid. Get hurt again, again, some people, they dead. Damnit, kid—you wanna be *dead*? You wanna *DIE*?" he bellowed at me, his face filling my world.

I had stopped breathing. When Edna yelled like this I got hit. If Mr. Punsalong hit me with all that emotion, I was *definitely* going to die *and* be dead. I waited for the blow, like a veal calf in a box.

"When my turn, you gonna *take* punch. Hit back. I don care you *clumsy*. You hit back. I don care you cry *and* piss your pants. You know, 'stick n' move.' Okay. You better *stick*. I don care if you don move. I better *feel* your glove, Ting. You *no* hit me, I gonna *whale* you. Hit me good, don hol' back, I pass on my counterpunch."

Pass on his counterpunch? He wasn't going to slap me around with his hands until I was a big bruise. He—the teacher—was going to punch me out with gloves in the *ring*. I couldn't figure out which was worse.

"I *know* I your nightmare. Not sorry, no sir! *You* beat nightmare outa 'self. You fear *me* mor'n you worry 'bout other boy." He didn't have to worry about that.

Mr. Punsalong taught me to let pain pass through me. I was never good at it, but I got the idea.

"When *punch*, don hol' back. Put hip into it and *give* it to 'em.

"You *get* punched, Ting, don hol' *on*. Let it go t'ru you, and away, like oyster down throat."

"Yuk!" I said. His eyebrows came down and it seemed the lights dimmed.

So I boxed Mr. Punsalong. It was like entering the ring with Godzilla. When I threw a half-hearted punch in his general direction, he knocked me down. Firmly, clearly, quickly.

"Get up, Ting," he said. "Now *punch*."

I tried, meekly, and was reflattened.

"Don be afraid, hit grown-up," he said. "You be afraid *not* hit me, got it?"

I closed my eyes against my karma, closed the distance, and threw a wild haymaker at him, at his hazing, at his insane urging to strike—to hit an elder.

"Yaass!" he cried, letting the glove whop him on his jaw.

I opened my eyes to see him beaming at me, so proud, so happy.

"Do again," he said.

18

MR. LEWIS

Mr. Lewis was the president and elder statesman of the Pug Council. He was Bossman, Head Honcho, and M.I.C., the Man in Charge. He wasn't necessarily the best fighter—that was Mr. Punsalong's credit. He was the best boxer.

"Misser Lewis bes' fighta?" I asked, much later in my fight career.

"Mr. Lewis," said Tony Barraza, "wuz the only fighter ever got outa the ring with more brains 'n when he went in."

Barney Lewis told us that boxing depended on brains first and combinations second. Physical talents were third.

We always got fired up when Mr. Lewis dressed for a lesson, trading in the starched whites for his gold silk trunks. He was finely muscled, ridges of gristle and sinew accentuating his arms, chest, and back, his abdominals looking like closely packed speed bumps.

We would stop breathing as Barney glided sibilantly forward, his black hightops stroking the hard canvas mat, his unnaturally low-slung left shoulder down, his muscled arms looking both tight and loose, shoulders fluid like Jayne Mansfield's hips, approaching the bag as a big cat closes on dinner. The concentration in his face was as foreboding as the bulging, coiled muscles in his body.

His well-defined form suddenly became a blur as he laid a blinding combination on the bag when we least expected it. He circled, punched, stopped, faked-left, right, combination punch, motor up, shoulder fake, combination punch, and reverse. That was the first time I realized what a boxer could do.

You can't touch him because you don't know where he is. You go crazy with the frustration and throw a bad punch and take his counter in your mouth or solar plexus. He circles you until you are dizzy, making you dance like an inebriated puppet at the end of a busted string and then knocks you out with a cyclone of punches designed to reverse the growth process.

Later, no one could agree on the number of shots, the sequence, or their identity. He controlled the huge body bag as if it were a speed bag. It danced as if charged with explosives and detonated.

When he backed away from the bag, he kept his eyes on it, as though it was a person he respected and maybe sent Christmas cards to every year. The gym echoed with his blows, now part of the history of dramatic sound that this high-ceilinged chamber had produced. He smiled as if all he had done was make a phone call.

"Top of the Morning, young gentlemen," he announced in his deep, crisp radio announcer's voice. "What you observed me demonstrate for you is a *planned attack*. It was thought out. It was *not* street jive. It was not a loose rapadiddle rhythm that is going to come out because you are cool and your daddy's cool and he killed a lot of Germans in the war. Attacking a bag or a boxer—that's *thinking*. It's *science*. What you saw was an attack flurry combination up, and then the same combination, reversed, down. If you have the gift, the natural, God-given ability to box for Golden Gloves, it will come from *thinking*." He was tapping his temple with his red bag glove.

"Thinking lets you win, in *everything*. My man, the bag, was hit in each target location twice. I set him up, I faked him, I made him think when he should have been punching, made him punch when he should have been moving." We looked at the bag and believed it. The bag had been faked out.

Mr. Lewis spoke like a movie actor. He was like a black Gregory

Peck—or Peck was like an Anglo Barney Lewis; both had deep, rich, brown voices, with meticulous articulation.

"When you speak clearly, Master Ting," he said once, "everyone listens more carefully. It means that you have an important message. Now I know that you need to learn how to fight. We're focusing on that. But when you get through your crisis, I will not accept your slurred speech anymore. It means, young man, that you will have to move your lips. You speak as if you are trying to hide your teeth."

Now he said, to the class, "If you are a simple palooka, just out there swinging, looking to feel good and lay down some bad leather, *you are out of there.* You do not belong in *my* ring.

"Now, gentlemen, plan your combos and box with your *brains.* Fail me with your combinations and I will know you're boxing with your gonads, and not your smarts."

I began to learn combinations. As the World Series progressed toward an inevitable Yankees hammering and Halloween approached, Mr. Barraza rubbed his ear and sat down next to Mr. Lewis on the folding chairs pulled from the office. The Intro class was pounding away on itself.

"Barney, I need two years easy 'fore Ting's body builds up. His bones, they're like sticks. Don't think I can pile on more meat on top. He's gained ten pounds, but his bones, 'at takes time. Never worked with a kid this small. Angelina says he ain't eatin much as he was. He still eats like a pig, but the edge is off. We got all the fast gain outa him we can hope fer.

"Wanta have him street smart, we gotta move him ta First Contact, have him chew the wax. Want 'em ta stand on his street by Christmas. Be the best friggin present we could give 'em."

Mr. Lewis looked at me. First Contact it is.

I was given the red wax plug, which I chewed and softened. Then Mr. Lewis molded it to my teeth, to keep the ivories from coming out. I had to open my mouth wide, looking at the red, wax-stained towel on his shoulder while his fingers worked on my teeth.

He looked very somber, his eyebrows in a shallow frown. Mr. Barraza was all smiles. I couldn't see Mr. Punsalong, which was normal. I missed having Toussaint by my side.

19

RING

I had already taken blows in limited left-jab and right-cross regimens with other kids. I had traded sequenced punches with the tall, the strong, the quick, the canny, the long-reachers, the gut-diggers, the vicious, and the meek. I could circle left and throw a punch at the same time while another kid was doing the same thing to me. I compared it favorably to learning how to chop off someone's head while he is returning the favor.

The next Saturday, after watching many bouts, I was in the ring. But this time, not to shadow-box, to merely practice circling and throwing punches inside the roped enclosure.

I was facing Connie Dureaux, my partner. He was a white kid, almost as bad as I was because he had had polio, with long hospital stays. His parents wanted to build his manly character through the Sweet Science. He was more unfamiliar with Third World culture than I, and was built like me: skinny. But before polio, he could play sports, which put him a leg up.

His dad drove him to the Y and picked him up after lessons. Mr. Dureaux loved to read the trophies in the lobby and talked to Mr. McCoo in the office. He would remove his jacket, roll up his sleeves, and play Ping-Pong with the kids. He smiled a lot, and looked at Connie the way kids gaze at adults who give them bountiful attention.

When I looked at Connie in the ring I thought I saw his father behind him, and I felt as if I were facing two people. This is not going to be a fair fight, I thought. Of course, I thought that fighting Tweety Bird would have been equally unfair. To me.

Rufus Monk looks at the Timex stopwatch looped around his neck with the black cord. He raises the hammer and hits the flat brass bell. It is the coda of the executioner, the knell of bloody doom.

Uh-oh, I say.

I, the world master of comic books, stand petrified. A couple of the older kids shout, "C'mon, Lame Boy!" and "Go get 'em, Blind Boy!"

"At ease!" Mr. Barraza breaks the sound barrier with an ear-smashing military bellow and the kids freeze, like me. We look like museum pieces, the echoes of his shout pinging off the ceiling and the windows.

" 'At's bush league, men," he said thickly, his head down, ashamed that any of the Duke's boys could be so low. A lot of young throats cough and clear nervously. My execution continues.

Connie moves to my corner and punches both gloves at the same time, the ring move of little children, delivering two bags of leather at the same time. Pattycake, Mr. B calls it. Connie hits hard enough to make my own covering glove bang into my mouth, and blood flows. It is the familiar metallic seasoning of defeat, melded in with wax.

"Belay that pattycake crap! Separate yur punches, *right now!*" shouts Mr. B.

I begin to wail and Connie looks worried and returns with little funny steps to his corner. But Mr. Barraza jumps all over him with the vigor of Edna on my sister. He tells Connie that the round is not over until the bell rings, and that when he sees blood he is to continue punching, but away from its source.

Connie is hitting me again, and I put my arms up just as I do on the street, covering my lowered head. I am now about as tall as a flattened cricket. The blows seem to have no ending.

"Sidestep. Hit the midsection, Master Dureaux," says Mister Barraza. "Master Ting is givin it to ya ona silver platter."

I look toward Mr. Barraza, the Turncoat, the Betrayer, the Thief of Boyhood Loyalty. I can't see him, because he's behind me and too far away, but I know the direction of his voice.

My gut takes a couple of hard punches before I cover my middle, and Mr. Barraza, who is nothing if not observant, directs Connie back to my head. I take the punches and my head hurts. My headgear twists so I cannot see. Obviously, this will now stop.

"Hit 'em in the midsection," says Mr. B, drily.

Connie hits me, and I can tell he is holding back. Mr. Barraza is yelling at him.

"*Never* hold back!" he screams, and the blows return. I think Connie is confused. I am not confused. I am definitely in a terror.

I hate gloves. They are so big, none of Connie's punches could possibly miss. If we were on the same continent, those gloves would find me.

While he yells and I cry, for what seems like half an hour, Connie's punches range over me and as I begin to run for the ropes the bell sounds, ending round one. It has been three minutes.

I collapse in the middle and Mr. Barraza escorts me back to my corner, resetting my gear.

"Ya stayed in the ring like a man. I like it," he says, full of enthusiasm, hitting me on my back, which hurts.

"Lissen. Master Dureaux jes threw all his punches. His gloves are pullin down his hands. Now it's *yur* turn!"

Ding! Roof hits the bell on the wood table again. It sounds like a fire alarm and enters my ears like a keening mosquito that I cannot reach.

I don't want to get up, glued to the little-kid, three-legged stool used for breaks. Connie's up, nearing center ring, conflicted.

"Getchur ass inna ring!" growls Mr. Barraza. I want his approval, not knowing what I would do if he stopped giving me his time. I stand and walk like an automaton.

"Gimme profile, guard up, head down," he says, and as I do he urges Connie to separate his punches, jab jab jab jab, cross. Connie has waited for me to get my guard up.

Mr. Barraza wants Connie to be a man and cares about his abilities, too, I realize.

I cry after each blow. I don't land a glove on Connie, who is nearly as afraid of my screaming as he is of Mr. Barraza's exhortations to close and lay leather.

The gym seems quiet, hushed by the unique sounds of weeping.

I screech when he hits me with a roundhouse and I lose my footing and fall into the padded corner post, into the ropes and through them. I am too small to be restrained, like a tiny bacteria flowing through a ten-micron screen. I bounce onto the soft mats that encircle the ring. Someone helps me back in. That was not the assistance I had been hoping for.

My cries make Connie back up, until he is shouted back by Mr. Barraza. When Connie finds Mr. B's voice to be more frightening than my screams, he uses the one-two on me in a steadily tiring routine until I hear Mr. B's voice telling me to clinch.

I throw my arms around Connie and hold him, and we stand there, two little guys spotted in my blood, gasping in the ring.

I love the sweet bell that ends the round, and hate its sour, dooms-day note when it signals the start.

I finish the three rounds. On my way to the wrong corner Mr. B says, "Didn't even hurt like a leech on yur unit. Didn't kill ya at all. Am I right?" he beams. He reminds us to shake hands, to touch gloves.

"Sorry, Kai," rasps Connie.

I shake my head as I shake his hand. I feel hurt and punished. These boxing students are as unimpressed with my spillage of blood as the kids on the block.

"Haay!" shouts Mr. B, vaulting over the ropes, entering the ring to grab me by my arms. I expect pain, but he merely moves me, like a broom, back to Connie.

"This boy, he's yur *mate.* He's yur *partner.* A fella troop a the Y.M.C.A., doin what yur doin." He turns to Connie.

"Don't *never* do *no* apologizin ta yur opponent fer boxin him. 'At's bush league. If ya *foul* him, ya apologize ta him, ta me, ta the Duke, ta God. An hope fer the best.

"But ya fought fair, no fouls. Got *nothin* ta apologize fer.

"You, Master Ting. Puchur glove out there and thank Master Dureaux fer his guts. When he touches yur glove, he's admirin ya fer *yur* guts."

I put my glove out. "Look at him," said Tony softly. I looked at Connie and said, "T'ank you." Connie said the same thing.

Connie's father, wearing a tie and sport coat, was waiting by the elevator, and his gaze made me uncomfortable.

I did not know then that he was pondering the indecipherable logic of uncaring nature, wondering why a kid as crippled, as ill-fated, as gimpy and lost as I would have such a healthy heart pounding magnificently in the middle of my flat, free-from-polio-chest. I knew. It was karma.

I had another bout on Monday, with Eugene Phillips, who at eight was tougher than a latrine rat. At eight and a half he fought like a junkyard dog. This was merely another opportunity to experience pain, but Mr. Barraza's attitude was clear: this is a fight I must do. I must now face a boy who is not in the least bit a friend, who will not hold back.

I got a bloody nose and began to truly hate the disgusting feel of a huge, stinking flattening glove smacking into my face and making my nose feel as though it had broken glass in it. Little pinpoints of light appeared while I tasted blood in my mouth and felt the bits of broken wax, knowing that more was coming. My blood dripped on the ring floor and turned instantly black, merging with the modern art collage of other stains.

Eugene reminded me distantly of the China Boy Bashers, of Willie Mack's confederates. He had a brooding anger that spelled pain for his opponents, the ring serving as a cathartic agent for the psychic doldrums that had closed upon him.

But I liked Eugene. He pounded me fairly, and did not hate me. He used me in the ring as people with other problems used Ex-Lax or aspirin. I was a curative for the pressures of his life.

I liked shaking hands at the end of the third round. It meant the fight was over. I also liked the Duke's Rules and the concept of a Tony Barraza ensuring that [a] there were no fouls and [b] the fight ended after three rounds.

"Eleven minutes, Master Ting," said Mr. Barraza. "All ya gotta do is stay alive fer *eleven* stinkin' minutes, an it's done like a Navy T-bone steak."

The Duke was God's Umpire, the scorekeeper in a striped shirt with a whistle around his neck who tallied up the points of each boxer's karma.

"Master Ting. When ya *jump* at the opening bell, fer all three rounds, ya get two days off 'fore yur next bout," said Mr. B, trying to work out the matrix of a skipped fight on his class fight card.

"Ya gotta unerstan yur not in there jes ta get ta the end. 'At's a big part of it, but the main course, the big samich, isa time 'tween the bells. Now. Lessee yur *try*."

I jumped at the bell. Pavlov, that foul master of fascist science, smiled from his study in purgatory.

I studied the bouts. I listened carefully to what Mr. Barraza said to each student, especially Connie, who was skitterish, like me. Most of the other kids had the hearts of great white sharks.

"Black, Spanish, better boxer," I said to Connie.

He shook his head. "Mr. Barraza, Mr. Punsalong, they aren't black or Latin. Joey Cohen, he's Jewish. Eric Kagiwada, he's Japanese, or somethin, and he could be tops, the best in Intro. And we're getting better, cuz everyone we fight's better'n us."

I nodded my head at Connie, knowing I had heard wisdom, not yet ready to learn it.

Joey Cohen was a kid who took absolute pleasure in swearing and in proving his toughness to himself. He seemed to care little about what others, beyond his parents, thought of him. He was Jewish and seemed, in some inexplicable way, to share a social ranking reminiscent of mine.

I liked Master Kagiwada, and Master Kodama, too. They looked like me, except they had been eating longer than I had, and apparently could see things not in my world. I saw them looking at me as I came shuddering through the ropes after being creamed and sensed their common, Asian shame for my lack of skill.

I remembered Uncle Shim's teachings about *pao chia*, collective guilt, the responsibility of family for the failures of any of its members.

"Sorry," I wheezed at them, and they nodded.

I found my voice, learning that I could shout and yell like other kids.

"Didja *see* that!" cries Mr. Barraza after he lets Rufus Monk flurry on him, his teeth and eyes bright like big Navy searchlights in the cavernous gym.

"Tell me what that demonstrates!" His Marine voice.

"*Boxer win, brawler lose!*" I cry with the others, my voice louder than theirs, gloves raised high, smiling in a great human chorus of physical joy.

20

UNCLE SHIM

Father was becoming increasingly American. He came home like the Army football team industriously tramping through the players' tunnel to play Notre Dame.

"I'm home!" he would shout in English, making all of us jump. I would run to the top of the staircase and smile as he charged up, his military cordovans pounding like bass drums. He would grin at me as he tossed his hat into his and Edna's bedroom, the first room to the right.

Uncle Shim arrived in our house like a tired memory, almost forgotten. I struggle now to fix his image, for his greatest presence occurred during the life of my mother, an era abounding with emotion but without many surviving monuments.

As Anthony Cemore Barraza, former Italianate heavyweight, began to assume a presence in my consciousness, I found myself thinking of

C. K. Shim, former Oriental scholar of the realm and wailer of Ming poetry.

In the days before Edna, I would hear the groan of the remote lock lever and the loud crack of our front door. The lever was a large magic iron handle that was at the left, by the top stair. If you pulled it with all your weight and might, it would make the front door—eighteen steps and one hard left turn down—open. It was, to my mother, the work of a small and minor, but appreciated, house god.

I can still hear Uncle Shim's soft footfalls and smell the chemistry of the mothballs and camphor that guarded his clothes. "Good evening, Learned Lady," he would say in his soft, hesitant voice, slightly inclining his head to my mother, making crumpling sounds with the paper sack in his arms. "I find you round, full, and lucky."

I loved many things about my uncle. He was gentle in manner, soft in voice, his kindness providing ample room for a child to operate within, without fear. He was like a tall and forgiving toy that never hurt, but expected full play and consideration.

He was invited into our household by my father the way Yip Syensheng had been solicited by my mother to provide escort out of Shanghai—by force of inarticulated expectation, by the power of suggestion, without direct words.

Shim Dababa was a "Chinese uncle"—a relative by virtue of proximity, and not of blood. Chinese uncles are as prolific as penitents on Judgment Day, and are as beloved by children as any people on earth. Their role is to spoil children, to grant what parents could never condone, to show the soft and accommodating side of adulthood. Uncle Shim's blood relationship to our clan has been explained to me intermittently since my birth, and as none of the stories is consistent I merely acknowledge the claim, for it is immaterial.

But for me, Uncle Shim was much more special than a familial soft touch. He was the last word, the prototype and the paradigm, of all good uncles everywhere. His gifts were personal.

"*Hau bu hau, Haushusheng,* Able Student," he said to me, in Mandarin, inclining his silvery head even lower.

I was on my knees, my forehead touching the hardwood floor, in a *kuuh duuh* in Songhai, or a *kow tao*, showing reverence to the grandest scholar available to our family in America. China, like my mother, had grown in modern times to distrust men who accomplished things with muscles and swords; Uncle Shim and Mother both liked brains.

Uncle and my father had gone to the same college. I used to think that this school was West Point, but that was the school my father loved and had not attended. The school that Father and Uncle Shim had shared was St. John's University in the British Concession of Shanghai.

"My education," Uncle Shim once said, "was completed when I left my tutor. St. John's was a place to learn the English language and to understand how primitive Western thought is."

The Shim family knew the Tings, and despite that fact Father liked my uncle. Although they were years apart and could not agree on politics, Uncle Shim was often described as Father's Closest Friend. Now, they worked together at the China Lights Bank.

"I thought Na-men was Baba's number-one *pungyoh*, his best friend," I had said to Mother.

"When your father thinks of himself, Na-Men is in his heart. When he thinks of you, and your young mind, he places your Uncle Shim in that place. This will be true until you are old enough to go to West Point," she said. "Then, Na-men will be number one."

"Your father sends you greetings, Able Student," said Uncle Shim to me. "He appreciates your efforts in learning. I find you looking very round, very full, very lucky, and a strong credit to your family." This was his recital of flattering greetings. To appear round and full was to exhibit the characteristics of prosperity and the patent outcome of regular meals. Luck is what the gods, who rule, choose to share with mere mortals, struggling below. To be a credit to the family was the justification for birth. Uncle Shim shared these thoughts both as a courtesy to our family and as instruction to me.

To emphasize the value of scholarship upon a young mind, Dababa gave me a *hong fung tao*—a small, square, bright red paper envelope with gold piping. He used bribery to lure me into the world of thought. Inside was a coin. It was Kuomintang money until my father reminded Uncle Shim that KMT cash was worthless in America.

"Uncle Shim," said Father, "is brilliant. And scholarly. And incredibly intellectual. He is not, however, very smart."

It was customary for uncles to give cash to young relatives on New Year's and at festivals, but Uncle Shim gave me envelopes almost every time I bowed to him and my forehead touched the floor. I treasured it as if it were Captain Kidd's gold, and knew that he gave me Chinese cash in order to strengthen my relationship to the past.

Uncle Shim was an aesthete, an intellectual devotee of protocol,

an elder who had attained the station of *Chien shur*, of Imperial Presented Scholar, during the twilight of the Chinese Empire. He had bowed
before the Empress Dowager and the Boy Emperor P'u-yi, even as the
entire architecture of the Empire began its collapse from the weight of
inaction.

He was an academic who respected women, a scholar who appreciated music, and a man who had loved his father. Dababa came from
a civic culture that awarded high office and direct political power to
men of proven moral character and scholarly ways; in traditional China,
professors were the rulers. He was skeptical about spirits, distrusted *feng
shui*, geomantic forces, believed in self-made good fortune, and loved to
debate. He was a perfect tea partner for my mother, for they had the
entire world of intellect in which to disagree and argue.

They were seated in their customary places in the parlor. Mother
had directed Megan to clear the room of the clutter of papers and books,
and to put the house in order to advertise the anticipated arrival of
C. K. Shim, Imperial Scholar, top dresser, bringer of food and coins,
chanter of poetry, and Chinese uncle.

Mother only struggled with matches to light joss.

"Light candles, Second Daughter," said Mother. She sat on the
sofa. Uncle sat in our father's large chair. I was on the hassock. Megan
had left.

"So," said Uncle Shim. "It's good that the T'ang poets were so
clumsy. Had their romantic poetry been more balanced, scholars would
have had a choice between valid learning and seductive poetry."

I looked at Mother. She knew most of the answers.

"I like choices," she said. "No choices means no judgment, not
knowing reality. I think the T'ang poets were lovely." She did not speak
to him directly, looking out of the corner of her eye, her head ever so
slightly inclined, as she would to Tutor Tang, in her youth.

"Ah. But what good are choices in the real world?" he asked, in
the style of the teacher, the Before Born. "In the real world, truth
changes every day; 'reality' does not apply to the world, only to the
mind. Choices—do not the gods laugh at them, as delusions?" I rotated
my head back and forth between them, never knowing who was doing
better. They would do this for hours until my neck grew sore.

Uncle Shim's neck would never ache because he was careful not to
move in any dramatic way. He was a traditional Chinese intellectual.

He was nonathletic and thought perspiration to be a bitter physical trick played upon the temple of thought. He regarded Father as a Chinese Errol Flynn, dashing, gallant, physically courageous, and utterly lacking in judgment.

American cinema runs in my veins. If Father was the rogue Flynn, then Uncle Shim was David Niven with a sprig of Alec Guinness's melancholy, a pinch of Clifton Webb's forbidding intellect: spare, dapper, finely mustached, impeccably dressed, exuding the aromas of mothballs and English cologne, dry of wit and long in tolerance. The very timbre of his voice implied rightness and the authority of the mind. Mother had great strength to duel intellectually with him.

He was shorter than my father, about five feet, eight inches. His fingers were long and muscularly lean, and the callus created by a lifetime's mortal grip upon a hard bamboo brush pen ran the length of his right thumb, an honorable tattoo of learning.

He constantly rinsed his eyes with cold water. He wore delicate, square, metal-legged, unframed glasses, cleaning them in the sink in a mountain of suds.

"Able Student," he said. "Always wash the eyes. A man without eyes cannot read. A man who cannot read, cannot live." Most of his axioms were unconditional.

He used two large teak brushes to groom his silvery white hair to the back, in the manner once employed to prepare his queue. In all he did, he was as methodical as the lead chef at the Cordon Bleu. When student revolutionaries opposed to imperial rule had cut off their queues in radical protest to the throne and the rule of the Manchus, Uncle Shim kept his. He removed his queue when, during the revolution, keeping it could have meant death.

"When confronting force, use reason," he said.

One afternoon, he announced to my mother, "See here, how do you expect your son to become a *Chu-ren*, a Recommended Man for Metropolitan Rank, if you do not read him the *Sheng-Yu*, the Sacred Edict, or the Four Treasuries, on the first and fifteenth days of every month? How will he learn of *shiao*, filial piety, falseness, scholarly practice, cultivation of peace, and *pao chia*, collective guilt, if you do not teach him?"

He would say this with the pacing of "My Momma Done Tole Me" on a seventy-eight record. With the same expressions, curled, wig-

gling eyebrow, and gestures, the first two fingers of his right hand pointing. His voice would beseech, climbing two octaves. For Uncle Shim,
this was high physical vigor.

"It is the father's duty to transfer scholarship, C.K., not the mother's," she replied. Uncle Shim's most recent name was Cheng-kung, or
C.K. This was the name given to him by Amethyst Jade Cheng, whose
brother, now dead, had named my father.

"Oh ho. Of course. The boy's father only wants to teach him about
killing other humans and about the foreigner, Thomas Jefferson! And
you were given the benefits of learning! You had the influence of a
Hanlin scholar! I never did! So do not toss customs at me when you
reject the True Traditions!"

"C.K.," replied my mother. "The entire system of *Hsiu-ts'ai*, of
Flowering Talent, is gone. What if My Son were to study to become a
Chien-sher? Who would proctor the pen? What post would he assume,
when we cannot even go home?"

"The true post is moral," said Uncle Shim. "It is not connected
to a mere chair in an ivoried hall. Heaven recognizes merit and piety,
whatever the transient circumstances." He smiled, happy with his return. With remarkable American delicacy, Mother stuck her tongue out
at her sparring partner. This would have been unimaginable in China,
and she laughed wonderfully as Uncle Shim shuddered. Chinese people
do not show the insides of their bodies to anyone, much less scholars.
But Mother liked to win.

My sisters were now in attendance. Jennifer and Megan were becoming Americans, too. They did not want to kow tao, so they arrived
fashionably late and missed the welcoming ritual. Megan always lit the
candles. Sometimes Megan would bow, and sometimes she would not.
I, who knew the least of Chinese culture, was not given a choice.

My mother would frown gently, and I would bow deeply.

Uncle Shim taught me calligraphy, bringing me my first inexpensive
rabbit-hair pens, ink tablets and heavy, black glass ink pots, and soft,
floppy books filled with empty graph paper, on which to cast the characters of the Chinese tongue.

Uncle Shim's calligraphy was reportedly stupendous; the sound of
his bold, wet brush, the stark, startling sweeps of bright black art on
simple brown wrapping paper, the aura of hushed silence created by his
spiritual intensity during the movements.

"*Attack* the paper, Able Student!" he hissed. "Hold the pen high in the hand, like a Turkestan scimitar!"

He coached me through the memorization of the sixteen edicts of the *Sheng-Yu*.

"You are diligent, Able Student," he said. "But you speak with the tongue a drunk monkey would spit from its mouth without a moment's regret."

"Why I talk like monkey, Mah-mee?" I asked.

"Tsa! Tsa! You do not talk like a monkey! You have a wonderful, happy combination of the northern dialects! It makes you very special, My Only Son!"

I didn't like Uncle Shim calling me a monkey.

"Little One," said my uncle. "Listen, here. Do not make that face! It is so like your mother's when she is peeved! Of course, learning the Great Masters is hard. It is supposed to be!

"Your young mind. It should bleed! It should be exercised so hard, so incessantly, that it swells in effort and draws all your blood! It does not matter that you are a world away from other young scholars, so distant from the *Chingsu*, the Pen Forest! Study! Study! Then study more!

"If you are not studious, your father will blame me! And you are all the family he has left in the world!"

Mother would make Grand Imperial Canal, Seven Wonders, Heavenly Fragrance, Good Fortune tea for Uncle Shim. All those wonderful thoughts—a wide, man-made river, the Great Wall and the Colossus of Rhodes, Heaven, good smells, and good luck—inside a little tea cup.

Uncle Shim brought high-tea lunches, dim sum, for us. He served me first, out of respect to my *fuh-muu*, my parents, and then served my mother and my sisters. Megan would make faces, protesting my status, while I stuffed mine.

When Uncle Shim overserved my mother, loading her plate with wrapped shrimp, mashed taro, and black-bean dumplings, she would scold him by grasping and shaking his arms with a broad smile on her face. Uncle Shim was above worry, his steady fingers dexterously moving the *kuaitze*, the chopsticks, absorbing the quakings of his friend, his cheeks gently reddening, the thinnest hint of a smile trembling beneath his mouth behind the trim gray mustache.

"Dababa, *ching*, Uncle, please," said my *tsiatsia*, my older sisters.

"Quote the romantic poetry of Jo-lee, her poems of love!" Jo-lee of Yunnan was a woman who wrote under the name of a man in order to be published.

" 'His' poems, young ladies," said Uncle Shim.

"Learned Uncle," said Jennifer. "Jo-lee's only son became a model governor and painted her portrait for the *Chingsu*. This is America. We can admit she was a woman!"

"Ah, ha," said Uncle Shim, flatly.

Uncle Shim would dab his mouth with a silk handkerchief, adjusting his green jade bowtie. He wore an elegant gold watch from Switzerland. This request made him check the time. Then he would recite, in his softly sad, gently longing, Songhai voice,

> *"Darkening night without end*
> *I cannot sleep.*
> *The full moon—a lantern in my mind*
> *Far off*
> *I hear the voice of my dreams*
> *And hopelessly I answer*
> *'Yes' "*

"Pay attention, Kai, even to poetry," whispered Jennifer. As Firstborn, she was the official chief of staff. I had been looking for wisdom inside my closed eyelids.

"Why Madame Cheng bank need poetry?" I asked.

"Shhh!" said Jennifer, pinching me.

"What you do in bank, Uncle?" I later asked.

"Oh ho. Such a direct question!"

"So. What you do?"

"Ask your mother, Little One."

"*Muu.* What is Uncle's job at the bank?" I asked, later.

"I think he is there to set an example of moral rectitude, of respect, of old values," she said.

"How?"

"He reads. And does not steal."

"Why he no tell me?"

"Direct questions to elders?" she asked me. Learning, schoolwork okay. Personal things, not okay, said her eyes.

I asked, "Should not ask you about him?"

Oh no, was her nonverbal reply; this is how it should be done. I nodded, understanding.

Ask indirectly, through others closer in rank or in family relationship. No charging straight ahead. Not for personal matters.

When my father left San Francisco on business, Uncle Shim climbed the long staircase from our front door and appeared with a paper sack full of calligraphy materials, high-tea foods, his underwear, and his toiletries. His place in the home seemed natural.

"Why does Uncle Shim always appear when Father leaves?" asked Janie.

"To provide us company," said Mother.

"But he moves in. Like he was Father," said Janie. "Why?"

"We are *his* family," said Mother. "For Chinese, family is everything. Uncle shares with you his learning, which is why we, the Chinese, are on the earth. It is our national skill. His gift to us is as special as Tutor Tang's learning was for our family in Kiangsu. A place to brush his hair, to clean his teeth, with women's laughter and the sound of a young boy in the background, is very little payment for the wisdom of China," she said.

When Mother died, the special dim sum no longer appeared. It took me a while to realize that Uncle Shim no longer visited. I asked Father about him.

My father said, "Uncle Shim is very sad. He lost his family in the war, his parents in the revolution. Now, he has lost his best friend," he said.

"I thought *you* were his best friend," I said.

"No," he said. "Your mother was."

During one of our trips to the bank with the briefcase filled with cash, I asked Father if I could visit Uncle Shim.

"Uncle Shim leave bank when I bring you," he said. "To see your face, also see your mother's face. Make him very, very sad."

Father switched to Songhai, and I closed my eyes, trying to catch it.

"Seeing you would spark his grief and make it difficult for him to do his job."

"Why he no cry when see *your* face?"

"Your mother and I were of the same heart. Not the same blood," he said. "You look like your mother. You look like her very much."

My father cleared his throat. He rubbed his nose. I knew that he wanted his pipe, but he was driving.

"The Chinese have this system, called Face Relationships," he said. I sat on my legs, leaning against the carseat, scarcely breathing.

"It means dealing with people whose faces you know very well. Family. These are the *only* ones the Chinese trust. For marriage references, business, contracts, burials, loans. Saving Face is important to Chinese.

"It means not having to say no to someone you have Face with. It is a special, a very deep embarrassment, to deny a service to family, or to those treated as family.

"If Uncle Shim sees you, he will lose Face, for he should comfort you with stories and candy, carrying out his Confucian duty of setting an example. But all he can do is cry, and fail you.

"It is a *stupid* system!" he shouted, pounding a big fist on the dashboard and, for a moment, driving like Mother. I recoiled.

"It keeps China from being strong and organized! The Chinese *only* trust people under their own roofs. Meanwhile, everyone else in the world is making atomic bombs and big cars, while the Chinese light joss, cry about bad spirits and *foo chi*, piss about geomancy, and do business like the male organ of a bug! *Harrumph!*" he said, clearing his throat again.

My father was proud of China's past, but saw it as an unbearable liability in the modern world. He saw old customs and superstitions as invitations to rapine, catastrophe, misery. He hated misery, as only one who has confronted it can.

Father was in an untenable position, forked on the cultural chessboard where the white squares of intellectual China met the hard black industrial squares of the West. To succeed in his new world, he was becoming increasingly anti-Chinese.

It had not helped to have lost his first wife, his army, his profession, and his sense of economic self-sufficiency during this transition between cultures.

"You must *decide*," he said. "Very smart men, just before the Empress Dowager died, tried self-strengthening, *tsu chiang*. 'Chinese Essence, Western Means,' they said, trying to be Chinese *and* European at the same time. They failed.

"So. Pick *one*. Be American. Or Chinese. And never change your mind," he added.

"Na-men Schwatz'd taught me that. It is what West Point had taught him. When you have to make a decision, *make it*! Because doing nothing is worse than making the wrong choice. Then, after making your decision, don't look back. Combat. Battle. They allow no regrets, only the guts to make another decision." He looked at me, wondering if I understood.

"It took courage to come to America. Courage to stay here, when I could have joined the American Army as interpreter, even as private of infantry, for Korean War! Ayy! Even courage to have a mixed marriage!"

I nodded my head. I understood.

"I pick Y.M.C.A.," I said to myself.

When Mother was alive, I had kept Uncle Shim's calligraphy books and my pen and ink pot on a compartmentalized shelf in the back of the redwood chest, that great, heroic repository that had traveled the world like a sea-tossed message bottle. The chest that was now ash, gray, cold windblown memory, an offering to progress, to assimilation.

In the attic that was now Janie's room, I looked at the spot where the crate had sat, so stolidly, so patiently, for all the years of my young life.

The strained and fogged light of the city filtered through the small twin windows of the attic, where God brought his light, where Janie and I had daydreamed of Mother, thinking of her in Tsingtao. When Janie had known that Mah-mee was dead.

I missed my books, and I stretched my fingers in the preparatory exercise Uncle Shim had taught me prior to using the pen. Like Tony Barraza, my uncle believed in warming up prior to work.

I performed kow tao to the empty spot on the attic floor. Oh, Dababa, I miss you. I miss your arguments with my mother.

"Jane. You miss Uncle Shim?"

"Uncle Shim. Ahhh," she said, shaking her head. "He's from Mah-mee's time. It's been—a year? More . . . I wonder how he is."

"But you miss Uncle Shim?"

"Well. Not really. He only came to visit Mommy, and you. He paid very little attention to me. I miss the dim sum, the *bargow*, the *wooguk*, the *suimy*."

"He talk to Jennifer. And Megan," I offered.

"That's what I mean," she said.

I handed her a piece of lined school paper and a pencil.

"You write retter to Uncle Shim? For me?"

She shook her head at me, a wry smile lightening her face.

"Boys," she said.

"Connie, I need favor," I said while we were jogging around the upper running gallery of the main gym.

I was a good runner. Outside of crafts, it was what I did best in the world. I could run forever. My legs had learned early that they served a crucial purpose. My psyche had never doubted the necessity of my legs.

"Sure." Pant, pant. "What is it?"

"Want to go bank, Chinatown bank. Fliday, for me," I said.

"Bank? How come?"

"Take retter to uncle," I said.

I waited at the corner of Jackson and Powell, three blocks below the China Lights Bank, by the Flowering Nation Grocery Store. I was leaning for concealment against a light pole, my cotton jacket crumpling the paper messages taped to its base. My mouth was dry, my heart pounding. I could not see Connie or the bank, but I knew that my *nabgwanging pungyob* was looking in his strangely confident way for a silver-haired elder with square spectacles, a gray mustache, and the name of C.K. Shim.

Large shoes connected to tall adults swarmed around me and the pole. I heard Connie, knowing his footsteps.

"Got him," he said.

"Wow! No lie?" I asked. Pause. "Lie! I say, lie!"

"No lie, guy. Mr. Shim's pretty important. Has a real big office. Gave me tea! Yuk! That stuff is *awful.*"

We stood there. I whispered the word "lie" triumphantly.

"What now?" Connie asked.

"Go back Y. I stay. Misser Balaza know I be late." I could hear my blood pounding.

I smelled camphor and looked up into the bright, sun-reflecting glasses of my uncle. Oh, Dababa.

I performed kow tao on the sidewalk, taking deep comfort from my respect, literally kissing the ground upon which he stood.

"Hausbeng," he said in a voice that sounded so small and strained within the bustling, negotiating clatter of Chinatown. He sounded old.

"I am very happy to see you. I find you looking very round, very full, very lucky, and a strong credit to your family." He hesitated. "You look, quite *Meigworen*," American. His eyebrows wiggled, and he coughed gently a number of times.

"What," he said, "is the sixteenth edict of the *Sheng-Yu?*"

In stumbling Songhai, I said, "Resolve, uh, animosities to give people, uh, life, uh—full respect."

"So, why, Able Student, do you have bruises on your face, and on your hands?"

"I learn war. Uh, *wu-shu*. Fighting, Uncle Shim," I said.

"What," he said, "is the sixteenth edict of the *Sheng-Yu?*" There was no irony in his voice, no reprimand. Only patience.

"Resolve animosities to give life full respect," I said. "Uncle, no can fix animosities—"

He repeated his question.

I answered by rote, again.

"Able Student. There is great weeping in the *Chingsu*, the Forest of Pens today. To see me secretly, behind your father's back, violates the *wu fu*, the Five Forms of Piety. Master K'ung would be so unhappy with you! But, this happens within your mourning period for your mother, and I forgive you that. You need family now, and there is little left.

"But to fight in this new land is miserably stupid." He looked away, over my head, to the left.

"When you confront force, use reason," he said, very slowly.

I nodded. That made perfect sense. I had tried to resolve animosities. I had given away my blood and clothes. I tried to respect life; I did not kill insects and I spoke to dogs.

"I cannot see you here, on the street, Able Student," he said. "When will you be in Chinatown again?"

"I go Central, Downtown Y.M.C.A. Monday, Wednesday, Friday, Saturday," I said.

He stood immobile, and I wondered if I had said something to offend him. He looked at his Swiss watch.

"Every week?" he asked. I nodded, Yes, Uncle.

He looked down at me, his face empty, his eyes liquidly bright. I stared intently back at him, trying desperately to squeeze his image into my memory, to hold on to the smell of the mothballs, the straining timbre of his familiar voice, the magically sharp melodic bells of his wonderfully scholastic Songhai.

"I will meet you at the hour of high tea, at the Y.M.C.A., two Saturdays from now."

"Dababa, you know where Y.M.C.A?"

He laughed. "The Y tried to create labor reform in China, when Shanghai workers were exploited. Do you know what I mean?"

I nodded, then shook my head.

"I no go Songhai. Go to Y, Dababa."

"Bring your calligraphy," he added.

I started to perform kow tao and he stopped me. I told him that I no longer had my pen and ink pot, or the writing tablets.

"Seventeenth Edict, Able Student: never lose your pen!" he said.

"What must you do before meeting me again?" he asked.

"Get pen," I said.

He shook his head, very solemnly.

"Ink bottle?" I asked. Again, no.

Not the ink? Then I got it.

"I tell Father. Ask Father for permission," I said. "I have a, uh, a new, uh, Mah-mee," I added.

He nodded. Of course, he knew. He had spoken to Edna on the telephone.

"Now, how will you remember to meet me?"

"No can forget, Uncle Shim. I never forget."

Uncle Shim smiled tightly, nodding, his scholar's eyes closed.

21

FOOD

"Master Ting. When ya counter-
punch, when ya land a glove, I'm haulin ya to my place an makin youse
a special lunch." Mr. Barraza knows that I love food more than I hate
pain.

A special lunch. Oyster beef over rice with black mushrooms and
wood ears; mu shu pork in wafer-thin wrappers; curried crab with
prawns; *mubr-deb; job diao* long-bean, and water chestnut duvu; Peking
duck with plum sauce. Noodles. And more noodles.

After five or six bouts, in which I resembled Jerry Lewis scrim-
maging the Green Bay Packers, I parried. Then counterpunched. I took
blows to the face, my headgear awry. I froze and stopped breathing.

"Breathe! Don't never stop breathin!" shouted Mr. Barraza.

I breathed. I landed a sharp left jab into the face of another equally
determined kid and was so delighted I grinned like Dopey, dropping my
guard and taking blows all over me, from the Cape of Good Hope to

Thule, Greenland. I felt this kid's anger from being hit by Master Ting, the Blind Boy.

That angered me and I attacked wildly, my huge gloves flailing air.

Mr. Barraza's shouts cut through the earholes in my headgear and I heard him exhorting my aggression, funneling it into the practiced moves of the ring.

Go left, he said, and I did. Guard up, close, and jab, he said. Smile through that blood, he said, and I did. I began to become a child's extension of his experience.

Tony and Mrs. Barraza and Tony Junior used to live on Prado Lane, one of the ritziest streets in the City's pricey Marina District. Prado is near the expansive teak-paneled St. Francis Yacht Club, in the center of the sunbelt, and Tony could do his patented L-bar pullups, his legs held straight out, parallel to the floor, on his chinning bar on the roof, with a perfect view of the Golden Gate Bridge. He could shop at Antonello's on Chestnut while Mrs. Barraza sang Puccini and cleaned the seafood donated by his fans at the wharf. Their meals, he later told me, were fit for emperors.

Now he lived in the Y.M.C.A. Hotel. The man who could once hookpunch for a shot at the heavyweight title of the world, who could cook like the chief chef at Tarantino's, now lived on uncooked and unheated spaghetti and meatballs from the can.

After the bout in which I intimated signs of life, I came through the ropes, smiling. I looked at Mr. Barraza. He was smiling. My stunted, shortsighted world froze as an aura of warmth shimmered through the gym. Boyhood pledges and rites of passage, boy pages learning skills of survival from men of iron. I looked at the other kids, but they weren't noticing. At the end of bouts kids would reenact the good punches, the hard blows, undergoing an emotional and technical debriefing, imprinting the lessons in their own minds and hands. All I saw was the magic of Tony's great gleaming false teeth. He was like Burt Lancaster.

The Junior Leaders had taken the Intro class to see a matinee of the movie *Vera Cruz*, with Burt and Gary Cooper. Out of deference to me, and for the eventual eradication of our corneas, we sat in the absolute front row. It was there I learned why people went to the movies. It made actors look even larger than bigger-than-life.

Cooper had lead billing, but Lancaster stole the show as quickly as a Slicky Boy cops a watch from an idle wrist. Burt Lancaster played bad Joe Erron. He wore a black shirt, black vest, black leather wristbands and was spectacularly athletic. All the kids cheered for Lancaster—not for his values, because he was selfish, slovenly, venal, and cruel—but for his sporting competence, agility, and power. He could shoot people with *his* back turned to them. He could do pullups with the ease of chewing gum. His muscular carriage was menacing, like Tío Hector's walk when he was angry, the way Mr. Lewis approached the bag, like Tony Barraza striding with his great, focused sense of purpose.

I loved Lancaster for his charm; Burt used a smile that made flashbulbs obsolete. He moved down the streets of Vera Cruz like a champ. Then he smiled. "Smiley! Yeah! Dat Smiley!" we cried, offending the grown-ups until the usher with his dreaded flashlight came down the aisle. I knew why I had always liked this actor.

"Dat's Smiley—he smile like Mr. B!" exclaimed Eugene Phillips, and we nodded. Burt Lancaster must have learned the smile, and his athleticism, from Tony.

I would stand in front of the cracked and fading mirror in the boys' locker room and flash my wistful Burt Lancaster smile, rumbling in a wild cacophony of half-forgotten Shanghai and imitation Texas drawl about the wonder of my teeth.

"Goddamn, Kai!" cried Norman. "Knock dat shit off! Make me think ya'lls chokin ona banana!"

Now I was with my own, personal, version of Burt Lancaster, talking about food—the special lunch—the purse for my great courage in the ring. Mr. B and I left the Y through the boys' department. He stopped on the top stair and with a critical eye surveyed the neighborhood. So did I. We were both looking for boys. Tony Junior and I were the same age, and I knew what he looked like when he was two. Which meant I had no clue as to his present appearance. I just looked for a short, clean-shaven Mr. Barraza.

We walked north to Turk Street, past bars that stank of dying stomachs and dead livers, past men who made the winos of my block look noble. Too early for the hookers, too late for the needle artists and just right for the Tokay crowd, the streets looked half-empty, or half-full, depending on one's tastes. It was sunny and bright, and we both had light feet.

I looked as we walked, which was silly, since I saw little. He gestured. He was a man who did not have to worry about people who lurked in alleyways. We looked like Superman escorting Howdy Doody, and I bathed in the light of his company.

Mr. B was talkative, expressive about the fight, the scars on his face mottling as he spoke and moved his huge hands.

"Master Ting. 'At was gen-you-wine hot shit! I loved it! Ya know, youse can be a good fighter. Really, I mean it. A good fighter. Ya got a sweet left. Ya got anger. I seen it in there. Ya fight good usin yur anger. It's better'n fightin fer a meal, specially after Angie's been curin yur gut."

He stopped, and looked at me.

"Whatya pissed off about. Uh, angry at?" he asked.

I shook my head.

"Yur pop beatcha?" he asked. I shook my head. He began walking again. Then he stopped.

"What's yur first name, Master Ting?"

"China Boy," I said.

"*China Boy? China* Boy? Jeezus. Well, 'at explains it. 'At's a pretty shitty name, ya ask me." We stood there for a moment while he looked down at me, as if he were looking for another answer to the one I had offered.

"It my name, sir," I said.

Me, a good fighter. I smiled with the silliness of the thought. Good painter, maybe. Good runner, good reader, you bet.

I was surprised that the pedestrians did not recognize Tony Barraza. Inside the Y, he was a celebrity. On the street, amid the detritus of modern times, he was unknown. But people paid attention to his size, his obvious muscularity. He seemed indifferent to both conditions.

We turned into the lobby of the Y.M.C.A. Hotel, and I thought I had blinked too hard or had missed the correct door. I had expected something like the Central Y, with high ceilings, impressive stone pillars, and marbled stairs. This seemed unrelated. Or forgotten. It looked like a place where the elephants came to die. It was large and unlit, old spittoons and mounds of newspaper left as memorials of lost health and accumulating obituaries. The lobby seats resembled our body bag and were filled by small men who did not move. I smelled stale smoke, new wine, old mildew, fresh stomach contents, Clorox, and Pine Sol. It smelled like the Panhandle, halfway across the city to the west.

He was talking about focusing, about aiming for specific targets on the opponent's body. When we exited the old elevator and stepped into the hallway, he grew silent. It was dark and dingy. To me it appeared normal. We entered his room and a strange brown squat dog came out of nowhere and jumped all over him, panting, its tongue out. I only had seen two dogs up close—Evil and the junk dog on McAllister, and I backed down the hall, also panting, my heart in my throat.

"Semper, geddown! Ya crazy mutt! Hey, say hello ta—Master Ting! Come back here! 'Iss is a good dog, won't bite ya."

"Doggie bite, Misser B'laza, he smell my fear!" I wailed, hating the dog and hating the gymnastics of Mr. B's name. He couldn't be a Cheng or a Luke or a Lew or a Woon. Barraza!

The first time I tried it I said "Blaza. Baza." Then, "Blaza."

"Blaza? Like City Hall Plaza! No, that ain't it, kid."

"Braza," I said, mustering every muscle in my tongue.

"No, not Braza," he said. " 'At's a singer. Or ladies' underwear. Fer God's sake, kid, work on yur *pranunciatin'*."

Now he was looking at me as I quivered halfway to the elevator.

"Will ya lissinta me? Master Ting. 'Iss dog is a Marine mutt and it will not *touch* yur holy body. Getchur ass inna door.

"I mean, getchur heinie in the goddamn door. Jeezus. Please— kid—get in here," he groaned. "Pardon my fuckin French, already," he mumbled.

I entered and Semper jumped all over me, making me moan in terror. He smelled my fear. But he did not bite. He licked me.

"Go ahead, siddown," he said, clearing his throat and pointing to a worn chair.

The room was a wild, tangled clutter of clothes, magazines, news-papers, gym gear, and boxing apparatus. A gaggle of black leather run-ning shoes was by the door. Mr. Lewis was of a like mind; these men had more shoes than two feet would ever need, enough for a battalion of road runners.

Every glove lace missing from the Y was on the worn carpet. He had undressed forty-five-pound weight bars, stacked plates, and dumb-bells on the floor. The deep depressions and worn, flattened rug fields revealed where he lifted iron and where he did his thousands of situps.

Water and food dishes sat on spread newspapers. Paper sacks filled with faded women's and boys' clothing were aligned beneath the large window.

As in every thirties' film noir, he actually had a view of the giant vertical neon Y.M.C.A. sign outside his window, facing Turk Street. At night, his room would be filled with the blinking of the decorative perimeter of red and blue lights that surrounded the letters. His room looked wondrous to me, full of history and the stuff of men. I think he liked his room but did not like the dark hallway. He was in his kitchen nook with the single plug-in electric burner. He sighed and rubbed his ears.

He said that he couldn't cook anymore. He was scooping up armsful of empty spaghetti cans and dumping them into an overflowing wastebasket.

"Yoosta be a good chef, Master Ting," he said. He was scratching his beard. It was eleven a.m. and he had to shave again.

I was missing my weightlifting. I didn't like lifting weights; I liked the identification it produced in me with Mr. Barraza. I never believed it would make me look like him. At the age of seven, I already distrusted consumer advertising and was not a believer in the Charles Atlas ads in the back of comics..

I was going to miss my open lunch at Angie's, but I didn't care. Being in Mr. B's house was like being in a fire station or at a secret Air Force base. A place for adults where kids always wanted to go.

It was just like Mr. Barraza to have an ugly dog that liked kids and did not eat them. Semper sat at my feet and looked at me with quiet, mournful eyes, as if we were related. He was half bassett and half basenji, and looked like a fat hot dog with a scorpion tail. When I petted him his whole pelt shifted across his body, and he pressed a cold nose and a wet tongue on my hand. I felt a new emotion in an arena once ruled by fear: trust. I sat back in the chair, petting a new friend.

I felt empathy for Mr. B's cooking problem. At least he didn't have any sauerkraut. And he definitely didn't have a bigger woman slapping him for a bad table setting. Good thing. Given the condition of his room, the beating would be extremely bad news.

I wondered why he didn't marry Angie Costello. I knew that he could definitely do worse. I didn't even know if Angie C. had a husband. A real one.

I already knew that there were dead husbands. And live ones who lived somewhere else, usually very far away, in places like Macon, New Orleans, Chicago, Pittsburgh. A lot of them lived in some place called Hell, where their wives had asked them to travel. And living ones that camped out nearby, dropping by on weekends at whatever time was rudest and the least convenient.

There were pictures of Mr. B in the ring. I got up and looked at his stance, which was wide in feet and tight to the opponent, good for close-in work. In one photo, he was throwing his patented left hook, the flash catching the delivery of the left, the high guard of his right, and the transit of his entire body to focus the power into the glove, in freeze-frame, inches from contact. His opponent was about to have his short ribs broken. I felt absolutely terrified for him. But I understood the photo, and nodded as if I were a sage.

"No Army pitures?" I asked.

"Naaaa," he said in the conventional "no" of the fifties.

"How come, Misser B'laza?"

He stood still for a moment. He rubbed his ears, both of them at the same time. He ran his hands over his loud whiskers.

"Kid. It was the drippy shits. I mean, cripes, they had *really* bad grub. Jes awful food. Bad smells. Hey, bad everything—inseks, rats, dengue fever, malaria, bad water, shit everywhere—and those were the good parts.

"War, jeezus, kid. Ya beat a guy there. . . . ya can't shake hands with a headless thing, a bag a ripped-up guts when it's done. Know what I mean? Naaa. Ya don't know. God, I hope ya *never* know, kid like youse.

"This," he waved at his place. "This is *heaven* compared ta Okinawa. Iwo. Saipan and Tinian. Shit. Parris Island, even. 'At. 'At was another life."

"My father in Chinese Army," I said.

"Uh-huh," said Mr. Barraza. "Great."

Barney Lewis was proud of his military heroism because it was an ironic advancement in human dignity for black Americans to kill Nazis in order to save white Europeans.

In an effort to stop Tony from swearing around the kids, Barney implied that the Marine Corps would not be impressed with a foul mouth. That was Mr. Lewis's only blind spot: he was sure that Tony Barraza had great pride in his decorated combat record.

"Yeah, Barney, I oath too much," Tony would mutter, hitting his own forehead with an open palm.

Barney Lewis was not envious of Tony's greater notoriety as a fighter, for his toast-of-the-town status, for his heavyweight press. He understood that an Italian–American would fare better than a black boxer. He certainly did not envy him his domestic problems or his resulting injuries to soul and face.

Barney Lewis envied Tony's Navy Cross, awarded for conspicuous gallantry and battlefield valor on Iwo Jima.

But Tony viewed the Corps as he would look at a gun he had used just once, to kill a rabid mutt in the neighborhood that was after the kids. You would be grateful for the piece, but he wasn't going up to the attic to kiss the damn thing every night and sing it a sentimental song about the glory of the Infantry.

Tony didn't care what the Corps thought, but he respected Barney's opinion. He always felt genuinely guilty when he swore.

"Kid, I'm sorry. I'm not a good man, really," he said. He was clearing a place to work in the kitchen.

"I'm gross. Dirty. I'm close ta leadin a foul life. It's wrong fer me ta drink, ta oath, ta have a dog inna room, but manager lets me cuz I was a fighter, and had a name. I was bad ta my wife, and it cost me, bad. I swear all the fu—, all the time, and I work with kids. I killed a lota people. Ah, crap, it don't matter."

I think that is why Tony and his colleagues gave their spirits to children, and made special efforts with lost causes. I persist in thinking that Tony's dalliance with pretty women had its roots in the Pacific, when life lost its customary promise and tomorrow was less a silent prayer and more a forlorn hope. He would have looked at a young and beautiful, fresh-faced, Noxzema-scrubbed starry-eyed girl, her hair bright and clean, her being emanating hope on two pretty legs, the empty autograph book open and offered. This was a tangible replacement for the nightmares of the Pacific, intestines and dysentery on your boots and the fetid bite of bloody death in your mouth, the memory of the dying scarred into retinas that continued to see, long after the fall of a heartless moon.

Mr. B made lots of toast and then fried eggs, sunny-side up. He scooped the eggs onto the toast, the bubbled whites hanging over the crusts. He salted, peppered, and doused them in paprika, sprinkling a light dust of sugar at the end.

He put toast lids on the eggs, squashed them down, making the yolks explode and run, and served them on badly scratched plastic plates. He had made eight Original Tonys.

"Egg samich," he said.

"Thank you, Mr. B'laza," I said, in awe of his work.

I sat on a footstool packed with newspapers and devoured the eggs. Sunshine came through his window and warmed the clothes in the paper sacks while our jaws did their work and Semper licked crumbs. The clothes were neatly folded and covered in dust. I knew what they were. They were icons of his heart, memories of his past, when the treasure of his wife and the richness of his son were his, forfeited to immaturity, stupidity, and the tariff of war.

The clothes were a symbol of faith in a future, a rabbit's foot for redemption. The place in the hallway where my mother's picture had hung was the same thing.

My mother will return, her spirit alive. I'll be a great boxer, a good dodgeball artist, a surviving swimmer, a less-than-disgusting basketball player, and maybe even learn music. No, I knew, that's not true. She will come back to laugh and read me books of scholars and hard-working sons. She will burn toast and let Jane cook a hundred meals of Chinese food.

She will do *something* about Edna.

Mrs. B and Tony Junior will return to San Francisco and Mr. B will smile all the time, just like Burt Lancaster.

That, dickbreath, I said to myself, is why Mr. B can't marry Angie Costello. He *has* one of those wives that's alive but gone. I had the family-planning abilities of a mad hatter.

When Semper got up and stretched in the warmth, he whacked the bags with his dinosaur-like tail, and the specks of dust filled the shafts of light like shooting stars in a summer night sky.

The kids would now be in Crafts. Mr. McCoo would be mixing clay and setting out the watercolor cases. Then he would make his rounds, making sure no one had skipped class, cheating by shooting baskets in the small seventh-floor gym, smoking on the ninth floor, or doing pullups in the gymnastics section. The Fish and Flying Fish were in the pool with the Hundred Milers. Beginners Swim wasn't until two p.m.

Mrs. Costello would be cutting the potatoes she had peeled and chilled at ten in the morning for the last orders of fries.

I was in Tony Barraza the Hook's home, eating egg sandwiches that he had made, without a schedule to meet, a fist to avoid, or a care in the world. A dog sat at my feet and ate crumbs from my sandwich.

"I happy, Misser B'laza," I said.

"Ghood, krid," he nodded, smiling with a mouthful of yolk and toast all bulging in his right cheek. He petted Semper and pulled out his notebook, recording his meal.

"Lucky, see? Ya don't havta worry 'bout bein fat."

He laughed. "An I don't havta worry 'bout eatin fancy," he added. The simplicity of his cuisine did not seem to bother him, but I felt sad for him. When a little boy grows into a big boy, he should have great Chinese food, the best meals, whenever he wants. That was what being an adult meant. Not this. I knew it was great for me, but bad for him. I knew women prepared the food in the world, and that, somehow, he was in trouble, eating like this.

"Missus B she come home sometime," I offered.

Mr. Barraza dropped his plate from his lap, the Melmac plate warping back and forth on the flat rug, throwing bread and eggs in random little tosses.

He looked at me, his mouth full of egg and mashed bread, his eyes glinting into small, angry slits. From his chest, a tortured pain far beyond *quab*, strange behavior. A twisted, almost odious, subvocal, otherworldly sound came from his throat, as if something very small were being strangled inside him by something very large.

"GODDAMNIT!" he roared, and I leapt to my feet in panicked horror as he shook his boulderlike head. He was suddenly up, hurling stupendous blows into the wall, his massive shoulders shuddering in contact. Somehow my plate had ended up behind me, egg all over the floor, all over my clothes. Semper had been alerted, the hair around his shoulders seeming to stand up, torn between running to his master, eating the eggs, or jumping out the fire escape.

Ohhh, no. I jerked. I had done this, and tears filled my eyes and ran down my face in salty rivulets and I trembled in the grip of a primitive fear of limitless loss.

Stupid, stupid, dumbshitratface China Boy say wrong thing all time.

He was crying. He peered at me, over his shoulder.

"Tony? That you, son?" he said, his hands still up, and I knew I had done something really, incredibly, terribly wrong.

I had to leave. I got up, shakily trying to pick up the plate, staggering as I bused it to his kitchen. I waved at Semper, saying good-bye. My spirit was breaking, my heart collapsing in a thousand little-boy pieces into the pit of my stomach, through bottomless feet, into an ugly, beaten rug.

When I cracked the door he said, "Haay, siddown," in a thin voice.

He faced me, his chest heaving. Turning to the wall as if he had forgotten something, he threw an air-popping lead right and two hammering jabs into it, grunting tremendously as he cracked the plaster and drywall, punching gaps into the stud behind it, half of his treasured photos jumping from the wall and cracking onto the floor, falling over shoes, boxes, and weights. A lot of glass broke. He blew out his reserve air.

"Lissen. Don't *never* bug out when som'un turns bad fer ya. Make a mess, stick around, clean it up." He beckoned with his head, his hard Brooklyn voice transparent, slower, pocked with fragility, dissipating opaquely into the musty air of his hotel room.

"Goddamnit!" he hissed, tearfully, his voice an agony of sound, reaching from a deep, aching hurt within him. "Ya do one fucken thing wrong in yur whole goddamn life an ya gotta pay fer it till kingdom come! Goddamn shit!

Then he said to himself, "Okay, maybe two fucken things wrong. Three," he said.

"Oh, God," he mourned. "Clara, Clara. I'm so fucken sorry!"

Suddenly he remembered I was in the room.

"An do me a fucken favor," he said hoarsely, pointing at me with that huge finger, looking at me as if I had put mucilage in his running shoes. "Don mention the missus. Ya see her walk inta the gym, don't say *nothin.* Ya *don't* see her, don't say nothin neither."

"Okay, yessir, Mr. B'laza," I said, crying.

He went into the kitchen and grabbed a bottle of Johnnie Walker Red. He popped the cap and tossed down several long gurgling pulls. He then rummaged in the drawers and found some Camel cigarettes, thrashed around for matches, and chain-smoked until it was time to go.

I found a paper sack and put the broken glass into it, not at all unhappy when I cut my fingers, bleeding for my terrible karma. The tinkling of busted glass, the sucking of his bottle.

He didn't record the scotch or the smokes in his book.

I did not say a word about his wife for three years.

"Sir," I said. "I no say nuting 'bout missus. Promise."

I put out my hand. We shook. He looked at the thin smear of my blood on his palm, and wrapped a small black towel around my hand. We returned to the Y.

Tony in the middle of his teach, at the point that I begin to understand what I am doing. I am in the ring with Arturo Torres, a fifteen-year-old Junior Leader and another pro prospect. Arturo has blinding speed and thinks the way Barney Lewis does, six punches ahead of his opponents. He, like Rufus Monk, has his AAU card. He will be a Golden Glove.

Right now, Arturo is holding back, serving, in his assistant-instructor role, as a mobile body bag. Arturo is a snappy dresser, and his whites have more starch than a pasta factory.

"Left up, keep it up," urges Mr. B. "Thumb at yur eyebrow. Forearm up, good. Putchur back forward, head down, eyes up, more left lead—gimme yur freakin profile! Show me more left side, Master Ting. Slide a shoulder. . . .

"Jab jab jab jab. Good snap. Combo One. One-two. Again. Come back ta vertical, ya droppin it like it weighed a hunnert pounds. Combo Two. One-one, two-two. Okay, gimme Four. . . . No, no 1-1-3-2, not 1-3-1! Hey whadya tryin to do, make me puke? Uh? Don't understand English? Oh yeah. Right . . . ya don't. Nah nah nah! Not rabbit punches, ya palooka! Punch through, punch through. Hit and go through, sluggo!

"Okay. Keep yur left up when ya drop fer yur cut. Here we go—shuffle up, head down, arms higher, arms's so skinny, wishful thinkin could hold 'em up. One-one-five, don't drop the shoulder. . . . Now cut! Okay. Not pretty, but wudn't the shits neither.

"Okay now cover, cover, damn ya do *that* right, uncover, clinch. Pop jabs, go ta yur left, light feet, light feet, good, ah—use yur right for guard! Keep yur goddamn head down! Now left hook!

"Circle—God ya positioned, Master Torres! Thank you, Master Ting, thank you. Gonna go ta Heaven. In 'bout five fucken minutes. Okay, Barney, no more swearin, yur right, yur right. Jeezus I'm sorry fer my French. Keep shuffle-steppin. . . . Now," he says, taking a deep breath, "Combo Three. Yeeeechh!"

Mr. Barraza rubbed his ears.

Swim lessons were canceled once to clean the pool in preparation for the Northern California Sectional AAU Intermediates. Most of the kids from Beginners went up to the mezzanine, where Angie had set up a soda and sandwich concession. I would clean it up later.

I ran the stairs to the gym.

"Misser Balaza," I said, adding the other syllable to his name. "Ya say 'punch trew.' Misser Punsarong, he say, 'lip punch.' I tink not same." I looked at him, frowning with inquiry. Mr. Barraza nodded.

"Lemme get this straight," he said.

"*I* say ya should '*punch through.*' Mr. Punsalong, *he* says, '*rip-punch.*' Right?"

I nodded, excited with the complexity of the communication.

"We're crowdin ya, Master Ting. Not yur fault. Lissina me. In *Intro*, ya punch through. Get everythin in yur gut poppin, explodin, inta yur opponent's body. Inta the midsection.

"Use yur shoulder, use yur back, put yur hips in an punch yur hand *through* the opponent's body. Knife through butter. *Capish?*" I nodded.

"In *Intermediate*, which ya ain't achieved yet, no way, yur three years off, Mister Punsalong, he teaches a buncha punches. *One* a 'em, it's a rip-punch. He don't mean ya ta do it, cuz ya ain't ready. Ya heard about it cuz Mr. Punsalong, he's helpin ya with individual lessons.

"When yur bigger, lots bigger, ya gonna deliver the blow ta the face when ya got a true mouthpiece and tournament gloves 'steada these here pillows.

"Ya gonna pop the punch *back* the *second* ya make contact. It opens the skin real nice and ya got a bleeder.

"Ya know already a bleeder keeps the opponent from seein ya. Go ta work, chop him down. With blood in his eyeballs, he sees like you. Blind like a bat.

"But lissen. Yur eyes bad, ya got no meat yet. Ya try ta rip-punch, yur jus gonna look like a hog fartin at ladies, 'scuse my French."

Sometimes I felt a mindless, uncontrollable rage, a consumption that ran through my chest to my hands. I ran to the bag and beat it, an imaginary Mighty Mouse pounding imaginary Bashers. This happened several times, and I only realized later that I needed bag gloves. I gasped air and saw the bright crimson of my skinned knuckles. The canvas of the swinging bag could be used as number-one sandpaper.

My legs were well in advance of my upper body. I quickly got inside a kid's defenses but had little to give him when I got there. I could punch, but without knowing it, I was holding back. At the end of bouts, my legs were fine while my arms and shoulders and chest ached.

Crawling shakily through the ropes, Mr. Punsalong grabbed me hard on my left arm and propelled me to a full-length mirror on the opposite side of the gym.

"Look at you," he said. "Your legs shake, not 'cause tired, but 'cause scared! I saw you make face at your blood. Wrong, Ting. Wrong. That not your blood! You jus gave blood to Y.M.C.A. blood bank, Ting! You say good-bye blood."

Say it, said his eyes.

"Bye-bye brud," I said.

I could stand in the ring and not run, parrying sincere head shots, even counterpunching for points. I did not cheat. I obeyed the Duke, and never hit below the belt, rabbit-punched, jabbed the throat, or threw a glove coming out of the clinch. I only clinched when I had to, and I learned to view minor injuries as passing fancies.

Big blows made me cry, struggling to swallow the sound of it, waiting, waiting, praying to be saved by the bell.

I lost again and again, but I did not care in the sweet moment when the hammer fell and the bell closed the third round. I began to shut out the sound of screaming kids as we fought, hearing only Mr. B, a sign of concentration on the task at hand.

When I delivered my first true follow-through punches in a planned series of combinations, Mr. Barraza rewarded me as promised.

He took me to the Crystal Palace Market on Tenth Street. It faced the city hall fountains and the underground construction of Brooks Hall. It was another cathedral, more of glass than concrete, airy, spacious, its glass-latticed, domed ceiling beyond the reach of my eyes.

"Kid, yur gonna love this place," he said.

The Palace was an emporium dedicated to the palates of the cosmos. It probably had food from Saturn. It was the FAO Schwarz of the stomach. It was so big and so full of edibles that I recognized it as the true cathedral to human existence.

Ay-yaa, I thought. The General Lew Wallace Eatery could be dropped in an aisleway in the Palace and never be noticed. Even my faith in Angie's Cafe and the Kuo Wah wavered. I was such a crass kid, a whore for food, willing to follow my stomach to hell itself. I looked for my pew, ready to give my coins to the god of this temple. How did I ever miss *this* church?

Rows and rows of food of every type and variety, from Jakarta, Juan de Fuca, Antwerp, Leeds, Vienna, and Singapore. Canned goods, fresh produce, fishmongers, breads, pastas, legumes of every variety. I was in Heaven, smelling everything, grinning from east to west with the salivary promise of an upended cornucopia. I was ready to eat it all, the wrappings, the glass containers, the windows in the walls.

Then we entered the meat section. Dead things dangled humidly from what seemed to be miles of cold steel racks, dripping discreetly onto thick sawdust. Whole animals without skin. Now I made the connection between little lambs, baby chickies, kidlet cows, and the things we put on plates. Dead meat with a light blood rain was everywhere. I shivered. It probably reminded me of myself.

"Plitty scary," I said in a small voice. I had the feeling that the animals had been killed here, on the racks, their pitiful cries making small children throw up. I wondered where they put the heads. And little feet.

"Yeah. It's so big, I could get lost in here. Jus' stay close, kid."

I felt superstitious. I wanted to tell the poor, sad carcasses that I had not killed them or wanted them dead or hoisted them so cruelly. I wanted to free them, and make them breathe again. Their karma must have been very, very bad.

He bought deli sandwiches with strange-looking sliced meats inside. The bread was a roll with seeds that kept falling off. The lettuce was cut up into slices and had a mustard with small teeth inside it.

With relatives of the luncheon meat hanging from the racks overhead, the taste seemed different. Meat never again tasted the same. It was like eating venison while watching *Bambi*.

Edna said I was an animal. I felt consciously that she was right. I ate, trying not to smell or look at the carcass above me, concentrating on the new mustard and the little seeds that fell from the bun onto the sawdust floor.

"Sub," he said. I wasn't sure if he was telling me to do something or was describing something.

"Submarine," he said, grinning. That didn't help. I think I smiled thinly, however, because he was.

I loved Mr. Barraza and I loved what he did for me. I loved his food. But I forgot to thank him for lunch in the Palace.

As he bought bones for Semper, he told me about the flurry.

"Frurry?"

"Yeah, the flurry. Wild, crazy thing. Come from the heart. God takes yur body. Takes yur arms and yur hands and He tells ya when they go, where they go, how fast." He made a wicked whirlwind of shortened punching moves, showing hooks, crosses, jabs, cuts, diggers, all intermixed with lightning speed. The air around us popped for an instant, the vortex of his heavy arms, snapping like tree trunks in cyclone storms, taking the breath from my lungs. I almost choked. I saw him punching the Y Hotel again, the world crushed by his huge fists. I could not believe that anyone in the world, even Mr. Punsalong, could stand against this huge, human hurricane.

He spoke while he swung away. "Putchur self two, three flurries inna row, yur gonna win big-time. Ain't no defense to it, 'cept ta bleed."

"Hey, ain't you Tony Barraza?" asks the butcher.

"Naaa," says Mr. B, dropping his arms. "How much fer the bones?

"Ya can't *decide* ta flurry, Master Ting. God decides 'at. But if He calls ya and it ever comes, and ya flurry one of those little pigs on yur street, Praise Jesus.

"Yur gonna be wunna God's children, and not a bruise bag, an ouch pouch, fer them dumb un-Christian bullies. I gotta tell ya, kid. I pray fer that, I really do."

"Hausheng, tell me this is not true!" urged Uncle Shim.

"Is true, Uncle," I replied. "I learning how move in water, like Songhai Yangtze yellow fish. And fight, with fist and glove. Inside fighting ring. And wrestle. On mat."

"Ayyy," he said, as if someone were pushing a needle into his head, one eye shrinking with the pain of the thought. It made him look a little like Mr. Barraza. He showed his teeth, then fluffed his jacket, filling the air with the scent of camphor. "In China, your father's brother, Han, was a boxer. He took the blow of a double fighting staff, a *liang-jiang*, in the head. He never thought very well again."

"Baba say Uncle Han break nose," I said.

"True," said Uncle Shim. "When he fell after being hit with the staff, he broke his nose on the ground. It was Heaven's final insult to a once-handsome man. A man so adept at this useless activity that he dueled empty-handed against swordsmen. See here, Hausheng, there is no benefit to pushing yourself in athletic endeavors." A tremor moved through him.

"Eventually, the body fails its last test. Push the body, it meets its limit. We are men, not gods! The man fails with the test! This problem does not exist in learning. There, every challenge presented to the mind only delivers more promise, more knowledge, and the musculature of the mind is unlimited! It grows ever stronger! Do you understand?" he asked.

I shook my head. We were seated in the Y.M.C.A.'s mezzanine lobby outside Angie's Cafe for our appointment, our meeting. A steady line of customers trooped by for tuna fish and bologna. I heard someone say, "Hey, lookit the Chinaman and the China boy."

"Wash out your tongue," hissed Angie. "That's not polite talk."

"Dababa, why you stare at me?" I asked.

"Young Ting," he said softly, shaking his head and removing his spectacles, blowing on the lenses. "You so resemble your mother. It is strange to see her face in yours, and to hear your voice, which is not at all like hers."

"I know. I sound like monkey," I said, dejectedly.

"Oh, no. You sound like a new American missionary, speaking *bwa*. That is not bad; it is just, unusual," he said.

"Able Student. What else do you do in this building? Tell me everything, please, Little Scholar, for I am feeling exceptionally brave."

I reflected a moment. "Oh!" I shouted, startling him. "I do gymnastics. Hang from bar, hang from rings. Do somersault. Work on a *ma*, a horse, with no head or tail, do vaults," I said, calming my voice, thrilled that I might say something that might please him. "Also, painting, clay work."

"Now! That is *excellent!*" he exclaimed, shaking a hand at me. "Those are very good activities! But it is notable that all you think of is fighting. Acrobats and artists are very admired throughout the world, even in the West. Boxers, well. This is hard to explain.

"Hausheng. In 1900, all the best boxers in the Middle Kingdom showed how badly they could use their brains, which were a great, vast emptiness. They created a *hui*, a *tong*, an association, and attacked all the European armies in China with their very hard fists and their empty brains. The European armies used machine guns and cannon. It is no overstatement to say, quite directly, that the boxers did not win. So now, to be all for *wu-shu* is to say, I have the brain of a peanut without the meat within it. Much better to be a good acrobat."

"I try be good acrobat, Uncle," I said.

Uncle Shim nodded, smoothing his hair, satisfied. Then he laid out a blank, cross-squared calligraphy tablet with brushes. Open at the top of the tablet was the *Boy's Book of Characters*, which I had not seen for over a year. It was open to the first page, which showed the simple figures for the numbers one, two, and three. In Chinese, they are depicted by single, double, and triple horizontal strokes, like supine Roman numerals with flared ends. I was starting over again. As I moistened the brush, sharpening it for its work and inking it, Uncle Shim removed the handkerchief from his breast pocket and wiped his eyes, sniffling.

I was on the fourth page, having finished the first ten numbers and was moving on to the basic radicals, and beginning the character *yu*, jade, on the brown grid sheet, when he asked me how I was doing with my new mother.

The brush jerked in my hand, the ink forming something closer to *wu*, a crow. Actually, it resembled a squashed spider.

"As I thought," he said. "Your new mother, of course, cannot be the same as the true mother. Your new mother is also from a different culture, and I am sure there is much she does not comprehend.

"Hausheng. This is a very wonderful opportunity for you. Having a new mother is like facing a very stern examination. An examination of the mind and spirit, your *chi*, your essence."

"Not *shigong*?" I asked.

"Different, but related. *Chi* goes to the inner strength of your personality, your character. *Shigong* describes the energy you possess when you are in harmony with Heaven and the Emperor and your father." He was peering at me, his eyes searching my face.

"I think your new mother does not cook food?" he asked. By food, Uncle Shim of course meant Chinese food.

"No Chinese food. No Songhai," I said.

There was a long silence. I waited.

"Does not the brush feel wonderful in your hand?" he asked. "Does it not feel like steamed jasmine tea on a snowcapped morning in winter?" He smiled, patting me on my head. "Of course," he said softly, "you have never seen snow. San Francisco is such a curious city! Yes, Hausheng, that is correct. Move down, then flare the brush as if I were holding it for you."

A shadow moved over my paper. "You Mr. Ting?" asked Tony Barraza. I jumped up, almost spilling the ink bottle. Uncle Shim stood, bowing slightly as his formally presented, delicate hand disappeared inside Mr. Barraza's hairy, mammoth fist.

"C.K. Shim," he said very slowly. "I am known to the young master, Kai Ting, as 'Uncle Shim.' I am a distant relative, a fifth cousin, and I knew the family in China." He withdrew his hand and looked at it.

"How do ya do. I'm Tony Barraza. Call me Tony. I, uh, we, uh, really like Master Ting here. Good kid. Tries hard. Yeah, he tries hard. Lotsa, uh, lotsa *pep.*" Mr. Barraza was grinning, his teeth bright, his bulk overshadowing both of us.

Uncle Shim said nothing, slightly nodding his head.

"So, Mr. Shim. Whaddya think a the changes inna boy?"

Uncle Shim lowered his silver head. A moment passed. Two moments. He slowly cleared his throat.

Tony asked, flatly, "Ya don't think the boy oughta be here."

"Kai Ting has much to learn, Mr. Barraza. It seems he devotes much time, much effort, to his body. Not quite so much to learning."

"Mr. Shim. He's learnin, and learnin real good. It's what counts. Ta him."

"The mind is always more important than the body, I think, Mr. Barraza," said my uncle.

Mr. Barraza blew out air. "See the marks on the boy's face? See 'em, Mr. Shim? 'At don't happen here. He gets them shiners an doohickies on his block. Boy lives on a bad street. It ain't a place for, uh, ya know, *thinkers.*" Mr. Barraza looked at me. "If he don't work his body, what he learns in his brain from school ain't gonna amounta spit. Mr. Shim, this boy, he lives in a hell's kitchen. Boys can't fight there, don't get ta *live.* Now you, and me, we don't wanna see this here boy dead. And it don't get no more simple 'n that. And please, siddown. Keep goin with what yur doin.

"Lissen," he said, trying to smile through a grim mouth, his bright teeth hidden. "A real pleasure meetin ya, and I'm, like, glad 'at Master Ting has ya. Has ya ta teach 'em the real hard stuff." Tony rubbed his ear.

" 'At'sa stuff I don't know too good." He put out his hand again, and sort of bowed to Uncle Shim. "I'm jus' helpin the boy out a little, with a basics." He took a breath, his head cocked to the side. "Help me with this thing, okay? Trust me. I know yur smart, college man an all, and can figger it. See ya, kid."

"Interesting man," said Uncle Shim, watching Tony march to the cafe. "You know, Able Student, that *moral* energy controls the world. Not fists. If the street is dangerous, do not venture into it."

"New mother send me street," I said.

"What do you mean?" he asked.

"She not want me in house."

"Do your sisters know this?" he asked.

"Janie know. She in very big trouble with Stepmother Edna," I said. "Very big trouble. Trouble bigger than my trouble."

Uncle Shim lowered his head. "This is very sad. But sad, or not sad, the authority of the parent cannot be disturbed. Little Janie, the quiet one, the Small Tail of the family. What trouble could she cause? See here, see here," he ruminated, pausing. "Your *yuing chi* contains deep mysteries. This is clearly a test, Able Student. You must be in harmony with the *Sheng-Yu*! No fighting!

"See here. Your father was a proud fighter. Guns! Airplanes! Lots of death! It brought your father nothing!

"Still, I cannot imagine what makes a man teach *children* how to fight. It is immoral and disturbs the harmony of mankind. You admire this man for what he teaches you?"

"Yes, Uncle," I said.

"Do you call him father—the highest title of respect?" he asked.

"No, Uncle."

He sighed gently. "Well, that is something. He is probably an interesting man. Can he write? Is he literate?"

I remembered Mr. Barraza struggling with the carpenter's pencil, his tongue sticking out as he wrote.

"He very good writer, Uncle," I said.

My uncle sighed again. "This is a very strange country. In China, a man so large would never fit in the scholar's chair. Everyone would want him to fulfill his role—as a soldier, or a woodsman, a carpenter. So why is your teacher so large?"

22

TENDERLOIN

In the Tenderloin, the boys of the Y.M.C.A. were given free rein. We stared at the hookers, skipped around the bums, cruised through the Army–Navy Surplus Store, and sipped Cokes with law students in the soda shops next to Hastings Law College.

What was a man's true yuing chi? Could you find out without having to live your life, to come to the final answer?

Leroy Jones, Connie Dureaux, and I went into Madame Chanteuse's Palmistry on Turk Street with a combined wealth of one dollar and eighty-three cents and the cumulative longevity of twenty-three years. When it was added up we knew we had to be worthy of some measure of adult respect. I wanted to know our karmas.

The door opened into one room. No bell, little light, and less space. There were many conflicting smells—musty scents suggestive of faded perfumes, herbal teas, and an aging woman. The madame was perhaps in her forties, of average size, which was disappointing. I expected someone very small or very tall. Her face was fine-featured, and rather gray.

She wore a sunbleached purple turban and presented fingernails long enough to make the spine shiver in sympathetic sensitivity. We were nervous and pretended not to be, and seeing her rig made us look at each other, nodding. She was the real McCoy.

"Some *true* interestin shit go on in *here,*" intoned Leroy.

The walls were covered with feathers, skins, small leather bags, and an array of dead and dried animals. Large and strangely colored playing cards sat in stacks on small tables. In the midst of unknown scents, there was no music. It was eerily quiet. I could not take my eyes from the carcasses, trying to discern what they had been before they had become wall coverings.

"Leave here," she said in a voice that matched the dark and small chamber of her workplace. She was tired. And poor.

Three months earlier I would never have entered. Two months earlier I would've split out of there like a boy fleeing a bath.

"I not aflaid," I gulped to myself, realizing that I had to go to the bathroom.

We looked at Connie, who spoke white English. He had said he would speak to her. "She's French, and so am I," he had assured us earlier. Madame Chanteuse was black.

"We have a dollar and eighty-three cents and we wanna have our palms read," he said. Leroy and I looked at each other. Connie's voice sounded high and young. And unimportant. We all wanted to sound like Barney Lewis, and Connie was squeaking like a juvenile banty rooster with a rock in his throat.

"Uh-huh," threw in Leroy, backing him up.

"Yep," I squeaked in accord.

Connie showed our coins.

"Riches beyond belief," she said, and we smiled. We had enough silver. But she was assessing our brass. Not our coins.

"All right," she said. "All of you. Sit down, place your right palms up, on the table. Do not mess the linen."

We had been with the Y for nearly four months. Fearlessly and together, like the Rockettes, we sat in wicker chairs, our hands opened, stretched out on the table. I blanched. Our hands were filthy.

She lowered her face and peered. I felt her breath and almost closed my hand, it tickled so. She felt Leroy's palm, touching, testing, smiling faintly at him.

"You," she said to him, "are very strong in your *septentrion.* You will marry and have children." Leroy's face scrunched with the ugliness of that fate, articulated plainly in the open, for all to hear. That is not what we came in here to purchase, or to learn.

My hand was next. "You," she said to me, "have a strong presence on your *midy* line. There is much activity along the perimeter of your *mort per melancolie.* Despite this, you will marry and have children," and my face fell. Leroy was trying not to laugh. Connie smiled, looking at both our faces.

Children. Only the Y.M.C.A. should have kids. Not families.

"You," she said to Connie, "will not."

We looked at her, then at each other, our hands still out.

"Nothing else matters," she said, knowing our questions. "I cannot tell from these," and we trembled as she ran her soft, warm hand across our palms, "if you will be good men, or bad. Or firemen or merchant sailors or bakers. Or convicts. Or, if you will marry pretty girls. Or, if your children will live. And, I have told you too much."

She reached out to Connie and rubbed his cheek slowly and solemnly. His face seemed so pale against the dark of her graceful, delicate hand. His lips seemed almost translucently blue. Connie did not tremble. I did.

She collected our treasury and returned it in a cascade of shimmering, tinkling metal to Connie's opened palms.

"Enjoy life, little one. Now go," she said.

We could run downtown forever. Woolworth's Five and Dime at Powell was in the heart of Market with the Cable Car Roundtable. When the conductor physically turned the car around on the car turntable to head back to the Wharf, everyone helped, especially the kids, pushing for all we were worth.

My buddies knew that I was lifting weights with Mr. Barraza. They presumed, in those days of comic books, that I was somehow magically stronger than anyone.

"Mister," said Leroy to the blue-capped Muni Railway bellman. "Betcha dis kid can push yo' cable car all by hisself. He lif's weights at da Y.M.C.A.! Hey, Kai—hey! Where he go?"

Angie Costello gave me a dollar a week to bus her tables and put the silverware into the soaking sinks. We could buy a big bag of popcorn, three lollipops, and a box of Sugar Duds at the five-and-dime for a quarter.

More importantly, I could get an order of chow mein at Kuo Wah's in Chinatown with the change. Food for my spirit. We could hoof it up to Grant Avenue and back to the Y with my food eaten on the run in forty minutes. Few of my buddies thought the food was worth the trip—they would rather go into the Crystal Palace—but it made me a happy boy.

Joey Cohen, whose guts and pure fighting ability reminded me of Toussaint, loved Jewish food and also liked Chinese food.

"Joey. I join you church?" I asked.

Joey gave me a look with which I was familiar. I had posed another dumb question.

"Kai. It's called a synagogue. You don't *pick* 'churches.' You have *one* faith. You keep it, and never change."

"Yeh I do," I said. "I been to Chrishten Science. Rutheran. Preboterian. Community. I been to Episcoparian. Baptist."

Joey frowned. "No way! But I'll ask my dad," he said.

The next Monday—he didn't box on Saturdays—he gave me the news.

"Dad says Gentiles can pick religions like groceries. Jews don't do that. You're born into it, or ferget it."

I felt a great sadness. "Sorry," he said.

"You guys, bein Negro and everything, don't get to go to Gentile weddings. I do. They got the *worst* food. Little bitty pieces of white bread with fat greasy meat inside. Big things of mayonnaise, by themselves. And then coffee.

"All that stuff, that's *Protestant* shit," he said. "Here. Try this. Mom made some for you guys."

They were kosher bologna sandwiches, made on rye bread with thinly sliced dill pickles.

"Ohh, Joey," I whispered, ingesting them with joy. They were delicious.

Next lifetime, if I'm *really, very* good, I thought—I'm coming back Jewish. Nothing against Reverend Jones or Mr. Lamport or Mary Baker Eddy or the missionary spirit.

23

CHINATOWN

There are times when I think that San Francisco was designed by the architects who laid out Disneyland. With the ease of a park visitor crossing from Fantasyland to Tomorrowland, a City tourist can leave the Tenderloin, traverse the business district, and enter North Beach or Chinatown. A tourist can stand on Broadway and Grant and see Sicilian, Chinese, Neapolitan, Bohemian, and Basque neighborhoods.

In Chinatown, the alienating difficulty of the Cantonese dialects scared me. They made me foreign, different, stupid. I was occasionally treated as if I were retarded. I was insulted by the presumption and hateful of the discrimination that was dealt to people who were mentally slow, or perceived to be so, and to those who *appeared* to be Chinese but didn't speak it. I did my best to avoid conversation, or nonconversation.

On bustling streets, there was a comfort in realizing that no one was speaking to me, for it made my incomprehension irrelevant. On Grant Avenue, I loved looking the way I did.

And the food! Families have their favorite restaurants, where a Face Relationship has been created. The proprietor knows that all possible business will be brought to his restaurant, and the customer knows that he and his family will be treated as the clan of the proprietor.

I had two favorites—Kuo Wah Gardens and the On-On Cafe— both on Grant within a block of each other, on opposite sides of the street. Kuo Wah was a first-class operation. It had a kitchen in which Wang, Na-Gung's fish cook, would have been a star. Its walls were lined with photographs of the dancers and singers from the Forbidden City Nightclub on Sutter and of famous Hollywood people. Bold golden dragons with cherry red eyes danced sinuously on deep green, finely tiled columns.

My mother used to tell me not to look at the photographs of the Forbidden City dancers. Years later, when I got taller, I realized why.

The On-On was a cafeteria. For fifty cents I got a huge caldron of rice overlaid with oyster-sauce beef, finely chopped scallions and on-ion, and a raw egg. The rice and beef were so hot that stirring the egg with the other ingredients cooked it.

I inhaled food. It was my addiction, my habit, my love. Chinese food brought more than splendid sauces, delightful flavors, wonderful textures, and all the pleasures of a child's innocent tastes. It carried a spiritual message of the past and suggested hope for tomorrow through the survival of continuity. My mother's spirit lay within the wafting aromas. I was the only kid in the Y who grinned while in midbite.

I ate quickly, lest it get away, or rude fortune interrupt my work, or a worthier child be found suddenly to receive my unfinished servings. Whether sitting in a restaurant or walking down a street, I could pack away a meal before the others had found their napkins.

Chinatown was like its host city—small and compressed in physical dimensions, boundless and ephemeral in spirit.

Like the old and no-longer-noble Victorian structures in the Han-dle, the structures of Chinatown were obtuse and complicated, filled with shadowed side alleys, curiously angled doors, hidden fences, gabled attics, brooding and silent second stories, quiet non-Anglo spiritualism, and dark unknowns.

I had seen much of the city by the time I was seven. The Mission barrios where Arturo lived, the hard, bitter streets of the Western Addition and the Fillmore. The museumlike quiet of St. Francis Woods, and the picture-book neighborhoods in the Sunset and the Richmond.

The Handle and Chinatown were neighborhoods that revered customs drawn from continents far distant from North America, whose features were now only memory. Both neighborhoods were filled with people who had arrived en masse—not as single family migrants. Most others had come to the City as economically independent families.

Both neighborhoods had a strong spiritual sense, a different musical culture, unique foods, and unappreciated patois. Everyone had black hair, brown eyes, and darker skin than the majority. That is, the majority in San Francisco. And everyone in both 'hoods seemed so chronically poor that poverty had become an integral expression of local culture. Stores in both districts carried inordinate importance.

I was energetically drawn to the Flowering Nation Grocery, which was where I had knelt to Uncle Shim after Connie Dureaux had asked him to meet me. The place was more zoo than store, more a museum of oddities than a grocery, more a continuum of East Asia than the fading recollections of China in our own home. It was a small, congested three-dimensional picture box of my heritage, and of my heritage's primary cultural activity: food.

I always thought that being in this shop was akin to reviewing the brown-paged photographs in our family album, the primary victim of Edna's pyromania.

Flowering Nation Grocery stood between a modest school-supply store called the Wing-Wing Company and a resplendent antiques and clothing store, The City of Kunming. The Wing-Wing sold calligraphy brushes, plastic screw-top ink pots, plastic pencil boxes with the multiplication table on the top, and cheap school purses, which boys and girls in Chinatown carried on schooldays. The City of Kunming sold the most expensive cheongsam dresses in the world—and had photos of Grace Kelly, Ava Gardner, and Paulette Goddard to prove it.

But neither shop had food. The Flowering Nation storefront was a bright red-tile front acting as a base for a huge plate-glass window. Inserted into the middle of the tile, below the picture window, was a smaller, rectangular window that was the front of an aquarium, in which catfish swam at the height of my knees.

Children knelt on the sidewalk. We waggled fingers at the slow, dull fish, circling in the dirty, tepid brownness of their confined world, dodging the impedimenta that threatened to overtake their environment. We would tap on the glass for hours, hoping for a response, for the beginning of communication, receiving as our only answers the swish of an indifferent tail, the streamlining of thick, uneven catfish whiskers. I looked carefully at these fish, knowing that people who had been terribly evil in the past could now be prisoners of their karma, swimming in the Flowering Nation's aquarium.

Above the window inside the store hung dead ducks, dead chickens, dead vegetables. And dangling sausages.

The Hom family ran the store. Mr. Hom spoke with the rapidity of an excited machine gun. He loved his store, his goods, his customers, and his trade, and it showed. Smiling, shouting, jumping, throwing money and packages, he surrendered his vital essence, his *shigong*, to his enterprise, and never looked back. He made Mrs. Timms look uninterested in her store, the Reliance Market, and she was a hard worker.

Mr. Hom was a perfectionist and a micromanager, attending to every detail, imagined or extant, historical or projected, frowning between his cajoling laughter, pondering problems with likely solutions.

I would edge up to the counter, my face concealed by dangling Chinese celery and ful some bok choy, watching him wrap meats and fish and produce, darting back and forth, shouting and laughing. After waiting in line, I put two pennies on the counter and pointed above to the sausages. Mr. Hom would shout, "Hey, Songhai!" and, without looking, pull down a *lop chong* sausage from above his head, dropping it into my hands, scooping the pennies into a cigar box deep in change, and jabbering to three people behind me as he began to extract and wrap their orders.

I skipped from the Flowering Nation, the sausages in hand, humming to myself as I bit off large bites and chomped them with great determination.

During the late autumn of my first year as a city cosmopolite, as I was closing my eyes with the dreaminess of the *lop chong* I was consuming, I bumbled directly into a tall stack of wooden produce crates. They tumbled down, flattening me into a posture altogether too familiar.

Helpful hands removed the crates and I stood, dazed, gasping and unnerved. People spoke, brushing me off, and I nodded dumbly and ran away, embarrassed by my inability to apologize.

Another time I was returning to the Y late on a Saturday afternoon, eating an early dinner as I hummed down Grant. I savored the sausage while trying to avoid people, crates, and questions.

Uncle Shim was facing me, his arms full of groceries. *"Hau bu hau,*
Able Student," he said, the sunlight glinting from his spectacles.

"Uncle!" I tried to say while smiling, my mouth full, struggling to
swallow while bowing.

"Ayy-yaaa! What are you eating?" he cried, startling me.

"Lop chong, Dababa," I said, remembering to offer him some.

"Kai Ting! That is a *pork sausage!* You cannot eat it without cooking! It has poisons in it! Spit it out! Spit it out! Eating raw pork! You
are as crazy as your father!" He was viciously waving his entire arm at
me, and I knew this was serious.

I immediately spat it from me, as if my mother were once again
gagging my throat, terrified that I was ingesting something so horrible
that Uncle Shim might administer Life Essence herbs to cure me. I spat
quickly, again and again, driven by fear of the unknown poison and
propelled by fear of the antidote.

"Kai Ting! *Never* eat pork sausages without cooking first!" he almost cried.

I spat again, worried by his urgency.

"Sorry, Dababa," I said. "Sausage worse than peanuts?" I asked.

"Peanuts?" he asked.

"Mah-mee say peanuts bad," I said.

"Well, of course they are," he said dubiously. He cleared his throat
and breathed slowly, calming his disturbed state.

"Hausheng. I apologize for criticizing your father. I was most
wrong. I—I was on my way to my chess association meeting." He
looked over my head, and then back down to my face.

"See here, Hausheng. I think it is time for you to let some old
men meet the son of Colonel Ting and Mar Dai-li. But, first, let's dress
you properly." We reversed course and entered the City of Kunming
clothing store through its glass doors.

"Mr. Fu," said my uncle in English. "This is my nephew. I want
him to look like a scholar, with a cap. I apologize for not knowing; do
you have clothes for boys?"

"Of course, of course. Stand, Master," said Mr. Fu. He was short
and rather emaciated, perhaps the age of my father and not tremendously larger than myself. He pointed, and I stood on a bright green
wooden block, as high as a stairstep, and he measured me, pulling my
arms out, pushing them back.

"Mr. Fu recognizes the scholar in you, Able Student," said Uncle

Shim. "He likes thin and sleek people, whose weights do not change because of bulging muscle, or added fat, requiring alterations."

"Boy not speak?" asked Mr. Fu in Cantonese.

"He speaks Songhai, some Mandarin," Uncle answered. "But we are encouraging his English language. He is very lucky, for his stepmother is pure American."

"Ohhh!" intoned Mr. Fu, measuring me more carefully. "You find Gold Mountain, Master. Such a stepmother mean big cash! You will talk *yinggwen*, English, numbah-one, like boss *lo fan*!"

Mr. Fu fitted me into a dark blue, cotton, high-collared jacket, and sewed a bright red vermilion button atop a black cap while Uncle Shim used a telephone to inform the chess club that we were coming. Again, he surprised me by shouting into the telephone. He was having an argument, but seemed to win in the end. Then he prepared me for my presentation to its members.

"Able Student. My friends are excellent thinkers. We had different histories, but we all stood to examinations in the old empire." He laughed gently. "We argue about who had the best tutor, who created the best eight-legged essay, who understood best the unsolvable mysteries of the *Analects*. We still write essays for the group, and then criticize them. We play chess, just like schoolboys who avoid their lessons." I was facing a mirror that held my blurred image.

A rich, deep blue jacket, faded and knee-thinned denim jeans, roughly beaten Keds with extravagantly long laces, and a cap that looked like a yarmulke. This was the kind of outfit that would invite a hundred beatings in the Handle. But I knew it would work in Chinatown.

"*Syesyeni*, Dababa, *syesyeni*, Fu Syensheng," I said, bowing.

"*Bukachi*, Hausheng," answered my uncle, while Mr. Fu returned the bow.

From behind me, Uncle Shim said, "It will gladden the hearts of my friends to see you. All of us are here without our wives. Without our children, and without the ancestral tablets. You—you look like home. You look tremendously wonderful! Let's go, Hausheng."

24

WOOD

W$_e$ walked down to Kearney Street, below Chinatown's main thoroughfare of Grant Avenue, and entered a familiar-looking building. It was the International Hotel, and its decrepitude reminded me of the Y.M.C.A. Hotel. Both structures were leading candidates for the wrecking ball.

"This home, Dababa?" I asked.

"No, no," he replied. "But I meet my friends here. I live in another hotel, called the Beverly Plaza. There are many, uh, working-class people here." I heard the wails of babies, the yells of young children, the elevated voices of animated mothers, the deep bass vibrations of closely packed humanity. I smelled the distant scents of my own young past—the smell of Chinese groceries being converted into meals, the humid waft of drying laundry, the strangely interesting smell of old vegetable parts awaiting the garbage man.

"Who Beve'ly Balaza?" I asked.

"Beverly Plaza," he said clearly. "It is a hotel, not a person."

We trudged up the stairs. I banged the little white dual-handled paper sack labeled in Chinese, "City of Kunming," against the iron banister. It was filled with the clothes I had worn into the store. Uncle Shim rustled his bag of groceries and stopped, breathing hard.

"Able Student. Do you remember the moves of the *ping*, the *chiang*, the *pao*?" These were the soldiers, general, and cannon of Chinese chess. I loved the cannon, for its name was based on the sound it made. I nodded.

"Do you remember the charge of the *shiang*, the elephant?"

"Yes, Uncle," I said.

"Now," he said, slightly huffing. "Where did *shiang-chi* originate, and how was it passed to Europe?"

"India to China, and India to Persia, for Europe," I said.

"Yes, yes, good," he replied. "The Indians were masters of inventing intellectual riddles. And of Buddhist teaching."

"Why no use rift?" I asked after we reached the seventh floor.

"I do not trust elevators," he said. "They are too, too, Western. What if the man who designed them was wrong? There is little tradition in the making of them."

In the hallway of the eighth floor, before Room 888, Uncle Shim smoothed down his hair, adjusted his bowtie, and knocked.

The door opened, and we entered. Twelve elders in a variety of dress, of different heights, and in descending seniority, stood in a semicircle around the entrance. The room was thick with cigarette smoke, rich in the accumulated scents of Chinese cooking, spiced with a history of anise-salted pumpkin-seed consumption and the preparation of strong southern teas. Countless pieces of writing-filled paper were taped to the dull red concrete walls. There was one rather cloudy window. A fan in the ceiling turned methodically, its pull-chain gently clicking.

"Honored Friends," said Uncle very slowly, in English, against the metronome of the fan. "I present to you the Only Son of Colonel Ting Kuo-fan and Mar Dai-li. You all remember that Ting *Taitai* was tutored by Tang Su-lin, a Hanlin scholar." He cleared his throat.

"This is Master Kai Ting, who has been honored by being selected out of thousands of American boys to learn the secret arts of American *wu-shu* and Western *gong-fu*."

I stood before them and performed kow tao as they murmured,

Ohhhh! and Ah so! I blinked at the old wooden floor with misunder-standing. Uncle Shim had been shamed by my physical training. He lifted me gently and, holding my shoulders, guided me into a position of attention.

"Hausheng. I am proud to introduce you to my friends." He was smiling as the first man he indicated hurriedly extinguished his cigarette.

"This man with the great gold teeth, the little round spectacles which he does not need to see all the moves, twenty steps ahead on the chess board, with the smoke coming from his mouth like a great dragon of antiquity, is the honorable president, Chan Yu-ying. He is the best chess player of us all, because he is seventy-seven years old and his clan, from Foochow, is famous for its sons." He inclined his head, and I bowed to him, bending from the waist.

"Next is Moy Ssu-fu, sixty-eight years. . . ." He was a little taller than Mr. Fu the tailor and dressed with much less care. He was bent with rheumatism, one eye glazed porcelain white with a huge cataract, the other eye twinkling, almost smiling, understanding how small and ignorant I felt in the presence of such grand elders. He methodically popped emptied pumpkin shells from his mouth, inserting fresh ones in their place. I bowed to each one, smiling whenever one of them gave me the opportunity. One had a secret face, without expression. Another was a big, broad-shouldered man proudly described as a former official for the Triads criminal syndicate.

The intensity of the introductions made me tremble, overtaken by the sheer weight of their status. Each of these men was a patriarch—a father to men such as my own father! This was such grand authority, concentrated, shoulder-to-shoulder, all in one small room. The men, except for a couple of exceptions, were friendly and kind, the ambience of their association hall pleasing and somehow familiar. But all of them, I recalled, were alone in the world. They had no families, and it was irrefutable that elders should be surrounded by those they had raised. They were looking at me and seeing other children, now grown, or dead, or lost without explanation to the great cavernous unknowns of the twentieth century.

They were too much like Tony Barraza. Good men, with incredible talents, shunted by error or happenstance into solo orbits around uncaring communities, left to remember the past while their days dwindled.

"Hausheng," said my uncle in a voice that almost succeeded in hiding his strain. "Please demonstrate for the *Chinshan Taishiangchi Hui*, the Great Chess Association of Gold Mountain, the learning you have received from Mr. Barraza." I turned, looking at him.

"You see, Uncle Tu—" and he pointed at a younger, bearded man in a red sweater, quite close to me—"is a supporter of your sport, and watched someone called the Brown Bomber box. Uncle Tu was a big fan of your teacher. He saw your teacher fight in one of the large foreign auditoriums!" There was no indication from Uncle Shim that the entire enterprise of professional, physical conflict disgusted him. It had cost my Uncle Han his brains.

I cleared my throat, licked my lips. I assumed the stance, directing my profile at "Uncle" Tu. I took a deep breath, and shuffled up, throwing strict left jabs, and shuffled back, hooking with both hands and throwing right crosses. The collar on my cotton jacket pulled at my throat, but I continued. I circled left, jinked my shoulders, and threw combinations.

"*Hao, hao!*" they shouted, clapping hands, and I stopped, red-faced, and bowed deeply to them.

Uncle Shim gave me a cup of hot tea. "Drink, little boxer. This will leach out the poisons of the raw pork sausage! This boy is so *fierce,*" said my uncle, "that he eats Cantonese *lop chong raw!*" and that brought another round of applause.

"Just like his father!" said the one named Tsong, who reached into his jacket pocket and removed a handful of red-and-white watermelon seeds, pouring them into my hands after I put down the teacup. He also gave me two *sumeh*, salt-soured dried plums, which I had not seen for a year. I did not like them, but I accepted them for the generosity intended, and ate them seriously, in memory of past days. It was a Chinese woman's snack item.

Uncle Shim removed the groceries. It was Taiwan beer, from Taipei, and Schlitz, and Moy Syensheng—Moy Dababa—without the aid of clear vision, began opening the bottles, offering me one.

"Not for the boy!" spat the one with the secret, unmoving face, between rumbling, liquid tubercular coughs.

Uncle Lee, the descendant of gangsters with traditions older than Christianity, said, "Ay-yaa! Let him taste the beer! Did you see his fists? The anger in his eyes? He needs the alcohol to calm his fires!"

Uncle Moy poured a small glass and I drank it eagerly. It tasted, as Toos would have said, like tomcat piss.

"Baaaghhh!" I said involuntarily, choking on its bitterness, and they all laughed. "Tea! More tea, please, Dababa!"

Uncle Shim invited me to play him one game of chess. I declined, but he made it clear that this was more than a mere invitation. The board was reset, and we sat down.

I was very lucky, moving my five soldiers energetically according to the first tactical board moves he had taught me. I heard the fan clicking and the bubbling of the hot-water kettle in the silence of the hall. Uncle Shim had somehow forgotten the rest of the pattern, allowing my elephants and cannon to clear a channel for my general to capture his. Again, the applause, and I blushed. I felt like a firstborn son.

"Stay for dinner!" shouted Uncle Moy.

"No, no, the boy must go home for dinner," said Uncle Wang.

"Honored Before Borns!" cried President Chan. "We forget ourselves. Please. Let us remember the boy's uncle?"

"Hausheng," said Uncle Shim. "It is your choice; you are as welcome here as you are in your own home. Shall we call your learned father and ask him for the honor of your young presence at the Far East Cafe, for dinner?"

"Please, oh please!" I said, and they laughed again, creating a music so sweet, so innocent, so connected to their own pristine youth and to the joy of life that it surpassed, for me, anything I had known since the death of my mother. I looked at these old men and loved them, trembling with emotion.

We ate a roaringly good meal. I drank more beer, holding my nose while I swallowed. I ate past need, surpassing pleasure and transcending pain as my stomach distended with gluttony.

When the platters were cleared, there was a great dispute as to who would take me home. Uncle Shim had to win this argument, but the other twelve men, including the fundamentally blind Uncle Moy, had to show their respect for both Uncle Shim and my family by vociferously demanding the right to escort me through the jungle of an American urban evening. Later, I learned that not one of these men owned a motor vehicle. Uncle Shim and I took the bus.

The evening ended with a final round of toasts. There was a great deal of shouting of "Gambei!" as glasses were emptied and Go-liang rice wine and clean glasses appeared. Everyone had been smoking, and after a full evening of it, my eyes were in a bitter uproar.

Uncle Shim rose, and a quiet slowly came over the large, round wooden table within our private, enclosed dining cubicle. Ashtrays stirred, and glasses were filled. Respectful waiters cried for silence back to the clatter of the kitchen. My uncle coughed discreetly, and cleared his throat.

"Tonight, we met the hope of a new China," he said, using his dramatic poet's voice. "A boy with a Kiangsu father who works for Amethyst Jade Cheng. With an American stepmother who went to Smith College. A boy who is the student of Barraza Syensheng, who is teaching him about iron, and who is learning about ancient literacy and the Indian elephant game from us." There were respectful noddings of heads and acknowledgments of *"hao, hao,"* followed by drinking.

"But this toast is to all of us. We are wood, my brothers. We are sinewy, old wood, old trunks with fading limbs and few leaves! Right? Is it not so? Oh, it is an old T'ang poem, this thing about our age, and learning. We are not base elements of the world, and therefore will not endure. We are not fire, we are not wind, we are not water. We go, as old wood rots, to join mother earth. We pass through, like the sailors of Cheng Ho, gone to Africa for all their lives, with no families to remember them.

"We were all born in the nineteenth century. We are men of the past age. This little boy," he said, pointing to me, "is our memory. We drink to ourselves, for our meager contributions to books, to scholarship, and to the Master Kang."

There were gutturals of affirmation, and drinking. Uncle Shim licked his lips.

"We drink to the boy," he said, "because we have our youth back again, for a night. Ha! When would we have *stood* for a child back in the Middle Kingdom! *Never!* But here, we have only the memory of what a child represents to us. We ask him to remember us, and thank him for being our collective Only Son. *Gambei*, Before Borns!"

"Hao, hao!!" they cried, emptying their glasses, smacking their lips, hitting each other on their arms, nodding their heads deeply, hiding their moistening eyes by gazing into the bottoms of their wine vessels.

It was an encore of a now infamous performance: the scion of the Ting family standing at the door of his home in the company of an adult male masquerading as an uncle. Now, in lieu of an unwelcome muscular Latin American auto mechanic in Navy khaki, stood an unwelcome Chinese man of letters, smartly bowtied and tipsy from an excess of both beer and emotion. Before, at my door with Uncle Hector, following my trashing at the hands of Anita Mae Williams, I had resembled something Evil the bulldog had spit out after an unsuccessful effort at digestion.

"You look like something—something from a flea market! An Arabian bazaar!" exclaimed Edna, looking at my Chinese scholar's jacket and cap.

Uncle Shim gently coughed. "Mrs. Ting, uh, good evening," he suggested.

"Yes, so it appears to have been," she said, sniffing the aroma of hops, the invidious virus of crossculturalism.

"Oh oh oh!" said Uncle Shim, sighting my father. "T.K.! What a pleasure to see you! Your son, your son did great service to your family name, tonight. Yes, yes. It's true!" he cried, making small little movements with his arms while bobbing in place. Uncle Shim, as many people did, was becoming quite exercised in the presence of my stepmother.

"Hello, C.K.—come in, please," Father said to Uncle Shim while staring at my clothes. "Very kind, very kind, to take the boy to the chess club," he said in an overloud voice. "Nice clothing," he added in an underbreath. Father was in his usual Army olive drab cardigan, with a tie on a white shirt, his jaw clenched tightly around an unlit pipe.

"Darling," Edna said. "He looks—he—Kai—looks totally *foreign*!"

"The clothes are Chinese," said my father.

"He looks scholarly, Mister and Missus Ting," said Uncle Shim. "He was with masters of the pen tonight. Men who have devoted their lives to learning. They would be American doctors, for all the years given to books!"

"They would all be bartenders, if you're any indication, Mr. Shim," she said.

"Is okay," I offered brazenly. "They not drink all beer. I drink some, too."

The ensuing silence indicated that I had not helped matters. I stared at my Keds, hoping for divine guidance. Or deliverance.

"You, young man," Edna said with barely masked intensity. "You hie yourself into your room this instant, and remove those—*clothes*. I will deal with you later. Go!" she cried.

The argument over the ability of Uncle Shim to exist in my life began in earnest that night, and continued unabated until his death. The fitted blue jacket and the small cap with the red button disappeared. I was filled with shame for my inability to retain gifts from elders whom I loved.

•

25

CARETAKERS

In the Y, we were in a contained space, working on supervised tasks of limited and monitored violence, protected by guiding adults, enveloping headgear, and filtering gloves.

I heard better. I saw more. I was becoming more aware, my senses activated. Running with Leroy Jones and Connie Dureaux—two kids with immense senses of humor—was rubbing off. Connie read *Boys Life* magazine, memorizing "Grin 'n' Bear It," the back page of jokes. He was the first to tell me the chicken-crossing-the-road riddle. I didn't think it was particularly funny but I liked his laugh.

Leroy was a great prankster, with a penchant for exchanging kids' jock straps, putting hair slick inside shampoo bottles, and jamming Silly Putty inside headgear, an act requiring the wearer to cut his hair to the scalp. I understood that, and we laughed until tears came—something that I could not understand.

Leroy would approach a man on the street. "Hey, mister," he'd say with the sincerity of an encyclopedia salesman. "Your cigarette's on fire." We would then hit each other in a celebration of comedy until the sheer pain of congratulation stopped us.

Leroy got us to help him simultaneously flush all the toilets and urinals in the boys' locker room to lobster cook the bigger kids in Intermediate who were always hogging the showers and denying us the soap. We shouted in pure delight, running and jumping in dizzying circles of joyous excitement when they screamed in great manlike curses and called us fuckentwerps.

I loved being a fuckentwerp. I loved the collective in the curse; I wasn't alone. I had never been so elevated in society, so unified with others, so accepted and true to the baseline ethos of boyhood.

My body put on weight and I began to trust it to do more than ingest food and run. I could skip a rope for half an hour and was learning reverses. I went from trip-trip-trip, to slap-slap-slap-trip. I could hit a speed bag and make it dance with the three-part rhythm of glove-bag-glove, knuckle-back-left-right-right. The rhythm was slow, but recognizable.

I could make the huge, heavy body bag creak on its chains and complain to my blows. The bag gloves were a size too big, but I closed my fist around the metal bar for comfort and swung away. Half the time I missed, misjudging the eccentric rotation of the bag and hurting my wrists. But my arms had utility, approaching the development of my legs. By Thanksgiving, I sniffled, but no longer wept, after taking a hard punch.

At the opening bell, I jumped up and clapped my gloves. Roof taught me shoulder fakes, which I did on blind faith. As I could not see the shoulder fakes of my opponents, I thought at first that they were of no value. But they set up my left jab.

Many of our best adventures took place in the Y after regular hours. Angie recognized my desire to work and to earn affection. So I started to open her cafe—making the coffee, warming the griddles, peeling lettuce leaves for the bologna sandwiches. She gave me a key to the main Golden Gate entrance and to her mezzanine cafe. The only hard part was reaching everything on the counters and making coffee into GI Very Strong and Regular. I got four dollars a week and gave it to Edna, who learned accounting from the Mafia.

Connie, Leroy, and I entered the Y on Sunday mornings, when

the entire building was closed. Leroy was available like I was—we had both been freed by our families.

Connie Dureaux had had polio and still did not enjoy perfect health. His mother wanted him home all the time, to protect him. His father wanted him to seize life in both hands, to do everything, to explore without limitation, to squeeze as much life and experience from his days as was possible.

I asked Joey to join us as well, since it was not his sabbath, but he declined. His family wanted him home, for the pleasure of his company.

"Shee-it," said Leroy.

"Makes sense," said Connie.

Wow, I thought.

The three of us stood next to the tall, grooved, pinkly gray Corinthian columns of the Y on that first Sunday morning, the sun bright on the pavement, and we made one of the big turns of our lives.

"Guys," I said. "No cop *nuting*. Crean, clean *everyfing* touch. *Everyfing!*" I was looking down at my feet. I couldn't take it if they weren't going to help me, if they were going to screw the Y.

"No sweat," said Connie.

"We be cool," said Leroy. We shook hands. I smiled like a fool.

We had the run of the weight room, the good leather body bag. We couldn't reach the high, beautiful, shining black speed bags unless we jumped. Ours were gray, the color beaten from them. We reveled in the big showers in the elite first-floor Golden Gate Club and dribbled the good basketballs the way jewel thieves would caress the Star of India. These roundballs had dark stenciled letters and pebbled grips on their hides—so different from the pitiful, skinned, and overworked spheres we regularly used. We could do pullups on the steady, immobile high bar instead of on our clanking, swaying ceiling pipes.

We always got thirsty and usually were hungry.

Leroy looked at me and Angie's key, which I wore around my neck on a chain.

"Sure could use a Coke," he said. Angie's wall fridge had two shelves of the bottles that came straight from the downtown Coca-Cola bottling plant on Howard Street, south of Market.

All the muscles—well, all the ones I had—moved in my shoulders. I tried to cover my ears with them. I didn't want to hear it.

"Don wan hear dat, Reroy," I said.

He looked at me. I looked down.

He sighed. "Gonna get some water, dudes," he said.

We became aficionados of water before Perrier was a name.

The cafe was on the mezzanine. A twelve-foot-high, half-circle window looked out over Golden Gate Avenue, and the three of us would sit on the floor and study the hookers, the drunks, the pushers, the men without labels, elbowing each other when we saw the vice cops. We knew they were police; both were members of the Businessmen's Club in the Y, and one of them, Detective Don Cooper, was an occasional Y.M.C.A. volunteer.

But mostly we liked to go up on the roof and watch Bruce Punsalong fight himself.

It seems preposterous that Bruce did not know we were there. Leroy was a very smart street kid, and I was furtive as furtive could be, but Connie Dureaux made as much noise as hippos procreating at midnight. I figure Mr. Punsalong always knew we were up there, spying on him.

The first time we went on the roof, Leroy said "Shhh!" and we froze. We saw Mr. Punsalong. He was killing someone with a knife.

Bruce was throwing the knife into a man who just stood there and got cut. I gasped, and as I put my hand up to cover my own mouth, Leroy's and Connie's arrived on various parts of my face as well. I crept closer. Bruce had a dummy. A stuffed dummy shaped like a man with a stake up his back. Bruce drove the stake into the gravel and asphalt roof—which graphically explained why the ninth-floor gym leaked—and paced off some distances. He left bright yellow banana peels as his marks on the tarred and graveled roof.

Then he turned his back on the dummy, masticating the fruit. Reaching behind him, he pulled out the K-Bar knife from its scabbard with a hard metallic zing, and with a shout of "Heart!" that made us feel like going to the bathroom without notice, he hurled it with a sharp, whipping wrist at his target. He usually hit the chest, and our teeth bared as the hilt of the bayonet quivered in the dummy.

Sometimes, he would shout "Head!" and that was where the blade would fall. When he missed, the knife sliced off a part of the dummy, the stuffing fluttering away in the high roof breeze while the heavy knife banged into a hollow vent or skittered along the gravel.

The first time the knife hit a fan housing we gasped as every pigeon in San Francisco exploded into sudden flight from the roof and the ninth-floor sills, whipping the wind with hundreds of panicked wings.

We checked ourselves, gasping, our little hearts lunging in our chests, ensuring that continence had not been lost.

Then he did *katas*, attacking the head, stabbed, and punctured the dummy with kicks, then with punches, and then with combinations. He was unbelievably quick, his hands, feet blurs in the high roof wind. He had a turn kick, rotating his body like a 78 rpm record, his back horizontal to the ground as his free leg punched into the dummy, making it bend on its stake and crack back. He cried, "Keee-YAT!" as he did his work. It was like watching Victor Mature kill the lion, or Big Willie do Kai Ting. This was *wu-shu*, the combat of my ancestry. Uncle Han knew how to do this, in China.

We had seen him kick the body bag before. But this made us think that we knew nothing about fighting.

"Dang!" hissed Leroy.

Leaving the Y one Sunday, we were surprised to find the sun down and the streets dark.

"I'm gonna be in trouble for being late," said Connie. Then he smiled. "But not real big trouble." I did not want to break up; I wanted to stay with my friends forever.

"Le's go Market Street?" I suggested and, grinning, we trotted down Leavenworth. A man in a wide-brimmed felt hat played a violin while his dog slept, a large metal cup attached to his collar. We listened, and dropped coins. In front of the Tufts Hotel, the Salvation Army Band played brightly mournful tunes while a large man sang in a larger voice.

"Pretty soon," said Leroy, "Santa Clauses be out, beggin coins." I pricked my ears up on that one. Santa *Clauses*? How many were there?

In front of Loew's Warfield Theatre, Connie stopped us. "Kai, ya gotta give this man a dime! You're gonna see somethin real cool!"

I pulled a dime and trustingly handed it to the man in front of us. He carefully deposited the dime into a coin changer fastened to the front of his belt. The man was cold, his broad shoulders hunched as he rubbed his hands together, blowing into them. Connie pushed me forward, to a telescope. I looked into it.

Facing me, a quarter of a million miles away, was the moon. It was round and bright. It was pocked with shadowed circles. I had stopped breathing, for what I was seeing was delineated in unprecedentedly sharp detail. For the first time in my life, I was seeing something in my world with the assistance of high-powered optics, and the surface of the moon catapulted in a brilliant, vibrant cascade of light into my pupils. I had never seen anything more beautifully clear, more startlingly defined, more captivating to the neural senses of my brain. My entire being became subsumed into the vastness and the minuteness of the world of that cold, forbidding, hotly exciting lunar landscape. For the rest of my life, the moon assumed magical proportions, becoming a symbol of clarity, of perfection, of otherworldliness against which mere mortal sentiments became motes of impunity in a galaxy of stellar potentiality. For the rest of my childhood, whenever the fogged nights of San Francisco would permit, I would think the moon was following me because I had seen it as few others had. In what seemed seconds, a loud click was followed by a shutter falling across the object of my adoration.

A minute had passed in a micromoment, and I spilled coins all over Market Street to recover the image. The man laughed, my friends hit me, and thereafter, on the subsequent Sunday nights that were illuminated by an observable moon, I was left to feed my addiction to Mr. D. J. Masuda's Magic Lunar Telescope alone.

"Kai, he got a *ba-ad* habit," laughed Leroy.

At home, Edna was in her final campaign against Jane Ming-li, who continued to defy the new order. She would not accord Edna the respect due a mother. Nor could Edna forgive Jane her offensive passive resistance. Jane needed to suffer, and Edna now kept her confined to her room with a myriad of housecleaning tasks and mild tortures.

"Jane, do what stepma want!" I hissed.

"No, no, no! She has no right! I didn't *do* anything to her!"

"No matta! She big, she win!" I cried.

"Jane," said Edna. "I'm sorry. I forgot to tell you that Donna Riley called for you."

"Can I use the phone to call her back?" asked Jane.

"Of course. The phone is now available. However, Donna said that you had to call her by eight o'clock last night. It was something about a movie tonight."

Jane returned the favor by constantly forgetting to buy the groceries Edna wanted, by misplacing valued items, and by scrambling the high order of kitchen implements. They made each other miserable, locking wills, disbelieving that the other party could long endure a war of emotional attrition. Misery, hard moods, and antagonism became the seasoning of the house.

"Jane. You okay?"

"Sure, Kai," she said, sitting with her knees tightly together in her new residence. Edna had moved Ming-li into the attic, which had once held the crate from China. At least she had a window, with a view of the ocean.

"This is a special place, just for you," Edna had said. "But do not use the bathroom without permission."

"How's the Y?" Jane asked.

"I love Y," I said. "How you friens at Anza?"

"Fine," she said. She looked so sad.

This made no sense. My sisters knew everything. They could do anything. They had learned so much in China, where they had Tutor Luke, who had even named them. They had lived in India, before arriving here, speaking perfect Oxford English and eating new foods without batting an eyelash. They spoke clearly in any language they wished. Their charm, warmth, and beauty admitted them anywhere in the world. And, with their brains and guts, they excelled.

They *fit* in the Handle, Berkeley, Chinatown, Shanghai, New Dehli, or Oroville. Two of them knew how to drive a car. Not like our mother, but more like Father.

I was the lame idiot. How could my life improve while Jane's was worsening? And I was doing it by assimilating into my nonmusical, nonscholarly environment.

Jane Ming-li was conforming her behavior to proper conduct: She was not violent. She did very well in school. She did not raise the ire of teachers. And she was failing in life.

For me, shoulder bumps and cries of "China Boy!" made me stop and cock fists. As a result, my life was improving. Some of the kids laughed at my artificial ferocity—the teachings of Tío Hector—but my fight frequency continued to decline. As that autumn wore through daylight saving toward winter vacation, some of the China Boy Bashers dropped out and let me be.

I no longer had the beat-me-stupid demeanor on my body, and was not as worthy of scorn, or as worthy a target, as in the past.

"Stepma Edna," I ventured. "No more brud on shirt, yes?"

She shook her head, without looking at me.

26

LUCKY

It was in the week after Thanksgiving, 1953, as the stream of GIs began to return from Korea, after the Yankees' victory in the World Series had become history, that I opened hostilities.

Jerome Washington's new nickname was "Lucky," which came from his proud smuggling of Lucky Strike cigarettes into the nighttime lodge meetings of the local Junior Pessimists Club. Jerome pocketed the smokes from his father. They met in the deep and damp cellar garage ramp of J.T. Cooper's house on Fell, drank copped alcohol, and took to calling themselves the Hot Smokes.

When we entered adolescence, they would be the first on the block to consider killing people who disagreed with them. Their spiritual adviser, their role model and beau celebre, was Willis In-Your-Face Mack.

Willie advocated a code of conduct. Anything he wanted was his, right now. If something pissed him off, he expected the Hot Smokes to take care of business, from the get-go. If a Hot Smoke needed Willie's intervention, they were free to petition, but holding one's breath was not recommended.

I could not imagine laying punches on Big Willie, who would thump me a couple of times just because he was bored, leaving me throwing up and stuck with a headache that would intermittently last a week. I always figured that I could have been another Thomas Edison had Willis Mack not robbed me of so many precious neurons during my developing youth.

Jerome's daddy was a sensitive man. He had delicate ears, incapable of tolerating a boy's question or a child's request. Jerome would open his mouth and Mr. Washington would try to shut it for him. When that only caused more noise to emerge, Leo Washington's sensitivity would be converted into mindless rage. Mr. Washington liked to hurt people. He figured that was why God had given him a son.

Life had been hard on Leo. Jerome would beat on me after his daddy belt-whipped him for asking a question; I was at the bottom of the slide of life.

The fists would travel down the social fight card on the neighborhood totem pole, from Leo Washington at the apex to the China Boy on the bottom. I guess I could have trashed Missus Hall or thrown rocks at Evil when he was leashed, but I knew that my badly bludgeoned karma could not endure that type of abuse.

Jerome was one of the original China Boy Bashers. His blows carried a memorable viciousness after his father abused him. At the Y, I would pretend he was the body bag. Jerome was built like a boy, instead of like the Rock of Gibraltar, and I could fantasize about hurting him.

Mr. Leo was one of the ogres of West McAllister, the street that drew the men in the 'hood. This was the Handle's civilized counterpart to the poolrooms, poker halls, and bars of the Haight. We had barbershops, garages, and markets.

Separating the Haight and the Handle was the park. Two streets, Masonic and Ashbury, ran across the park, connecting the 'hoods. The boys of the Haight would cross the park on Masonic, unconsciously walking closer to each other. Masonic was cool for kids because it was wide and open, full of early visual warning and rich in running spaces.

The men of the Haight used Ashbury Avenue to traverse the 'hoods because it was narrow and it masked their movement. Ashbury's shops had a remarkable row of pretty women employees and hangers-on who were unaffected by the tugs of neighborhood allegiances.

The vaunted Haight, the Hate of my youth, the place of death, would become the Haight-Ashbury, or the Hashbury. But that would be the sixties, an eon away.

Mr. Washington was one of the few men of the Panhandle who went the other way, south on Ashbury, to frequent the Haight. A salmon who went downstream to spawn, and to kick. He fit better there. Men fought with bottles and knives, and with guns within easy reach. He wore tan work pants and old brown army boots laced with a neatness that reflected his interest in using them on people rather than on concrete.

Many of the returning Korean War veterans were not as hostile to whites and nonblacks as they had been before they left. They had seen a way to live with others. The U.S. Army, at its worst an instrument of genocide and internment camps, was fast becoming the leading integrating force in the entire world.

But Leo Washington had missed the learning. He took the wrong lessons, fortifying the original bitterness that had turned his soul putrid long before. He was a vicious pool player who seldom got games because he would stick-whip the winner, snapping the cue in the center and using the splintered base as a bludgeon and a nightstick. He would smash with the hard round base, gouge and slash with the jagged broken end.

I had seen him do his work. Strangers who came calling to pay court to single women in the 'hood did not know that Mr. Washington was a sucker puncher. Most of the men in the Handle became quiet when words failed and violence was about to become the solution. Leo Washington was tricky, cursing up a huge storm, pretending to be all mouth, just as he unleashed a brutal genitals-first attack on the noise-distracted victim.

Kids crossed the street against bad traffic when he lumbered his way down the pavement, his large, overweight bulk exciting genuine fear deep into our teenaged years.

I can still remember, with heart-pounding terror, the hot Indian summer night Mr. Washington bounced his wife down the stone stairs from their second-floor stoop to the street. We had heard yells and wailing as a car roared away. Then Mrs. Washington came down the stairs, like a life-sized Winnie the Pooh. But this was no Christopher Robin pulling her.

The corner of Lyon and Golden Gate had regular traffic, and as the sun went down the cars almost hit them as he beat her. He trashed her with a knowing fury. He wanted to kill her. With half the kids in the world watching, he kicked her until her nose bled and her heart-stopping screams ceased and she passed out. Her blood was thick and bright crimson, coursing on the sidewalk like a living thing. I was sure she was dying and I was filled with panic that froze my chest. I felt great sorrow for Jerome. I was reminded of the meat section in the Crystal Palace.

Mr. Washington mumbled something about telling her to shut up. He looked at the people of the neighborhood defiantly.

"*Fuck you!*" he spat, and silent children began to cry.

Toussaint, Titus, Jerome, Alvin Sharpes, a few others, and I thought we ought to do something. There were no teenagers between us and the grown men, who, for the most part, were not prepared to die to protect Leo's poor wife.

We did not know that someone had tried to intervene, just minutes before. Mathey Roache, a decorated Korean War hero, had heard Mrs. Washington's screams. He was reputed to be one of the best-looking men in San Francisco. His mother, a New York seamstress who made all his clothes, knew that Mathey had a future in Hollywood.

Mathey had changed from his travel-worn khakis just hours before. He came down from the third-floor apartment and entered the Washingtons' flat.

With a cold beer in his hand he came up behind Jerome's dad as Leo methodically slugged his wife's bleeding face.

Mathey suggested that Leo stop, to let the missus up.

Mr. Washington put a knife in Mathey's guts. Guts that had tightened under enemy gunfire, that had processed mean, cold, and ugly C-rats in slushed mud trenches and on hard-rock, artillery-scarred hills, that had hugged the ground as the rounds came in and had burst in blood when the shrapnel slashed through.

Leo Washington twisted it to the hilt, cursing as Mathey's civvy beer spilled on Leo's blood-spattered pants.

Mr. Brooks, who owned the mortuary, provided free services in view of the deceased's war record. Ex–Staff Sergeant Roache, Infantry, decorated with a Combat Infantryman's Badge, a Bronze Star with "V" device, a Purple Heart, Presidential Unit Citation, Korean and U.N. Service and Good Conduct medals, was put to rest in the Golden Gate

National Federal Cemetery in San Bruno, near the new international airport. He had died as Toussaint's father had died—surviving a war to perish at home. Mr. Washington missed the funeral.

When his dad, drunk, incoherent, and miserable, finally stopped kicking Jerome's momma, I drew breath. It was one of those times when I did not know if I was going to soil my pants or go blinder than I was.

"Jelome, le's help yo' momma upstairs." I said it without thinking. It was what Toussaint might have said. An offer of water. But Jerome was not my friend.

Jerome looked at me with tears in his eyes.

"Don touch my momma you chink mothafucka!" and he pushed me on the ground and kicked me a couple times.

Toussaint called him off.

"Jerome, you remember ya'self. Ya'll help yo' momma, right now," he said.

It was the son's job. Cops never came.

"Leggo me!" cried Jerome. "I'm gonna fucken kill dat goddamn chinkface right *now*!" He was hot to imitate the beating he had just witnessed, his brain exploding with its savagery, its violation of his mother, its destruction of his nascent soul.

"Stop it, Jerome," said Anita Williams. "Don't be showin no more of that *shit* to *any* kid on this block."

Anita had a hand on her brother Aaron, whose eyes were open and wet, blasted into shocked expansion by the trauma of violence. Anita was speaking like a mother.

"Now everyone, calm down, right now," she said. "For particular, I'm talking at *you*, Jerome."

It was now three months after Mrs. Washington survived that nightmare attack. With the concentrated exposure to bigger and more delinquent kids in the new term at Fremont, Jerome was on his way to becoming Lucky. It was approaching Christmas and dark came early to the streets.

Mr. Washington had neither been arrested nor punished for killing Mathey Roache. The culture of the Panhandle did not include calls to the police.

"The Good Lord's going to do in Leo Washington," said Momma LaRue, "and He's going to use Leo's hand to do it."

Mr. Washington was not in the spirit of the holidays and to prove it he whipped his son, flaying skin, bruising bones. Jerome was on the pavement, fighting his tears, struggling against the fear of his own father, hot for someone else's pain to displace the terror and the misery in his broken heart.

"Whatchu lookin at, chink mothafucka!" he cried.

I knew what that meant. Friends said "whatcha." Enemies said "whatchu."

Alvin Sharpes had been assigned to me by Toussaint. He had just shown me a treasure. It was a Borden's Dairy Selector, a little plastic device that the milkman read in the empty bottles on the steps by early-morning light, to figure out what to leave. There were at least five people on our block alone who had milk service. There was no lack of theft, so the subscribers appeared in the early morning like ghouls at their doorsteps to receive the processed products of cows.

The selector was like a deck of cards, fastened by a metal rivet at its base and connected to a smaller, vertical stem that went inside the lip of the bottle. You could fan them out, and a rainbow of colors appeared. Red for milk; blue for eggs; yellow for butter; green for buttermilk, all matching the color of the cartons. The colored fans were plastic-laminated and felt smooth and magically expensive in our hands. Alvin Sharpes and I smiled with the delight of it.

"You cop?" I asked.

"Shee-it, dude. Course. Whatcha think, I'se gettin milk?"

Alvin Sharpes liked his last name as much, or more, than his first. Titus would say, "Hey, Toos-dude!" or, "China, you crazy boy." Or, "Dig it, Al-vin *Sharpes*!"

Alvin Sharpes's daddy had been an Army engineer in the war. Now he conducted the Ingleside trolley for the Muni Railway. He loved his sons, and Alvin Sharpes loved his family name. Alvin Sharpes saw that a licking had been laid on Jerome. He got up slowly, and looked at him.

"Fuck you," Jerome said.

Alvin Sharpes stiffened, torn by conflicting obligations. But he knew this was my fight. Heck. Jerome Washington's focused and pent-up hatred was so virulent that no denial could possibly work. Not this night. The squirrels in the park knew this was my fight.

Alvin Sharpes sprinted on his long legs for the LaRue home. That was his job. No one could fight a boy's fights but himself. He went to get Toussaint to make sure a murder didn't happen. I appreciated the insurance.

I was still seated on my own steps, no longer thinking about smooth yellow butter markers or the happy prospect of my sisters' return from school for the holidays. I turned the multicolored selector over and over again in my hands, treating the cards like rosary beads. My bottom felt cold against the stairs, as if it were already two or three in the morning.

"Don wan no twuble wif you, Jelome," I said nervously. I knew better than to mention his mother. Like, "And say hi to your mom, Jerome." I was learning.

"Jus leave me alone," I enunciated carefully, hoping that Barney Lewis's admonition about clear speaking would now have some magical effect.

I did not want to fight him. It was dark and my night vision was less than special. I was pinned to my porch, with nowhere to run. Like the ring. I could parry some of the weaker kids. Jerome scared me.

I heard Mr. Punsalong say: You wet paper sack's dream fight.

"I'm *Lucky*, not 'Jelome,' you pissass mothafuckin cocksucka! Come down *here* and say dat, you fuckin slanteyed chinkface China Boy fuckshit!" His words almost paralyzed me.

Mother had said that we could change our names to our advantage, to improve our luck. Jerome had just changed his, but he was nonetheless still in a very bad mood. The angry facial maneuvers and *walkando* I had practiced with Hector would not help. The 2d Armored Division might not help.

I could hardly see Jerome. This was going to be it. He was Lucky. I had to be Mighty Mouse.

I stood up, my heart hammering, hyperventilating. I had no spit. I missed my gloves, my headgear. For the first time, I missed the wax mouthpiece. I missed my three teachers. I missed the womb of my mother.

My legs galvanized for a hot-legged sprint down Golden Gate to Hayes Street, where I could dodge traffic and maybe kill my pursuer under the wheels of a bad driver. Mr. Barraza had told me that I had bad eyesight. *I* would be the one who got creamed by a fast car. I wondered for a moment if Hector would take me in, but I knew he wouldn't. I didn't know where he lived.

But I had spent four months using my arms, hands, legs, head, and blood to stop this type of fear. Then I saw it: Jerome looked like boys I had already fought. With Mr. Barraza's guidance.

Was he with me? I looked down at my hands, now constantly swollen with hitting. I dropped the Dairy Selector.

Jerome could be Eugene Phillips's brother. His *younger* brother. I could box Eugene. I should be able to box Jerome.

I listened for a bell inside me, and stood up. I felt dizzy with the unaccustomed height. I said to myself: Don run, China Boy. Don run, Master Ting. Give profile, show left. Shuffle up, circle left. Head down eyes up. Make contac', combo. Punch thru an don hol' back. Stan up, box him. Stick 'n move. Rule Three. Give, no receive.

My legs were shaking. They no longer belonged to me. Fear and the Jell-O Company owned them.

Unknown to me, the reflection on my choices of action, of reviewing fight or flight, was slowing me down, quelling the natural panic that precedes anticipated pain.

"Think! Think!" I urged myself, struggling with my swamping fear, my trembling guts.

I saw Mr. Lewis in front of me, heard Mr. Barraza shouting, and I got it. Yes, oh yes, just Combo Four, a 1-1-3-2. Jab-jab, left hook, my opening left hands moving him to the right, to meet my right cross. I would really have to deliver a right cross. And not miss. I would have to keep my eyes open, on this dark, dark night.

I clapped my gloves together, surprised when my bare knuckles smacked each other.

Back up and set. Go down the order to Combo Three, Two, then One. The simplest symphony in the Y.M.C.A. Book on Queensberry. It maximized my chances for making solid contact by starting with the tough ones and ending with the one-two.

Jerome did not know why I was saying "T'ink! T'ink!" but that is what he had to do when I lined up two feet from him and assumed the stance, shoulders squared, left profile leading, my skinny guard up, dukes ready for three rounds. I trembled like a tuning fork, but my shoulder fakes absorbed the worst of the shaking.

When he moved for me, it would be my bell. My heart was booming in my chest. I was sure he could hear it.

I am seven years old, it is winter's night, my fists are up, and I am sweating.

He wants to do foreplay, have a little appetizer and push me. I am at the main course, ready to give fists.

"Mothafucka!" he hisses, puts his fists up high, arms out to the sides, hands at eye level, protecting nothing. Some boys have arms so long they can guard their guts by closing their elbows in the center. Jerome is using his to practice flying like a bat. I have been trained to concentrate on the movement of his midtorso. His stupid stance fills me with wild hope.

Jerome steps into me on his left foot, bringing a tall falling right. I jab his fist, deflecting it as I shuffle back. I bring my left back, keep my right up, and pop the jab into his right cheek, without the snap I expected. I am accustomed to the added inches and weighty payoff of a big one-pound glove, and my hand hurts now from two shots. I think of Mr. Barraza. Jab jab jab. Circle left. Stick 'n move, close and deliver.

I jab smartly, snapping out into his unsuspecting face and make solid contact against his nose. Ah ha! take that! I show you! I hesitate before hooking left and Jerome is on me with punches to my head. I did not see them coming in the dark. Angry from my blow, he grunts as he tries to down me with a storm of fists. They hurt, the sound of the blows echoing off my body. I feel the rush of panic, my quadriceps flexing for flight.

Instead of running, I shuffle back, as taught. My guard is up and complete, parrying, rolling my shoulders, head low, hands high, elbows flying, catching his fists on my arms and shoulders, feeling his knuckles on my bones, jinking and backing up, and I hear Toussaint scream, from far away:

"YEAH CHINA YEAH!! Duke 'em!"

I stop, balance, and circle him, going left. My arms sting as if lighted matches had been stuck into my flesh, but my head and guts are absolutely intact. I feel like cheering, and I smile.

I start again with Combo Four, 1-1-3-2. My first jab is wild and misses, but I bring it back high, gasping as it blocks his following, counterpunching right. The flesh on my hand burns again, but the pain is familiar, and not threatening.

"Tsou go wan bah dan!" I cry. Boxing and streetfighting are related! I had just called Lucky the Offspring of a Tortoise and a Running Dog in Songhai, showing him that I had an equivalently dirty mouth. Call *me* a chink! I call you a mongrel turtle's egg!

I feel like a historic rebel, a Chinese kid with the mouth of a renegade warlord, ready to tear the roof from Heaven itself.

I snap the jab into his nose, still a bit short for the lack of the glove, and cheat myself, not recovering it into defense but cranking it as fast as I can, and hooking it into his head. It lands hard. Pain sizzles up my arm, and I take the comfort, knowing that I have hurt him, and instantly hook again.

That is how Tony Barraza fought his last bouts, hastened by blood lust and uncaring about injury, digging his whistling hooks into the opponent's ribs while his own face got broken.

My hook is short, but the hard tight swing takes some of the skin from Jerome's high upper cheek and I can feel his pain in my hand. My fist returns and I snap it again, now into his nose with a loud fleshy *whap*. Blood appears, a shining dark sinuous presence. *His* blood.

"Mother-fuck!" he says in a high voice, the pain adding elocution to his oath. Jerome is confused, not knowing how to carry his arms, where to put them. He has discovered that he does not know how to box a boxer, even a junior neophyte like me. He rushes me, and I jink and move, almost too late. I am wearing down. But tears are in his eyes.

Breathless, I throw my right into his wet, shiny face, pulling it just before it crushes his nose, and shuffle back, dancing nervously on my feet. I breathe, sucking air while circling left. I had flinched on that one, holding back.

No wonder I tired, I think; I had stopped breathing.

I had broken four rules. I had dropped my guard and I did not punch through. I had let his blood stop one of my attacks, which was correct for Intro but wrong for the street. I had forgotten to breathe. But I am alive and have committed no fouls. I feel like singing, warbling, yodeling to Mr. B and the Duke. My heart races with the wild unbelievability of events.

The blows have tired Jerome. I am adding insult to his daddy's whipping, to the fear and hurt that had led to his calling me out. Having the China Boy bust his face was not the crowning glory to an otherwise outstanding day.

Worse yet, he cries. He is eight, and no longer carries the cultural authorization to loose tears.

He rubs his cheek, the hand coming away wet but without blood; it is on his lip, flowing from the nose. He grunts and throws a wild swinging right. I keep my guard up, backshuffle and he collects air, losing his balance. He looks at me, knowing that I could have kicked him or headpunched him as he stumbled past on dead feet. He feels my commitment to protect myself regardless of what he does.

"Fucker," he hisses. From him, on this night, it is a compliment.

Jerome stops. Standing before me, his chest heaving, swabbing the blood and tears from his nose and wiping it on his pants with shaking hands. I put my guard down.

Under the pale light of the old glass streetlight, he turns around and heads home, cursing and talking about another day in a voice vibrant with the minor keys of bad fate. I keep my eyes on him like Mr. Lewis would, until Jerome disappears in the dark.

His misery ached inside my own heart as I thought of him returning to Mr. Leo and his belt. This was so stupid, I thought. So stupid. But I won. . . .

I tried to hold the thoughts in my head the way any kid strives to cherish the moment of first victory, the first touch of tape on the chest, the first game-winning RBI. The smell of roses atop the dankness of effort, of struggle, of boyish pain and a child's sweat. Of feeling the brush with power, and the greed of pushing defeat onto another child.

In all my fights at the Y, I had never won a bout. Not even a split decision. But I had just whipped a Basher. A tough Basher.

Toussaint was grabbing me and screaming words in a babble and Alvin Sharpes said, "You one tough titty, China."

Titus McGovern put out his hand, the broad palm of it low and open, and I shook it warmly. I was moved by his offer. He wanted to be indifferent to me, and his handshake cost him. We still were not pals, but the edge was off. Lucky Jerome was a kid who, in the last year, had been fitted for the role of Bad Kid. The prologue to Bad Guy, which was the prescription for, Dead Man. My fighting him, the extension of Mr. Leo, was cool.

I felt grand and we chattered like little squirrels who have saved all the acorns for winter. Later, I went in the house on fast feet, happy on the frayed carpet as I threw a wild flurry of punches at defenseless air.

In front of the place where Mother's portrait had been, I sang, "Heah I come, to save day. Dat mean Mighty Mouse he on his way."

"You be proud of me," I whispered. "Mah-mee. I follow *all* rules." I looked down at my hands. The knuckles were skinned, and the brown stain of Jerome's blood mottled my fingers, the backs of my hands. I washed them, trying to sort out my feelings, my thoughts. These rules of mine belonged to the Duke, the Mark-something of Queen-something. A Y.M.C.A. house god. They were not my mother's rules. But my mother had fought in China, with knives. I held that thought close to me, and felt better.

There was talk about that fight. I began to think that I could whip anyone, and I chased off a couple of smaller kids who approached me by putting up my dukes and swearing in my ferociously hybrid street English. I felt like the King of England. The China Boy Bashers were put on hold.

"Gonna knock you *out*!" I shouted at a menacing gaggle of kids.

Toussaint was happy, but watched me carefully.

"Don get crazy wif yo'self, China. Don be no Big Willie asshole bully, now."

"Not me!" I chirped back, throwing punches, shadow-boxing against little Aaron Williams, showing off how I could make my snapping jabs slap air into his startled eyes, making him flinch.

Toos grabbed me by my collar. He pulled me so close I could smell his breakfast grits.

"China. Don push yo fists on little kids. Rev'ren Jones say dat wrong. My momma say dat wrong. I do a lot fo' you. Ya'll do dis fo' *me.*"

27

NEW YEAR

On New Year's Day, parties on the block were loud and continuous. New men I vaguely recognized were running around in army khakis, bellowing musically funny words like *soju* and *yobo sayo!* at each other. Thirteen years later, in Korea, I learned that the words meant "rice wine," and "hello!"

We all admired the ones who had shiny black paratrooper boots and bright silver airborne wings the color of courage itself.

"We gonna do dat too!" Toos and I yelled.

Then voices would drop, the rhythm of speech slowed. These young men would talk about Blood Ridge, Pork Chop, and the Punchbowl, of fathers who did not return to the Handle.

They called the Handle "The World."

"I'm in The World, Momma, and I ain't gonna go back to no mo' chill-my-ass, freeze-my-butt Ko-rea!"

They talked about killing chinks and gooks and commies.

I knew what chink and commie meant. "What 'gook' mean, Janie?" I asked.

"It's the Korean word for 'country,' for 'nation,' " she said. "It's the same as our *gwo*. The men who went to Korea learned some of the words, and I guess the Koreans said that they were 'Han-gook,' which means 'Korean.' All the GIs remembered was the last part. 'Gook.' "

With growing paranoia, I started talking loudly, if not clearly, about my father shooting commies, but no one cared. I was deeply relieved. I couldn't take another bout of discrimination while I was struggling up the totem pole.

I did not know that Zeke Daniels had a dad until half the 'hood went to the Golden Gate National Federal Cemetery in San Bruno to pay final respects.

Reverend Jones began to show a bend in his back that year, as the infantry regiments heavy with San Francisco men took the last brutal Chinese assaults to fix the DMZ line in Korea. All the eulogies he offered seemed to be for the men who had been the cornerstones of the neighborhood. Cutty lost Tom Molineaux from the garage; the barbershop lost a small, young apprentice named Joe Dance Bethune. Farrell Benneker, Mrs. Timms's senior grocery clerk, came back an invalid and died in the Veterans Administration Hospital. The woodworks on Central, Fremont Elementary's custodial staff—all had lost people. We had not had a lot of fathers in the Handle when the families trekked out from the South, nursing their wounds from the World War. Now there were fewer. Even Rupert and Dozer in the Eatery put out American flags and seemed to make a halfway peace with each other. Their disagreements had been trivialized.

We all knew that J.T. Cooper's daddy had gone to Korea, and he came back dead as well. Mrs. Cooper took no pleasure in the rightness of her prediction, the accuracy of the bereaved cockroaches in her kitchen. Mrs. LaRue and Mrs. Timms paid respects at Mrs. Cooper's home again and again that winter.

"Missus Cooper don't remember our visits, Toussaint," said his momma. "We keep goin and hold her, and cry with her, but it ain't never done with her. She's got it terrible bad."

Death was on the street. For some, the world had ended.

The stars went up in the windows. Zeke and J.T. became quieter youths. J.T. dropped out of the Hot Smokes, forcing them to meet elsewhere. The widows had great respect, and even Big Willie wouldn't defy Mrs. Cooper's feelings by smoking cigarettes in her driveway.

J.T. started having a lot of trouble in school. He challenged Mr. Isington to fight him, tears raining across his face.

Big Willie told the Hot Smokes that his dad had died over there and they had buried him in Korea. "Dat's where dey bury da *real* heroes," he said.

I did not even know where Willie lived, and no one believed the story about his father. No one had ever seen his mother.

"Missus LaRue," I said to Toussaint's momma, "who Big Wirry's momma?"

"Don know, Kai," she said. "I think Willie has some relations in the West Addition, and stays there, sometimes.

"I have offered that boy to come to church. I gave him a warm look and offered him food." She sighed. "He once liked me, a little. But he turn the corner. 'Bout two years ago, I got some candy from Cornelia Timms and gave it to him. Willis, he threw it in the gutter, and cursed me. From then on I knew that he lost his soul. His momma, wherever she be, done lost him for all time. And he still alive.

"You know, honey," she said. "Willis Mack is the loneliest kid on the street. It used to be you. Oh, he run with the Hot Smoke chil'un, but that boy's as lonely as lonely can be."

I thought: give me Willie's size, and I'll be lonely too, anytime.

Christmas was not a time of solitude for me. My sisters were home and Jane and I heard wondrous stories about college, professors, restaurants, interesting people, and food. I sat on the old leather hassock, which was my seat, and watched and listened while my older sisters spoke and laughed and my heart filled with a sense of richness and appreciation. Jane felt better with Jennifer and Megan as conversation partners. They made a great deal more sense than I.

I loved to listen to them, the music of their words, the doors their thoughts opened. I learned about scholars who had been to war and had done manual labor before their library days, about the books of ancient history, science, Western writers, a world of people who spoke and listened. Berkeley sounded like the Golden Mountain Chess Association—filled with smart people who could write. I learned that there were thousands of men pursuing my sisters, who seemed not the least bit concerned.

I wanted to tell them about Tony Barraza, Barney Lewis, Bruce Punsalong, Mr. Miller, and Mr. McCoo, but I sensed they would not be too interested.

Suddenly I got it: they were girls, and this is what the difference between us meant. They would never box. Or wrestle.

I wondered if that meant I would never be smart.

Edna wanted Jane to move out. I wanted my sisters to move back. I began to think that anything was possible. I skipped through the neighborhood, singing off-key songs.

I liked songs about trains, and mothers.

"Momma she say, when we be so small,
Yeah, oh, yeah.
We eat our greens, and grow us up tall.
Momma she say, when our pants climbs high,
Be stayin' away from Debil Woman, or die.
Die, oh, die.
Momma she say, when dat woman walk by,
Go jump yo'self some track, or die, or die."

Willie Mack came out of nowhere in broad daylight and opened my face with a series of crushing right hands that banged all over my forehead, mouth, and nose. I don't think he missed a shot. He hit my skull with dull clonks.

A second punch can erase the pain of the first, reviving the senses. But his second, which caromed off my left cheek and opened it like a zipper, was just as bad. Then my ribs collapsed, pain erupting from the center of my face and nose, and my mouth exploded under his big, hard searching fists.

I did not remember hitting the pavement, but I kissed it with my forehead and nose, leaving signatures that lasted the month. My lip leaked blood like a busted spigot.

He pulled my Y.M.C.A. Keds from my feet while I grunted and wept helplessly with the hurt, trying to keep my shoes away from him, believing that I had been killed. Then the pain came in strong, and I knew that teeth were loose, and that I was still alive. My socks came off. I did not have to feel the slick coppery wetness in my mouth and on my face to know that he had opened me up like a tin can.

He wished me a Happy New Year and a MerryfuckenChristmas

and said, "China Boy, you a *mess?*! You'se bleedin *everywhere*. Want me ta teach ya'll some Fist City? Wanna fist wif me? Like wif Lucky? Lissen, and lissen real good, chink boy. I's time ta come ta *Jeezuz.*"

He faked one of his rights and I covered up and cried, long darts of pain lacing through my chest with every choked blubber. He was so offended by my cover that he spat on me. I felt my work had been undone. It had.

Before the end of vacation, Lucky Washington called me out. I had no heart left. He punched me through my ineffective left guard, in my teeth, making him cry in pain with the resulting cut. He kicked me on the ground while he shook his hand, cursing over my tucked body until he got tired. I left my body while he did in my cracked ribs. I saw him kicking me, a detached observer hovering ten or twelve feet from the sidewalk, at a height where only ghosts and spirits could reach me. My scuffed Buster Browns, now too small for my growing feet, had been knocked off. The good thing was, they looked so bad that even Big Willie would not deign to take them.

I avoided Hector, Toussaint, Titus, and Alvin Sharpes, meaning that I had to shun my streets. I went to the Holy Christian Church, and sat on its steps, telling Reverend Jones that I did not want to come inside, just wanting his stairs.

I had risen to Olympian heights at Christmas, but the return to earth after Big Willie's surprise attack had been more painful than anything before it. I knew in a deep and fundamental way that I did not deserve elevation or success. No way could I fight him. I could eat until Angie ran out of food and punch the body bag until it collapsed from its chains and the roof fell in and I had defeated every kid in Intro. Willie was like a grown-up. There was no hope.

Mighty Mouse had been a bad joke, a sad child's fantasy in a Willie Mack world.

I tried to figure out how I could move in with Mr. Barraza without anyone, including Mr. Barraza, knowing about it. I wanted to live like Semper, a quiet low beast who was fed, watered, given old newspapers, and petted and otherwise left completely alone. No more challenges in boyhood, no more hurdles to leap on the way to manhood. I wanted to be a dog with a kind master.

I was absent when boxing classes began in the new year. I boarded the Five McAllister, forgetting to say hello to the cheery Muni driver. I disembarked at Market, as I had now done a hundred times.

I did not want to go to the Y. I used another punch on my new Muni ride card to take the first rumbling Market streetcar headed west. It was the "L" Car/Taraval Street, and it took me the length of Market, past the outer Mission, climbing past Church Street, to the Castro and the Twin Peaks Tunnel. The Tunnel was black inside, the lights in the car bright and brittle on the eyes. The car swayed as the tracks clacked, mesmerizing me, a continuous mantra to steel and to cold unfeeling. I gave myself to their soothing monotony, the comfort of repetition like a patient and loving mother's voice.

The car went all the way to the beach, stopping below the level of the dunes and the thick ice plant on the shore side of the Great Highway. I stepped off the car and remembered this place, this place of my mother.

I slowly approached the parking areas that bordered the road, looking at the diagonal and parallel parking slots where she had never solved the riddle. I ran, as she had, through the wet mist and the hard pungent smells of seaweed and ocean, across the Great Highway and Route 1, to the seawall, past the undertow warnings, onto the beach, and to the surf. I sprinted as if my speed could catch her, and I could find her arms and her eyes and her laugh once more.

I imagined keeping my shoes on and swimming to the Farallon Islands, which I knew were there, but, like many things, had never been seen.

"Where are the islands?" I had yelled in Songhai, free in the wind like the gulls wheeling overhead, in the days when we had been a family of Mah-mee, Baba, and tsiatsia.

"There, Kai, over there, to your left," Jane had said. "Don't feel bad. I can barely see them myself."

Now I knew I could not reach them. I would drink water, without Coach Lee screaming at me, and die.

I did not know if my mother was really in the water, waiting for me. She wasn't in Tsingtao. I didn't know where else she could be. Why should she be so hard to find? I had loved her so much that I would not have misplaced her, lost like a meaningless toy. Where did God keep lost mothers?

I put my shoes in the wet sand, standing still to let the waves hit them, drenching my pants, looking for a sign from her, something to draw me into the water.

The water was colder than the Y.M.C.A. pool. This was not a swimming beach—the frigid waters, the sucking undertow, the passing sharks, and the cold, wind-whipped air produced a landscape-quality vista—but no one was reminded of Malibu, four hundred miles south. This was like Dover, or Land's End.

The surf crashed loudly, deafeningly. I blinked, seeing a choice, feeling it, the cold inviting me, offering relief.

"Hey, kid, get your feet outa the water!" shouted a fisherman in waders, his pole embedded in the sand at a high angle, his voice vibrating in the roar of the waves.

"You're gonna catch your death of a cold! Go on! Get outa there!"

Mr. McCoo called Edna, asking where I was.

That night I was solidly whipped. Edna said it was because she was worried. I knew it was because she had been embarrassed.

I returned to the Y, listless. I had been a big enthusiast, a cheerleader, with louder noises coming from my throat than from my gloves. Now I was morose. I started coming out of the stairwell late, my laces loose on my shoes. Mr. Barraza crinkled up his face and rubbed his ears. I had the feeling I was disappointing him, and it filled me with a dull continuous inner chest pain.

He got me another pair of lost-and-found tennis shoes.

I asked to return to Crafts and to drop weightlifting. I was getting creamed in dodgeball. My basketball had always been hopeless, and would be until I got glasses, but Coach Oliva got angry. He blew his whistle, which was reserved for serious hacking fouls.

"If you're going to be a girl out there, wear a skirt, damnit!" he shouted. He was not a pathbreaking feminist. Nor was he an egalitarian. He tried to mask truth, but he liked tall players and disliked kids with glasses. I knew how he felt about me—a short blind boy who hated leather basketballs. I was two stages below a troglodyte.

My swimming resembled the spirited effort of a rock falling from a tall cliff.

"Lay off lessons till you get your concentration back," said Coach Lee.

I resolved not to return. I began to have trouble sleeping at night, having to fight a creeping narcosis in the classroom.

In school, my lack of glasses should have pushed me to the front row, but an oblivion to visual events led me in the opposite direction. I picked the back. I had been a withdrawn pupil from the beginning, unable to associate the teacher's English language with the unseen and mystic markings on the blackboard. The teacher's questions were unrelated to anything in my mind.

In the back row, I was surrounded by children who were failing for other reasons. I used to be considered shy but smart. Now Mrs. Halloran was not sure. I was not paying sufficient attention to know, but I think I was becoming inattentive.

"Kai. Are you trying to anger me?" she asked. I didn't know.

Toussaint knew that Big Willie had taken my shoes.

He gave up lunchtime kickball games to sit next to me. Mrs. Halloran was yard monitor and her penny loafers were next to him. He looked at the game he was missing, his head nodding with the action.

"China. Ain't no kid in da Handle kin stan up ta Big Willie. I think he kin beat Missa Leo Washington, truf be known."

I looked at Toos. He *knew* that wasn't true.

"Okay, den. He kin take Missus Halloran's shoes in his *sleep*," he whispered. I couldn't say anything. Big Willie had become the juggernaut of my life, exemplifying the uselessness of effort.

"Is okay, Toos," I said. "Go back game."

I thought of telling Angie Costello that I was having trouble sleeping but she would only feel bad, unable to make spirits move away through the threat of overfeeding. I realized there were problems that could not be solved by eating.

I felt that I had done wrong in trying to be different from what I was supposed to be: a loser, an out-of-step, cultureless, skinny, offensive, myopic, babble-mouthed, rock-talking, clueless, fool punching bag for other people.

I began to lose interest in food.

28

AIR

Ghosts and spirits have variety.
Good spirits lived in the boxing instructors' office. It was a holy crypt
of male function. All the things in it had meaning; each of these men
had closely considered what they wanted to bring into the cramped
space.

Once it was just Kurt Miller and Bruce Punsalong teaching all
classes. Then Mr. Miller was promoted and Tony arrived. Mr. McCoo
joined the staff, but after a few months he showed up in Mr. Miller's
office, his fine gray hat in his big, swollen hands.

"Mistah Miller. Don't wanta teach little kids how ta box, no mo'.
Tisn't in mah heart. Asa mattafack, it *hurt* mah heart."

He reached into his windbreaker and pulled out a piece of paper.
Mr. Miller grabbed his desk and stood, ready to tell Mr. McCoo that
he would not accept a resignation from him, that they could work it
out. McCoo was such a kind and hardworking man.

"I paint pretty good, Mistah Miller. And, it be fittin, I tell da boys 'bout da Good Lord, now an again. When dey might lose it a little in dere young mine's.

"You'se got a close-up craf' shop on da t'ird floor. Oughta be usin it."

He unfolded the paper. It was a watercolor of a gum tree leaning in the Pacific winds in the Presidio and the startlingly bucolic Army base in the north City, built originally by the Spanish to protect the Bay from English raiders. The Marin headlands were in the background, far away.

It was beautiful. Mr. Miller took it in his hands and studied it, marveled at it.

"This should be in the Maxwell Gallery, Eugene," he said.

It hung in the reopened craft shop, surrounded by the paintings and scrawls of children who did not have pencils and drawing paper in their homes, who drew inspiration from the art of this big-muscled man who spoke to them of kindness in life.

"Don get no confusion in da mine, young gennamens," he said. "Da Golden Rule, it fo' boxer boys. Da's why ya'll don foul. 'Cuz dat ain't fair, and tisn't right, and da Good Lord, He want all His people be good ta others. When ya'll ain't in da ring, don' be hitting people. Flash yo' fists, ta defend yo'self, yessir. Da growed men here dasn't hit you. Ya'll dasn't hit others.

"You young gennamens see dis shield of da Y.M.C.A.? It have 'John 17:21' writ on da Good Book, open on dis here triangle. Lissenup, gennamens, an' hear what John say." Mr. McCoo cleared his throat, flashed his gums and flexed his neck, pushing his chin out to relax it. In his deep voice, he continued: " 'Dat dey all may be one; as thou, Father, art in me, and I in thee. . . .'

"See. Da Good Lord say: we's all be da same. We's all be like da dee-sigh-puls, bruthas. Hollywood rich, dirt poor. Negro, Messican, Indian, Oriental, white. Hunter' Point, Mission, China-town, Presidio. Girl, or boy. Young gennamens—ain't dat somethin? Nod yo' heads at Mr. McCoo, show me dat John got insides ya."

Eugene McCoo's transfer to the arts left a hole in the pugilistics faculty. Barney Lewis became the last member of the cadre.

Mr. Miller's selection of a black as the chief of instruction was a dramatic move in the early 1950s, and there was bad talk for a while.

It came from club members who had nothing to do with boxing. Their sons were not in the classes. They themselves had not studied the Science. But they had opinions that demeaned a bright black man with all the talent and strength God could pour into a single soul.

Tony hated moving the watercooler out to make room for a third desk, but when he looked at Barney he knew that a good man was in their midst.

Barney had done something unique for men. He placed his mind and his heart in his eyes, intentionally. He hid very little because he had defeated fear in the ring, had knocked out any remaining self-doubt in crossing France and Germany, and had abandoned vanity in broad daylight, for all to see.

Tony, like many boxers, relied on his eyes to tell him the truth of men. Words, alone, were less than cheap.

"We are here," said Barney, "to teach kids the manly art of self-defense. I want to do it the Christian way, if that meets your approval." He paused and looked at them. It was okay.

"I mean the Golden Rule." He looked up. "Outstanding. So we impart *values*. We are not building a stud stable of future pros.

"I want them to learn rules. Discipline. Control, and self-reliance. And faith in others, particularly in *us*. Adult men. If a boy in the full program goes bad, it will be *my* fault. I want to teach them about violence so they can control it *early* before it gets them. But I do not want to go too far down that road.

"No pugs. Pure Marquis of Queensbury. In Intro, no blood. No Golden Gloves through this program. We can coach fighters individually, because I understand the reasons, but it will not be through this office. Once a kid goes AAU, he no longer belongs to the Y.M.C.A.

"You will not like something I do. That is inevitable. I was Army, you were Marines and Navy. We have different tactical approaches. I *like* that. I want you to talk to me about beefs. I have much to learn from you; you might learn from me. Nothing gets stowed in back pockets. You lay it out and give it to me. We make the effort to agree. I do not enjoy pulling rank, but I do not tolerate unmanly gossip and backbiting. Or breaches of the Golden Rule.

"Gripes or questions or anything else?" Barraza and Punsalong shook their heads. Bruce grinned. Tony's head was down.

"Were ya an officer," asked Tony.

"No, I was not. I wished I had been," said Barney. He knew that his three years of combat performance had merited a fistful of battlefield commissions.

"Officers. Buncha crap, fer the most part. But I forgive ya. Ya was a good fighter, very tough. But ya talk like an officer. Ya know. Long-winded. Maybe Army officers were better 'n those salutin fools the Navy kept siccin on me. I think I can live with ya. Sign me on," said Tony, extending his hand.

Barney put his hand out, and the three of them shook in a pile of knuckles, and Bruce laid a bear hug on Barney that robbed him of two inches of girth he never recovered. All they wanted was to avoid having an asshole; they instead got a very good leader.

Mr. Lewis greeted the class on Saturday.

"Top of the Morning, Young Gentlemen. Today we will concentrate on the inside hook, the digger. It will take all your attention, so please give it. Master Ting, in my office, please." Why was I being called in? Were they going to kick me out, for being sourpussed?

Their office. I loved the trophies, the military photos, the smell of old leather, Mr. Punsalong's stale cigarettes, their lunches, and their aftershave lotions. I smelled Johnson's Baby Powder, rubbing alcohol, gym chalk, Irish Liniment, and Mr. Punsalong's bananas. Peels and Angie's sandwich wrappers were in the waste cans.

Mr. Barraza had photos of himself all over the wall. They were professionally taken, like the ones in his hotel room. One of them was with Red Carlson, the heavyweight who tagged after Tony through his good years. Another was with California Attorney General Pat Brown, and one was with Mayor George Christopher.

"Good guys, Master Ting," Mr. Barraza had said. "Rich like the Rockefellers but they're still people, like us."

Only one picture on his desk. It showed a beautiful dark-haired Mrs. Barraza and the infant, Tony Junior. Both of them were smiling, the world a bright and lovely place. It was in a brass frame, corroded from the steam of coffee and spilled Cokes. I loved Mrs. Barraza's picture because I cared for Tony and I was infatuated with anyone who might be a good mother. His desk looked as though it had been dropped from the roof and had never been reassembled.

"Rook messy, Misser B'laza," I once said.

"Haay," said Tony. "It looks like your face, first day you walked in here."

Mr. Punsalong had no photos, no trace of origin, no indication of interest other than bananas on his desk. Inside the desk drawer was that Marine K-Bar knife and scabbard, Chinese three-section and two-section fighting staffs connected on chains, Chesterfield cigarettes, cloved pumpkin seeds, and a pinup painting from Esquire magazine by an artist named Varga. He did not like us near his desk and always closed it fast if kid sneakers padded up to the office door.

Above Barney Lewis's desk was an autographed photo of General Patton. It said: "To the Best of the Black Panthers, the Most Magnificent Fighters in the World Against the Greatest Number of Enemies, Foreign and Domestic. Bravo! Thank you. Geo. Patton."

A group photo showed his tank company on the eastern bank of the Rhine River. Everyone was black and frowning.

There was one picture, cut from a newspaper, of Barney in his black hightops, in a bout. He had boxed in the Army before he had become a tanker. Articles from *The Chronicle* described him as "The Malice at the Palace," a junior Sugar Ray full of tactical thought, fast feet, and deadly hands. The articles of Arthur Ronald Constance, the famed ring columnist, lined the walls in ancient, browned, curling tatters.

Barney Lewis's desk was very ordered. When we needed tape, Mercurochrome, Band-Aids, Ace bandages, aspirin, liniment, or laces, we went to his desk. Mr. B's was no help and Mr. T's was dangerous.

"Sit down, Master Ting." I sat. He closed the door, a first.

He sat on his desk.

"Tell me what is bothering you."

"Nuting, Misser Rewis. Mr., Lew-is."

"That's not true. I expect you to dig deep and bring it out and *give it to me*. Whatever it is, it interferes with your work. It interferes with my promise to Mr. Miller. I guess that goes back to Mr. Miller's promise to your father. These are things that must be honored.

"You have no decision in this. Tell me what is making you unhappy."

Unhappy? I thought. I thought of Big Willie Mack and the Hot Smokes. Of Lucky Washington. I thought of sleep, of Edna. Of looking for my mother in the sea, my fear of joining her, my fear of staying in the world. My mother's face. I could not remember it. I saw the place where her portrait had hung, the dark unfaded wall paint outlining its true former existence, but the recall of her was coming up blank. Her mouth, a nullity, a bland smear of beige on cream enamel.

I had lost her face and I felt my own features fall apart like an old brick hotel in a Frisco earthquake. My mouth trembled and I made a strange sound that could not have come from me and I tried to recover, to not cry in front of Mr. Lewis as tears ran down my cheeks. I bent over and began to weep seriously, wrenched by an open yawning fear that I would never again have the comfort of her face inside me, feeling crummy for my lack of control.

I had lost her until I too died. The fear of it was beyond words. I tried to say, "Dere no piture of her in house," but only wet blubber came out.

Mr. Lewis gave me a towel and set a swill bucket by my feet, like a cornerman prepared to sop blood between rounds. He knew a lot about pain, and seeing it, particularly when he had not caused it, troubled him not at all.

Barney was an advanced thinker, a believer in catharsis. Most men, white, black, yellow, or brown, would have said, Stow those tears, boy. What are you, a skag skirt?

I think I cried about ten minutes in great sobbing bursts of noise, tears, and snot. Mr. Lewis waited it out. I think he ate one of Mr. Punsalong's bananas and filled out boxing evaluations. Or did the daily crossword puzzle.

I had refused to show Edna my vulnerabilities. I had stored my grief. I cried for my mother, for Jane Ming-li, for my broken toys, my busted spirit, the misery of our home, the Big Willie beating outside, the slapping and kicking inside, the lack of simplicity in my life.

"Did you say, picture? Picture of who, Master Ting? Uh, whom?"

"Mah-mee. Momma," I said.

"She died, didn't she. When?" he asked.

"Aprir, ninetin fittee two," I said. A year and a half ago. An eon in the past.

"Got a new momma?"

"Yes, Misser Rewis."

"Like her?" he asked.

I hesitated. "Chure, yep," I said.

"*Really* like her? Do you like her as much as Angie Costello?"

"No," I said, inaudibly. I pursed my lips and shook my head. Again I cried, my shoulders shaking, producing more fluid than I believed possible. My legs were wet with tears and my mouth had turned to sharp salt. Crying twice in front of Coach, and I wasn't even in the ring. I felt like emotional waste matter.

"Is someone in particular trashing you on your block? You took some bad head shots where the headguard sits. You have dry blood in your nose and contusions on your forehead and nose. You have a cut cheek that could have used a stitch. By the looks of it, he was mighty tall." He put his head next to mine. "Did a grown-up do this to you?"

"No," I said, not wanting to talk about Edna. "Master Mack."

"You do not have to call him 'Master' here. He's not a student. What's his first name?"

"Big Wirry."

"Master Ting, what would you have me do to help you?"

"Ret me move in Y Hotel, same rike Misser Balaza," I said.

He laughed deep, making a warm, rumbling sound.

"No, I can't do that." He punched me on my arm.

"Coach," I said, spontaneously. "What Big Wirry mean, he say, 'Come to Jesus'? Uh, Misser Rewis," I added. "Lew-is."

"Coach" is what the Junior Leaders called the faculty.

"What exactly did Big Willie say?" he asked.

"He say, 'It time, come to Jesus,' I think," I said.

Mr. Lewis, Coach, nodded his head, his lips tightly compressed, his brow wrinkled like his abdominals.

"Well. That's wrong for him to say. Yes sir, that's very wrong. Using the Lord. . . . " He took a breath. "Ministers say that, inviting the parish to come to God, to be open to love. I guess Big Willie means for you to meet your Maker. That's a troubled lad. I must tell you, Master Ting, that this Willie Mack is one bad actor. I do not like his conduct. He has too much crust." Mr. Lewis looked at me very intently.

"Say 'Wil-lie.' "

"Wir-ry."

"No. Try again. Watch my lips. Wil-llie. . . ."

"Wir-llie," I said.

"Good. Practice that." He licked his lips.

"How about we teach you how to whip Big Willie Mack and make him walk funny for the rest of his days?"

I didn't think that was possible. The thought of fighting Lucky again made me sick to my stomach and my flagellated ribs ached. Fight Big, *Very Big* Willie? I wanted to flee my body, evaporating into space, becoming a wood nymph or a ghost, invisibly integrated into the air.

That would be best. Better than being a dog, even a well-cared-for one.

I looked up at him, feeling like an expired Kleenex. He was smiling, his belief in me, in my ability to fight Goliath, as obvious as the mass of muscle in his arms. If Coach, if Mr. Lewis, really believed I could do this . . .

His head was close to mine. He looked like all the versions of Jesus Christ advertised in every church in the City of San Francisco.

29

WIND

Mr. Lewis was a methodical thinker. He began on my approach to Willie Mack by doing homework.

"Tony. We should do this in two parts.

"First. We show him ring blood. Desensitize him. It's cruel, but I don't see the option. Why don't you take him up to Hazard's Gym. Let him watch some pros.

"Second. We give him a specific fight plan. A streetfight plan. I'll do that."

Mr. Barraza led the hike up Leavenworth, a hill no steeper than Central Avenue in the Handle. "This's Hazard's. Fat guy named McQuillan, toppa the stairs. He'll letcha in. Stay outa the lanes 'tween the rings. Walk 'round the edges. Don't sit in no chairs, they ain't yurs. Stay till they kick ya out. Lookit the fights, careful. Real, careful. *Capish?*" I nodded. He turned around and went down the hill. I went up the stairs.

McQuillan looked like an ancient, pale bloated whale with a poke

of a cigar pointing out of corpulent lips. Looking like his universal opposite was Ben Bain, senior trainer and former middleweight. He was
an Anglo version of Barney Lewis—chiseled muscle graced by a tight,
observing intelligence. Mr. McQuillan grunted at me as if he had bad
gas. Mr. Bain waved me in, as if a small Chinese boy in this adult
Western pugil palace were a customary condition.

I watched fights objectively. The savage, sinking blows, the small
tournament gloves going through the opponent's body, the fear, the
courage, the hopes, the enduring pain. Stone hands crunching hard,
prepared muscle.

Men getting savaged off their feet, collapsing on nerveless legs, the
years of muscular addition meaning nothing in the moment after a jolting, heart-stopping punch. Men getting off the canvas, weak as kittens,
putting their hands up for more.

Mr. Bain was desensitizing my feelings about blood, to prepare me
for my baptism of boyhood. He was letting me see adult courage. I
watched and gulped a great deal.

Mr. Lewis had an immaculately chromed, whitewalled, powder-
blue 1952 De Soto with wire rims. This was the first car I loved, an
American machine at the height of American empire, when General
Motors meant cars, smart kids wanted to design them, and "epic" meant
the annual Autorama and its cascade of free gifts for drivers and future
drivers. No one ever made cars like this before, or ever will again.

It was a pleasure to sit in the De Soto and smell the clean leather
and the perfume of his wife. For years, that was all I knew of her. She
smelled like flowers—not like Edna, not like Mother.

"Top of the Morning, Master Ting. Hey, now take your nose off
my car! Lord, I know you like to smell things but that is *disgusting*! We
have to get you glasses."

During lessons on a Monday afternoon in April, he told me to
meet him in the Leavenworth parking lot. He drove me to the corner
of McAllister and Masonic. It was the Municipal Railway Car Barn,
two blocks from my house.

"Mister Barraza and Mister Punsalong have been teaching you
how to defend yourself. How to move, how to find the punching lanes.

"I am going to teach you to win a streetfight. *Win* for you means
to get through it *and hurt your opponent*. And that is the truth, son,
even if you leak all your blood right here on this street and you can't

see for your eyeballs being in the blood. There are no bells and no three-minute clock. You have no corner.

"Your mission, Master Ting," he said in a deeper, more intimate, more casual voice, "is to *endure* a streetfight with Willie Mack. Just like you endure the ring, twenty times now. Like what you did with the other boy, Jerome, at Christmas.

"All you do is stand, take the blows you were going to get *anyway*, and hurt Willie just enough so he leaves you alone for the rest of your life. Dig it: You are going to get bruised by these kids until *you stop* Willie Mack, President of the Pack. Tell me if I'm right."

"You light, Misser Rewis, uh, right. Mr. Lew-is," I said. He nodded at me. Then his eyes narrowed. I was seeing another part of him.

"There he is now," he said. "You're going to have to take him. You know the street has rank. You're good enough to be average." He smiled. "That's progress. Forget rank. Go for the champ."

I looked at him, trembling inside.

He pointed a huge index finger at me. "Lookit here. Instead of doing ten, twenty fights on the street, do one. Because you beat one bad skinny dude at the bottom, all of them are going to line up for you—and the odds are against your reaching the finals. Too many contenders, too many fights and scratchings for rematches. It doesn't matter that he's older, bigger. You go to Mr. Champ. You hold your ground with him, take your best shot, one fight, it's over.

"Watch Willie Mack now. Study his high right hand."

Big Willie was at work in the Barn yard, abandoned after the winter's big quake collapsed half of the old brick roof. Brave, crazy, nothing-to-lose slum kids played on the collapsed roof, dancing around the holes, daring death as loose bricks cascaded to the ground below to shatter in great dust clouds. Willie was making another kid take his shoes off. When the kid hesitated, Willie kicked him. No overhand right. It was okay. I had seen it before.

"He has to be *twelve* years old," said Mr. Lewis. "He's built like a smaller version of Roof, who's going to go as a welter." That topped 148 pounds.

"Willie is so big, he'll *never* be smart, doing everything by size. I'll tell you, Master Ting. About his age? I think his mother got confused or the hospital did. I came down here last week and watched him do his stuff. Okay, here's Mr. Pueblo now." He looked at his watch and smiled. He got out of the car, and I collected my gear and followed him.

Hector Pueblo stopped in front of us. He was holding something.

"Nice car, *hombre*! Didn' see dis baby when you come by. Hey, chico, *cómo dice la buena vida?*" What says the good life. Hector took off his baseball cap, a Yankees cap, and put it on my head. The brim went down to my nose.

"*Amor y pesetas*, Tío Hector." Love and money, Uncle, I said from within the dark of the brim. This was like seeing Superman shake hands with Captain America. The first time I had seen Mr. Lewis I was reminded of Hector. Here they were together, tall, dark, handsome, strong, confident. I smiled, lifting my chin so I could see them.

"Master Ting, you told Rufus about Mr. Pueblo. Rufus mentioned it to me. Roof," he said, with some concern in his voice, "hates the idea of any Y boxer getting his clock cleaned by a street bully. So we worked this out.

"Listen, Lesson One," said Mr. Lewis, facing me, wiggling the fingers of his hands in excitement, standing in his ready stance, his collected power making me breathe fast.

"Wind. You have better wind than he does. Wear him down, dance, circle. Make him tired. Willie's a one-punch Charley who loves his overhand right. He winds up and sends it big, his body behind it. He aims worse than you. He's wild. He telegraphs like Western Union. So you can dance with him, and wear him down." He smiled. It was one of the familiar expressions in class.

"Lesson Two. Keep him in front of you. He knows you duck and dodge. Hector says that Willie suckerpunches you, coming up behind and using a high right hand, a cross that starts above his head. He throws about four of those and one of them hits and you go down. Makes sense," he said, nodding. "Willie punches like a woodchopper bringing down an axe. He's as big as a house and could bruise his daddy.

"Never has been a question, you have *no* reach. That means: *never* turn your back on him again. You walk like he was behind you all the time. Face him and keep moving.

"On fight day, you *move inside him* and without slowing, hit him in the eye with a rising right cross, giving him Rule Three. Better to Give." BAM! Mr. Lewis had slammed his right fist into his open left hand, making my heart jump.

"In the eye! This is a Two-Two-One.

"You recover, left up, and play the same tune again. Hit him! Low rising right cross, in the throat. *Whack!* In the *throat!* Your second Two, in the throat.

"Eye first, because he is tall, and that will be your toughest shot. From there, they get easier because you'll be moving down—throat and then throat again.

"This is not the ring. Mr. Barraza is not going to get down on you for throat-punching, and Mr. Punsalong is going to train you to hit it.

"Master Ting. The moment you bang through his throat, you move out on the express shuffle-back, keeping your left warm. Willie will try to clinch you. You don't have the meat for that.

"On the way out, pop left jab in the throat again. . . . That's your One. If he clinches, beat on his eye, or both of them, with Combo Two, again and again until he drops blind or you are KO'd.

"Don't run. Do not run. I know you'll want to. He's a very scary dude, isn't he? Your legs will shake, you want to run so much.

"Don't run. Don't escape victory. Stand in the ready position, guard up. If *all* your punches miss, *box* and hook him like Mr. Barraza until you have *nothing left inside*. You have good wind. Big Willie has no wind, Master Ting. He has no need of it.

"Mr. Pueblo, please tell Master Ting what you told me."

"Chico, pretend you be Toussaint LaRue. No fear *nada*, an punch 'em out till he all red mush on de sidewalk.

"You 'member what I tol you. Glove mess you up, it get dere too early. Fist, alone, wif no glove, it gotta reach *mas cerca*, close, niño. You unnerstan?"

I nodded.

"Fist, hurt *muchísimo* when you hit bone. Use fist, hit eye, nose, throat, jus' like doctor." I didn't get that one for years.

"Stay 'way from hit de head. Wif eye, de *ojo*, you be careful for de brow, cuz it hard. Niño, hit soft tings, jus hard as you can."

"That's Lesson Three, Master Ting," said Mr. Lewis. "When you boxed the other kid, did you pretend that you were Toussaint LaRue?"

"No," I said. "I pleten' I Mighty Mouse."

"Well, hell, son, you can't lose," he said, laughing. "Just remember that you are, underneath everything, a boy. A very good boy."

He paused and looked away from me.

"And he's an *asshole* bully who will respect your guts. So *show* them. *You* control your will. If he beats you dumb, you win, because you will still make contact with him and he'll never call you out again. Just by standing tall, you'll be too much work for him. If you beat him, it's done. See, if you leave him in the dirt, or leave all of yourself on the pavement, either way, your pounding days, they are *over.* One good fight, with the Big Ugly Dude, and you are on Strut Street *for life.* Lesson Four."

Mr. Lewis encircled my arm in his viselike hand and squeezed it, shaking me as he brought his face so close to me I flinched. His Old Spice aftershave and minty toothpaste seemed to catch on my eyelashes. He spoke with an intensity that made my eyes bulge while my frame shook and my left arm grew numb.

"Spend it all, kid. Spend *every* fucking drop of blood in your body. Leave *nothing*! Goddamnit, kid, *NOTHING*! No rematch with this pig. One time. *Do or Die.*"

I had never heard him swear before. He released my arm, almost pushing me away, cementing the emotion into my left, my jabbing arm, the arm that guarded me. He glided away, keeping his back turned to me.

Hector was talking. He told me to start the bout by insulting Big Willie. He said it was very important to get Willie excited, when his small brain would be swamped by emotion.

"Watch out, chico, 'cause he start go down, he try to kick you in de nuts. Willie, he love his shoes, his PF Flyers, chico," said Hector. "You take dis jar of crankcase oil, you pour on hees shoe in de yard afta school. Chico, you hear dat school bell, you get ready to pour. Den you say, 'Sheet, Willie, you shoes, dey *ugly.*' His blood, it be up. Dis oil, come from a tractor axle, all broke down at de yard. Is *bery* bad sheet, almos no fluid in dere. Is all grutch. You do dis to his shoes, chico, in de hopscotch area, where dere no fences or steel poles. You stay 'way from dem tether-ball poles, chico, cuz Willie, he try to kill you on dose."

"When you pour the oil," said Mr. Lewis, "assume the ready position, guard up, head down, eyes up, left leading. Stand *inside* his defense. As Mister Pueblo said, remember that without your fourteen ouncers, you have to be closer when you punch. That's why we teach follow-through, and punch-through. Use them."

"*Desegundo* dis cholo cock his *brazo,* you do it to heem. Real hard, my fren', *real* hard, eye, nose, throat." Hector pumped his muscular arm, like he had that first night in our house.

I tightened my lips, resolve humming through me.

"Two-two-one," said Mr. Lewis. "Two-two-one." He had a roll of black electrical tape and a laundry pen. He wrapped the tape around my wrist, similar to the wrapping of hands before a bout. But this had adhesive. On the tape, in white ink, he wrote large numbers. I turned my palm up and read it: *2 2 1.*

"Flex your fist. Feel that strength? This tape gives your left wrist more power and will keep you from popping the wrist when you make contact. You have a sweet and fast left. Use it.

"In war, the fellow who picks time, place, and method wins. Hector's told you the place: the schoolyard by the hopscotch. I've told you the method: don't turn your back; two-two-one, inside, eye, throat, throat. Spend it all. You pick the time, Master Ting. When does Willie Mack usually do his bully-fighting, his kid-beating, shoe-collecting clothing drive?"

I thought. "Monday," I said.

"Does he eat in the cafeteria?" I nodded. "When do they serve pork and beans?" Thursdays, I said. I knew my food. Beans, they disturbed the gut.

"What day do you think you should box Master Mack?"

"Tursdey," I said. Socrates smiled.

"How much more time do you want to prepare?" he asked.

In ten years I would be in the Army. In twenty years, if I kept up the weights and did not lose Angie Costello, I might be a real big guy. I knew those were wrong answers.

"Two week," I said.

My heart kept rising from my chest and I lost a week of public instruction. I was there, but Mr. B would have been proud: I was too busy making sweat to listen.

I prayed to the Chinese household spirits with whom my mother conversed. I sat in the dry bathtub and sent a desperate message to my grandfather, and my Uncle Han, Father's brother, my boxing relative, in Shanghai. I bought joss sticks at the On-On Cafe and burned them in the ninth-floor gym, chanting a litany of courage taught me by Hector and Mr. Punsalong.

I had practiced my inside move, my eye and throat shots, my

stance, until I could do it without thought. I was able to do the whole routine fast, slow, or medium.

It is the first Wednesday.

"Do it medium," said Mr. Lewis. "You will be hyped, so your pace goes up. It will come out faster than you think. But go medium in your brain, and you will hit your marks, and win."

Win. The thought of it made me faint, my breathing rapid. Mr. Lewis thinks that I will win. That I *deserve* to win.

I kept the jar of crankcase oil on the floor under my bed. Sometimes I looked at it and felt comfort. Other times, it looked like a bomb about to explode, quietly vibrant with its symbolic violence, its promise of war upon a frightening bully who could blow buildings down with his breath.

Friday and Saturday. Mr. Punsalong helped me practice the routine. He walked me through the combination on him, while he was on his knees. He stepped up the pace until I hit him, gloved, with all my strength. I hit him in the throat and he choked, his face reddening, and as I began to apologize he floored me with a fierce head shot that made my brain ring and he shouted at me to get up. His emotion was fearful.

"*NEVER* 'pol'gize in ring!" he yelled in a cracked voice, his face so close to mine it seemed that he was yelling from behind me.

"Mess up in fight, *never* 'pol'gize. Hit *good*! I feel it! See, Ting, you hurt grown man! Willie Boy a *kid*! How that feel?"

I knew the question by now.

"Feel good, on target, tru' the lane."

"I know you boo'shit me, but okay. Hit *good*!" Mr. Punsalong beamed and rubbed my right glove on his white gym shirt.

"Do again," he said.

Mr. Punsalong tried again to teach me *chi*, focusing my energy at the point of contact, drawing from my center, my abdomen, and transferring it to the target. I practiced it on the body bag. He was not impressed.

"An you *ni chung-kuo ren*," he said. You are Chinese. I stared at him with my customary opened mouth. "Ting. I part Chinese. Don't make me lose face by losing to a chump."

As soon as I was done I went up the stairs from the main lobby to the mezzanine. I dropped a nickel into the pay phone and dialed the China Lights Bank, which was open on Saturdays.

"Shim Syensheng, *ching*," I said.

"Mr. Shim on business, in Taipei. Back here in next week," the voice said.

What would my Dababa think about my hitting an elder? Of preparing to fight in school? Of pouring oil on a person's shoe? What would my uncles in the chess association say?

He would say: *Haushuhsheng*, do not fight. Use reason. Be a formidable chess player, a thinker, a scholar, a man of thought, a meritorious candidate for the Forest of Pens. Someone in whom the Emperor, the Son of Heaven, would invest trust above all else. Do not become a rude American brawler, a ruffian, a man of muscle who will never be able to recite the T'ang poets. Reject the physical world.

But he had been proud of my teacher. He had never spoken of Mr. Barraza after my dinner with the Gold Mountain Great Chess Association, allowing his momentary admiration to remain as an unsullied memory.

I had demonstrated Western fighting to my elders. They had said, *Hao, hao.*

Events had led me here. My yuing chi, my karma, was to offer my body to the gods of boxing, of *wu-shu*, of child battle, of the schoolyard. I had decided, as Father had urged me. Pick one, and don't look back. Stand tall, like Father, and Na-men, and my Y.M.C.A. teachers.

I knew that I had to fight Big Willie. And do it very, very well. The choices had been made before me by the gods who had taken my mother.

Monday. Mr. Punsalong argued with Mr. Barraza to let me do the body bag instead of weights in preparation for my bout. Mr. Barraza said that I would lose the ground I had gained.

"Groun? What, a dirt clod? Ay-ya!" snorted Mr. Punsalong.

"Tony. What Ting do, Willie Boy head-punch from behind? Ting roll up sleeve, show arm? Pop bicep? Show def'nition of deltoid? Squeeze trap'zoid for Big Willie? C'mon! Tony!"

Mr. Punsalong hit Mr. Barraza in the chest with his two-inch punch, something from karate. It really hurt. Mr. Barraza's eyebrows beetled and the muscles in his massive jaws flexed.

"Boy need zing in punch. *C'mon!* Letim do bag!"

Bruce grabbed, squeezed, and shook Tony's arm, making Tony's head wobble. If Bruce Punsalong had been a Nash or a Studebaker salesman, those cars would still be on the street. If he had ever met Mr. Tupperware . . .

I did the bag.

The bag was a canvas version of me—a catchall for the blows of uncaring youth. The Men's Department had the new gear. The boys' had the broken-back and dilapidated bag with frayed, blackened duct tape wrapped around its middle. It was hung to match the torso and head target of a ten-year-old, so the top of the bag was clean and cylindrical while the bottom looked like a forgotten athletic supporter.

I attacked the bag with *chi*. I pretended it was Willie, and the bag scared me. I tried to beat the stuffing out of it, to beat it silly. Thinking about my harmonic essence reminded me of Mother, and it gave me the resolve to punch the bag hard, even if I imagined it to be Willis Mack, King of the World.

Mr. McCoo talked to me in the Boys' Department office, in the lobby.

"Don be hatin dis boy, Master Ting. Da boy bin done painted wif da wrong brush; ain't his fault. Box 'em, Master Ting. Don' be tryin ta kill 'em, or bruise his soul. All dat ugly stuff, it come back ta haunt ya when ya try ta sleep at night. Lissen, young gennamen. I see yo' face. It so angry! Relax yo'self!" He grabbed my cheeks and pulled them until I had to laugh.

"Hear dat? Dat laughin? Dat's *you*, pardner. Ya'll hold onna dat. . . ."

I began replaying Mr. Barraza's instructions at night, to fight off the nightmares that seemed to pursue me. "Head shot, Master Ting. Temple. Hook for the temple on the head and drive through the temple. Don't get delicate on me, Mister. . . .

"Rib shot misses, get arm. Arm shot, get base of the delt, kill the nerve, make 'em think he been kissed by a hot wire.

"Kidney shot, follow through. Hey! Good! Now don't look at me—the other guy, he just killed you. Yur dead meat. You let Master Torres just kill you dead all over the place.

"Coulda taken yur head off. *Never* lookit yur trainer, never lookit yur corner. What if this goon's buddies shout at ya like I just did, loud—ya gonna drop yur guard and look around like a freakin tourist in Chinatown? No, kid, yur not. Uh, no offense."

Tuesday. Big Willie almost caught me during lunch. I was not ready. I sprinted away from him back to my classroom, his taunts and the hot slap of my shoe leather echoing in my ears.

I had trouble not hating him. Sorry, Mr. McCoo, I said. I hate this boy, very much. I thought of him, the terror of him, and all concept of laughter fled.

Wednesday. "Toos," I said, "gots talk." We ate lunch on the stairs to the schoolyard, facing McAllister, watching the buses, the trucks, the mothers, and the drunks. I ran a pencil along the concrete cracks, loosening weeds and small grass.

"Tersday, I fight Big Willie."

Toussaint looked at me. He looked at my jam sandwich, sitting on wax paper on the sidewalk. He frowned, suspecting that it contained a baby Mickey Finn, a poison, something that made the mind stop working.

"Howzat, China?"

"One fight, Toos. Don hav win, jes fight hard, win anyway. I start fight. I pour glease, grease, on shoes. Den say, 'Hey, Willie, you shoes, dey mighty *ugly?*' Den, I box 'em." I licked my lips. "Light?"

"Right!" he cried, slapping the calico patch on his painfully skinny knee. "Dang, China, on da nose! But, man, dat take *guts?*! You got dat much shit put away, stan up ta Big Willie? An do his *shoes*, too?!"

He thought. He looked at me with his deep, shining eyes, so much smarter than my own.

"Want me ta help?'Tween two of us, maybe no one git killed."

I looked at Toos very hard, imagining for a moment being dead, and never seeing his face again. Not hearing his strong voice.

"Oh, Toos," I said, "maybe yuing chi, karma, want me dead. Maybe dis way, see Mah-mee."

"Who want you dead, China?" he asked. "Who Mistah Young Cheese?"

"Karma," I said. "God."

"Nah," he said. "God don wan ya'll dead. But Big Willie. He might try to poke yo' eyes out."

I nodded.

"Okay," I said. "If he kick me in head, and I knock out? You get Misser Isington."

At the Y that afternoon, Mr. Lewis told me to stretch, practice one routine with Mr. Punsalong, hit the bag, and eat. Mr. Lewis sat down on the stool next to mine.

"I got this from your sister, Megan, at Cal," he said.

"You know Megan?" I asked.

"She sent Mr. Miller a Christmas card in December. Introduced herself to him through the card, and gave a phone number for the International House over there, in case we ever needed to get ahold of someone in an emergency." He looked down at his hands.

"We needed another emergency number for you," he said cryptically. "So I called your sister," he added.

He handed me a wrapped package. I slowly and carefully disassembled the thin paper, not wanting to tear it. Christmas paper.

A picture frame. Inside was a blurred black-and-white photo of my mother, her long thick hair tied in a bun at the nape of her neck. She was wearing one of her light, mandarin-collared dresses. An orchid sat behind her left ear. A white jade earring hung like a small teardrop beneath it. The picture was small, but it consumed my vision, my mind, and it seemed that my spirit began to leave the cafe, the building.

Mr. Lewis rubbed the hair on my head.

"She'll be with you, Master Ting," he said, "when you face the bully and show him what Y.M.C.A. boxing is all about." He took a deep breath.

He said very loudly, very slowly: *"I do not think that Willie Mack likes your mother. I think you should do something about that."* Hearing this made my heart pound like a huge drum, vibrating my chest, and I found myself breathing quickly, as if I had been running for an hour, as a light-headedness swam through my brain.

When I looked up, my eyes filmy, I was alone.

On my way out of the Boys' Department, I hitched up my jeans, secured the photograph, and checked for my bus card.

Rufus Monk opened the door behind me, yelling, "Hey, tiger, ya'll teach that boy some *religion*, and beat the stuffin outa him." This was very good karma, coming from Roof. I made a fist and cocked it; he did the same, and made a gesture at me. I squinted: he's showing me a finger—a thumbs-up. Whew! I felt grand as I headed down Leavenworth for the bus.

"Hey, Master Ting!" shouted Tony Barraza. I turned around.

"Yessir," I said. Mr. Barraza was barreling toward me in his street clothes—a heavy brown plaid shirt with brown workpants and his cleanest black running shoes.

"Yur fight's tomorrow," he asked in his funny way, without the question mark.

"Yessir," I nodded.

"Ain't helped ya much, gettin ready," he said, twisting his lips around as if he were sucking a lemon. "Bothers me, teachin a kid, a little kid, ta knock another kid in his google. Beezer, no sweat, do it inna heartbeat."

"What 'google'?" I asked. "What 'beezer'?"

"Beezer's yur nose. Google, 'at's yur Adam's apple," he said, pointing to the center of his throat. " 'At's a foul." He looked down at me, squinting. "I love the rules, kid, I really do. They're all we got. Crap, kid, we *gotta* follow the rules. *Capish?*"

I grimaced with the thought of fighting Big Willie *and* offending the Duke.

"But 'at's inna ring. I'm talkin outside the Y, and I ain't in uniform. Now I'm talkin like an uncle. Like yur Uncle Shen, or whatsis phedinkus name. Yur fightin a big street lummox who kicks. I figger it's jake fer ya ta do it.

"Lissina me. When ya close with 'em, drive yur hand through his google lika locomotive kickin a cow. Punch 'em like ya had my arm ta do it. Knife through butter, kid."

I looked down at my arm. It didn't look like Mr. Barraza's.

"Jes punch 'em like you was the meanest sonavabitch in San Francisco. I ain't gonna say 'good luck' to ya. Jes 'member that all youse gotta do is lay fists onna lunk and youse done good."

As I rode the bus, I felt the warmth in my chest as I hugged the picture to myself, seeing all of the details of her face in my mind. I didn't like the blackness of the photo. Although Mother looked very beautiful, the photo seemed historic, and ancient, suggesting that she was an archive from an earlier world. But she was my mother, and she was with me again, the wonder of her face, her presence, slowly seeping into my being. I clutched the frame to myself as if it were a lifesaving ring in the midst of a catastrophe at sea.

I entered the house with dramatic obsequiousness, the frame inside my sweatshirt, making it to my room and hiding it under my pillow as if I had actually smuggled my living mother into this place that was once hers.

I had been having nightmares. I knew that I did better at the Y whenever I had slept well the night before. I needed to sleep soundly. I thought of sleeping on Toos's steps, and remembered how cold it was. I looked at my bed, not wanting to sleep there.

I took my jar of tractor oil, Hector's Yankees cap, my pillow, blanket, and picture frame to the bathroom. I slept inside the bathtub, the cap on my head. I lay awake for an hour, my mother's photograph on my chest, and replayed Mr. Barraza's Monday coaching. I held Angie's cafe key on its chain in my hand, a small fetish of an adult's trust in me.

I marveled at Megan, at Mr. Lewis, for recovering the picture of my mother's face. I vowed: I will never lose it again. I clutched the cold metal photo frame to me, my eyes tightly closed, embracing my mother, selfishly absorbing all of her quiet energy and love.

I fell into deep and dreamless sleep.

30

FIRE

My father rose with the dawn, bounding out of bed with instant energy. He knocked on my door and I struggled out of the tub, running to my room with my icons to dress completely before returning to the bathroom.

It was one of Edna's rules. Father, son, That Girl, and the Bathroom Minuet. I wait for Father. I cannot leave the room to use the bathroom until I am completely dressed.

"Young men cannot show their bodies before ladies," she said.

Jane must wait until I am done before she can use it. She's a pretty teenager with long and complicated, time-consuming hair. I'm a skinny rail who has no use for a mirror I cannot see. But Edna has ordained me with bathroom priority because it is something Jane wants and something about which I am indifferent.

Jane had made our father's lunch the night before. I ate *tze*, a

Songhai rice porridge, while he read *The Chronicle*. Edna was still in bed, the only way we could manage to have Chinese food.

When Father, smartly dressed in one of his two suits, left with his lunch, Jane appeared, finished the *tze* and washed away the evidence. She left for Roosevelt and I prepared for Fremont. I wore my thickest clothing and tied my new laces very tight.

"Never let yur laces break inna middle of a bout," said Mr. Barraza. "Embarrassin as hell, yur shoe comin off."

If I survive the day, I thought, I will show Jane my picture of Mommy. It was a big incentive, for I knew that Jane would love it and feel the love of our mother, just by looking at the memory of her face. I made my bed and left it under my pillow, facedown. I tightened the black electrical tape with my game plan around my left wrist.

"Kai," whispered Jane. "Good luck!"

I looked at her quizzically.

"You talk in your sleep," she said. "I can't believe that you're sleeping in the tub."

School took forever. Two-two-one, I said to myself, holding the jar of oil. It was in a Dundee Marmalade crockery jar. Some kids wanted to taste it. It's nothing, I said. They persisted. I opened it and told them it was Chinese food, the statement not contradicted in their minds by the noxious metallic aromas. They made faces as they surrendered their interests in culinary cosmopolitanism. I was developing a sense of humor.

"Why chicken cross road?" I asked.

"Aw, China Boy. We heard dat one!"

I asked Blade Brown, who sat next to me and could read the far wall clock, to tell me when it was 3:05. I then asked Mrs. Halloran if I could use the bathroom, and she said of course, and that I Do Not Have To Come Back.

I stood in the playground, near the hopscotch grids, far from the tether poles, with my jar at my feet. I was breathing very fast, bouncing on my feet, stretching my calves. Quads for flight, calves for fight. I blew air out like Mr. Barraza in the weightroom.

I rolled my shoulders, popping my elbows in practice jabs and hooks. I didn't stretch my high-rising right cross; it felt better tight and coiled, ready in a nervy, tingling way, saved for Willie as a special gift from my teachers.

I remembered the things Hector told me.

The west sun was behind me, and would be in his face. I loosened my shirt collar and retied my shoes, a hundred times. I thought about the way he hit little kids. Mr. Lewis, Mr. Barraza, and Mr. Punsalong didn't like that. Mr. Pueblo thought it stank. Me too. I set my face to angry. I pissed! I said to myself. I stood tall, rolled my shoulders back like Toussaint. I thought about rolling up my sleeves, decided against it. One more layer of protection. I said my Litany of Big Willie, as Hector and Mr. Punsalong had taught me:

"I know I 'flaid, 'fraid. I know I feeling, velee very, big-time. Big Willie very big strong boy. I know my heart jump. I sweat, got no spit. I keep breathe, alway keep breathe. Don rike hit, brud, blood. I *hate* boy who take my crows, clothes, my shoes, my Keds. Spit on me. Ain't cool. Not fair!

"So, Y.M.C.A. boxer keep stance. Head down, left up, shuffle, combo, all time, big-time. I hit with *chi*, from gut. Hurt him, big-time. Do one time, onry one time. I spen' everyting. Leave nothin. Do or die. No rematch wif pig. No, sir. Ain't cool. He a chump. Think Toos. Think Mighty Mouse. Think Burt Rancaster. Hit google like train kick cow." I thought of Barraza, Lewis, and Punsalong. Mr. Miller. Tio Hector. I closed my eyes, keeping them inside me, in the place where my mother lay shimmering as a cool but enduring memory. The pantheon for my *try* and my trial was complete.

The 3:10 bell rings and slowly, as an amoebic mass, the kids emerge. Big Willie is easy to see—a big head above the crowd of children. As he comes closer, he slaps another sixth-grader on the arm and points at me.

The blood roars in my ears as if I have already been hit. My heart is tripping wildly. My stomach churns in a sour, acidic compression of anxiety and raw fear. I unhinge the wire lock on the jar with frightful, fumbling fingers, almost dropping it, and I realize that I am whimpering like a baby rat.

Willie walks directly for me and the glare of the sun; his head seems immense. When he steps on my shadow I express-shuffle up—advancing fast with my guard up—and tip the jar over his shoes. Nothing happens. Then the dark gunk burbles out, spilling on his shoes.

"What da fuck?" he says and jumps back, banging into other kids, knocking them down like tenpins. One PF Flyer hightop looks like it came from the La Brea tarpits. The other is splotched. Some of the stuff, a blackish slimey sludge that smells like wet bitter ore drawn from the subcore of the earth, is on his jeans.

Willie's face is captured by disbelief. Intellectual dissonance rules his mind, his concerns about being first to grab french fries at the Eatery suspended for the moment. He was about to laugh about my funny shuffling approach to him and then all this shit lands on his *Flyers*.

Someone takes the jar from my hand. It is Toussaint.

"Jee-e-zuz Lord!" he exclaims in four syllables. He is staring goggle-eyed at Willie. "Duke 'em!" he hisses, and shakes my arm. I am looking at Willie's surprised face, enjoying his confusion. "China!" he cries. Toos hits me, hard, on the arm, awakening me.

"Oww!" I cry. Then I remember. "Uh, yo' shoes. *Ugly?!*" I say, loud as I can. I sound like a mouse, my voice lost in the crowd, my mind swollen with the effort to maintain mental focus and control over my skyrocketing emotions. "Dey *ugly?*" I shout.

I go into the stance, and Big Willie looks as large as a building over my fists. He is larger than the body bag. My brain is tripping at light speed, calling up the fifteen parts of my body and organizing my training for the bout. My adrenaline is pumping hard.

Top of the Morning, Young Gentlemen, announcing the bout for the mind, body, spirit, and future of China Boy Kai Ting, the superlight featherweight in the blue jeans on the hopscotch corner, who is going to touch gloves with a welterweight, the boy as big as all outdoors, Big Willie Mack, wearing tractor crankcase oil, ugly Flyers, and an expression that makes China Boy's gonads feel like returning to base.

My body's in the right attitude and I have my feet, my profile. Willie is trying to produce profanities, but he is still stuck with the enormity, the stupidity of what I have done to his sneakers. He keeps looking at them and at me, trying to add it up. His mind clears.

"You—you fuckin—fuckin muthafuckin *mutbafucka!*" he screams. The words mean nothing to me, but I know he is being neither friendly nor imaginative. I flinch.

I guess that he was thinking about Lucky and our Christmas fight, about having pulverized me on New Year's Day, and about the number of people now around us. Big Willie did not fight for crowd approval. He fought for the pleasure of taking things that were not his. The Car Barn in early evening was his venue. Not high afternoon in the Fremont schoolyard. The pupils are out, with teachers in the mob. I can't tell who they are. They create a natural ring for us.

No one had stood up to Willie for a couple years.

I squint and in my mind I hear the echoes of my four guiding fathers, their advice melding: all I have to do is hurt him, to give, not receive. Spend it all, leave nothing. Don be afraid yo' own *sangre*, chico, you got lots. Two-two-one. It's gonna hurt like leeches on your dick, but when it's over, you are a free man.

My shoes are tight, his prized sneakers have tractor grutch on them, I am thinking, and he is having trouble getting his curses out. The spirits are with me. My ears tingle as I yearn to hear Mr. Barraza's voice in my corner. I feel him in my hands.

Make your move, Master Willie. I not running.

Willie shouts, which makes me flinch from my laces to my tonsils, but I keep my guard up. His right hand moves for me, and I hesitate. It is coming so slowly I think I have somehow inhaled too many fumes from the Double Olive Bar. He has a huge fist, and I watch it come near as hobos see trains approach from the smoky distance. Do it!

I shuffle fast, but stiffly, inside him, willing myself, forcing myself, to close with him, to approach his hulking menace. Lifting my left foot and pumping my right to jam me inside his punch, I keep my left high and my head low, protecting the left side of my head and face. I bring my right cross up with all my back and my hips. I know it is a great punch before it reaches his throat. When I make contact with his neck, I still have most of the power waiting in my shoulder and upper arm, and I let it all go and punch through with everything in me. I grunt as I smack it in. I feel the long contact with the details of his Adam's apple against my knuckles. The force from my legs and back transfer into his throat. He makes a gargling noise like Evil trying to inhale a hot dog inside the wrapper. Then Willie's right hand hits my left guard, in the center of the bone in my upper arm, where the deltoid meets the biceps and the triceps. I go numb, knowing I am in trouble.

"Ahhhh!" I moan.

I shuffle back for time and space, stop, will myself to move in, lunge and throw my right cross again for the same spot, his throat, punching it solidly. It is like hitting the body bag because he has not moved laterally, and my wrists have the shock that comes from little kids laying fists into the huge one-hundred-pound sack. I feel the black electrical tape supporting the circumference of my wrist as the other hand bangs into him. His arms come up.

Now I really shuffle back, feeling his clinch, and jab my left toward his eye. It does not get there. My left arm, deadened from his big fist, disobeys the command to strike, and it leaves my shoulder slowly, without power, fizzling and missing his face. Everything is still moving in slow motion, and the pain in my arm is acute. I feel as if I have just been inoculated by a telephone pole.

Remember, says Mr. Punsalong's voice, pain, it not for you, let it pass t'rue, don hol' on to pain. Pain in your arm, not *your* pain. Give back. Shake it out. I shook my arms.

Big Willie is not together. Coughing, his legs spastic. The fingers of his right hand splayed, searching for a grip while he holds his jumping throat in his left. I have never hit another kid so well, so true to original aim. Of course, I have never fought the broad side of a barn before, either.

I keep my guard and move in, humping my shoulders, offering fakes, circling left, throwing numbed and decorous jabs. Then I use the jab as a parrying foil and with my right I get some hits on his arms, his hands, his shoulders, stopping when he lands hot spiking punches on my left.

I go right, away from his punishing blows, sucking air, feeling something building inside my body.

Fighting is funny. Not funny like Danny Kaye and Lucille Ball, but funny as Aristophanes, as the Periclean Greeks, would have it.

If a kid starts a fight by pushing, pushing will be returned. If it starts with kicking, kicking is the theme. That is why one should never bring a knife to a gunfight, a worm should not challenge Godzilla, and a chump should never box a boxer.

Willie, the mugging artist, is trying to box. He looks at my stance and guard and imitates it, but it is monkey-see, monkey-do.

I lower my guard, he lowers his, and I step in and punch him hard with my right, crossing into his nose, crossing into his damaged throat, putting my back into it, delivering it smartly with *chi* from my center. Right hook temple, left jab face, left jab face, right hook temple, and left hook temple, now my best punch. The nerves in my left arm are back. Punch through! I cry. Find the lanes! Deliver!

Willie tries to defend himself. He tries to hit me. He telegraphs his right, he sends warnings about his left. He has no fakes, no counter-punches and is moving like molasses in January. I have time to brush my teeth and fold clean towels between hammering him. I am now doing target selection, like Mr. Lewis in his silks, beating on the bag. I dance around him.

My crosses splash on his nose and face. The first right hook gets good solid temple, enough to really zap my fist with a series of internal electrical misfirings, and the jabs connect on his face and chin. I know I am hitting him solidly because my hands and wrists hurt and ache as the skin comes off. I want to look at them but do not.

I concentrate on keeping my numb fists tight, resisting the muscles' desire to relax and open, to release the small pains.

The second right hook misses because my fist isn't up to another contact, and I flinch before it crashes into his hard, almost-adult head. The left hook gets him below his floating ribs and I can tell by his whimper that this is where he will hurt as much as anywhere, maybe even more than in the throat. I hate peanuts; Willie hates being hit in his flanks.

I bang them as hard as I can with sharp hammers and diggers, making the sounds of a small child-machine at work, mewing with my effort, taking smashing knocks on my shoulders and arms that rob me of feeling and strength. He succeeds in deflecting me from his ribs, and I hook into his face.

His nose is bleeding from both nostrils and he gags with pain. Confused about having the China Boy hurt him, about the Sweet Science of the Duke, he struggles to not cry and forgets to curse.

He drops his arms, spent, finished, his tears leaking. I know how they feel on bruised cheeks. Hot, without salve in them. I see the unbelievable as he stumbles away from me, out of the relative clarity of my vision.

I drop my guard, my arms heavy and worn and throbbing in swollen pain. It is as if he has been fighting me with a baseball bat. My knuckles are ripped and bleeding.

I look down and see Willie's thin, almost transparent blood on the white numerals on my black taped wrist. My breathing sounds like a symphony of spastic winds, the air whistling through my lungs like a cyclone through trees. I have better wind than Big Willie! I notice that now I do not hear his breathing.

I hear Toussaint scream as I go down hard on the yard, leaving skin. Lucky Washington had seen my inattention, and he put his hands on Willie's back and pushed with all his strength, driving Willie into me.

Willie took one giant step and hurled his bulk into me, throwing a clean shoulder into my chest that chopped me down like a farmer's wheat scythe. I roll as if I were playing dodgeball, breaking some of the fall but losing all of my air as his foot sinks into my stomach and another kick pitches me two feet in the opposite direction. I try to get away from him on hands and knees and empty lungs.

I am like a hen chasing peas down a steep hill. I try to cover my face and get up to my skinned knees and he kicks out my legs. I move my arms down and a foot lands on my head. I roll and he kicks my back, following me. I am a burn victim, all aflame, my rolling efforts failing to dampen the fires.

His kicks slow as he aims and sends big windups into my curled body, hearing his oomphs, his delicious sounds of vengeance, as his foot goes through me, jarring spine and stomach and an array of nameless internal organs. I feel my strength dissipate with each kick as the clock begins to slow. He gets me in the mouth, snapping my head back and I absorb the bitterness of the tractor oil as I desperately spit through a sudden flood of warm choking blood that gags me before I can empty my mouth. His foot slams me in the eye and I feel the swamping consumption of deep bodily fear as a warm black cloud wafts through my vision.

Willie gets on top of me and with one ferocious foot stomp crashes my head into the schoolyard and the stars come out in a rich fiery burst that makes me think my head has broken open like a melon. He has ended it. I sob in blind, dark, shadowed pain, uncaring about the humiliation, now only wanting to live, wanting the next blow to be the last, for all time.

Through a roar in my ears that made him sound wonderfully distant, I hear Big Willie swear about his own blood, and then he liquidly laughed, a deep rich basso rumble, full of pleasure, filled with glee, backed up by a wolfpack chorus of Hot Smokes chuckles and whistles.

I hear a teacher shouting to Mr. Isington to get the police—a futile call in the Handle.

I hear odd sounds. It is the kindergartners and first-graders making the sad small noises of dismay that little children emit when they see traffic accidents, domestic violence, and the labor of bullies.

His laughing changes me. I had given up, flirting with the mysteries of unconsciousness, wanting to pass out rather than feel another foot stomp.

Not nice, I think, laughing at small kids. Kicking them and laughing. Letting little kids see this. Like Leo Washington. This person, this bully, does not like my mother. Mr. Lewis told me that!

Big Willie pauses in stomping my face; it is guffaw time, and I feel the opening. I gather to rise, but nothing happens. Messages are not getting through. Then my arm jerks. On my hands, knees, face, elbows, and wild hope, I scrabble like a broken-backed crab, banking on a surviving ability to move and stumble to my feet. I fall down on absent legs, and get up again, staggering away, trying to gain ring space. My guard comes up like a baby blade of grass, seeking sun.

My head is compressed, with a roar of dizzying pain. I brush the sticky gravel from my face, spitting spools of red blood, the smack of his heel burning in my head, the source of blood universal, the memories of his feet in my gut, my back, my neck and arms, my chest shuddering from his crushing body block. My ankles hurt and I feel where his body had snapped my legs from the ground. With all this going on, I am still crying, which bothers me. All that teaching, for this. To cry in front of Big Willie, looking like something a southbound freight had played with for an hour. Everything is red, and moving my head causes lances of pain to buzz through my aching skull.

I am wobbly. I know my face looks worse than his, but he registers surprise when I get up. He hadn't expected that. His expression, his widening eyes, fortify me like iced Kool Aid on a hot day. Like spinach for Popeye. I stop snuffling and spit again to clear my throat. My lips are puffy, blood rushing into the trauma.

I have the power of an oppressed minority—little guys who are lunch for asshole bullies who laugh at the pain of others. This ugliness is where the Mr. Washingtons come from. I am pissed at myself for being in this situation, for being knocked down after beating my opponent on points. I am pissed at him for enjoying it so much. I am going to resolve it by beating the crap out of him.

I set my stance and clear blood and grimy tears out of my eyes. My body is a hormonal atomic bomb, splintered in pain, propelled by adrenaline, crazed between mortal fear, uncontrollable rage, and mindless fury. I feel a raw, bleeding hunger in my fists, which is a dangerous condition in a boy whose passion is food. I want to box Master Mack into the nineteenth century. Maybe the eighteenth.

I have become a small, hard doubled fist pointing at my torment. Emotions boil within me, and I babble at him in my excitement, my urgency to do my duty.

"Kick me, Big Willie, you twy, you jes' *twy*," I say, feeling the strength of my mother. She fought bandits, *dufei*, and would never give up. I spit sourly on the schoolyard, hating the coppery taste of my own blood, wanting it to stop so I could get on with the fight. No corner bucket for mouth swill here, and it was against school rules to spit. I have kicked out a lot of blood, even for me, and a huge thrill of fear trips up through my spinal cord.

"Sorry," I say to the rule, and to the yard.

The taste pisses me off. Stupid, I think. Never drop guard. Never drop. Never, never. Mah-mee, Mah-mee.

Willie frowns like an angry bear, raises his arms, and then stands stock-still. I shuffle left, bunch myself tight, and circle. I fake right and glide left. I close with snapping jabs, aiming for his eyes. I don't care what the brows might do to my hands. I need to put him down. Willie throws his high right and I jink and it hits me hard on the left shoulder as I back away to his grin.

He isn't moving in slow motion anymore. I realize that I had been in a state of grace in the earlier part of the fight, one of those rare moments when time becomes an ally instead of another enemy. I try to get it back, but I do not know how. Just box, I say. Just box.

Guard up, fists high, elbows out, inviting him to punch my mid-section. Willie goes for it and I parry his right and keep my right guard high, pivoting left.

I punch my recovered left hook into his temple, putting all my weight and will behind it. He staggers and I recenter and follow with the right hook, whistling air out with the effort, hitting the other side of his head so hard it rattles my teeth. I jab his nose, front hook into his belly, back up as I see his leg moving and catch his PF Flyer on my right shin. That hurts and I want to rub it and I back off, circling, regaining my guard, spitting like a rude drunk on McAllister.

Kids have been yelling and I suddenly hear them as if wax has popped from my ears. I can understand none of it, like gibberish in a foreign song before Toos has slowed it down and translated it for me. Like any song in America.

He tries to trade punches with me and grab me, alternately, some-times moving, sometimes still, unable to form a plan, and I cannot think of my combinations, my mental control slipping as my arms tell me that they are tired and my head hurts and says my mind is tired as well. Wind, my wind better. Iron, I iron like weights. Water. Your tears, Big Willie. Fire, this is fire, fire in hands, for you, Willie. Earth, my mother is earth.

When he bangs me with a surprise left fist in the face, lights exploding in my eyes, certain that everyone has seen the flash, my legs wobble and my knees turn to water and I desperately throw myself back, skidding on the ground on my butt and doing a back flip, using the distance to recover and rub my face before he can get his greased sneakers on me. My whole face hurts. He has hit me in the same place he bashed me on New Year's, and the old scab pops and bleeds heavily. My cheek is swelling and my right eye shrinking, knowing it will close as faces do in Hazard's Gym. I have a grand, Big Willie headache, but I'm not even close to throwing up.

But I have to hurry. If I had been boxing a kid my size, I would've won twice already. Instead, I am up to my neck, have used my best punches, my head is exploding, and my eye is closing.

Hook inside. Too big, can't KO him, just hurt him. Make him sorry. Take best shot. Just punch him. *Leave nothing.*

I shake my head, keeping my guard up and trying to get the ache out. My mouth still bleeds and I see that I have grease on me.

This is the third round.

Willie is overloading me with data. He shows everything at the same time—anger, confusion, hurt, fear, isolation, frustration, fatigue. It is too much for me to figure out, to use tactically. I just know I have to do better than he does.

I hurt more than he does, and I am tired. But he does not know pain very well and is gutted. His main effort is drawing air. I can do that. He is not taunting me anymore. No more invitations to Fist City.

"Come to Jesus, Big Willie," I whisper, inaudibly.

I shuffle into him, almost staggering, finding my path with left jabs, ducking his huge roundhouse rights. I power up my jabs, putting more effort into them, causing my right guard to drop when I snap. I know that Willie will not counterpunch. He will not exploit the lanes I offer him by my own blows. Every one lands, and they establish in me a rhythm that begins to sing in a unified chorus throughout my body.

He slips while backing up, his wet sneaker sliding, and I take it. As he moves his arms for balance, I stay with him, in his front pocket, exploding hammer gut blows, drawing from my hips and back to drive my hands through his body, left left right left right right, taking his floating ribs, his chest, his face. I follow with a baseline uppercut that starts at my flexed knees and sinks into his chin, jarring him, making him bite his tongue and cry in pain.

Jab-jab-jab, into his eye, nose, eye. Left hook, temple, left hook temple. Jab-jab, nose. Right cross with *chi* into his high chest, his heart. Right lead to the nose, return to the throat, feeling his air escape. Jab-jab-jab eyes, right hook, temple. Left hook, temple. Uppercut, chin. Jab-jab, throat. The blows thud home and I know I am beating him. He swings at me and I parry him without thought. He is banging my arms, making them ache deep down, and I repeat Mr. Punsalong's chant of passing pain through me, trying not to keep it. Sweat pops from my face every time I hit him, and I feel his slick sweat on my knuckles. My fists are becoming numb inside and have the sensation of an amputated leg. I feel nothing in my head, while my face hurts.

I have little defense and he has less attack. I am chopping him down, freeing myself from his meanness with my fists. I breathe and gather and circle and chase and throw hands like Toussaint and I hear Toos's high voice screaming near me.

I take a hard surprise punch from him on the right side of my head, jolting me back, but I am on my own path. I shake my exploding head, throwing disciplined punches as fast as I can at him, willing myself to keep going, to take the air I need, to endure, to keep throwing, to keep the lanes open for my fists. I drive the fists into him, trying to punch them through his body, wanting them to go through him like a knife through butter.

I got it. I am rocketing a rhythmic bombardment of punches without thought, my arms and shoulders working in an unseeing delivery of sequenced blows that my mind could never have designed. I am flurrying. I am one of God's children, as described in the Book of Barraza, as prayed for by my teacher in St. Bonifas Church to the Catholic God of the Tenderloin.

The punches come out faster, harder, truer than ever before in my life in fluid combinations that come from a part of me that is awake when I sleep. I marvel at my arms as I flurry Big Willie with both hands in combinations that Rufus Monk would envy. I feel that God or Uncle Han or Hector or Tony has touched my shoulder and unlocked instinctive reflexes. My jabs are interspersed with hooks, crosses, hammers, and diggers, and I lay them on his head and torso. I breathe air in mechanical whooshing gusts and my arms windmill and thrust as my hips turn and my back flexes and in a chorus of blind will they urge Willie to kiss the canvas. I do not see him consciously, all my blood coursing into my hands. My fists are in another world, propelled by ancient spirits, supported by all the ancestors in the Ting clan, whipped forward by Bannermen in blood-red armor beating their chests with glinting weapons of East Asian wars.

He is out on his feet and I keep him up by hooks and crosses, wobbling him like a cooperative body bag on a broken chain. I am frustrated as he slowly collapses like a slinky going down stairs. I want to keep hitting him until next year.

He becomes shorter and shorter and I grimace as I jab his face by punching downward, his head snapping back on a rubber neck. No hard fall, just a gradual vertical folding of the body.

He is horizontal and looks like the Jolly Green Giant resting, his chest heaving, blood pooling beneath his face. Even on the ground he does not look like a kid.

He looks like Missus Washington.

I stand above him, bent forward, dripping, my thin chest working like busted bellows, my arms pumped up as if I have been banging iron since the first day of school, the veins thick and the muscles in my child's body corded swollen and tight. I have trouble stretching them. My hands are shot; they look like the pitiful stripped and boned limbs of butchered beasts in the Crystal Palace. Blood and sweat coat me in a slick mist of pinkness that seems paradoxically gentle.

I cannot roll up my sleeves or button my shirt, which somehow popped open. My mouth bleeds and now I cannot spit enough while trying to suck oxygen. I am moaning, keening for reasons unclear, whimpering to fate, to an ill-defined but badly tampered karma. I rest my hands on my knees, gasping, mindless.

Mr. Isington reaches down and shakes my swollen, numb little skinless hand while Toos keeps slapping me on my back. The success of the moment seems blurred, and then Willie gargles something and everything occurs in a fog.

I hobble to him, shaking, going in strange little angles, tacking like a child's bathtub boat. I kneel by Big Willie and offer him my swollen, red hand. It trembles and jerks with involuntary internal spasms, the index finger on my right and the little finger on my left twitching spastically, individually, at curious angles.

Willie's face is red with blood, so bright on his dark, bruised head. He looks at me, unseeing and unfocused, and I regret not having the smelling salts that Mr. Lewis keeps in his desk.

He wasn't going to shake my hand. I was about to pull my hand back, trying to find the synapses that move the wrist, trying to communicate with my aching shoulder. Then Big Willie reached out and dropped his huge fist in my open palm, knocking it into the ground with a soft splat.

I looked at it as if it were the winning Irish Sweepstakes ticket. Manna from Heaven. The final bell. Deliverance via the Y.M.C.A.

"It over, Big Willie," I tried to say. "No more bully?" I added.

"Bully?" he said, dully, suddenly belching a thick spittle of blood on his own shirt, struggling to rise, mindlessly pressing his entire body weight on my bruised hand to sit up. Then he bent from the waist, blinking as gunk from a forehead cut went into his eyes and he noisily retched onto the hopscotch boundaries, holding his gut, rubbing his sides while he whimpered, fighting to get up while he twistingly dumped brown vomit on the schoolyard. Pork 'n' beans.

"Ooooh, dat's gross!" cried some of the little kids in high musical Munchkin voices.

Willie got up, and sat down. He waited a moment, and shakily stood, wiping his face with his trembling right arm.

Toussaint stepped over to him.

"He mean, no mo' bully asshole boolshit on da block, Willie Mack, no mo' takin udder kids' clothes an shoes an quarters, an standin on dere faces at da Car Barn, talkin' big 'bout Fist City," cried Toos.

"Yeah, dat's right!" screamed a hundred short, shoeless, underdressed, empty-pocketed children.

Willie shook his big head.

"Fuck you, LaRue."

Toos closed his fists. I tried to move, but my joints were locked. My hands would not close, and fear ran through me slowly, like the tingling of a sleeping foot. I had no fight left.

"Shee-it," said Big Willie.

Then he laughed, hollowly.

"Da's cool. No mo', not today," said Willie. He started to wobble, his knees failing. Mr. Isington helped him and looked into his eyes, searching for shrinking pupils.

Willie took shuddering breaths and kept wiping his face and coming up with fresh blood, and he looked at it in a strange, befuddled way, trying to figure out how all that red had gotten on him. It was dark on his shirt and pants. It painted the yard. Both of us were spitting, as if we had both ingested raw *lop chong* pork sausages, or peanuts.

I was looking at my bleeding knuckles and skinned hands when my right eye closed. I had never felt freer. I had a red cape on, a small mouse with a big chest flying through the clouds.

The shock of fighting Big Willie set in. I started to cry, my shoulders jerking, tears leaking from my eyes and running down my cheeks. I bent over, locking my arms onto my legs again, trembling, leaking fluids onto the pavement.

"Tsou gou wan ba dan," I muttered wetly. I shook my aching head and smiled awkwardly with the wonder of it, my swollen mouth downturning when I thought of the fight. It was confusing, but wonderful. Liberation was sweet. I had just gotten an "A" in life. It ranked up there with having an open-meal ticket at the Crystal Palace Market. In the vegetable section.

I felt no shame in the tears. I needed to give something, to shed something, to balance the blood I had spilled, the karma of my water for his blood. I wept as I thought of Mr. Barraza's tears for his boy, the goodness of his spirit and the hardness of his life, merging with the solitude of the men of the chess association, of my Uncle Shim. I saw myself as Mother might see me, cringing with her horror for the bloodied, physical condition of her Only Son, the unmusical, nonscholarly, brutish sport which her offspring had adopted as a way of life.

Oh, Mah-mee, oh Mah-mee, I cried, crying for all of us, the forever dead, the lost, the injured, the pained, the recovering.

"Bravo, chico, you meanass streetfighta!" shouted Hector Pueblo from far away, from the fence. I looked up, smiling blindly at his voice.

"Gracias, Tío Hector," I tried to call, but only a whisper came out. Oh, Coach—Fathers. Thank you, Fathers. But I couldn't speak.

Willie was standing, rubbing his gut, still spitting blood on the yard.

"China Boy," he wheezed, "where da *fuck* you learn ta box like dat?" He spoke thickly, slowly, his own spit and blood and swollen lips fighting him.

I tried to clear my throat to speak.

Toussaint put his hands on Willis Mack's heaving chest. He was reaching up to do it.

"*You*, Big Willie," said Toussaint, giggling his silly high spastic donkey laugh.

"Fist City, 'member? *Ya'll* invited him ta Fist City! *Ya'll* taught 'em. An' I wouldn' be callin him no *China Boy* no mo, if'n I be you. He ain't fo' yo' pickin-on no mo'."

31

EPILOGUE

I looked at the door that had once
been my portal to safety. I trembled as the world seemed to slow, its
many choices narrowing.

My face and arms were still wet from Momma LaRue's cleaning
me. "Good Lord, Good Lord," she had said, clucking her tongue while
she swabbed and swabbed, searching for the cuts.

"China done *pound* Big Willie, Momma," Toos had said.

"He did? My, my, I'm happy to hear that. But—hold still, now
chile while I pull this skin tag off. I surely don't feel like clapping han's
and singin 'Hallelujah.' I think a finger's busted. Kai, your stepma not
gonna colly your clothes lookin like this."

I looked down at my clothes and agreed; my garb did not look
good. I took a deep breath, and rang the doorbell. My doorbell. The
doorbell that had once called up the small little chime god for my

mother. "I know," I said, "I 'fraid. I know I fear, very, ι
Willie very big strong boy . . ."

Edna looked down at me. "Oh my God," she said.

I squared my shoulders and puffed out my chest. "I donι
Big Willie," I said with great clarity.

"I don't care *what* you have done. It is not dinnertime, and
have no business ringing this bell."

"I want go inside," I said. "I want drink water."

"Why, you little—," said Edna, raising her hand.

I brought my guard up while presenting my profile, my head down.
There was no ache, only the comfort of a familiar stance, the security
of the now-routine geometry of arms presented for defense. One finger
stuck out of my right fist, like a small flag.

"You—you would raise your fist—to—to your *mother*?" she cried.

I kept my guard up. "You not my Mah-mee!" I said. *"I ain't fo'
yo' pickin-on, no mo'!"*

Printed in the United States
by Baker & Taylor Publisher Services